ON CALL

Anita Burgh

BCA

LONDON NEW YORK SYDNEY TORONTO

This edition published 1998
by BCA
by arrangement with Orion
an imprint of Orion Books Ltd

CN 8934

Printed and bound in Great Britain by
Mackays of Chatham PLC, Chatham, Kent

For my granddaughter, Savannah Leith, who, sadly, for one so young, knows too much about hospitals, but whose courage has never failed her.

ACKNOWLEDGEMENTS

It is many years since I was a none too successful student nurse. Hospital routines, discipline, staff structuring and rotas are all altered. The NHS is different today. Treatments have changed beyond recognition and procedures once only dreamed of are now routine. Diseases which in my day were life threatening are feared no longer, new diagnoses have emerged. But one thing never changes and that is the spirit and the dedication of good nurses.

In order to learn about that changed medical world, I have been helped greatly by the following busy people who took the time to correct, advise and instruct. They are Barbara-Ann Patterson, RGN, OHN Cert.; Judith Pearce, RGN, BA; Margaret Jones, RGN, PN Cert.; Dr Brian Pearce, MB, BS, LRCP, MRCS, D.Obst. RCOG; and Dr Mark Patrick, MB, BS, BSc, FRCA. My debt and thanks to them is enormous.

No man, not even a doctor, ever gives any other definition of what a nurse should be than this – 'devoted and obedient.' This definition would do just as well for a porter. It might even do for a horse. It would not do for a policeman.

Florence Nightingale *Notes on Nursing*.

PROLOGUE

For one hundred and twenty years St Edith's Hospital had stood on the top of South Hill, as if standing sentinel over the inhabitants of Fellcar, a small town in the far north of England.

Erected at a time when no building was regarded with civic pride unless suitably crenellated, turreted and embellished, St Edith's was a fitting testament to the stone-mason's art, even if, with the passage of time, its maintenance was proving expensive. The long Italianate windows, their surrounds decorated with an intricate latticework of stone, let in too much heat in summer and far too much cold in winter for the comfort of those who worked, or languished, inside.

The people viewed the building with various emotions, which were dependent on what had happened to them, or those close to them, within its granite walls. To some it was a source of hope and happiness; to others a place of despair, to be feared. For a lucky few it was merely handy for checking the time as they glanced up at the large clock tower, which was known as Old Tom's but few knew why. But for everyone the idea of Fellcar without St Edith's to care for them was difficult to envisage.

The closure of St Edith's was a rumour that had circulated at regular intervals since the end of the Second World War. Until now the hospital had remained because Fellcar was a marginal parliamentary seat, and no government had been prepared to take on the inevitably angry townsfolk who, at each whispered hint of such action, became mightily vocal in their disapproval. Fellcar was marginal no longer, and St Edith's was yet again under threat – which, as yet, was known to only a handful of people.

CHAPTER ONE

I

It always rained on Thursdays or, at least, on the important Thursdays in Chrissy Galloway's life. She'd been born, 'with far to go', in a dramatic June storm. When she'd left home for good, on a Thursday, she'd been soaked to the skin. It was also unfortunate to have chosen that day of the week for her wedding, when dress and photographs were ruined by a torrential downpour. There was little she could do about the day of her husband's funeral, but inevitably the gloom of the day was accentuated by a seeping drizzle. And now she peered out of the window at Fellcar station, through the driving rain, and remembered that it was *that* day.

She smiled to herself. The man in front, choosing that moment to turn, saw her smile and looked as if he'd been stung. He moved a good six inches away from her, as if she were infectious. So much for the legendary friendliness of the northerners. What else, she wondered, had changed here in the sixteen years she'd been away?

The line shuffled forward as a cab pulled into the station yard, its wheels spraying water in great arcs on the passengers who had rushed out too eagerly for it. Chrissy pushed her heavy holdall along the floor with her foot.

It wasn't that she expected things to be as they had once been here. They couldn't be. Her leaving and then marrying had not only altered her life but her parents' too. Without her to consider, they had set up new routines and taken on new interests, of which she was not a part. Even her bedroom had been redecorated and turned into a study; it had been quite ridiculous of her, but she had not liked that being done – not that she'd ever said.

Then, three years ago, her father had died and that had changed everything irrevocably. He had died at a time when she was looking closely at how she felt about many things in her life. She'd wanted to talk to him and ask his advice, and hoped he'd help solve her problems with his keen, analytical mind – but she'd left it too late.

Another taxi pulled in. The queue moved.

How many of her school-friends were still here? Only a few, no doubt: during their last two years at school they had whiled away many hours planning how to escape from boring Fellcar. Chrissy had eagerly left for London and her teaching hospital, discarding the past without a regret. Time, however, had taught her it was familiarity from which they were fleeing. Now, after so many upheavals in her life, it was that which she needed, and which she hoped to recapture.

At her interview at the hospital last month she'd felt a stranger in her home town; that same feeling was back today. She'd only herself to blame: she'd not returned often enough, which was remiss of her, especially in the last three years with her mother on her own, but the problem was that she and Iris had never got along. Her mother had fussed over her and nagged her as a child, as a teenager and as a married woman. No doubt she'd meant well, but the constant interference had driven Chrissy away and kept her away. At the funeral of Chrissy's husband, Ewan, Iris had been hysterical – far more so than at her own husband's burial – and Chrissy had known then for certain that she could not see too much of her mother, not until she had recovered a measure of equilibrium in her own life. Heavens, she thought, she'd only just arrived here and already she was beginning to wonder if she had made a mistake in coming back. Bit late for doubts, she told herself firmly, but it did not make the tendrils of worry disappear.

Lynn was the only school-friend she could be certain still lived here. When she'd first left they'd written, but that had quickly deteriorated into an exchange of Christmas cards. Although she was looking forward to seeing her again, she was also nervous at the prospect in case they didn't get on any more. Or, worse, that they might not like each other.

The queue inched further along. If she thought about it, what did they have in common? Lynn had married the only boyfriend she'd ever had – Terry Petch. Chrissy didn't even like to count up the affairs *she'd* had over the years – the number always made her sound promiscuous, and yet she'd never thought of herself as such. Terry was a builder and years ago Lynn had sent a photo of them standing proudly in front of the modest bungalow he'd built with its net curtains, flowering cherry and silly name. Chrissy, meanwhile, lived in affluent muddle in a Cornish village, in a house so pretty it appeared on local postcards and tea-towels. Lynn had two children and Chrissy had failed miserably on that score. And Lynn was happily married and Chrissy was widowed and struggling towards normality. Still, she brightened up, they had nursing in common, but then the optimism evaporated, for experience had taught her that she didn't necessarily get on with someone just because they shared the same profession.

Finally Chrissy was at the head of the queue. She was standing closer now to the automatic doors, and each time they swished open, the keen wet-laden wind hurled in from the sea. She dug her hands further into her pockets; that was something she'd conveniently forgotten – how cold it could be here.

Clutching her bag she dashed through the rain and wrenched open the door of the Ford Fiesta almost before it had stopped. She settled into the taxi, looking forward to the drive ahead and seeing the town again, the mix of building styles that had evolved over the centuries.

Down by the harbour they drove past the sixteenth-century fishermen's cottages, huddled together against the storms, now gentrified beyond recognition. The houses, pubs and sail-lofts were scattered haphazardly, with no thought of planning, as if they were toy buildings thrown down by a fractious child.

The fine Regency Assembly Room loomed ahead, built when 'taking the waters' was all the rage. Beyond were the solid Victorian villas, converted into offices now, and the Grand Hotel, which still kept going, if not with its former style, but rather like a dowager fallen on hard times. High on North Hill were the expensive middle-class houses, one of which was her mother's.

In just over three hundred years the small fishing village of Fellcar had grown and changed until now it was a town of almost fifty thousand people. But the fishermen and their boats had long gone. Many of the hotels were divided into flats. The holiday camp, which had flourished in the fifties, had been beaten by cut-price air fares to Spain and Florida and was now a conference centre. On the outskirts of town there was the latest saviour of the community: a computer factory.

'You look deep in thought, Miss.'

Chrissy looked up to see the taxi-driver, reflected in the mirror, watching her.

'I was remembering the amusement arcades down on the front and they've all gone.'

'Ages ago, Miss. We don't get many trippers, these days. Can't say I'm sorry, they left a load of litter behind them and didn't use taxis. Now, the factories are a different kettle of fish – good trade there.'

'Factories, you say? I thought there was just the one.'

'God bless you, no. Once Sunflower Computers came others followed. There's ten at least out on the industrial estate. Where've you been?'

'Cornwall. I've only been back for the odd weekend. We never got round to talking about factories. Well, you don't, do you?' She grinned.

'I went to St Ives once – nice place.' The driver stopped chatting as he negotiated the busy roundabout at the base of South Hill, and they began to climb up the steep incline on which stood St Edith's.

'Daft place to put a hospital, I always say. If you're ill, by the time you've climbed the hill, you'll be dead. Cost-effective, I suppose.' He laughed, pleased with his remark, which sounded too practised, as if he made it often.

Chrissy looked out of the window as they passed the hospital where she was to start work in a week's time. That's where she'd been born, had her appendix removed and, she supposed, if she stayed here, that was where she might die. Such a thought made her shudder and pull up her coat collar protectively.

'You're from round here, then?' The taxi-driver, having negotiated the difficult hill, wanted to talk again.

'Yes.'

'Back for a visit?'

'No, for good this time.'

'You married?'

She had to smile. Another thing she had forgotten was the obtrusive curiosity of the natives round here.

'No.' Since Ewan's death, she had learnt not to say she was widowed: it led either to an embarrassed silence or to an outpouring of sympathy, which she found difficult to deal with. She had also found that, to some men, her widowhood encouraged blatant pursuit, as if they presumed she was desperate for them.

'Got a job?' They were motoring across the moor now, which crept to the cliff edge in this part.

'I've a position at St Edith's,' she said carefully. She knew that if she said she was a nurse then not only would she be told the driver's ailments but those of his wife, children, mother and best mate also.

'What, as a secretary?'

'Bigton is next left along that lane. The last house.' She had neatly side-stepped his question.

'Bet it gets a bit blowy up here.'

Chrissy felt a surge of excitement as the taxi bumped along the unmade road on the top of the cliff, through the hamlet of Bigton Wyke, which everyone knew as Bigton only. The car swung onto the small driveway, past the lopsided, five-bar gate, which had a wooden sign hanging by one nail with End Cottage carved on it. The taxi halted on the weed-encrusted drive. The garden was overgrown with only a few scraggly shrubs, which were probably all that would grow in such a salt-wind environment, she thought.

The house stood empty, sad and neglected in the rain. She climbed out of the cab and stood a moment looking at the building. Her house, her very own! She felt a great surge of peace and contentment, emotions she had not experienced for too long.

2

The corridor stretched far ahead, and from the tall windows, positioned at regular intervals along the outer wall, shining cubes of light illuminated the tessellated, well-worn floor. Kim Henderson, bringing up the rear of the small group walking along it, wondered how many square metres of space such long, wide corridors wasted if all of them in the hospital were added together. A tidy sum, he reckoned, enough for an extra ward or department, no doubt. He looked up at the false ceiling – put in several years back to cut the height and save on heating and, by covering much of the ornate plasterwork, save on cleaning costs too – and imagined how many spiders and how many kilos of dust and debris lurked up there. The administrator in him approved such measures; the admirer of Victorian architecture mourned such necessities.

He smiled at a young and pretty nurse who had stepped aside to let them pass, and thanked her. Since he was the only one of the group who had, she smiled at him in return. He looked over his shoulder, admiring her slim retreating figure, groaning inwardly at the black-stockinged legs, and was rewarded by seeing her turn and watch him too. He cannoned into his boss, Craig Nutting, who, with the others, had stopped in front of the large glass-panelled front door of St Edith's.

'Watch where you're going, matey. Ignore the crumpet!' Craig said good-naturedly.

'Sorry.' Kim felt himself begin to blush. He grinned apologetically at the only woman in the group, but Glynis Tillman, the hospital's Clinical Services Manager, indicated by the set of her lips, the arching of her brow, her disapproval of anyone leering at *her* nurses. Kim felt his blush accelerate.

'Right. Well. Thanks for your time, Glynis.' Craig's hand was extended towards her and reluctantly shaken.

'My pleasure, *Mr Nutting*.' She emphasised his surname.

Kim looked away, embarrassed for his boss being put down so obviously. But when he glanced back at him Craig seemed not to have noticed. His arm was around Miss Tillman's shoulder as if they were the oldest of friends and he appeared oblivious of the rigidness of the woman's stance.

One by one the others took their leave of her.

'Thank you, Miss Tillman.' It was Kim's turn. He'd known her for years but he'd never quite lost the feeling of awe he had for this uptight, very private woman.

'Give my regards to your aunt when you next see her.' She smiled at him as she shook his hand.

'Today – we're having lunch together.'

'Lucky you,' she said, before turning on her heel and retracing her steps along the endless corridor.

Bet she was stunning when she was young! Sad that lovely women like her and his aunt had to grow old. Kim pushed at the door and followed the other men outside.

'Phew! What a tyrant! Is she normally like that?' asked the oldest of the group.

'Afraid so, Minister. The trouble with our Glynis Tillman is that she thinks she owns this hospital. I've always thought what she needs is a bit of how's-your-father, know what I mean?' Craig Nutting, the Thorpedale and Fellcar NHS Trust's chief executive, smirked as he made an obscene gesture with his clenched fist. The other two men laughed, but Kim became interested in the shine on his shoes. He liked Craig, but there were times when he thought him a total prat.

Craig was in his early forties and still ambitious. Kim knew that he could learn a lot from him, if he wanted to. The trouble was, he wondered, sometimes, if he could be bothered any more. Maybe he should have gone into medicine as his father had wanted, then he would have been doing some good rather than causing problems for patients and staff alike, which was what this job seemed to entail. He was distracted from this line of thought by Craig laughing loudly again. Craig had lank, russet-coloured hair, the exaggerated thinness of the dyspeptic and the pale skin of one not used to daylight. His laughter stopped abruptly and he was serious, except that his expression of seriousness always made Kim think of a small, scruffy boy trying to keep a straight face when hauled up in front of the headmaster. 'So, Minister, what do you think?' he was saying – joke time over and back to business, Kim noted. He had often seen him work this way.

The round, pasty face of the Junior Minister for Health crumpled with concern, reminding Kim of dough being balled ready for kneading. He rocked on his heels momentarily in the way of one making portentous decisions; at least, that was what he hoped the others would think. 'I'd like the figures to study. Let's say on my desk before Christmas?' Hell! thought Kim, they'd never do it in time – or, rather, *he* wouldn't: he couldn't imagine Craig toiling over the hospital budget figures day and night.

'And when do you think we can expect a decision?' Mark Fisher, the local Member of Parliament, asked. He had a worried expression and was sweating slightly. It was a chilly autumn day so Kim presumed it was from nervous tension. What a shower, Kim thought, and then had to struggle not to laugh at the aptness of his choice of word.

'Now, now, Mark,' said the Junior Minister, 'you know as well as I do these matters take time.' Kim, noting the warmth of the Minister's smile, realised he could afford to bestow such a smile for Fisher was regarded as a dull back-bencher of no note, undoubtedly idle and unlikely to make waves whatever the Minister decided to do about this hospital. 'Is that clock right?' the Minister asked, looking up at the tall bell tower. 'God, what a monstrosity!'

'Don't let the electorate of Fellcar hear you say that – you'll halve my majority!' Mark Fisher protested. 'That tower was raised by public subscription in memory of a certain Alderman Thomas Yates, a gentleman of propriety, duty and stunning pomposity, long forgotten by all but his descendants, and rarely thought about by them either, truth be told! It's known as Old Tom's, even if few know why.'

Kim looked uncomfortable and wished he didn't. It was stupid of him to care. He tried to smile, but it didn't quite work.

'You all right, Kim? You look put out about something,' Craig said.

'I'm fine.'

'Christ, I forgot. You're a Yates, aren't you? On your mother's side. Hell, I'm sorry, Kim.' Mark Fisher put his hand on Kim's sleeve.

'No, I'm no relation at all. Old Tom is related by marriage to my aunt, that's all. I don't care what you say.' But he did mind, he'd always been proud of his tenuous link with the old buffer.

'I'd no idea you were so well connected, Kim.'

'I'm not, Craig. Really.' He wished someone would change the subject.

'Well, gentlemen, I must be off.' The Junior Minister swung round towards his car.

'A pleasure meeting you again, Mr –' He shook Craig's hand. 'And, of course, you as well, Mr –' With a faint nod he acknowledged Kim – presumably as a lowly assistant: that was all he warranted.

'Safe journey, Minister.' Craig waved as the minister was driven away. 'Cretinous, slimy, inadequate creep!' he said to the departing car.

'I thought you liked him,' Kim said, puzzled.

'Me? You have to be joking. What I could tell you about that useless little turd would make your flesh creep. You'll learn, Kim.' Craig put his arm about him in a comradely way.

'Nobody likes the toad. Twists himself into all manner of contortions rather than commit himself. No guts. Word has it he's got an interest in a bit of skirt in these parts. Not that his wife or the tabloids have twigged yet.' Now that the minister was safely away, Mark Fisher appeared to be bursting with confidence.

'But you'll be setting that little matter straight at some time, Mark?' Craig found this highly amusing.

'Depends on several issues, Craig. You coming? We've things to discuss – alone.' Mark looked pointedly at Kim.

'I've got a lunch appointment with my aunt. She lives here,' Kim explained, feeling suddenly awkward and in the way.

'Your dad's one of the local GPs, isn't he? I know him, nice bloke,' Mark said, also putting his arm round Kim's shoulder, as if to make amends, as they walked towards the car park.

'So, what did you think of the old battle-axe, Kim?'

'Miss Tillman? Bit on the rigid side, isn't she? But you've got to admire her, haven't you? I mean, she really loves St Edith's.' He wasn't sure why, but Kim felt it was better if he didn't let on that he knew Glynis.

'That's something else you'll learn too. She's a pain in the arse.'

'Still, you can understand her attitude. She's obviously worried. At her age it wouldn't be easy to find another job like the one she has here. And I agree with her, I don't see the point of closing this hospital. It works, it's needed.' Kim was far from happy at all the talk of St Edith's being closed. It had always been there, throughout his life, a looming but comforting presence.

'It's inefficient,' Mark offered.

'Then make it efficient,' Kim said, a shade too diffidently for his comment to have substance. He felt he was being put on the spot and it made him nervous since he was new to this job and already did not like what he was discovering.

'Kim, my boy, you've got so much to learn,' Craig said, in an almost affectionate way, apparently unaware of Kim's discomfort.

'But if we closed St Edith's could Thorpedale hospital absorb all the intake?'

'No problem. Need a bit of moving and shaking down, but not impossible.'

'And what would happen to this building?'

'You do go on, Kim. I told you, the other day. Apartments. Nice little earner for the Trust,' Craig said, as he unlocked his car.

'Still, it would be a shame, wouldn't it? A fine old place like this, which has served the community all these years . . .' Kim looked up at the sturdy, strangely beautiful building.

'Don't get sentimental on me, Kim. Just 'cause your grandpa built it . . . We've got to be practical. Cuts have got to be made, waiting lists have got to be shortened and that's an end to it,' Craig said, as he got into his brand new Rover 827, his by courtesy of the Thorpedale and Fellcar NHS Trust.

As he gunned the engine he did not hear Kim protesting, yet again, that Old Tom Yates was nothing to do with him.

3

Twenty-two was no age to kill oneself. But, given the way that Buck Marston was weaving his way across the forecourt of the Fox and Fiddle public house, that seemed to be his intention.

'*Happy Birthday to me!*' he was still singing as, unsteady on his feet, he leant against his car for support as he searched for his keys.

'Buck! You're too tanked up to drive,' Wayne Freeman shouted after him.

'Mind your own sodding business,' Buck yelled back.

'We ought to stop him, Jason.' Wayne turned to his elder brother, who had just appeared in the pub's doorway.

'He'll be all right. He's driven pissed enough times. Why, that car probably knows its own way home by now!' He slapped his brother on the back. But Wayne, less drunk than the other two, did not look too sure. 'Come on. It's nothing to do with us. It's only half past one, time for another. Why the silly sod promised Cheryl he'd be home for his dinner beats me.'

'You're right, it's down to Buck, isn't it?' Wayne turned to re-enter the pub but paused at the clatter of the defective exhaust on Buck's car, made worse by his over-revving of the engine. A cloud of acrid blue smoke billowed out as, with a rowdy banging on the horn and a two-finger salute, Buck shot out of the pub car park.

Andrew Basset was in a hurry to get home. He was feeling pleased with himself: it had proved a shrewd move changing jobs to Sunflower Computers – his commission would be double here for sure, enough to consider taking out a mortgage, and with less travelling. He glanced at his watch. Maybe he'd surprise Rachel – he'd collect details of the house on the new Mulberry estate that she had set her heart on. If he got a move on perhaps they could be in for Christmas! He laughed with excitement at the idea and, leaving the trading estate, instead of turning right at the crossroads for Thorpe-dale, he turned left towards Fellcar.

He wouldn't have chosen Fellcar himself, too quiet by far. But, with the baby on the way, it made sense that Rachel wanted to be closer to her mum.

He leant forward and pressed the eject button on the player as the cassette of *Runrig* came to a halt. Fumbling, he dropped it on the floor. He glanced down just for a second to locate it, his car wavering over the white line as he did so. The man in the car behind hit his horn in warning.

Andrew looked up just in time to see Buck's battered banger sweeping around the bend towards him, too fast and too far over on his side.

The combined force of the two cars crashing together, at the speed they were both travelling, made a hideous noise, as metal tore at metal, shards were separated and flew through the air with the force of bullets. The screeching noise battered the trees, bounded down the Tarmac and then everything was suddenly silent. A scream of intolerable pain was heard by other motorists as they rushed to help, and the man in the car behind Andrew's dialled 999 on his mobile phone.

The Accident and Emergency department of St Edith's, known to the staff as A and E and to the town simply as Casualty, was situated to the side of the hospital. It was a comparatively modern single-storeyed building, rendered in cement. The outside had been painted in what was called Adam Green, but which the residents thought was more like the colour of processed peas. It was connected to the main hospital by a glass-enclosed walkway. The staff had attempted to decorate the windows with cut-outs of flowers and cartoons, to cheer the patients up. This rarely worked since most of them were too stressed at being there to notice.

The department was quiet. In her small, cluttered office Sister Betty Greaves was taking this lull in the population's mania for damaging itself to have a quiet cup of tea and to catch up on her paperwork, especially as November and December were busy months. Betty looked at public holidays differently from most people: August meant drownings, Guy Fawkes' meant burns, and the run-up to Christmas meant crashes and fights, the harvest of drunken office parties. As if the department wasn't busy enough, the amount of information the managers required grew constantly. Betty could see that age, sex, social conditions, number of smokers, type of accident and disease were relevant. However, some statistics demanded, she felt, were pointless: how many left-handed patients, how many with brown eyes and how many six-footers were treated, were some she remembered. Sometimes she longed to put a third column after the question *Sex*, M for male, F for female, − mark it D for doubtful, just to annoy. What happened to the statistics she conscientiously collected she was rarely told. She had stopped asking so as not to get too cross at the waste of her time. Her final conclusion was that it was the managers justifying their existence.

'Yes, Margaret, what is it?' she said, to a young student nurse who had knocked nervously on her door. Although she was irritated at being interrupted she spoke kindly. Nurse Margaret Harper was a Project 2000 nurse, whose first week in the department this was. This system of training, brought in in 1990, with the intention that all nurses would be trained under it by the year 2000, was more academically weighted than Betty's own training had been. These students spent longer hours in the classroom than at the hands-on learning on the wards Betty had enjoyed. Many staff rejected the new regime, and the unfortunate students, with ill-concealed irritation. They were like Luddites with their intransigence, Betty thought. She acknowledged there were disadvantages: it was one thing to be taught a procedure from a book and on a dummy; it was totally different dealing with noisy, often smelly and belligerent patients, something only experience could teach. But Betty saw advantages too: hopefully, the profession would come to be better respected and paid; it might halt the often maudlin gratitude of the general public, which was all very well but did not pay the bills. And, she often pointed out, how much of her own training had been wasted in repetitive tasks which less-qualified people were quite capable of doing? Only time would tell. Betty was aware of how frightened most of the staff were when beginning a placement on A and E. They could never be sure from one minute to the next what they might see, what they might be asked to do, and if they would know how to do it.

'Sorry, Sister, but there's a young woman in Cubicle Two. She's got a severe abdominal pain. Staff isn't back from lunch and the patient says it's getting worse.' Nurse Harper's eyes, behind a pair of round spectacles, looked alarmed.

'Has the duty houseman seen her?'

'No, he popped off for a coffee – it was quiet, you see. She's not pregnant, though. I tested her urine,' Margaret said proudly.

'That's very good, Nurse.' Betty smiled her approval as she bleeped for the doctor. 'You've no idea how often, when the patient is a young woman, nurses forget that a complication with pregnancy is the first thing to eliminate. I'd better come and see.' She began to stand, a dark-haired, small, birdlike woman, but her size belied her strength.

'No need to bleep, I'm back. Which cubicle? If it's not written on the bloody board, how the hell am I to know where to look for the patient?' John Playfair, the A and E junior houseman, popped his head round the door. His expression and tone matched in aggressiveness. The student nurse seemed to shrivel and looked even more anxious.

'Margaret was just about to write it up. She was reporting to me, John. Cubicle Two.' Betty spoke in a no-nonsense manner to prevent further criticism of a member of her staff, whom she protected fiercely at all times.

John, looking exhausted, shuffled out without another word. Betty hadn't been able to warm to him, not as she usually did to her young housemen. Most of the newly qualified doctors were happy – in fact, frequently relieved – to acknowledge that, after fifteen years in this department, she had forgotten more than they knew. John Playfair wasn't one of them – he bridled at any helpful suggestions so Betty was doing what she always did in such situations: while keeping a keen eye on him, she was letting him get on with it. Sooner or later he'd learn.

With Margaret Harper dispatched to help the doctor, she returned to her reports and it was a good ten minutes before there was a further interruption. Freddie Favour, their consultant in A and E, barged into the room.

'I've got another one for your statistics.' Freddie was waving a letter triumphantly. 'That young woman in Cubicle Two – peptic ulcer or I'm a Dutchman.'

'Which GP referred her? No, let me guess – Dr Giles Middleton.'

'The very same. Up to his old tricks. So pop it on your list, Betty dear. I'm off to pen a note to him forthwith, while I'm still steamed up about it.'

If this hospital or this department closed it would be the Dr Middletons of this world who would have helped it on its way, Betty thought, as she took a notepad from her desk and entered the case to her lengthening list.

Everyone knew that GPs sometimes referred patients directly to A and E not only to jump a lengthy waiting list but also as a way of getting a patient admitted if a particular ward was full and so closed to routine admissions. They knew that she and her staff would move heaven and earth to get a sick patient a bed. But Giles Middleton was up to different tricks: doctors like him were not thinking of the well-being of their patients but, rather, of their pockets. Dr Middleton belonged to a fund-holding practice and, along with a couple of other GPs, had quickly found a money-saving loophole. If they referred a patient to a specialist at St Edith's, their practice paid for the consultation and treatment. However, if they referred patients as an emergency, and if the hospital doctors decided to admit, the practice did not pay, the hospital did. It was becoming harder for the hospital to keep to its own budget. This year already they were heading towards a serious overspend. A hospital like St Edith's, old and expensive to maintain, was always at risk from closure, and the Dr Middletons were helping to distort the figures: the hospital appeared to be out of favour with too few referrals. The sooner this system was axed the better.

At the first ring of the telephone she picked it up. 'A and E. Sister Greaves here . . . Yes . . . ETA? . . . Fine.' Calmly she replaced the receiver, alerted the resuscitation team and the consultant, and walked out into the main area of the department. 'Margaret, is Staff back yet? Right.' She took off her cuffs and rolled up her sleeves. 'There's been a serious RTA just along from the Sunflower Computers factory. Two victims, both will need the Resus room.' And she bustled out with a terrified Nurse Harper, who had never seen an accident, in her wake, and was still not sure what she was supposed to be doing.

As is the way, with an emergency due, the quietness of the department began to shatter and there was a sudden influx of patients. And she was lacking two members of staff. As Betty walked quickly through Reception she straightened a chair here, a table there, picked up books and toys, tutting at people's untidiness. She looked around for Margaret. Where was the girl? 'Nurse Harper?' she called.

'Sister!' Margaret Harper ran towards her.

'Walk, Nurse. Were you not taught that a nurse runs only in case of fire, haemorrhage, and if she is a member of the resuscitation team? Are you?'

'No, Sister. Sorry.'

'Right, then, come with me.'

The doors to the outside hissed open at their approach just as the ambulances, sirens stilled now, ground to a halt and the patients were unloaded. Betty quickly assessed both men, looking for the least hurt to give to Margaret to accompany to the resuscitation room. It was not an ideal situation since the young woman lacked experience, but as yet there was no sign of the teams who were on their way. There was no one else to call upon. Since both patients' heads were swathed in bandages, and since both were unconscious and had the same ashen colour, there was nothing to choose between them. 'You take that one, Margaret,' she ordered. And a white-faced Margaret Harper trotted alongside the trolley accompanied by the ambulance man.

'Here, you, come here.' Back in the department a loud, garrulous voice rang out.

Betty stopped in her tracks, the procession wheeling the trolleys going on without her. She looked about her and saw a disgruntled middle-aged man pointing at her. 'Yes, you in the blue. Are you in charge?'

'I'm the sister in charge, yes. If you could just speak with the receptionist . . . She began to move on. But the man was on his feet in a trice and grasping at her sleeve.

'Don't you walk off like that when I'm speaking to you.'

'I'm sorry, sir, but we have an emergency –'

'And what do you think I am? I've been here over ten minutes already.'

'What appears to be the problem, sir?'

'I've broken my wrist.' He held out a bony wrist, which showed no signs of damage. 'The Patients' Charter says I have only to wait five minutes to be attended to and I'm overdue.'

'Your name?'

'Mr Brighton.'

'You will be seen as soon as a nurse is available to take your details, Mr Brighton. Until then you will have to wait, Patients' Charter or no Patients' Charter.'

'I'll report you.'

'My dear man, do as you wish,' she called over her shoulder, as she sped away.

Forewarned of the severity of the men's injuries, the department was buzzing. The consultant and his housemen were joined by the registrar, the resuscitation team, and on their way were the 'head' men, as the neurosurgeons were irreverently known, with the 'bone' men – the orthopaedics team – in hot pursuit, with anaesthetists and X-ray personnel bringing up the rear.

It was controlled pandemonium in the starkly lit resuscitation room.

The ABC of emergency treatment – airway, breathing, circulation – was under way. Buck and Andrew were rapidly attached to equipment supplying vital oxygen and fluids, while other machines clicked, whirred and flickered the progress of their vital signs.

Orders were barked in a short-hand unintelligible except to those who followed them, as the group moved in an urgent and familiar routine.

'There's not a hope in hell here.' Freddie Favour stood up from leaning over one of the young men. 'Any relatives with him? He's fit and young – try to get hold of the relatives before it's too late for him to be a transplant donor.' And he turned his attentions to the other.

'Margaret, go through his clothes, find out his identity and bring it to me. Then clean him up,' Betty ordered.

But Margaret Harper stood by the trolley, her face white, tears streaming down her cheeks, and shook visibly as she looked at the blood and gore that had once been a vibrant man. 'But he's so young . . . I never saw anything like this . . .' she wailed.

Betty nodded to a staff nurse, Dawn Allyson, as she entered the room and told her to take over. 'It's all right, Margaret. Come with me. It's hard the first time. It doesn't get better but you just get more used to it. Come and sit down,' she said softly, remembering her own reaction all those years ago when she had been just as scared and just as sickened as poor Margaret Harper.

4

Glynis Tillman, in overall charge of St Edith's, an elegant woman, immaculate, her posture rigidly perfect, had been at her desk since seven thirty that morning. She was smartly dressed in a navy suit with a crisp high-collared blouse, which looked rather like the old uniform of a senior sister which, in truth, she would have much preferred to be wearing. This alteration in dress for senior staff was just one of the many changes she had seen in her profession, few of which met with her approval.

She was studying the surgical bed allocations and matching them against the proposed operations listed by the various surgeons to be done next week. She was not aware that she frowned as she worked; the lines caused were the only ones on her fine-boned, pale-complexioned face. It was a difficult task she was doing but it should have been simple: a surgeon had a fair idea of his patient's progress and when he was likely to be discharged, so knew when he could admit a new one to take their place. But chance invariably interfered with neat order. An unexpected deterioration in the condition of the recovering patient; a patient catching a cold and having his operation cancelled; a waiting patient's state suddenly worsening; the acute illness of someone who didn't even know they were poorly in the first place – any of these occurrences and the whole system was in danger of collapsing.

In the past, beds were kept empty, 'on the door' they had been called in the hospital where she had trained, always ready for emergencies. Now no bed was allowed to stand empty: all were booked to achieve the highest occupancy rate possible. The problem with this was that when an emergency cropped up and a bed was required a patient booked in had to be cancelled. This meant that patients were required to telephone on the morning of their admission to check if a bed was available for them. It was not a pleasant duty to tell them that their admission or operation was cancelled and that another date would be allocated. If a spate of A and E admissions happened, as had taken place this weekend, then the juggling began.

An even worse scenario was when the pressures on the wards were such that patients who had already been admitted and were undergoing tests were told that their operations had been cancelled and that they must go home and wait for a recall. Everyone hated this situation. They were fully aware of the worries experienced by patients, the effort needed to control that fear before entering the hospital, and what a blow such decisions must be, how frustrated they must feel. Understanding all that, however, did not help Glynis accept the anger that the staff frequently had to withstand from these people, as if they had rescheduled out of spite rather than necessity. Often she was called in to soothe irate patients or their relatives. Patiently she would try to explain the reasons behind their decision.

Glynis's commanding presence, learnt over many years in this profession, usually calmed the situation, but recently she had noted a rather more belligerent attitude appearing. The threat of litigation was often bandied about noisily; she had even had to outstare a man with raised fists. But at least no scurrilous stories had been leaked to the press about hospital malpractice, as some of her colleagues in other hospitals had had to endure.

Many times she wished that people could be ill to order or that she had a rubber hospital that would stretch to meet demand. In many hospitals this bed-allocating task was done by administrators, but she preferred to do it herself. The patients were her responsibility and she saw this as part of her job.

She attacked her chart with a rubber. From the surgical ward where most of the patients were long-stay, she rubbed out a name. Taking her pencil she booked the woman into surgical ward 6 – with keyhole surgery for gall bladders, these days, the recovery rate was quick. The first bed was now allocated to a bowel restructuring, who would be in for longer. Fortunately, with Russell Newson, the orthopaedic surgeon, away for a week and his surgical waiting list on hold, she should be able to resolve the influx with no cancellations for once.

The wards might be numbers now, but she still thought of them by their old names, Holly, Rowan, Willow. Such pretty names, less frightening for the patients than Medical 4, Orthopaedic 2. But the administrators had scrapped all that, her objections ignored.

'Come,' she said, in answer to a knock on the door. The frown deepened: she had specifically asked not to be disturbed. 'Well, what is it?' she asked, with marked irritation to Sister Shelagh Morris, her deputy.

'I thought you should see this.' Shelagh crossed to the desk, a newspaper in her hand. 'It's the *FD*.'

Smiling at her from the front page of the local weekly newspaper, the *Fellcar & District News*, known to all as the *FD*, was the face of a small boy. The bold headline seemed to leap at her from the page. '*Child of Four Refused Operation*'. She did not really have to read more to know who, it was alleged, was doing the refusing. She quickly scanned the story.

Brad Gordon (4) of Willow Close, Bracken, after waiting over a year for a critical operation, was turned away from St Edith's Hospital, Fellcar, on Wednesday. His mother, Tracey Gordon (22) told the *News* that he had already been settled in his bed in the children's ward when staff told her the operation had been cancelled.

'It's disgusting! He was crying. We've waited so long, and to be treated in this way,' said ·blonde, blue-eyed, five-months-pregnant Tracey, close to tears.

Bret Short (22) a sales representative, Ms Gordon's common-law husband, has written to Mark Fisher, MP for Fellcar. 'What do we pay our National Insurance for, I'd like to know? This child's health has been put at serious risk. I shall be in talks with our lawyers.'

A hospital spokesperson said, 'These things happen.' The *News*, as always working in your best interests, is demanding to know why!

'Oh, really!' Glynis whipped off her spectacles with annoyance. She put out her hand towards the telephone.

'Sister Plumpton's on her way. I called for her as soon as I saw it.'

'I had just this moment been thinking, At least we've never had any complaints to the press, and this happens! Yes,' she said shortly, to the tap on the door.

'You wanted to see me?' Sister Marge Plumpton, well named for her large, comfortable, soft-breasted body, appeared in the doorway. The apron covering her navy blue uniform had Mickey Mouse emblazoned on the front. The sight of it did not offend Glynis as much as her untidy appearance: her shoes needed cleaning, her hair looked unbrushed – but, then, Marge Plumpton had always been the same, and Glynis was the first to admit that her untidiness had never interfered with her efficiency as a children's nurse.

'I'm hoping you can explain this to us.' She handed over the paper and Marge began to read. With amused astonishment, Glynis noted that she mouthed the words ever so slightly as she did so, just like her little patients, she thought. The telephone rang.

'Yes?' Glynis answered it shortly.

'Glynis? It's Craig, I'm on the mobile. Seen the paper?'

'Yes, Mr Nutting, I'm looking into it at this very moment.'

'Good, get back to me soon as. Before the proverbial hits the fan.'

Glynis replaced the receiver, unaware that she shuddered slightly as she did so. Craig Nutting was an unpleasant cross she was resigned to bear. As chief executive of the Thorpedale and Fellcar NHS Trust, based in the large city eighteen miles from here, he was her senior, and a person she despised and mistrusted with the management of *her* hospital. An accountant in charge of her precious patients was a state of affairs to which Glynis had not adjusted well or gracefully.

'I knew that man, Short, was going to be trouble the minute I set eyes on him. Aggressive, bullying. He was angry when we postponed and the mother burst into tears. But the little boy didn't, he was a dear.'

'Yes, Marge, the character analysis is interesting but I'm more interested in the facts. What was the child in for?'

'Here are his notes.'

Quickly Glynis scanned them. 'I see. We cancelled the op because he had a cold and a chest infection.'

'Yes. I explained this carefully to the mother. He was sent home with a course of antibiotics and the assurance that we would fit him in as soon as possible.'

'You're sure you explained the risks inherent in giving a general anaesthetic in such circumstances?'

Marge Plumpton gave her a look as if she thought Glynis was half-witted. 'Of course I did.' She sighed her displeasure for good measure. 'And I thought the stupid woman understood.'

'It would appear the litigious patient has arrived in Fellcar, after all. Any idea who this so-called *hospital spokesperson* is?'

'I've no idea. No one on my ward,' Marge Plumpton said, indignant at the very idea.

'And who's going to admit they said it?' Shelagh Morris added.

'Exactly!' Briskly Glynis turned the newspaper towards her and leafed through it. 'Where's the phone number?'

'Six, seven, six, eight, six, nine. I looked it up before I came in,' Shelagh said, with a smug expression that, Glynis had noticed, was becoming more frequent.

Glynis punched in the numbers while the other two women stood waiting, Shelagh looking nosy, Marge anxious. 'Is this the editor?'

'It most surely is. And to whom do I speak?'

'The Clinical Services Manager of St Edith's. About this article –'

'Now, why on earth did they change from calling you the good old matron? Gave one confidence knowing Matron was in charge.' He laughed.

'I've no idea,' Glynis replied sharply, not taken in by his efforts at bonhomie. 'The article about young Brad Gordon. I wish you had checked your facts with us Mr – I'm sorry I don't know your name.' She did, it was McPherson and they had met at several functions to do with the hospital, but Glynis was no fool and knew the value of one-upmanship, especially in a situation like this.

'McPherson, Malcolm. Don't say you've forgotten me, Miss Tillman?' He laughed again as if he did not care, but she knew better.

'I would have preferred it, Mr McPherson, if you had had the courtesy to phone my office before publishing this account. I would have been happy to tell you that young Brad was suffering from glue ear – a common complaint in young children. He was in hospital to have a grommet fitted. You've heard of grommets? Unfortunately, due to the child's chest infection, we had to cancel for his own safety. He will be rescheduled as soon as he's better and we have a bed for him. And who is this so-called *spokesperson*?'

'I'm not at liberty to divulge my sources.'

'In other words, there wasn't anybody.'

'Well, then you'd be wrong.'

'I wish you to print a retraction in your next edition. If not, it will be a case of you hearing from our lawyers. Good day, Mr McPherson.'

Sister Plumpton clapped with pleasure as Glynis replaced the receiver. 'You were wonderful! Thank you so much.'

'As if we don't have problems enough without people like this making dramas just because they want their photograph in the newspapers. It's pathetic. Our first priority is to find out who spoke to them,' she said decisively, even as the telephone rang again.

'Glynis? Craig here. Any news? Before we know where we are I'll have the *Sun* chasing me.'

'I've already dealt with it. The newspaper will be printing an explanation. It was all a storm in a teacup.'

'You did *what*?' Craig's indignation exploded down the telephone, necessitating her holding the receiver away from her ear. 'How dare you?'

'I dare, Mr Nutting, because this is my hospital and I will not have its reputation besmirched. I found out the problem and I dealt with it immediately.'

'All media queries have to be handled by us at Thorpedale General. I am the spokesperson, not you.'

'I didn't think it was that important. It's not as if the BBC was on your tail.'

'It could have been, and it could have been serious.'

'Well, it wasn't, so I don't see what the problem is.'

'The problem is, Glynis, that rules are rules and you are not above them. I shall be amending the agenda of the meeting later today. This situation has to be clarified.'

'As you wish, Mr Nutting. Now, if you're not busy, I am.' And without waiting for his reply she put down the receiver.

'More trouble?' Marge Plumpton asked, anxiety flooding back.

'Just Craig Nutting wanting me to know what an important little bureaucrat he is. He's amending the agenda of today's meeting.'

'*Adding* to it?' Shelagh Morris asked, appalled.

'Have you ever known him shorten one?' Glynis smiled at her own remark. 'Did you manage to get hold of Miss Galloway?'

'She was due to arrive on the one o'clock train. She should be here by now. I left a message with her mother.'

'Is that the new sister? Poor soul. Fancy having to attend a managers' meeting on her first day,' Marge said, with feeling.

'You met her, Shelagh. What's she like?'

'Young, pretty but not flashy. Rather a withdrawn creature, I'd say. But pleasant. She's a local girl, which always helps them settle, I think.'

'I look forward to meeting her,' Glynis lied. She wished Shelagh's assessment had been different, that she was old and ugly. All her insecurities rose at the news that the new sister was neither of these.

5

Standing on the terrace overlooking the steep garden, Kim Henderson watched his aunt climb the steps she'd had cut into the slope. 'Want a hand?' he shouted down.

'I'm not on a Zimmer frame yet!' Harriet Yates, known to all and sundry as Floss, though no one could remember why, called in reply. 'Bloody cheek,' she said, as she reached the terrace.

'You'd have moaned if I hadn't offered.'

'Indubitably.' Floss grinned broadly. 'What's the point of getting on if you can't be a cantankerous old cow when you want? Kiss?' She was so short that he had to bend to kiss her cheek.

'You're looking well.'

'Ah! Fatter than ever, you mean. At this rate I shall be as wide as I am tall. If I slip, no doubt I'd bounce like a rubber ball. You're early.' They were entering the large house as she spoke.

'Meeting ended sooner than we expected. Rumour has it that the Minister who came has a bit of skirt on the other side of Thorpedale. He was certainly in a hurry to get going.' He helped his aunt out of her voluminous coat. 'This is wet.'

'Sling it over the radiator. Nap and Jo, did you miss me?' she called with delight, as two elderly and overweight bulldogs shambled towards her and from somewhere dredged up sufficient energy to welcome them. 'If there's one thing both Napoleon and Josephine loathe it's the rain – it *disgusts* them. Now, large gins are in order, don't you think?' In stockinged feet, her wellingtons kicked to one side, Floss led the way into her drawing room. 'Right, where was I? Large gins?' She waved the bottle at him.

'Small. There's a meeting at St Edith's this afternoon.'

He watched Floss as she busied herself with the drinks – he'd given up offering to pour them, She liked to do it, she'd told him, Then she could ensure that her drink was strong enough for her taste. Kim's monthly lunch with his aunt was never a hardship, but something to look forward to. He enjoyed her company and, childless as she was, he knew that she adored him as substitute for a child of her own – even if he was happy to acknowledge that she loved her dogs more. Floss was unconventional, even if she could never see it herself. Instead, as she often told him, she felt that it was the rest of the world who were off kilter. It never failed to amaze him that his conventional, rather prissy mother and Floss were sisters – how two such different people could be the product of the same loins. Makes you think! He did just that as he stood in front of the window in Floss's drawing room in the large, rambling mansion she refused to give up on the top of North Hill overlooking Fellcar.

'Just like twins, aren't you? St Edith's on South Hill and you up here.'

'Same architect.'

'Really? I never knew that, but now you say it it's obvious.' He took his drink from her. He sipped it gingerly for one of Floss's small gins could still be lethal.

'Seen my prune-faced sister? She doesn't like you coming here, you know. She thinks I'm corrupting you.'

'I didn't know you'd seen her. She didn't say.'

'Oh, I haven't – I never do, if I can help it. No, Molly Pratt – you know old Molly, dipso and nymphomaniac to boot – she told me that Fiona had been carping on.'

'Molly's sixty-five if she's a day.' He laughed.

'So? The elderly have hormones too, you know. You wait and see. Anyhow, it was she who told me your mean-spirited mother resents our friendship. I sent a message back saying, "Fine, I won't see your son again, but if so then I'm leaving everything to the Battersea Dogs' Home!" I've heard no more. In fact, the silence is deafening!' She chuckled merrily at this snippet and seemed unaware that her nephew was not smiling. Sometimes, in his experience, ideas sown as jokes had a nasty way of becoming facts.

'How's the hip?' he asked, to change the subject. He hadn't much time for his mother either but, it was an odd thing, he always felt uncomfortable if Floss sounded off about her.

'Don't like me wittering on about your mother? Fair enough. I like your loyalty even if you mustn't expect it from me. Look.' She swung her leg high. 'Brilliant, isn't it? Best replacement hip ever. Russell Newson should be sanctified.'

'He's a good surgeon. We're lucky to have him. I've heard his wife would prefer they moved to London.'

'He'd never go. He likes it here – he told me so. Not a London type. In any case, all those waiting lists you read about at other hospitals would upset him, he's so conscientious. No, he's better off here.'

'Thorpedale and Fellcar have horrendous waiting lists. It's staff shortages mainly. I mean –'

'I didn't have to wait. I was in hospital within two weeks. All this waiting-list stuff you read in the papers, it's all exaggeration. Another gin?'

'No thanks. As for the lists – we're working on them, but I put in a word for you and so did Dad.'

'You what?' Floss put the gin bottle back on the tray with exaggerated slowness. 'You mean, you arranged for me to jump the queue?'

26

'Something like that,' Kim said, with pride.

'You interfering creeps! You had no right to do that. How dare you and your boring old fart of a father compromise me and my principles in that way?'

'I thought you'd be pleased.'

'Pleased! I'm incandescent with rage. You know I'm a Friend of St Edith's. You've compromised me, made it look as if it's an advantage over everyone else if you're a Friend. I don't know if I'll ever forgive you.' She turned away with an angry gesture and poured half a tumbler of gin to which she added a mere dash of tonic.

'Aunt Floss, I wouldn't do anything to upset you, you know that.' Kim was horrified.

'Bit late, then, isn't it? You've done just that in spades. I'm mortified.'

'I'm sorry, but people tend to change their principles when it's they who need treatment.'

'I wouldn't,' Floss said staunchly. Before he could stop it a cynical look flashed across Kim's face. 'You don't believe me, do you?'

'I didn't say that.'

'You didn't need to. Now I can't prove myself to you.'

'Floss, you're the last person who needs to prove herself. You're right, it was unforgivable of me. I should have consulted you, but when I saw you in such pain I had to do something, don't you see?'

Floss shrugged her shoulders. 'Oh, well, it's done now. I'll forgive you, but just this once. Next time something goes wrong or falls off me, don't interfere. Ever!' She wagged a finger at him and smiled, her anger, as so often with her, quickly over.

'I promise. Honest.' He held up his hands defensively and grinned, he hoped apologetically.

'Then we shall eat. Come.' In procession, led by the bulldogs, they filed into the dining room where the table had been beautifully set for two by Floss's cook-cum-housekeeper.

The smoked salmon and vegetable terrine was finished and replaced with roast pheasant.

'Scrummy. Beats hospital food.' Kim tucked in enthusiastically.

'How's the job?'

'It's not what I thought it was going to be. I suppose I was stupid – I'd had an idea I'd be helping people. All we seem to do is make everything more difficult for them. The medical staff are so devoted, all they think of is the patients. Then we come along with our "unit controls" and "rate of throughput", and it's their patients we're talking about. I thought we'd work together, but instead it seems to be "them" and "us" and outright sniping and warfare. It's getting me down.'

'Oh, sweetie, I *am* sorry. Then you must change it.'

'Dear Floss, I'm so junior. It'll be years before I make any mark.'

'Rubbish! Make waves. I would. If you see something you don't like, then speak up.'

'You would. I'm different. I mean –' He stopped talking as if he was changing his mind.

'What? What is it? Tell me.'

'It's difficult, Floss.'

'I'll help.'

Kim looked at his food, at the patterned Turkey carpet, at the ceiling. 'A friend overheard . . . I might have misinterpreted. I'm probably wrong . . .'

'What?'

'I think they're planning to sell off St Edith's.'

'Oh, don't worry, that rumour comes each year like the swallows – for apartments they usually claim.'

'But it's worse than that, Floss. I think the talk of apartments is another smoke-screen. I think they want to privatise the hospital.'

'Who? Who's planning this? The government?'

'Individuals. My boss for one.'

'Report him.'

'I can't do that!' Kim looked appalled at the very idea. 'He has lots of faults – he's bossy, a bit like a tank – but he's got an odd rough charm to him and he can be funny. And he's fair to work with. And I can't snitch!'

'Only he wants to ruin a perfectly good hospital, endowed originally, if you've forgotten, by my husband's great-great-grandfather. Sounds a charming bloke.'

'I know.' Kim looked even more miserable.

'I shan't let this happen!' Floss banged the table.

Having run out of places to look so as to avoid Floss's eye, Kim concentrated on the palm of his hand.

'Who else, Kim?' Floss asked softly.

'My father's partner, so I'm forced to presume Dad too,' he said finally, his voice filled with misery.

6

As she waited for the removal van to arrive Chrissy explored her cottage. It was smaller, and the hall, more of a corridor if she were honest, was darker than she recalled. If she hung the heavy gilded mirror here and put a lamp in front that would help. But empty like this it looked so sad.

'Cooee! Anyone home?'

'Gran! I wasn't expecting you. How lovely,' she exclaimed. Her grandmother, a large wicker basket hooked over her arm, was standing in the doorway. 'You're my first visitor.'

'You didn't get a taxi, did you? All that money. I told your mother we should have checked the station. Where's your car? When's the furniture due?' All this was asked in the familiar, gravelly, smoker's voice, as the older woman bustled into the kitchen. 'Oh, this is nice, I like oak. And what colour curtains do you plan?'

'I thought Black Watch.'

'You sure?'

'Well, almost. As for the rest, the removal men are due any time. I caught the earlier train. Yes, I took a taxi. My car died, I left it. Anything else?' She giggled.

By now, her grandmother was busily unpacking the cleaning materials in the basket.

'Do I see coffee in there?' Chrissy asked.

'It's only instant. Don't let your mother know you've had some – she thinks I packed it for the removal men.' Daphne Galloway snorted derisively as she spooned coffee granules into two brightly coloured mugs. 'It's all my Frank's fault, I'm afraid. He could be an insufferable and snobby little creep about the oddest things.'

'That's your son you're talking about,' Chrissy said reprovingly. 'But you shouldn't –' She stopped abruptly.

'Speak ill of the dead? Is that what you were about to say?' Daphne scoffed. 'I'm not saying anything I didn't say to him when he was alive. He must have driven your mother mad with his pernickety ways. It's no wonder she's kicking up her heels. She's enjoying the liberation.'

'Is she? Liberation from Dad?'

'Don't listen to me. I'm just rambling. It's my senility,' Daphne said, with the confidence of one who had nothing of the sort. 'Gets us all in the end!' She began to laugh, but her breath caught and she started to cough.

'Are you all right, Gran? You're not still smoking?'

'No. I gave it up. Got the patches,' she managed to say finally. 'It's just a bit of cold left over. Can't seem to shake it off.'

'Go and see your doctor.'

'I hate going to the doctor.'

'Don't we all? But you should at your . . .' She paused. 'Well –'

'*At your age* . . . Cheeky minx!' She pushed Chrissy playfully.

They sat on the window-seat, their coffee mugs in their hands, and both looked out of the window at the rain and mist outside.

'There really is a wonderful view out there if only we could see it,' Chrissy remarked.

'You don't have to justify your purchase to me, dear. Mind you, I bet it'll be parky up here in winter.'

They sat in companionable silence. It was strange, Chrissy thought, the way her grandmother so often seemed able to read her mind. Was it an ability that came with age? She certainly hadn't got it – it might have come in handy once or twice if she had.

Outside the rain had stopped but the wind had strengthened and the sea mist had increased in billowing swirls. There was a pervasive dampness in the air, and she hoped it wasn't often like this, or she might end up regretting not only her return but buying this house.

'Why have you come back, Chrissy?' Daphne asked kindly, but it didn't stop Chrissy shivering at how she'd hit the nail on the head again.

'I don't really know, Gran. No cut and dried reason – just a vague feeling that this was where I wanted to be. After all "East, west, home's best." Isn't that what they say?' She trotted out the glib words in a light tone, not wanting to explain anything, not even to this woman she loved.

'Do you want to talk about it? About Ewan?'

'No, Gran. If you don't mind.' Chrissy pointedly looked out of the small-paned window at the mist rather than at the other woman to see in her eyes the sadness she felt for her.

'Where's Mum?' she asked, when she thought the moment had safely passed.

'She's gone to get some champagne and Harpic. I'm sure the last owners have left the house clean, but it won't be up to your mother's high standards. What's that?' The elderly woman looked up sharply.

'The removal men are here,' Chrissy said, at the sound of a large vehicle inching down the narrow lane.

Two hours and several cups of tea later, the last of Chrissy's possessions had been unloaded just as Iris drove her Volvo estate, a shade too quickly, through the gates.

'Chrissy!' Iris kissed the air beside her daughter's cheeks. 'Unpacked already? You *have* been working hard!'

'There wasn't much, I've sold a lot of stuff. I like your hair.'

Iris patted her newly cut and highlighted hair and laughed skittishly as she made for the door. 'Poky little place you've bought. Personally I think you're mad.'

'Excuse me, Miss Galloway.' The foreman of the removal men approached Chrissy, a form in his hands for her to sign. Chrissy accepted the men's good-luck wishes and dug in her pocket for the tip she had ready and folded. Despite the mist she decided it would be polite to stand and wave the large lorry away – her last link with Cornwall.

In the kitchen, her grandmother was unpacking and washing china, and her mother had begun to make sandwiches from the groceries she'd bought.

'Why did that man call you Galloway? Your name's Watson.' Iris waved a cucumber at her accusingly.

'Not any more.'

'Well, what a thing to do!'

'Iris, leave her alone. What she calls herself is up to her, not you,' Daphne intervened. 'You took your time.' She changed the subject abruptly, as if heading her off at the pass.

'I had to go out to Sainsbury's, the traffic was heavy.' Iris sounded defensive. 'When your father died I didn't change back to my maiden name. I'm proud to be a Galloway.'

'That's very nice for you, Mum. Right, I'll start on the packing cases in the sitting room.' Chrissy stood up decisively, not wanting to get into an argument, and left the other two women still bickering.

In the next room she cleared a space on the low coffee table, knelt on the floor and began to unpack the first of the cardboard cartons.

First out was a china cat, won for her by her father at a fair when she was eight. It had improbable green eyes and its body was encrusted with a scattering of brightly coloured flowers. 'Are you sure that's what you want?' her father had asked in surprise at her choice of prize, or perhaps it had been horror.

Had he been as difficult as her gran had said? She had never been aware of it. How could the perfect father she'd known be anything but a perfect husband too? She placed the cat on the coffee table.

From the box she took an intricately engraved silver bowl. It was the first present Ewan had given her. She'd been overwhelmed by his generosity. He'd laughed at her expression, and picked her up, smothering her face with sweet, urgent kisses. She'd been so happy, so proud of this new, unbelievably handsome, talented boyfriend. Such happiness! She sighed as she placed the pretty bowl beside the gaudy cat. Two such different objects from the two most important and equally opposite men in her life. Her conservative, careful, bank-manager father could never have been expected to understand the free-spirited, dangerous man in his daughter's life – and he never did. He'd never stopped worrying and fretting over her well-being. If only he'd known, if only she'd talked to him. If only . . .

'You need the light on.' Iris flicked the switch and everything in the room looked even sadder.

'My possessions look as if they'd come from a car-boot sale.'

'They're disorientated. They'll be fine in a few days when they've settled. Tea's ready or, rather, the champagne is. Pity that ghastly cat didn't get broken.'

'I love that cat.'

'A taste bypass.'

Chrissy laughed as she followed her neat-figured, cashmere-dressed mother back into the kitchen.

Wafer-thin smoked salmon and cucumber sandwiches, a cake-stand crammed with cream cakes, blue bone-china plates, damask napkins and crystal flutes awaited her. 'You went home to collect all this? How sweet of you, Mum. How elegant it looks.'

'Oh, it's nothing.' Her mother waved her hand dismissively, but for all that she looked pleased at the praise. 'Gracious, I nearly forgot. The hospital phoned this morning.'

'And?'

'What? Oh, I think they said you were to phone back – yes, as soon as you got here. I'll forget my own head one day!'

Chrissy covered the surge of irritation she felt at her mother's vagueness as she went into the sitting room to look for the phone.

'Was it important?' Iris asked innocently, when she returned.

'You could say it was. There was a hospital management meeting they wanted me to attend this afternoon.'

'I'm *so* sorry.'

'Never mind. It would have been bone-numbingly awful, ending in arguments over money, or the lack of it.'

'We should drink a toast to Chrissy's happiness here, Iris.'

'It's about time she found some,' Iris said gloomily. 'I can't help thinking . . . He was so young . . .' And Iris dived for her handbag and took out a scrap of lace handkerchief to dab at her eyes. Daphne looked with concern at Chrissy.

'I'm to see the Clinical Services Manager tomorrow instead,' she said brightly, and hoped it didn't sound too bright.

'What a mouthful. I remember when Gladys Simpson was matron of St Edith's. Everyone was terrified witless of her – but, by God, that hospital was run like clockwork. Not a speck of dirt would have dared alight there. And she cared. She didn't just know the name and condition of every patient, but their home circumstances too. Patients felt they were important.' Her grandmother, she realised, was deliberately steering the conversation away from the subject of Ewan.

'Instead of just "*throughput*".'

'That isn't what we're called these days?' Daphne looked horrified.

'Not at St Edith's, I'm sure,' Chrissy lied reassuringly, aware of her grandmother's concern.

'I don't know why you've come back to such a tin-pot operation. That hospital just lurches from one crisis to another. If you want the honest truth we'd all be better off if it *was* closed,' Iris said sharply.

33

'And what if you had a coronary and the ambulance had to high-tail it to Thorpedale General? Great news! You'd be dead by the time you reached the ring-road, Iris.'

'So, is it better that a run-down place like St Edith's has to be kept open because of a few heart-attacks?' Iris looked angrily at her mother-in-law as she spoke, and Chrissy realised that they'd disagreed on almost everything so far.

'It's more than a few, Mum. Fellcar has so many elderly, retired people that coronaries and strokes are probably a major problem.'

'With all your qualifications, Chrissy, you should be working in a senior position at a major London hospital.'

'Mum, we've been over this. I'm more than happy with this job – after all, it's what I've done all those courses in oncology for.'

'What's that when it's at home?'

'Cancer, Gran.'

'Then why don't they call it that?'

'They've a staffing crisis and have asked me to do some nights to help out.'

'Won't you find nights tiring?' Iris asked, helping herself to more champagne.

'I always liked nights. But, anyway, it will only be for a couple of weeks. The builders are behind with the new ward. Once that's done I'll only do nights in rotation with the other staff.'

'That place killed your father,' Iris suddenly said.

'Mum, it didn't. The clot on his lungs after his operation killed him. Nothing could have saved him.'

'We should have sued.'

'Dr Henderson explained it all to you at the time. There was no one to sue but God.'

'Chrissy's right, Iris. He'd had that pain for years, and what did the silly man do? Downed enough Rennies and Milk of Magnesia to sink a battleship, and boasted he was as fit as a flea, never needed a doctor. Then whoosh – he'd an ulcer and needed an operation. He was stupid.'

'Sometimes, Daphne, your callousness about your son is quite chilling.'

'I'm just better at facing reality, that's all.'

'Hi, everyone. I'm still here!' Chrissy waved at the other two across the table.

'I'm sorry, Chrissy. How rude of us.' Daphne apologised.

'She always thinks she knows best,' Iris said.

'Won't this cottage be super when I've finished with it?' Chrissy steered the small talk.

'I'll never understand why you bought it. It's small and dark and stuck out here.' Iris looked about her disparagingly.

'I like it. What would you have preferred? That I lived with you?' Chrissy said, preparing herself for the inevitable argument.

'Certainly not,' Iris said, almost hurriedly. 'That wouldn't have worked.'

'Exactly,' said Chrissy, but, illogically, she felt hurt at her mother's swift response. Iris had certainly changed since her husband's death – Chrissy hadn't realised how much until now. She looked up. Her grandmother was smiling a knowing little smile at her.

7

Although the meeting had not yet started, the atmosphere was already hot and heavy in what had once been the hospital governors' boardroom. Now it was where the senior doctors, nurses and managers of the Thorpedale and Fellcar NHS Trust met – too often, in the opinion of the majority present. The poor air quality would not lead to rapt attention, but even if the windows had been open it was doubtful that the deep boredom, from which most would soon be suffering, would have been eliminated.

This meeting at St Edith's had been called unexpectedly by Craig Nutting. Since the end of the financial year was not until April, and it was still only November, no one had been too concerned initially. Until they read the agenda. Tucked away among the items for discussion – work rotas, pay structures, ground maintenance – was one that had jumped out at those present: Managing Disinvestment, grey-suit talk for *cuts*. The heads of the various departments were talking among themselves. Some were quietly resigned, others were noisily adamant that their departments would be making no further cuts. But overall, given that all of the medical staff were very busy people, resentment was bubbling that they'd been called away from more important matters.

'Anyone know where Matthew Kersey is?' Craig Nutting asked irritably, looking up from the stack of papers in front of him. His expression was almost resigned when no one answered since the medical staff and the managers did not get on and probably never would. 'It might be an idea to start this meeting an hour earlier, then we might all manage to get here on time,' he said acidly. Still no one reacted.

The door opened and Russell Newson mouthed his apologies. 'Thanks so much for coming, Russell. So kind of you.' Russell took his seat, ignoring the other man's sarcasm. Kim Henderson, sitting at Craig's right hand, moved in his seat, not from any physical discomfort but from embarrassment at the animosity that was obviously mounting. Tiffany, Craig's secretary, sitting at his left, concentrated on her shorthand pad.

'Right, then. If you're all fit? No point in waiting for Matthew. The minutes, Tiffany.'

Just for once he hadn't told them to pin back their lug-holes, for which they should be thankful, thought Glynis, positioned at the top of the table. As Tiffany droned out the minutes of the previous meeting, Glynis studied the others present. The medical staff sat at one side of the table, the administrators at the other, as if they were two teams – which, in truth, they were. And that, of course, was no way to run a hospital, as she also knew well.

Her sharp eyes noticed that Russell Newson's eyes were closed. Glynis was worried about him. They were all overworked, but Glynis saw more than tiredness in Russell. He'd always been a private person, but recently he had become withdrawn and, she did not think it was her imagination, sad. He was one of her favourites, inevitably since he had trained at her own London hospital, which had made a lasting bond of loyalty. She could have wished he'd married someone a little more serious than the pretty but somewhat vacuous wife by whom he had been chosen – Glynis was fully aware that it was invariably the woman who decided such matters. Still, Sabine was popular with the other staff members, so she must have depths not evident to Glynis.

Late as always, the joy of Glynis's own life, Matthew Kersey, noisily entered the room. The quieter he tried to be the noisier he was, she noted with indulgent amusement.

'S-o-r-r-y, s-o-r-r-y,' he mouthed to all and sundry, tiptoeing across the carpet and barging into a side table, which rocked alarmingly and the ornate Victorian ink-well, fortunately empty, crashed noisily to the floor. There were muffled laughs and Craig rolled his eyes heavenward with frustration.

'My apologies, ladies and gentlemen.' Matthew bowed as if he was an ex-student of RADA rather than of UCH.

Glynis smiled, fully aware that in anyone else she would have found such clumsiness intolerable. Fortunately, the only spare seat was beside her, so for as long as this meeting took she'd have him near her – infantile on her part, but something she could do nothing about.

'Miss Tillman,' he acknowledged her formally.

'Mr Kersey,' she replied, while laughing inside at their subterfuge. It never failed to amaze her how they had got away so long with their relationship undetected.

The meeting settled again and it was Craig's turn to drone on: only the faces in the large oil paintings of former hospital governors and local worthies appeared to be taking any interest. This was nothing new. Each doctor's passion was for their own department, for which they would fight to the bitter end. However, once Craig got on to cuts and acquisitions the change in the meeting would be electric.

'Glynis, have you found out who shopped us to the newspaper?'

'No, Mr Nutting.' As always she emphasised his name. The use of Christian names was too common these days – another of those changes she was far from happy with – but at least it gave her the chance to register disapproval when she wanted, as now.

'I trust you're on to it.'

'Of course I am, Mr Nutting.'

'Well, I want it noted . . .' And Craig was away, lecturing how press enquiries were to be dealt with at such length that he only stopped when Matthew yawned pointedly.

'By the way,' he said, in a vague sort of way, 'next month I've arranged for the time-and-motion bods to have a dekko at A and E.'

'No!' Freddie Favour, the accident and emergency consultant, was immediately on his feet.

'Got a problem with that, Freddie?'

'You know damn well I have. I've been here eight years and I've lost count of the times we've been disrupted by the clip-board men. Not again!'

'Got to be done, Freddie. Sorry.' Craig smiled in what he confidently thought was a charming way, but which none of the others saw.

'Why, when things are hard, is it always A and E that faces closure?'

'Did I say that, Freddie?'

'No, Craig, you didn't, but we're not stupid. It's what you're leading up to – *again*.'

'If there *are* to be cuts – I didn't say there would be, only *if* – then I admit A and E is, in my opinion, the logical one to go for. We have an ageing community here, we have other priorities to think about. Other calls on our time and money.'

'It's because we have so many old and retired people, prone to fractures, that we need an efficient A and E twenty-four hours a day so don't give me any of that "daytime coverage only" crap! But I see where you're leading, Craig. The old can't be patched up, is that what you're saying? Do they take up too much bed space, not fast enough throughput for you?' Freddie was barely controlling himself.

'If you're thinking along such lines then presumably the ortho-paedics department will be the next at risk too. Take away the car-crash and sports injuries, and the majority of our patients are elderly,' Russell said calmly. 'Surely, Craig, if you target one section of the population it will have a knock-on effect on the other departments.'

'We have to prioritise.'

'We do that already, Craig,' Russell said quietly, to a murmur of approval.

'There's only so much money in the kitty, Russell, me old mate. Decisions have to be made.'

'I didn't come into this profession to treat patients on financial rather than clinical grounds.'

'Russell, my old fruit, I dislike it as much as you do.'

'I doubt it,' Russell said as an aside, which Craig apparently had not heard since he made no reply. Instead he began to shuffle pages officiously. But Kim had heard.

'I'll tell you how money can be made.' Freddie was on his feet again.

'I'm all ears, Freddie.' Craig smiled.

'A and E is being abused by certain fund-holding GPs in this area. They're referring patients to us as casualties in the hope we will admit them to save on their own funds. And they tell patients to come to Emergency because they're too sodding idle to attend them. That's how beds get blocked. Talk to them.' He burrowed in his briefcase and produced a folder. 'Study that. Those are our admission figures for the past six months. Look at Dr Middleton's in particular, would you?'

'Not my responsibility, old boy.'

'I'll study them.' Kim put out his hand.

'That wouldn't be proper, Kim. I'll see to it.' Craig grabbed at the file. 'Kim's father is the local GP, Dr Henderson. We don't want any conflict of interest, now do we?'

'Excuse me. While we're talking money, a new incubator is imperative. One of the old ones is working on a wing and a prayer. I can't take responsibility for it much longer.' Their dedicated paediatrician spoke quickly.

There was a swell of noise about the crowded room as each head of department began to add what their needs were.

'Look, all of you, keep your hair on! All I'm trying to say is we're running in over budget and when I say over I mean OVER. We've got a lot of aggravation ahead and I'm just trying to get into your noddles that cuts are going to have to be made. No ifs or buts. Personally, speaking for myself, the logical one is A and E. But,' he held his hand up, warding off the uproar that threatened, 'I'm open to suggestions on any savings. I want you all to look at your budgets, see where savings can be made next year, and if I could have them before Christmas. Ta.' He swung round to face the paediatrician. 'What about the Friends of St Edith's? Can't you ask them to rustle up the money for your incubators?'

'They paid for the last one and are flat out raising money for equipment for the new oncology ward. There's only so much they can do. There is such a thing as fund-raising fatigue,' Glynis interrupted, but she might just as well not have bothered as the arguments flowed back and forth.

'One thing.' Craig had almost to shout to be heard. 'As from today no replacements to be taken on for positions vacated. No advertising for new staff.'

A great roar of 'No!' filled the room.

'Hang on a minute.' The Occupational Health Sister was on her feet. 'My secretary's leaving next month. I have to have a replacement. I'm always out in the community, advising in factories, offices. How can I continue without help?'

'Get an answering-machine.'

'Craig, it was you who rejected my request for one and it was you who told me to get out and sell our expertise to businesses to generate more money for the Trust. How can I be in two places at once? What do you want? You decide.' She sat down again, and looked as if she was bored with the whole subject – but Glynis knew better.

'Once recruitment starts again are you planning one-year contracts?' Glynis asked quietly.

'Sorry, Glynis, I'm not with you.' Craig looked innocent.

'Good gracious, Mr Nutting, I can't believe you haven't worked out that if all staff are on short contracts then no redundancies are payable.' Glynis spoke with heavy sarcasm, knowing full well what his plan was and how other hospitals had already fallen prey to this practice.

'Good on yer, Glynis. Good thinking!' With exaggerated gestures Craig made a note.

'Oh, come on, Craig. We were warned. And I'll tell you this, the staff won't stand for it. It leads to insecurity – and that leads to inefficiency. The one thing we can't afford.' Russell was on his feet leaning across the table, his face angry, one fist bunched. The others shouted their approval.

'Well, Russell, inefficiency on the wards is down to you lot. Me, I'm just an administrator who tots up the figures. Falling off of efficiency – that ball's in your court.' Craig smirked; Kim looked uncomfortable. 'By the way, I read about a good idea the other day, might interest you all. Maybe we should be paying you doctors on how well the patient assesses he feels after his treatment! Good idea, isn't it?' Craig laughed loudly, but he was the only one who did.

On days like this, Glynis could wish she had chosen a different profession. As demands on the service got greater and were not matched by the necessary funds – would they ever be? – the arguments and horse-trading got worse and more frequent. It was appalling that such talented people should have to spend so much of their valuable time trying to balance the books, she thought, as she looked with concern at her colleagues.

8

Russell Newson worked methodically, folding a stack of T-shirts, which he then packed into a large black-leather holdall. He looked about the room, checking to see if he'd left anything out. He stretched. He felt exhausted but knew he would sleep on the plane. No doubt, the tiredness had been caused by that meeting he'd attended earlier. If only he could ignore the administrative side of his work and be free to concentrate on surgery alone. Still, that was the luxury he'd be enjoying in this coming week.

'Have you ever thought that I don't want you to go?' Sabine, prettily blonde, pouting and dainty, appeared in the doorway of the bedroom. Russell looked at her momentarily and responded with a derisive-sounding snort. 'You don't believe me, do you? Why don't you answer me?' A tear emerged from one large clear blue eye and rolled down her cheek, followed by another. She let them fall. 'Please! Russell, please!' Russell, unmoved, watched her. It never failed to fascinate him that whenever she cried her prettiness was never marred – if anything, he supposed, it enhanced her looks, adding a sad vulnerability to the prettiness as if a Dresden china ornament was crying. 'Please, speak to me!'

'There doesn't seem any point any longer. And do me and yourself a favour, turn off the waterworks.' Russell spied a stack of socks he'd forgotten.

'You're cruel!'

'Whatever you say.' He began to ball the socks into pairs, which he slid into the crevices in his packing.

'You don't care what I think, do you?' She patted at the tears on her cheek and sobbed dramatically.

'Not particularly. And don't forget, Sabine, I know that you can cry at will. You've tried that trick one time too many.'

'I hate you!'

'Then you won't mind my going, will you? I'm doing you a favour.' He laughed, but it was a chilling sound, as laughs are when devoid of all humour.

'I only hate you when you're like this. When you won't listen to me.' Before he was aware of what she was doing, Sabine rushed across the room, grabbed the bag from the bed and tipped the contents onto the floor. 'Don't go! Not like this!' She kicked at the T-shirts, socks and toiletries.

Russell wrestled the bag back from her. He bent and picked everything up, his mouth set firmly. He placed the bag and his clothes on the bed and began to repack as if nothing had happened.

'What do I have to do to make you notice me? What?' Sabine's normally low, husky voice was becoming shrill.

He turned and faced her. 'Sabine, what game are you playing now? You should have thought this through. You don't want *my* attention. That's the last thing you want.'

'I'm so upset.'

'No, you're not, you just enjoy the drama you're making.'

'I asked you to stay!'

'What for? I *have* to go. I promised. I can't let them down.'

'What about *me*?' The tears began again just as the telephone rang. Sabine answered it before Russell could reach it. 'Sabine Newson,' she said, on a sob. 'No, no, I'm fine. Really . . .' She tossed her long blonde hair, as if that could control the tremor in her voice. 'You're so kind!' Her voice caught again. 'He's very busy. He's leaving tonight, he's flying out . . . Please, a moment . . .' She turned her head from the receiver and began to cry noisily.

'Who is it?' he said, annoyed, and snatched the telephone from her.

'Russell Newson here.'

'Mr Newson, is Sabine all right?' Milton Curtis, his senior houseman, asked.

'She's fine.'

'I thought I heard her crying.'

'You did.'

'Oh, I see.' There was a long, awkward pause. 'Anything I can do?' Milton sounded puzzled.

'No,' Russell answered shortly. He had no intention of explaining himself to anyone.

'Ah . . . yes . . . Well, it's Mrs Norman. She's complaining of pain.'

'Milton, what were your instructions?'

'To refer everything that worried me to Phil —'

'Exactly.'

'But I just thought . . . I mean, Mrs Norman never complains.'

'Then discuss it with him.'

'Since you were the surgeon —'

'I'm perfectly aware I was the surgeon, but Phil is competent to deal with any complications. Now, if you'll excuse me, I've a plane to catch.' And Russell replaced the receiver, picked up his briefcase and checked the contents. He looked calm as he worked, but in truth he was upset. It wasn't that he minded what people thought of him, he didn't, but these endless scenes with Sabine were wearing him down. He longed for some peace in his life, a lack of sniping and hysteria.

'I'll give you a call,' he said finally.

'Why, thank you so much,' Sabine said sarcastically, no sign of a tear now.

'God, he's a cold sod,' Milton said, as he hung up. 'I never know what's the best thing to do. If I didn't tell him I'd be in the wrong, but when I do . . .' He shrugged his shoulders. 'And how could I tell him his registrar's out on the booze?'

'At least you've covered your back,' Lance Travers, the department's new junior houseman, said from the desk where he was finishing making up the patients' notes for the day.

'Do you like orthopaedics?' he asked suddenly.

'Odd question. Yes, I do. And you?'

'I'd have preferred something a bit more glamorous, you know, like brain surgery — help pull the birds.'

'Don't forget, orthopaedics is a growth industry. With an ageing population we'll always be in work.'

'Coffee, you two?' A nurse's head appeared around the door.

'Hello, hello! *Who* are *you*?' Lance asked, with exaggerated interest etched on his face.

'You needn't look at me like that,' she snapped.

'Just keeping a beady eye open for any possible new talent.' Lance smiled confidently at her.

'Do you know the biggest drawback in this profession? Sex-obsessed doctors like you. Don't you ever think of anything else?'

'Not if I can help it!' Lance guffawed.

'I reckon you're a waste of space, Doctor.'

'Is that a nice thing to say to an overworked, overtired houseman who sacrifices himself for the good of others?' asked Lance flirtatiously.

'You? Sacrifice yourself? I've no time for your moaning. A few years from now, when you're a consultant, you'll be pulling in the money like there's no tomorrow, while we nurses will still be overworked, underpaid and having to put up with creeps like you. Right, your coffee. Sugar? Milk?' The nurse turned on a heel and, with head held high, swept from the office.

'Did you see the way her rear wiggled? She's a corker. And I like them with spirit.' Lance stretched with contentment.

'I have an idea she meant what she said.'

'Rubbish. We all know why women go into nursing. It's hardly for the money, it's to snare doctors like us. Not that they'll get me.'

'If they wanted you,' Milton said, under his breath, and returned to his notes.

'I'd begun to think that there was a dearth of fab women round here.'

'You haven't met Newson's wife then, Lance. She's gorgeous. Heart-shaped face, blue eyes to die for.'

'Problem with doll women like that is I find it's a bit like shagging the fairy from the top of the Christmas tree – bit off-putting.'

'Odd – we always had an angel on ours!' Milton responded.

The door swung open and a nurse backed into the room, pushing the door with her large bottom. Her sturdy legs were like inverted bottles, and the size of her large feet was not helped by the plain, sensible lace-up shoes.

'Your coffee.' Auxiliary Nurse Alex Oldham put the tray noisily on the desk, slopping the coffee over the sides of the thick, catering-style cups, so that the equally thick saucers were awash with the pale brown liquid.

'Where's the other one?'

'Sylve? She's got more important things to do than wait on you lot. This isn't a sodding hotel, you know.'

'Don't you like us, Alex?' Lance grinned at her.

'If you must know, I loathe all medics. I think you're conceited, useless prats . . . Oh, good evening, Mr Newson. We were told you'd gone. Can I help you? Do you want to see the staff nurse?' Alex spoke in a breathless rush, her face quite pink. A smile even flitted across her dough-like face.

Russell nodded at his housemen, who had hurriedly jumped to their feet, both looking as guilty as if they'd been caught scrumping.

'Mrs Norman's notes, please.'

Alex barged across the small office leaving a trail of body odour, much like the froth stirred up by a passing liner, and pulled towards her the carrier on which the patients' files were suspended. The notes were in bed rather than alphabetical order, a system new to the ward, and to which she was not yet accustomed. The resultant minor delay aggravated Russell's already irritable mood, and he drummed his fingers on the desk.

Once the notes had been found, he wheeled smartly out of the small office and into the corridor that bisected the ward. Lance and Milton trotted along behind him, followed by Alex, looking frantically about her for Sylve, the senior nurse.

There was still activity on the side wards positioned off the main corridor. The last of the patients were being settled for the night – pillows puffed, water jugs checked, heating pads placed, where necessary, goodnights whispered.

All was dark in Mrs Norman's ward, apart from the blue light that glowed over her bed – always an indication that procedures would be necessary through the night. Alex hurriedly pulled the curtains to isolate the bed, the noise disturbing other patients, who muttered petulantly and fidgeted.

'Good evening, Mrs Norman. I'm told you're feeling a little poorly?' Russell smiled down at the elderly woman who, her family had noted when visiting that evening, seemed to have shrunk to half her normal size.

'I don't want to make a fuss, Mr Newson.'

'You're not, but even if you wanted to, why shouldn't you?' Russell sat on the side of the bed. 'Now, this pain. Perhaps you could

45

describe it to me. Is it a dull ache or a nasty sharp one?' As he spoke he took her hand comfortingly in his and gently, kindly, urged out of the worried woman her symptoms.

Minutes later, in the office, he refused Alex's offer of coffee. 'She's all right. I really can't think what you were fussing about, Milton. I've written her up for an increased dose of morphine later if she persists in complaining. I don't think she will. I think she's frightened. Keep an eye on her temperature. Half-hourly obs to be on the safe side. All right, gentlemen? Right, can I go now?' he said sarcastically. 'I'll see you in a week.'

'Good luck,' Lance called as Milton escorted Russell to the ward door.

'Shit! Was that one of the consultants?' Sylve asked anxiously. 'Alex, why didn't you come and get me? You know the rules.'

'I couldn't find you. He was in a hurry – there wasn't time,' Alex snapped back. 'Don't flap. I handled him. He's a puss-cat, our Mr Newson.'

'If he's a cat, he's a bloody snarling tiger,' Lance interrupted. 'He's bad-tempered, bossy, unpleasant.'

'He's a brilliant surgeon so he's allowed to be,' Alex retorted.

'I was told he was on holiday.' Sylve frowned, annoyed that she should be caught out.

'Newson? Holiday? He couldn't even spell it. No, he's off to Bosnia, quite the little saint he is. He patches up the amputees.'

'But the war's over.'

'Yes, Sylve, but no one remembered to tell the land-mines.'

9

As the transport aeroplane flew over the Alps, Russell Newson looked out of the small window in the fuselage at the mountains below. The moon was shining on the glistening snow and the peaks looked close enough to touch. Momentarily he longed to be able to step out of the plane, lie down, let the snow enfold him and carry him gently away . . . He shook his head at this, too fanciful for logic, but, for all that, an attractive idea.

'You all right, Russell? You look a bit doomy.'

He looked up to see Georgie Wallace smiling down at him, proffering a whisky.

'Where did you get that?'

'I've always got supplies. Purely medicinal, of course.'

'Of course!' He grinned as he took the plastic cup from her. She sat down beside him, settling herself as if for a companionable chat. He wished she hadn't: he liked Georgie, and she was a fine theatre nurse, it was just, with so much to think about, he'd rather be alone. An innate politeness made him shift in his seat as if giving her room.

'Are you all right?'

'Right as rain, Georgie. You're turning into a mother hen.'

'It's just . . . I've known you a long time, Russell, and you've changed, you know.'

'Have I?' he asked guardedly.

'You know you have. And in the past year. You can tell me what's bothering you, Russell, I'd never breathe a word.'

'Georgie, love, if there was anything bothering me you'd be the one person I'd turn to for a good dollop of sensible counselling. I'm sorry to disappoint you but I'm afraid there's nothing. Just the same boring old me.' He forced himself to smile at her.

'I'm not fooled, you know. Still, have it your own way.' She shrugged her shoulders, as if she didn't care. She did.

'You're looking a bit peaky yourself.'

'I'm pregnant. A laugh, isn't it – at my age?'

'You're not *that* old, for heaven's sake. Is this good news or bad?'

'Mixed.' She gazed at him over her plastic cup, which he now realised was full of orange juice and not whisky, her normal tipple. 'I never expected to be, not at forty. And until I found I was preggers I didn't even know I wanted to be. But I am, and, well, I've come round to the idea.'

'Who's the dad?'

'Don't ask me.' Georgie chortled at his shocked expression. 'Don't get me wrong. I do know, but he's not the sort I'd want to settle down with and I'm certain he's got no desire to be a dad. So – it's bubs and me alone, I suppose. The sad bit is, this'll probably be my last trip with you. I've enjoyed them.'

'It's different, isn't it?'

'It's been real medicine – patching up innocent people, real victims. Instead of supervising ops on people who, a lot of the time, have brought misfortune on themselves, drinking, eating, smoking too much.'

'Falling off skis. Smashing up cars.'

'Exactly.'

'But it's not for us to judge, Georgie, is it?'

'I never did before. I didn't even think much about it. But after coming to Bosnia that first time everything changed. I began to despise a lot of my patients.'

'Dearie me. Sounds as if it's time you got out,' he said teasingly, at her proselytising.

'Georgie, anything left in that bottle?' Ship, the anaesthetist, called from several rows in front.

'A bit.' She stood. Russell watched her move along the gangway. He could imagine what a comfort it would be to unburden himself to someone like Georgie. It was an attractive thought, too attractive. He turned and looked out again at the sky, blacker than normal in contrast to the snow. It might be a nice idea, but it wasn't his way.

Chrissy had thought she was so tired she'd get to sleep immediately. Instead, two hours after going to bed, she was still tossing and turning. Everything was too strange, she reasoned, that, and the wind howling outside as if hungry to enter her little cottage and spirit her away. Despite the noise the wind made, she could still hear the sound of the sea pounding noisily onto the beach below, like an express train that had no destination.

The newness of her bedroom, nature's sounds, were good excuses, but they were not all, as well she knew. Nights like this, so similar to the night Ewan died, always acted as a trigger, making her mind return to that time and worry, and wonder at all that had happened, and whether she could or should have done more. But she also knew that constantly going over the past prevented her getting on with her future.

She turned her pillows for the umpteenth time, searching for a cool spot. Making a conscious effort not to think of her dead husband, she began to worry at her grandmother's comments about her father. Chrissy did not know if she could bear to learn that he hadn't been as she had thought him to be. If it was so, then it meant she'd been duped again and that made her feel such a fool.

Iris Galloway lay in Bob's arms and felt content. She put her hand up to his face and touched him gently, as if making sure he was there. As he kissed the tips of her fingers she sighed.

'That was a big sigh.' His voice rumbled in her ear. 'Any problems? You can tell me, you know you can.'

Iris elbowed herself up and looked down at him. 'I can't believe you're real.'

He sat up, feeling for his cigarettes and lighter on the bedside table. Iris smiled to herself: she'd never allowed Frank to smoke in the bedroom but she didn't mind Bob doing it. 'So, what's the problem? Worried about what your daughter will say?'

'Silly, no,' she lied. 'It's none of Chrissy's business. Shall I make us a cup of tea?'

'Do you know what made me fall in love with you, Iris? You're the only woman I've ever met who understood the need for a cuppa after a good fuck.'

'Oh, Bobby. You're so bad!' She slid from the bed and slipped on her dressing gown. 'And how about a bacon sarnie?'

'At this rate I'll have to propose!'

In the kitchen, the cherry tree outside the window clicked against the panes as it was lashed by the storm. She was still smiling as she busied herself with kettle, bacon and frying pan. She smiled a lot these days. And all thanks to Bob.

When she thought of her husband now, it was with a dreadful anger. Why, for all those years, had their love-making been a quick, groping coupling once a week on a Saturday? She had sometimes wondered if that was all there was to it, since their sex had been nothing like the noisy sighing and rutting she saw on TV and at the cinema. Once she'd queried if, perhaps, their love-making was lacking a certain something.

Frank had looked at her in horror, as if she'd suggested wife-swapping. 'Really, Iris! At our age? We're a married couple,' he'd said, with disapproval and, she realised, embarrassment too.

But she wasn't old. She'd been in her forties when she'd asked, fifty-two when she was widowed. That wasn't old, not these days.

She turned the sizzling bacon over. What would have happened if she hadn't met Bob, and the wonderful uninhibited world he'd given her? Today she'd resented every moment spent at Chrissy's cottage in case she missed a call from him. He dominated every moment of her waking day. He only had to look at her and she felt her nerve ends start tingling. And when he used language never allowed in this house before, she felt a wave of sexual excitement that was almost unbearable. She'd tried saying that word herself, the F word, when she was alone and longing for him and his body, but it never worked, not like when he said it – especially when he was lying naked in her bed.

She'd hoped to say something to Chrissy about him today – a hint, perhaps, a warning – but her stupid mother-in-law had insisted on going to help unpack. And how could she say, 'Chrissy, I've met this man, he's giving me the most wonderful love, real sex for the first time in my life, and I feel reborn, and by the way he's fifteen years younger and I think I want to marry him,' with Frank's mother sitting there? She sighed loudly as she drained the bacon and placed it on the bread. Chrissy would go ape, she was sure. She'd see it as a betrayal of her sainted father.

She pushed open the bedroom door. He was pretending to be asleep – she always knew when he was playing. She stood awhile looking down at him, sprawled naked on Frank's side of the bed. She liked that bit best of all. They'd been away for odd weekends, but she always enjoyed it best here. It was as if she was cocking a snook at Frank beyond the grave.

Daphne could not settle. She'd made herself tea, taken paracetamol, but her head throbbed and sleep would not come. One moment she was hot, the next shivering with cold. She put the electric fire on, closed the window against the storm and climbed wearily back into bed.

For a couple of days she had known she was going down with something. She knew she should have seen the doctor. She knew why she hadn't. She was afraid to be ill. She felt that if she gave in she would be swamped by helplessness and she couldn't bear the thought of being dependent on anyone. 'Not yet, dear God, not yet,' she said aloud. She sighed deeply and winced from the pain of it. She was so tired. She couldn't fight, not any more. So tired . . .

St Edith's, standing exposed on the top of South Hill, was being buffeted with such ferocity that the wind seemed to be in a frustrated rage with the hospital. As the storm intensified the rain lashed at the old granite, beat against the tall windows, angrily demanding entry. As the lightning forked from the billowing black clouds, it illuminated the long corridors, puddling light on the highly polished floor. The thunder, distant until now, roared overhead, as if nature was calling up reinforcements.

In the hospital there was a restlessness that, with the speed of the storm, raced from one ward to another until the building was full of tossing, turning, sighing forms. Overworked nurses zigzagged the floors, tending to their patients. The young women cajoled and calmed, turned pillows, tucked in, made hot drinks, doled out sedatives, wishing the patients would settle so that they could put up their feet again.

The great building creaked and groaned, as if it were a ship on high seas. The noises fed fear into the souls of the nervous while the fearless slept on, oblivious to the tension and racket.

On Ward 2, once called Beach, the elderly fretted and moaned. Gwen Fortune, having a nightmare, woke screaming into another.

'There, there, love. It's only a nasty old storm,' the student nurse crooned, as Gwen screamed on.

'Can't you shut that stupid old cow up, Chelsea?'

'She's frightened, Jazz.'

'I'll give her something to be frightened about.' And, before Chelsea was aware of what was happening, the staff nurse lashed out and slapped Gwen hard.

'Jazz, you shouldn't have done that!' Chelsea Mottram's own hand shot to her mouth with shock.

'Well, I did! And it worked, didn't it? Any complaints?'

Gwen slumped back on her pillows, and cowered with a new fear. She began to cry silently, tears rolling down her wrinkled cheeks.

In Maternity, as the lights flicked and faded and the emergency power cut in, Jessica Carr, after an almighty push from her mother, emerged into the noisy world.

At the same instant, on Male Medical, beneath the blue light that marked the bed of those who would need tending or of the seriously ill, Ted Potter slipped gently away. Even in death he'd no wish to be any trouble to anyone.

CHAPTER TWO

I

In the morning, the sea was free of mist. The sun was shining and everything looked fresh and washed.

Chrissy inspected her face in the mirror tiles above the bathroom hand-basin. Since she had turned thirty, she checked for any wrinkles that might have sneaked up on her in the night. She was not sure why this ritual was necessary. She was not neurotic about being thirty-four – she looked younger, anyway – and she was not dreading being forty. And yet, each morning, the search was made, she never missed. Perhaps she was more worried about ageing than she realised, or maybe it was a hangover from . . . She shook her head, stopping that particular thought before it could take hold. The movement distorted her image in the tiles, making her look like a fitting portrait for Picasso. These tiles would have to go!

When she'd decided to buy this cottage she had thought it perfect but although she'd been here less than twenty-four hours her list of faults was growing. The bath was taking too long to fill – she needed a shower for speed. She'd had dreams of quiet evenings by a log fire burning merrily in the inglenook – until last night when she'd nearly choked on the acrid smoke billowing out. A wood-burner was now a priority. She needed a new car and these problems would dent her budget alarmingly. How was she to afford to have the lovely oak floors sanded and polished and scattered with as yet unpurchased rugs?

'You'll regret it,' Daphne had counselled. 'More trouble than they're worth, wooden floors. They're dusty, draughty and noisy. In my day we scrimped and saved for fitted carpets. Bare boards were for the poor. Now, a nice bit of parquet – I can understand that!'

Chrissy smiled at the memory of her grandmother's voice last night as she sipped her sherry and worried at Chrissy making a wrong decision. Daphne had had a hard life, working as a cleaner to put her clever son, Frank, through grammar school. And yet, if she began to talk about her past, he had invariably cut her off short: he must have been ashamed of her. How sad. Chrissy stopped her face-cleansing, cotton ball poised in the air. Why had she only just realised this? Why had she not thought it through sooner? Too obsessed with herself and her own problems, if she was honest, which, at the moment she wasn't sure she wanted to be. She stripped, slipped into the bath-water and shut out such uncomfortable thoughts by washing herself briskly.

On bare feet she crossed the tiny landing with its head-threatening sloping eave and entered her bedroom. It was this room that had sealed her decision to buy the cottage. Its sloping ceiling, which at one point swept down to only two feet from the floor, matched the walls, which were covered in a paper patterned with small blue, white and yellow daisy-like flowers. Whenever she came into the room she felt as if she was stepping into a millefiore paperweight. The curtains she'd bought from the previous owners matched, and even the fitted cupboard's doors were papered the same.

'It's a nightmare!' Iris had exclaimed.

'Isn't it somewhat busy?' Daphne had asked.

'I love it. Just as it is.' Chrissy had laughed at their disapproval. 'My pale blue sheets will match perfectly.'

'Rather you than me. All those fiddly flowers will make you dizzy and give you nightmares!' Iris had shuddered.

It hadn't. She had slept finally like a dream.

Since her dressing-table was still covered in bubble wrap, Chrissy sat on the floor and propped a mirror against the wall. She rubbed in her moisturising cream and applied a light foundation; she needed little for she had inherited a good skin from Iris. A touch of beige eye-shadow, a flick of black mascara, a whisper of kohl pencil, and her dark brown eyes shone. She outlined her full lips with pencil and filled in with a bright lipstick applied with a brush. When she was young she'd hated her mouth – 'Rubber Lips', they'd called her at school. Those same girls would envy her mouth now, she knew.

Her long, straight dark brown hair brushed, she wondered what to do with it. Anchored with a scrunchie and hanging down her back was a little too casual for her meeting, so she coiled it up, winding it around the scrunchie into a neat, heavy bun.

What to wear? She wanted to look smart without overdoing it. She finally chose a mid-calf fine brown tweed skirt, which she topped with a black polo-neck sweater and a short brown velvet jacket. She pulled on her flat black leather boots, looked at herself in her cheval mirror and decided she would do.

A quick coffee and an apple were her breakfast as she waited for a taxi. She leafed through the local paper and saw a car that might suit her and was within her price range at Potter's Garage; she could go there after her meeting. Then, for something to do, she wrote down her list of wants for the house, realising she was nervous, which was silly since the job was already hers. How odd, she thought.

2

Glynis Tillman smiled secretively at the piece of paper in her hand. It was one of many, notifying her of telephone calls made to her while she was off-duty. 'Cancellation, Saturday possible,' said the message and was signed 'A. B. Hausmann', which was neither very original nor discreet, and no longer funny after all these years as Matthew Kersey's pseudonym.

For sixteen years their secret had held. It was incredible how fast that time had flown. Yet they had spent so little time together, the odd snatched evening, the hour in the day, the miraculous long-remembered rare weekends – if they were all added together this romance had been going probably for only a year in hours spent together, no time at all.

It was sad that this was how it was, and more so now that she was in her middle years. These days she found herself often thinking of her retirement, not because she looked forward to it but from fear of it and the loneliness she expected it would bring.

Not this weekend, though. Incredibly he would be free for her birthday on Saturday. She'd long ago resigned herself to not seeing him then — that that was a family day. Lord, how much she had accepted.

Saturday! She clutched the message to her, her excitement at the contents no different from a teenager's, even though she was forty-six this week. At least he had kept her looking young — even her disapproving mother had agreed on that. Her mother's censorious attitude had been a constant wearying nuisance until she died, but then Glynis realised, with her gone, she had no one in the world she could talk to about him.

'Come.' She looked up, flustered, as if whoever was at the door would be able to read her thoughts.

'The new F grade sister has arrived. She's early. Do you want to see her now?' Sister Shelagh Morris asked.

'If you could give me a couple of minutes to finish noting my calls, Sister? Then arrange some coffee?' She smiled at the other woman, whose lips twitched a mild response. Glynis knew Shelagh Morris did not like, approve of or want her here; that she lusted after her position. Well, she'd have to wait. Glynis had no intention of retiring a day before it was necessary. This hospital was her life — well, almost.

Her messages sorted into piles of varying urgency, she stood, a slim, upright woman who, given her height of a good five foot ten, had an imposing bearing. She crossed to the door to the outer office.

'Miss Galloway?' she called.

Chrissy jumped to her feet and in her confusion immediately dropped her handbag. Confronted with this smart, somewhat imperious woman, she was glad she'd thought out carefully what to wear. She looked the sort who set great store by appearance and, no doubt, polished shoes. As if in confirmation, she was aware that her boots *were* being studied.

Glynis held the door wide open for her and Chrissy stepped into the Clinical Services Manager's room. It looked more like a study than an office, with cream, glazed-cotton curtains, a nice selection of water-colours, leather-bound books and chintz-covered armchairs either side of a coal-effect fire.

'Would you care to sit?' Glynis indicated one of the chairs and settled opposite, just as a woman, in the blue and white checked overalls of a cleaner, appeared with a tray on which stood a silver coffee pot, bone-china cups and saucers. 'Cream? Sugar?' Glynis asked, as she poured the coffee.

'Just a little cream, please. This is a lovely room.' Chrissy looked about her appreciatively but, since there was no response, wondered if she should not have commented and then felt cross with herself for being intimidated.

The cup was handed over and Chrissy found herself being studied long and hard by two clear blue eyes, which, she could imagine, might be quite frightening in anger. 'I'm sorry I wasn't here in August to interview you personally.'

'They told me you were on holiday,' Chrissy said, though at the time she'd been surprised at her absence.

'Yes. Well . . .' Glynis hoped she hid the annoyance, which still rankled, that such an important appointment had been decided in her absence – the deft hands of Craig Nutting and Shelagh Morris at play. 'As you know we were promised that the oncology ward would be up and running next week. Unfortunately it's delayed – builders, you understand.'

'Yes, Sister Morris telephoned and warned me.'

'We've the added problem that one of our junior sisters has had to leave abruptly and a senior sister is having to take sudden early retirement.'

'Yes, she told me that too. I said I didn't mind being a float pro tem.'

'You seem to know everything, Miss Galloway.' Glynis gave a glacial smile.

'Only what she told me. I hope you had a nice holiday,' Chrissy added lightly, to try and dispel the chill atmosphere that was building.

'It was most co-operative of you to agree to help out with some night duty.'

'My pleasure.' Chrissy smiled, though if she had known how unfriendly the woman was she wondered if she would have been so keen to help.

'Of course, it's only because of this wretched flu epidemic. I'm worried that you will find yourself on wards with patients whose conditions you may be unfamiliar with. It's the main problem with nursing staff, specialising as they do. In the old days a nurse could take over any ward at any time.'

'Don't worry, I'll muddle through,' Chrissy said encouragingly.

'That is what I fear, Sister.' The voice was deep-frozen with disapproval. 'If you could outline your career to me thus far,' Glynis continued shortly.

'Well,' Chrissy began uncertainly, caught off-guard by the woman's obvious dismissal of her attempts to gain her confidence, 'I worked for two years as a staff nurse at my teaching hospital, University College, male surgical and oncology. I left to do my midwifery at Addenbrooke's in Cambridge.'

'Why not at UCH? An excellent maternity hospital.' It was at this point that Chrissy registered the Clinical Services' Manager was wearing the familiar silver and blue brooch, which was her own hospital badge. They were colleagues, it was a bond of loyalty, and it always stood one in good stead. Chrissy immediately relaxed.

'Well . . . I met a feller.' Chrissy immediately wished she hadn't said it, since a frown flashed across the other woman's face and all thoughts of swapping anecdotes about their old hospital faded. 'After my midwifery I applied for a post as a staff nurse on the oncology unit and did six months before becoming a junior sister and making that my specialist subject. Then I married. We lived at first in Cambridge and I held that post for three years.'

'Did you stop nursing because you had children?'

'No. I'd intended to keep on but my husband didn't want me to work. You know how it is?' But from her expression of cool disinterest Glynis Tillman obviously did not know, and it looked as if she didn't care either.

'You're a widow?'

'Yes, my husband died two years ago.' She paused, wondering if she should explain about the shock she had suffered, but decided not to. 'Then I thought I'd like to get back into the profession. I did the Back to Nursing course. As you know, I could choose which wards to do my placement on. I chose oncology. I worked as an E grade for six months and was fortunate to get a permanent post at F grade at my local hospital. I saw your advertisement in the *Nursing Mirror*. I wanted to get away . . . you know, memories . . .' There was no reaction from Glynis. 'I was born here – so, hey presto, here I am. It seemed a nice neat closing of the circle.'

'You are fully recovered from your husband's death? I ask because nothing must come between you and your work. The position you have been awarded is one of great responsibility and nothing must interfere with your care of your patients.'

'I'm fine.' Chrissy looked down at her hands, which she always did when Ewan was being discussed to avoid the sympathy in others' eyes. She allowed herself a small smile, however, since she knew that the hospital had been overjoyed to take her: staff shortages were becoming a nightmare and, with her experience, she'd been an ideal candidate. She said nothing, though. Let this woman play her power games, if that's what she wanted.

'I should explain that I belong to the old school, Miss Galloway. I will not have anything worn other than the designated uniform. And no perfume, ever. I expect total dedication. Whereas some of my senior staff are happy for staff junior to them to use their Christian names, I am not one of them.'

'But of course, Miss Tillman.' This woman must be one of those who was having trouble moving with the times. She could easily feel sorry for her – it *was* proving hard for some – but, on the other hand, with her being so unfriendly, why should she bother?

'Where are you living? With your parents?'

'No. I've bought a cottage out at Bigton Wyke.'

'Is that wise? Your contract is a short one.'

'I realise that. I didn't want to lose it. The house, I mean. I fell in love with it the minute I saw it.' She knew she was babbling and wished she could stop, furious with the way she thought she'd got the measure of Glynis Tillman only, seconds later, to feel the initial intimidation flood back. Why should she be worried? She was a good, competent nurse: there should be no reason why they wouldn't renew her contract. Or was there? Professionalism apart, she'd forgotten one factor in the equation. Personality conflict. She was certain this woman didn't like her, had, in fact, taken an instant dislike to her. Maybe she'd live to regret the house, returning, trying to build her new life here – everything!

'Miss Galloway!'

'Sorry,' she said, flustered, unaware that Glynis had been speaking to her. 'I was miles away.' And that was something else she shouldn't have admitted, she realised.

'Is there anything further you wish to discuss?'

'I've been thinking I would like to start a support group for my breast-cancer patients. As I'm sure you're aware, research is beginning to show that those who have this help live longer. And I do believe it helps raise the spirit – controls fears, helps depression.'

'Funding would be difficult,' said Glynis, mindful of Craig Nutting's warnings on cuts. But, seeing the disappointment in Chrissy's face, she added hurriedly, 'I think it sounds a splendid idea. We follow up patients for their physical well-being, why not mental too?' Chrissy wondered if it was her imagination or if she had actually said something that had met with Miss Tillman's approval.

'I wouldn't mind running it in my own time.'

'Then you have my permission. Would you like me to take you on a tour of the hospital?' Glynis was already standing. 'To familiarise you with the building.' She smiled at last.

'That would be so kind of you.' Chrissy got to her feet. The last thing she really wanted was to spend any more time in the company of this rigid, unfriendly woman.

3

With Kerry in bed and her teenage daughter, Katya, out with friends, Mo Fordham was enjoying a leisurely bath before Robbie returned from the pub and took her out for a promised meal to celebrate her thirty-fifth birthday. How the hell she'd got to that age was a total mystery to her. One day she was twenty, newly wed, a happy life stretching before her, and wham! here she was, the big four-oh just around the corner.

She played with her sponge, filling it with water and then squeezing it out. Where had all the time gone, all the things she had meant to do? She smiled at her pessimistic thoughts: she sounded like an old woman, or a condemned one. But she knew only too well why she thought them.

Whoever had written 'they lived happily ever after' should have been shot, preferably before they had penned the phrase. Did anyone ever achieve such a state? She doubted it. She and Robbie hadn't, that was for sure. You had to have time to be happy, time to sit back and realise you were, and time was a commodity they had always been short of. Mo, with the house, the children, her teaching job, had had little time left for fun; generally she was too exhausted. Even tonight, her birthday treat, she was so tired and her feet ached that she'd really much rather have a take-away, hire a couple of videos and curl up in front of the telly. She had hinted as much to Robbie, but she'd seen the look of irritation on his face and had speedily turned her lack of interest into concern at the expense.

'We never go out. For Christ's sake, let me spoil you on your birthday.'

She'd kissed his cheek, wishing she hadn't said it, and began there and then to plan what to wear.

They were drifting apart, she knew it. That kiss on the cheek said it all really. Time was when she'd have kissed him thanks full on the lips, and he'd have grabbed her and fondled her, and they'd have told the kids to go and play and would have fallen into bed. Sex had been so good, once. Now it was a rarity. But what made that situation even worse was that she didn't mind its infrequency.

Robbie had always worked long hard hours, but now in the free time he had he was often out. In the past when he'd invited her to go with him to the pub or the club she'd always said she hadn't the time. Now he never bothered to ask. And now, she knew, often he wasn't at either – she squeezed her sponge tight, as if to hurt it. The water cascaded out, and as she released it, the pressure made it fly like a champagne cork into the air and fall on the bathroom floor. Mo sank back in the bath onto the frilled, rosebud-sprigged bath pillow Katya had given her for Christmas. The thought she didn't want to consider slid back into her mind. 'He's got a bird!' she said out loud. There. She sat bolt upright. She'd allowed herself to say the unthinkable. She sat listening, as if expecting to hear her own voice repeating it. She laughed at the anti-climax she felt. What had she expected – to feel different? To be made different by admitting to it? She'd sensed it for a couple of months now so it wasn't exactly a secret to her.

Half of her wanted to hit him for being so weak, so disloyal and bringing down the shutter hard on 'they lived happily ever after.' The other half found she couldn't blame him, they weren't happy and hadn't been for some time. And what sort of wife was she when she found that him not wanting her sexually any more was something of a relief?

'Come on, Mo. It's your birthday. Stop this! Think about it tomorrow.'

She leant out of the bath, fingers stretched for her sponge which lay just out of reach. She liked her sponge, bought on a holiday in Greece, and always soaped herself with it. Instead, she had to pick up the soap and lather it in her hands.

She washed her arms and her neck. She began to soap her left breast, her hand flat and moving in a rhythmic circular motion. Suddenly she froze, sitting completely still, not even breathing. Then her hand moved away from her body as if it had been stung. She took a deep breath and gingerly touched herself again. The water, which was still hot, felt like ice. Waves of fear started accumulating in the top of her head and then trickled down her body to the very tips of her toes at an ever-increasing speed. Quickly she got out of the bath. In front of the mirror she tried again, hoping that by standing upright the lump she had felt would disappear. That it was all in her imagination. It didn't. It wasn't.

She sat on the lid of the lavatory seat and began to shake, her eyes flitting sharply from left to right. She felt dizzy and realised she was holding her breath. She forced herself to inhale deeply. The fear inside her skidded from organ to organ like a skater out of control on the ice. Mo had never felt so alone.

4

Glynis poured herself a moderate whisky and added an equal measure of water. From her collection of CDs she selected Mahler's Third and put it on the player with the volume low. Carrying her glass she crossed her sitting room, pleasingly decorated and furnished in cream and sage green. In the kitchen she checked that the chicken with tarragon that she had cooked was not drying out. She looked at her watch. He wasn't late yet, not by his standards – only by her own.

On her return to the sitting room, she lowered the writing-flap of her desk and from her briefcase took out a folder. The interior of the desk, with its row of pigeon-holes, was immaculate and remained so as she placed the folder perfectly straight on the leather top, opened it, then laid her pen and pencil precisely beside it. From their case she took her gold-framed half-eye spectacles and began checking the rows of figures in front of her. Ever since the management meeting she had been working on this, trying to do the impossible, to make savings for the next financial year.

Although it was an integral part of her job, it was not, and never had been, a favourite task. And, as always, so much depended on these wretched figures – people's health, their jobs and, what was becoming evident, the future of the hospital. Cost-effectiveness was the mantra of the accountants. While being the first to agree that economies should be made wherever possible and that waste must always be guarded against, it seemed now that money ruled everything; every decision was money-orientated, money led. The needs of the patients were becoming lost, almost unimportant, it seemed to her, against Mammon. She had always laboured conscientiously over these matters, determined that, by remaining vigilant, in her hospital it would be the clinicians who made the medical decisions and not the 'suits' with their clip-boards and calculators. It was a stand that was becoming harder to maintain.

An hour later, her task still not finished but weary now, she looked at her watch and then the telephone. Her hand stretched out towards it, but she retracted it sharply as if she hadn't wanted it to act in that way.

He wasn't coming, that was evident. What had she expected? He'd never come on a Saturday before, and it had been mad of him to have thought he would be able to get away. She had been mad too, for allowing herself to hope that, just this once, he'd make it for her birthday.

How childish of me, she thought. Ridiculous! She stood up purposefully. In the small dining room, the table laid with her best silver, she lit the dark green candles, which exactly matched the green of the walls.

Before settling to her meal she rang the office in the hospital. Change-over from day to night staff must be almost completed.

'Yes.' A voice spoke abruptly, and Glynis frowned. She wished that Shelagh Morris had a better telephone manner.

'Sister, I'm just checking all's well.'

'Everything's fine.' Shelagh did not even bother to try to disguise her annoyance. Once she put down the telephone she'd probably complain about her 'snooping' – she was such a stupid woman.

'Staffing levels adequate?' Her voice mirrored her amazement. Staffing to safe levels was becoming a nightmare.

'Just about. No one's called in sick.'

'Excellent.'

'Have a happy birthday dinner,' Shelagh said, quite kindly for her. Glynis often wondered what she knew.

'Thank you,' she said simply, and replaced the receiver.

Her first course was Dublin Bay prawns with an aïoli sauce she had made herself. She sat, upright as always, at one end of the table and wished she'd removed his setting from the other. But, then, if she did, it was as if she was acknowledging he wouldn't come. Such an idea made her stand up abruptly, yet again despising her childishness. She stacked his unused china, silver and glass quickly and decisively, as if she was afraid that if she didn't act rapidly then she might change her mind.

In the kitchen she served herself a small portion of the chicken. She placed the strained vegetables in a dish, but she ignored the potatoes. At the table she helped herself to peas and broccoli, swallowed a vitamin pill with her mineral water and poured a glass of the Gewürztraminer she had chosen specially.

The problem with such disappointments was that she had no one to blame but herself – though knowing that didn't help much. On nights like this she had invariably to rein in her thoughts and remind herself that this was her chosen life and to stop feeling sorry for herself.

Sixteen years ago she had been thirty and well set on her promising career. She had had several chaste relationships for she had been a beautiful young woman – naturally blonde, with eyes of a remarkable blue, effortlessly slim with cheekbones that were envied. She had a lot of style, she'd often been told, although she was never exactly sure what that meant. But none of those men had meant more to her than her career.

Glynis picked up her glass of wine and looked thoughtfully at it, a small smile at a happy memory playing about her mouth. Her work had been everything, until she'd met Matthew. Nearly six years younger than her, he was newly qualified, a junior houseman, the lowest of the low in the medical hierarchy. She was enjoying promotion to junior theatre sister at UCH, the prestigious London hospital that had trained her. It was a role she had worked for, planned for and, she thought sometimes, would have killed to achieve.

Some people meet and in the moment of meeting they know they have met their destiny. So it was with her.

On their first date he'd ordered Gewürztraminer, which afterwards they always drank on special occasions. They had negotiated with other staff to arrange a weekend when they were both off duty, all done with no mention of each other and why, for no one must know. The gossip would have spread rapidly around the large hospital. In a hotel in the New Forest, to his astonishment, he found she was still a virgin. It was a present she gave him, together with her love, for life.

There was no way of knowing that it was to be the last truly happy weekend of her life. On their last night together, he confessed that he was married. She was called Wendy. He did not love her but had dutifully married her because she was pregnant – a mere month before he'd met Glynis.

Glynis had sat still as a rock, her face rigid as she battled to control her emotions. Her world was shattering at his words. He had assured her that, once the baby was born, he'd ask for a divorce and they'd marry as soon as possible. But instinct told her it would not happen like that. Wendy's baby was stillborn, and its death meant the death of their plans. Wendy could not be told about Glynis, not until she recovered from her understandable depression.

Wendy never did recover. Her depression lurched on. Less than a year later she was pregnant again – even though he'd said they never slept together. He'd explained that Wendy had got tipsy one night and seduced him. Glynis made herself believe him.

This child was born with a defective heart and an uncertain future. Again, she agreed, Wendy could not be told.

He took a post as registrar in general surgery at Inverness. Six months later, much to everyone's surprise since Glynis's career in London was on target for an administrative post, she followed him.

It was as well she had, for she was the nurse in charge when, during a routine gall-bladder operation, he had made a clumsy mistake and the patient had died. In the subsequent enquiry she was able to cover up for him. It was not an incident she was proud of – it was a blot on an otherwise perfect career. But Glynis was a victim to love, as so many before her had been; and where Matthew was involved – when morality and love clashed – love won.

Wendy tired of the Highlands. He moved to a consultancy at Fellcar. Another discreet six months later Glynis followed to take up her post as senior night sister. Fortunately Wendy liked Fellcar, so Glynis took promotion until, two years ago, she'd applied for, and been appointed to, the post of Clinical Services Manager.

Patrick, the sickly son, grew into a healthy rugby-playing teenager. Glynis waited patiently until two years ago, at her prompting, Matthew finally confessed to Wendy. He massaged the truth a mite by implying it was a recent event rather than a love affair as old as her own marriage, and no mention was made of Glynis.

Wendy ranted, screamed, begged and entreated through the evening, well into the night until, exhausted, she collapsed in a heap on the floor. Matthew, feeling battle weary himself, carried her to bed. Told her he was sorry, stealthily left the house, and drove to Glynis to tell her he had done it, they were free.

The remainder of the night they spent making love and planning their future together. She had tried to mirror his confidence but found, after all this time, that doubts were not easily eradicated.

She was right. During the day, the news that Matthew Kersey's wife had been brought into Casualty was phoned to her office. Out of courtesy to a member of staff's wife, she had to attend her. She no longer cared to remember her thoughts that day as she walked quickly towards the department. Suffice to say that they had been unprofessional and unChristian.

Wendy had taken an overdose. She was saved.

Her unmarried sister, Jenna, had moved in with them so that she was never alone. Matthew felt he could not risk leaving her, not yet.

In uncharitable moments which, to Glynis's shame, were rather too frequent, she was sure that Wendy had never intended to kill herself, had planned to be found. That she was blackmailing him.

On nights like this, with whisky and wine inside her, Glynis could see clearly the hopelessness of her situation – something she normally tried to keep buried deep inside her. *Matthew would never leave Wendy!*

Sometimes she dreamed of telling Wendy everything. But it

remained a dream, for Glynis was a loyal creature and her love for Matthew was genuine: she could never hurt him. And so she endured.

Endured. What a harsh, hard word to describe her anguish. *Anguish* was not an exaggeration, either. And fear loomed: fear of what the future held, how she would manage, how to survive.

Her meal lay untouched. She sat at her empty table and felt such a dreadful sadness. Tears, which she never normally allowed herself, tumbled down her cheeks and fell silently on to her fine linen napkin. Glynis shuddered for suddenly she realised that she had never felt such loneliness.

5

Mo Fordham was beginning the preparations for the roast, as she did every Sunday. She hoped the familiar routine would help stem the fear that swirled around inside her. It didn't. This fear was not like the normal day-to-day variety that, for a mother, was part and parcel of living. That familiar fear with its familiar list of worries: where were the kids? Were they safe? Would Katya let her know before she did anything silly with a boy? Was she trying drugs? What about Aids? Meningitis? How to find the money for the electricity bill? Those fears, real as they were, were as much part of her as her nose or her heart. Often she'd joked that if these disappeared she'd have to find something else to worry about, to fill the void their absence would make. If only she'd known! If only she hadn't tempted fate in that way!

Above her head she heard Kerry in her bedroom, no doubt playing with her precious Polly Pockets. Mo gasped and stuffed her hand in her mouth to stop the sound but there was no stopping the tears that slid down her cheeks. How would the children manage without her? How could Kerry, eight next birthday, cope if she was not here? And Katya was only fourteen and needed her more than ever now. Who would guide her, protect her? Her legs felt weak and she sat down on the kitchen stool. She felt dizzy from anguish and then, hearing Katya call from the hall, she shook herself, forcing herself to look in control.

She grabbed an onion from the vegetable rack and quickly began to peel it.

'Mum, guess what?' Katya rushed into the room, hair flying, cheeks pink from the cold, her new coat unbuttoned.

'Have you been walking about like that? You'll get a chill.' Mo used the nagging as a shield.

'I've been running. I'm hot. Guess what? Mr Stevens says he's going to start up a club for us.'

'Can I join?' asked Kerry, appearing in the doorway.

'No. It's only for teenagers. Brats aren't allowed.'

'Mum, that's not fair!' Kerry began to wail.

'You've got the Brownies.' Katya pushed her.

'I hate the Brownies.' Kerry stamped her foot.

'Stop it! Both of you!' Mo shouted, and the tears began again.

'Mum, what is it? Why are you crying?'

Mo wiped at her eyes with the edge of her apron. 'I'm not crying, silly. It's the onions.'

'Oh, is that all? Can I join?'

'I expect so.'

'Mum –'

'Kerry, don't start. Now, if you're not going to help, clear out.' She shushed her daughters away and she smiled, for the first time that day, at how easy it was to be shot of them. They were both so afraid of helping. She began to peel the potatoes. She was lucky with her girls – oh, they fought and argued, but with such a big age difference that was understandable. Otherwise they were good and helpful and never cheeked her. So whoever – she gulped audibly. She wouldn't even allow such thoughts to enter her head.

'I'm off.' Robbie's head appeared in the doorway.

'When will you be back?'

'Hope you've cheered up by the time I get back.' He ignored her question, he often did these days.

'I'm sorry . . .' she began, but he'd already gone.

Last night's birthday celebration had been a disaster and it had been her fault, she knew that. But knowing it didn't make it any the easier.

Robbie had tried hard with the evening, she'd give him that. They'd gone to the Lotus Blossom for her favourite, Peking Duck – and everyone knew how expensive that restaurant was. And he'd bought her a red rose from the flower-seller whom he normally told to piss off. There, he'd given her a CD of Dire Straits – her all-time favourites – to play on the new mini-deck he'd given her before they left home. And then they'd gone to the Indigo, the club where they'd done most of their courting, to find all their friends gathered there as a surprise.

The attention he was paying her, the fuss, the expense made her wonder if his fling was over and he was making amends. It was a pleasant thought, but not one that lingered long. Soon she was wondering if this was being done out of guilt. But such concerns, which normally would have been eating away at her, didn't bother her nearly as much as her breast and what was happening in there.

She had sat on a banquette in the half-light, her arm across her chest cupping her left breast protectively, afraid it could be hurt, afraid it could be made worse. She had tried to join in the banter and the fun, but she couldn't.

'Anything wrong, Mo?'

'What's up, Mo?'

'You down in the dumps, Mo?'

As one friend after another questioned her she forced a smile.

'*Anno domini* . . .'

'Feeling me age . . .'

'Birthdays are coming round too fast for comfort . . .'

'You look really sad, Mo. Anything I can do to help?' Ashley Straw, Robbie's friend and partner in their central-heating company, leant over her, looking anxious.

'Honest, Ash, I'm fine. I don't know why everyone's getting at me.' She tried to keep irritation out of her voice – it wasn't fair on her friends, they didn't know what bothered her.

'We love you, Mo. And you know I'm always there for you.' Ash squeezed her hand.

'I know, Ash. Thanks. But honest –' She forced herself to laugh.

She could fool the others, but not Robbie.

'What the fuck's got into you? Aren't you ever happy?' he'd whispered angrily into her ear.

'I'm fine. A bit tired,' she'd said, while longing to have the courage to shout, 'I've got a lump in my breast and I'm frightened I'll die. And

I'm afraid you'll leave me if they cut it off,' but she didn't. 'Sorry,' she said instead.

He'd driven her home in silence but hadn't got out of the car. He hadn't explained anything, just gunned the car and shot off into the night. Mo had lain in bed, staring at the ceiling, while fear multiplied like a virus. She was still awake when he came home as dawn broke, but she'd turned on her side and pretended she was asleep . . .

Once the potatoes were on and the Brussels sprouts peeled she made herself a coffee and sat at the kitchen table. There were times she wished she smoked and this was one of them. If only her mum was alive or she had a sister to talk to. She had friends, but no one to whom she felt close enough to unburden herself, not about something like this.

The rest of the day stretched ahead: how to deal with that and with Robbie when he came back? If he came back.

6

Chrissy had the whole of Sunday planned. As she pottered about she found her concentration wavering and slowly became aware of a strange, insidious feeling of unease. Since she was normally pragmatic, she tried to ignore it, except that it would not go away. Instead, it intensified into a certainty that something was wrong.

When she called her mother and grandmother there was no reply. While she was not surprised that her mother was not in, it was worrying that Daphne did not answer the phone: she rarely went out and certainly not on a Sunday. This decided her; she forgot her plans and called a taxi.

Two bottles of milk stood ominously on the doorstep of Daphne's modest Victorian terraced house. They had often nagged her about the danger of a key on a piece of string inside the letter-box but today, as she fished for it, she was relieved that her grandmother had not listened to them. As she pushed the door open she called out, even though, by now, she was certain there would be no response.

Chrissy felt sick with apprehension as she ran lightly up the stairs.

She paused outside the bedroom door and forced herself to take a deep, calming breath.

'Gran, it's me.'

The only light was from two bars of an electric fire, which was making the room intolerably hot. She felt her shoulders slump with relief at the sound of breathing, but stiffen again as she registered how shallow and rapid it was. She made her way to the side of the bed and felt for the switch of the bedside lamp.

Daphne was lying on her back, her mouth agape, her face flushed. Gingerly Chrissy touched her hot forehead. Her action woke the older woman: her eyes opened slowly and she looked at Chrissy with an unfocused stare. She coughed and winced with obvious pain.

All the years of training, all the patient care, all Chrissy's knowledge was doused, in a second, by a great blanket of fear. Chrissy should have been registering her symptoms, reaching conclusions, but she could not remember anything, only that she feared her grandmother was dying and fear began to give way to panic.

'What . . . are you . . . doing here?' Daphne asked, with difficulty.

'It's me,' Chrissy said inanely.

'I know it's you.' She gasped for breath. 'I'm not senile, you know.'

'You should be sitting up.' Sense began to edge back into her mind.

'I'm comfortable . . . as I am, thank you –' But the sentence was too long for her and she began to cough and to struggle to sit up herself. Chrissy linked her arm into her grandmother's and helped her upright.

'That's right, indulge me . . . Here, sip some water . . . Can you lean forward, I'll plump your pillows up . . . There, see? Isn't that better? Isn't that easier?' The familiar nursing actions began to calm her and she forced some order into her mind.

'I'm glad you came . . . I'll be all right . . . now . . .' The painful cough intervened.

'Try not to talk, Gran. Try to relax.' Chrissy felt her pulse, noting its speed. She leant forward to look more closely at the red eruption on Daphne's cheek. 'I'll go and call the doctor.' She stood straight and decisive now. 'Is the number –?'

'No fuss . . .' Daphne was struggling, as if she was trying to get out of bed. 'No . . . not on a Sunday . . . The poor man . . . Tomorrow

'. . . surgery . . .' But the effort was too much and she slumped back on to her pillows, exhausted.

'It's his job to come,' Chrissy said briskly. 'And *you're* not going anywhere tomorrow. I'll just be a tick.' And to prevent further argument she quickly left the room.

In the hall she tapped her foot with impatience as, having heard her call rerouted, she had to listen to it ring and ring.

'Yes?' a man's voice said abruptly.

'Dr Henderson?'

'Middleton.' The voice offered no further explanation.

'I'm calling on behalf of Mrs Galloway – seven, Prince's Row. I think you should call, she's running a temperature, she's –'

'Are you a doctor?'

'No. I –'

'Bring her to the surgery tomorrow. There's a bug about,' he said brusquely. Chrissy thought she heard a woman's laugh in the background.

'I beg your pardon?' Her voice wavered with disbelief. 'I assure you, Mrs Galloway needs to be seen –'

'In my experience –'

'It's my experience we're talking about here, Doctor.' Her anger made the panic finally roll away. 'My grandmother is ill. She . . .' Using medical parlance she methodically listed all the signs she had observed.

'If you're not a doctor, have you swallowed a medical dictionary?' There was amusement in his voice, and this time she was certain she heard a woman wheedling and cajoling him.

'I'm a nursing sister at St Edith's, Dr Middleton. And, in my professional opinion, you should be in attendance as soon as possible, *Doctor*.' With that she slammed down the telephone on its cradle, having injected a satisfactory degree of sarcasm into that last word, and felt a shade better for it.

When she returned Daphne looked agitated and had slipped down the bed again.

'He's coming. A Dr Middleton.' She helped the older woman back up the bed and placed a pillow at her feet to prevent her sliding down. 'We need to keep you sitting upright. It will help your breathing.'

'He doesn't do house calls.'

'He does today.' She wiped her grandmother's face with a flannel she'd collected from the bathroom.

Ten minutes later Daphne was sitting up, hair brushed, with a clean nightie on. The curtains were pulled, the window slightly open and Chrissy had done a quick tidy-up, for the thought of the doctor seeing her room in a mess was bothering the old woman more than anything else.

'I'm fine. I don't need a doctor. You'd better call and put him off.' She was speaking almost normally now.

'You do need him and it's too late, he's here,' Chrissy said, as she saw a car pull in to the kerb in the street below.

Dr Middleton was handsome, arrogant and in his early thirties. He did not smile at Chrissy in greeting but his disdainful expression told her clearly how inordinately pleased he was with himself – and how angry he was with her for having the temerity to tell him his job. Certainly a loaded look, since it said all that, thought Chrissy, as she led him up the stairs.

'You were right to call me, I'm sorry,' he said later, in Daphne's sitting room where he was writing out a prescription.

'That's all right. It *is* Sunday.'

He smiled at her now, a mixed smile, half apologetic, like a naughty boy found out, and half flirty.

'I'm amazed I haven't seen you around – someone like you.' The smile this time was smooth and practised.

'Is it lobar pneumonia?' she asked, hiding behind the barrier of medical matters, distancing herself from his obvious interest in her.

'Afraid so.' He finished writing the long prescription. 'The chemist in Station Road will be open.'

'Shouldn't she be in hospital?'

'I think she's better off here.'

'How can you be sure? You don't know her circumstances.'

'You're here.'

'But I do work, Doctor.'

'I find these old people recover faster in their own environment,' he said quickly.

'Not clogging up beds and eating into funds, you mean.'

'Look . . . I'm sorry. I don't make the rules.'

She wanted to argue with him and tell him to make a stand, to care, but suddenly she knew there was no point. He'd decided. And probably Daphne *would* prefer to be here, people her age were frightened of hospitals – convinced that if they went in they'd never come out again.

'I'll stay here today and tonight. Then my mother can take over,' she conceded.

'Any problems, let me know. I'll arrange for the community nurse to call. Antibiotics, rest, fluids plus – plus, well there's no need for me to tell *you*.' He was on his feet, all smiles and amiability. The room was small and over-furnished and he was tall and, she suddenly felt, too close. She stepped towards the door.

'I shall look forward to meeting you again,' he said, as he passed her in the narrow hall, his jacket brushing against her even though she had pressed herself back against the wall. He held his hand out to her and held hers a fraction too long. 'Well . . . I hope to see you around.'

'Inevitable,' she replied, looking down at the floor. She opened the front door and stood back to let him pass.

7

Lynn Petch was late. She cursed herself for oversleeping – she'd known yesterday evening that watching that late-night film was a mistake. She looked at her watch, as she began the steep drive up North Hill. She had less than an hour before Terry began to throw a wobbly over his Yorkshire puddings. The man was a saint, she decided – not for the first time – as she carefully manoeuvred her car through the gates of Tall Pines, the large, expensive home of the practice's senior partner.

It was damn cold, she thought, as she pulled her coat closer to her and waited for her ring on the doorbell to be answered.

'Morning, Mrs Henderson,' she said, with forced brightness since the older woman had a pained expression at the sight of her. 'Doctor about?'

'It's *Sunday*. Really, Mrs . . .' Her voice trailed off. 'Dr Middleton's on duty.'

'I know. I need the surgery keys. It's arranged.'

'Then you'd better come in.' Fiona Henderson held open the door as if reluctant to do so. Lynn waited for her to add, 'I suppose.' She did not but sighed extravagantly instead. 'I'll see if my husband can see you. He's a busy man, you know.' And she wafted away trailing a cloud of Arpège.

Lynn waited in the panelled hall, amused at the charade she had just been part of. Mrs Henderson made a point of making them all feel like paid retainers and her name, she knew, had been 'forgotten' on purpose. It always was.

'Lynn, sorry to keep you, I was in the bog.' Dick Henderson, a broad grin on his face – tanned from his many hours on the golf course – came towards her. His blunt honesty made his wife's attitude look ridiculous. He unclipped the surgery key from his key-ring. 'You shouldn't be giving up your Sunday.'

'I'm not doing that, just an hour of it. It's my Well Woman clinic tomorrow and if I don't get the pharmacy order done now I shall be catching up for the rest of the week.'

'Did you enjoy the lectures?' he asked, referring to the family-planning seminar she had been to on Friday and the reason that she was now behind with her routine.

'It was great.' She took the key and pocketed it. In fact, the seminar had been a waste of time, she had learnt nothing that she did not already know, but she'd enjoyed the gossip with other practice nurses. If she told the truth, Henderson might think twice about sending them on other courses.

'Family well?'

'Great, thanks.' She had the door open, but there was nothing Dick Henderson liked more than to natter and she had Terry to get home to. 'Thank you, Mrs Henderson,' she called to Fiona, who hovered behind her husband like a malevolent spirit. It was no wonder the old boy liked to chat, having that sour-faced old puss for company, she thought a few minutes later as she drove back down the hill towards the surgery.

Since she knew that the car park at the back of the surgery would be locked, she left the car on the street. She had long ago given up trying to park at the front since she and her car had had several disagreements with the huge beech, Dr Henderson's pride and joy. The tree was set bang in the middle of the forecourt and to negotiate it needed some pretty nifty driving. She walked quickly towards the building. She'd have to hurry or she'd be late for the meal. How many men were there who, working as hard as Terry did, would turn round and cook the Sunday lunch when she had things to do? Not many, in fact a minuscule number, she reckoned, as she turned in at the gate.

Lynn let herself into the building, purposefully slamming the door. She paused and deactivated the burglar alarm before entering the large reception area. The chairs were in rows, the magazines neatly piled, the toys in their boxes. It looked so much tidier without patients cluttering it up. It took all her courage to enter the building when it was empty like this. There weren't many drugs stored here that were of any use to addicts, but the addicts did not know that and saw the surgery as a gold mine – and didn't she know it. Two years had gone by since she'd been attacked here by a crazed drug addict and she doubted if she'd ever recover. It wasn't that he'd hurt her, he was too doped to aim straight and she'd suffered only a glancing blow, but it was the fear he'd instilled that had damaged her, and it wouldn't go away.

Still, she straightened her shoulders, no point in dwelling on that. She entered her own office and from her desk took her drug stores book. From the doctors' surgeries she took their scheduled-drug books in which they entered which drugs they had used, on whom and when – that was the theory but, rushed off their feet as they usually were, it was a hit-and-miss affair and usually involved Lynn in trawling through the patients' notes on the computer to find out for herself.

In the treatment room she unlocked the outer green steel-mesh door of the drugs cabinet and with a second key the inner lock. She quickly counted the ampoules nestling in their racks and checked the resuscitation equipment, which was kept there. Then she turned her attention to the non-scheduled drugs, also locked in a cupboard but one that was less like Fort Knox. She noted those that needed re-ordering and made notes before returning to her own office.

Back at her desk she began to make out the prescription for the pharmacist in the morning, ready for one of the doctors to sign. It seemed that a lot of tamazepam had been used. She should check it out but, then, Terry was waiting.

A stealthy noise outside her office made her heart helter-skelter. She held her breath. As quietly as she could she opened the instrument drawer and gingerly removed a scalpel with blade attached. She winced as she turned her door handle, but blessed her rubber-soled loafers as she tiptoed towards the sound coming from Dr Middleton's room.

The door was open. She sighed audibly at the sight of Giles Middleton hunched over his bag.

'Oh, you gave me a fright!' she said, laughing, but feeling foolish. She hid the hand that was holding the scalpel behind her back.

'What the hell!' Giles Middleton swung round to face her. 'Are you spying on me?' he asked angrily.

'Don't be silly, Giles. What a thing to say!' She began to back towards the door as she spoke.

'I'm sorry, Lynn. I don't know why I spoke to you like that. I suppose you gave me a fright too.' He laughed, but it sounded false. 'Where's your car?'

'In the street. The beech tree and I don't get along.'

'Oh, I see. I didn't even notice the burglar alarm had been deactivated. Getting sloppy . . . So . . . Just replenishing my bag.'

'I must be going. Terry's cooking the roast.' She returned to her office and locked the door. ''Bye,' she called out, as she retraced her steps. That was odd, she thought, as she let herself out of the building. Why had he looked so guilty?

Giles Middleton ran up the stairs two at a time.

'I thought you'd gone for ever,' the woman said from the bed.

'Not likely.' Quickly he began to remove his trousers.

'Anything important?'

'No, just a silly old cow with pneumonia. Nice granddaughter, though – lovely boobs!'

A pillow flew across the room. He ducked, laughing.

'Look what I've got for us, though.' He held up a carton of pills in one hand and and rattled it; in the other he had a bottle of vodka. 'Treats!' He really laughed now as he jumped onto the bed beside the beautiful woman.

Russell Newson stood outside the bleak, shell-pocked building that passed for a hospital here in Bosnia. It was unseasonably warm, with no smell of winter in the air. He looked about him for physical signs of it to reassure himself that he wasn't hallucinating from overwork and thinking himself back in summer. The trees were bare of leaves, the small flower-bed denuded of plants. It was winter, all right.

He never understood people who said they hated a particular season and couldn't wait for the next one, virtually wishing their lives away – Profligate lot, he thought to himself. He'd admit to a sadness at summer's end since he enjoyed it so much, but it was short-lived for there was the beauty of autumn to anticipate, then winter to follow and, with luck, some snow. Then it was the surge of spring and back to summer. All of them made him content. He was lucky in that, he supposed, even if he wasn't so lucky with love. He frowned as the image of Sabine wormed into his mind, spoiling this contentment, marring the day.

'You look down. What's up?' Georgie pushed him playfully.

'I didn't hear you sneak up. I'm fine.'

'Then do me a favour and look it. It's such a brilliant day, isn't it? We're going for a walk, we need a break – join us?' She pointed to the small group of volunteers walking towards the gate.

'Sure.' He hauled himself away from the wall he'd been leaning against. 'A break will do us good.'

'The surgery seems never-ending, doesn't it? It's the kids that get to me. Poor little sods with their mangled limbs. I could personally strangle the evil bastards who laid the mines.'

'More point in strangling the ones who gave the orders.'

They had caught up with the small group outside the hospital gate.

'Where are we going?' Russell asked.

'Apparently there's a spectacular waterfall a kilometre that way.' Ship pointed along the steep valley, its sides heavily wooded with pine trees.

'Is it safe? What about the mines?' Georgie enquired.

'I asked. If we keep to the paths we're safe – they've been cleared,' Ship reassured her.

The group of six set off along a path beside the fast-flowing river. One by one they removed their padded jackets as the heat got to them, and the fast pace at which they'd set off soon slowed.

'So, where's this famous waterfall?' Russell pretended to complain.

'Listen,' Ship said. They paused. Ahead was the unmistakable roar of tumbling water. They quickened their pace. Suddenly the trees were bigger, the undergrowth lush. The promised waterfall cascaded down between the high rocks of the gorge.

'Look at that!' Georgie exclaimed.

'They haven't got much, here, have they? But at least they've got the most marvellous scenery as compensation –'

That view was the last thing Ship saw, the last thing he said as a mine hidden at the side of the path exploded and then another, triggered by the first, then a third. The terrifying noise was magnified as it ricocheted from one rock of the gorge to another, while birds, calling hysterically, flapped away from the disaster. In the unnatural stillness that followed, two of the party stood rooted in shock, wide-eyed with horror, as they saw the carnage in front of them.

CHAPTER THREE

I

What was her class of six-year-olds getting up to, Mo thought, as she sat in the waiting room of the doctor's surgery. She fingered the numbered plastic disc in her hand nervously. She shouldn't have come on a Monday morning – everyone knew that the skivers swelled the numbers of the genuinely sick, making it the busiest day of the week. She should have waited and made an appointment, then she could have seen nice Dr Henderson who'd always been their GP. Instead she was to see young Middleton and she'd never even met him. How was she to talk to a total stranger about her worries?

Looking around the crowded room it was obvious that attempts had been made to make the place cheerful. An elderly woman kept glancing irritably at a group of toddlers playing in a fenced-off area crammed with toys. The walls were painted yellow – hadn't Mo read somewhere that that was the colour of hope? On the tables, in front of the rows of canvas and steel chairs, were stacked fairly new-looking magazines. She hadn't bothered to pick one up, she knew she'd never have concentrated on it. Instead she read the posters on the walls, which was a mistake – information on Aids, meningitis, sexually transmitted diseases, the dangers of smoking, dental caries was hardly likely to lighten her mood. She resolutely turned her head away from the posters concerned with smear tests and mammograms.

Of the people here only the young mothers and a couple of old women chatted contentedly and looked relaxed. These were familiar surroundings to them, a thought confirmed by the arrival of another young mother who was welcomed loudly by the others, as if they were all members of a club. The other, non-members sat isolated, cocooned in their worry and discomfort.

Mo was working herself into a state. She was aware of it, but she could do nothing about it. Her fear had a life and momentum of its own, pulling her along with it as she held on to its coat-tails, unable to let go, even though she longed to.

The loud click of the number indicator rattled, a large twenty-three shone out and a buzzer sounded, just in case the patient wasn't concentrating sufficiently on it. She checked the disc in her hand as if she did not already know that that was her number. Maybe she was checking it in the fond hope that it had miraculously changed.

As she entered his surgery, Dr Middleton was tapping at the keyboard of his computer. She stood waiting, but when he did not acknowledge her she sat down. She doubted that her legs would support her any longer – they seemed to have lost all strength. He said, 'Good morning.' Mo felt her mouth dry, her heart thud, and was convinced she would not be able to speak. She nodded in greeting instead. 'And what seems to be the problem?'

Mo swallowed hard, fighting the rising panic, forcing herself to speak. 'Well . . .' she began, in a whisper. She coughed and tried again. 'I've found a lump in my breast.' She winced mentally. Just saying it frightened her, as if verbalising it made it even more real. If only she could have kept quiet about it, perhaps it would not exist. She had to clear her throat again. 'I found it on Saturday,' she said, sounding more in control while her mind was screaming, '*Not me, not my breast!*'

Less than five minutes later she emerged into the reception area, white-faced and looking close to tears. The speed of his examination had made everything seem even more unreal.

'Yes? You. Standing there. What's the problem?' snapped the fat-faced receptionist, Enid, whose comfortable shape and many chins would have better suited a kindly soul.

'I'm not sure what I'm supposed to do.'

'What did the doctor say?'

'I can't remember.' Mo knew she sounded pathetic but she seemed to have lost the ability to think.

'You'd best sit down, I'll get someone for you.' The receptionist picked up the telephone. 'There's a woman here, looks as if she needs attention.'

'I have got a name,' she mustered the spirit to say, but Enid was already out of earshot.

A minute later a uniformed nurse appeared, the receptionist pointed at her, and Mo felt that everyone in the surgery must be staring at her too. 'It's Mo, isn't it? Mo Fordham, hello. How are you? Silly question to ask in this place.' Lynn Petch smiled kindly at her.

'Lynn!' Mo felt relief surge through her at the sight of the cheerful woman in her comforting navy blue uniform. But she wished she didn't sound so kind, she feared it would make her cry.

'Are you all right? No, you're not, are you? Have you seen the doctor? Yes? Do you want to come into my room for a minute?'

'Please.' She allowed Lynn to take her hand. She found herself suddenly unaware of the people or the noise. She held on to Lynn tightly and felt, oddly, that she was a child again and any decisions had been taken out of her hands. Lynn ushered her into her office.

'You sit down there. Now, what's the problem? Do you want to tell me?' Lynn sat down too, beside her, not behind the desk, which Mo thought was nice, as if they were preparing for a cosy chat.

Mo's hand went to her left breast and she cradled it. 'I've got a lump here. It's scared me witless.' She shuddered. 'I don't like to even say it.'

'It would scare anyone, me certainly. But try not to be too frightened. As I'm sure the doctor told you, nine out of ten of these lumps prove to be harmless.'

'I didn't. I mean he didn't say. Is that really so?' Mo grasped at this information and felt a tiny spot of hope begin, a long way away still, but there. If that was so, why hadn't the doctor told her? Or was Lynn just saying that to make her feel better? 'All he wanted to know was if I had private health insurance. He didn't seem interested in me.'

'Ah, well,' said Lynn non-committally, but thinking, typical, that just sums up the problems of GP fund-holding, and Giles Middleton's attitude in particular.

'I'd always used a sponge in the bath, you see, but I dropped it the other day and had to use my hand to wash, something I normally don't do. And that's how I found it. So I don't know how long it's been there. I've never bothered to examine myself. I felt fine. I'm only thirty-five – I never thought it could happen to me!' The words tumbled from her now.

'Did the doctor say he'd make an appointment for you to have a mammogram?'

'He said he'd make an appointment but I don't know what for or when. I hope it's soon – I mean, I can't wait long, not in this state!'

'I understand totally.' And Lynn understood more than that. By the time Giles had dictated the letter for the clinic, the secretary had typed it and he'd signed it, and they waited for the appointment to be made, and that to be posted, Mo could have had half a dozen mammograms. 'Look, Mo, if I were you, I'd make an appointment for a private consultation.'

'We can't afford to go private.'

'Not just the one consultation? It'll save all the agony of waiting for a hospital appointment to find out that it's nothing, after all. Tell the specialist you can't afford private treatment and then he'll swap you over to the NHS – but only if it's *nasty*.' She consciously chose the word. 'Dr Stratton in Thorpedale is a sweetie. Shall I get Dr Middleton to make an appointment for you?'

'That would be great. The last two days have nearly driven me mental. There was so much I wanted to ask the doctor, but he didn't give me the time.'

'Then ask me. I might be able to help,' Lynn said modestly.

'I'm not holding you up?'

'I've all the time in the world for an old school-friend,' she lied smoothly.

2

Sabine Newson let herself into her house. Having dropped her shopping on the floor, the first thing she did was to check the answering-machine. It showed that a dozen calls were waiting for her. A dozen! Someone must need to talk to her, but it was hardly likely to be Russell. He'd phoned to say he'd arrived in Bosnia, and she didn't expect to hear from him again while he was there. She wanted to take a shower before her hair appointment. Should she check out the phone first? She began to climb the stairs, the decision to have the shower first having won, but then she changed her mind.

All the messages were the same. They were from an RAF hospital in Lincolnshire. The voice that gave this information sounded bored repeating the number, which she now dialled. She gave her name and waited impatiently to be connected. She'd be late for her highlights at this rate.

'Mrs Newson? I'm the nursing sister in charge. I'm sorry, Mrs Newson, but I'm afraid we have your husband here.'

'But he's in Bosnia.'

'As a patient.'

'A patient?'

'He's been in an incident. A mine –'

'Is he hurt?'

'He was knocked unconscious but was conscious when he arrived here. We've done a brain scan and can see no apparent damage.'

'So he's all right?'

'I didn't say that. We have to do further tests and observations. If you'd like directions to the hospital. It's –'

'Can't he be moved?'

'It would be inadvisable.'

'But if you can't see any injuries, I don't see the problem.'

'Unconsciousness is never taken lightly. As it is – well, I'd rather you came.'

'What is it? I insist on knowing.'

'He won't speak to us, Mrs Newson.'

'Won't speak? What do you mean? Is he damaged?'

'No, not physically.'

'You mean mentally? Then he'd be happier here. I know him – he'd want to be in his own hospital with his own people around him. He's probably sulking.'

'But, Mrs Newson, I really can't –'

'I know my husband and what he'd want. I'll leave it to you to arrange – as quickly as possible, if you don't mind.' Sabine replaced the receiver so that the discussion could not continue. And she ran up the stairs, undressing as she went.

'She's a lot better, Mum. We caught the pneumonia early enough.

Anyhow, she's nattering like nobody's business today.' Chrissy and Iris were standing in the narrow passage that was Daphne's hall.

'I don't know. I go away for a weekend and this happens!' Iris tutted as she lied.

'She didn't look well last week at my cottage.'

'You didn't say. I told her we didn't need her, but your gran can be so pig-headed when she puts her mind to it.' Iris was taking her coat off as she spoke while Chrissy was putting hers on.

'People of Gran's age like to be needed.'

'Sometimes you sound as old as she is.' Iris laughed. 'Is there anything to be done?'

'The nurse has been and gave her a blanket bath. I suggest a little light broth for lunch. The bedpan's in the bathroom.'

'I can't lift her! Look at the size of me. She should be in hospital.'

'She can get on the bedpan, she just needs a steadying hand.'

'Can't you stay?'

'No, Mum. I'm to pick up the car I bought on Saturday. I didn't get much sleep last night with Gran. I want to try to rest this afternoon otherwise I'll be worse than useless on my first night.'

'When will I see you?'

'I'll pop in tomorrow morning after work. I'll phone later this afternoon. Okay?'

'No, it's not okay, but I suppose it'll have to be,' Iris said petulantly. She wouldn't see Bob now. 'We'll have to make some other arrangement if this situation is to continue.'

'I forgot. Did you have a nice weekend?' Chrissy decided not to pursue her mother's griping – best to ignore her when she was like this.

'Brilliant.'

'Where were you?'

'Bournemouth.'

'What on earth for?'

'At a would-be writer's seminar.'

'I didn't know you wanted to write.'

'You don't know everything about me.' Iris was giggling at how easy it was to lie as she closed the door on her daughter.

As Chrissy walked towards the garage a possible problem, to which she hadn't given any thought, zapped crisply into her mind, lacking only a fanfare to announce its urgent arrival. What on earth would she do if both her mother and grandmother became dependent upon her? If she was to work full-time, caring for elderly relatives could become a problem. Was she to find that she'd come home to the possible trap of being a full-time carer? But still, she thought, in a more positive way, as she strode along, if that transpired, wasn't it better that she was here already? She knew that if she'd still been working in Cornwall she'd have dropped everything to be here. Much better that she'd come home, she decided, as she turned into Potter's Garage.

3

The new car was handling a treat, Chrissy thought, as she drove along the narrow lanes that crisscrossed the top of the cliff. At the junction with the main road into Fellcar she stopped and sat waiting her chance to find a gap in the traffic flashing by.

The road was busy, which was odd for a cold Monday night in November, but eventually she was able to slip in behind a large articulated lorry. For a couple of miles they sped along until everything shuddered to a halt as they joined the line of traffic held up at the big roundabout on the outskirts of town.

The engine sounded smooth as she waited patiently in line. She had told no one about this car, and with reason. It didn't take much effort to know what her mother's reaction would be to the bright red BMW – undoubted disapproval that she hadn't bought a Mini or something equally sensible and economical to run when she had so much expense with the new house too. Still, she thought as she fiddled with the car radio, it was second-hand but it would last for ages. German cars did, the man at the garage had assured her.

'I'll call you Rommel,' she said aloud, to the car. 'And, in any case, it's my money and I'll do what I want with it, won't I?' Suddenly aware of what she was doing, she looked sideways at the car to her right for fear that the occupants might have seen her talking to herself. But then, what if they had? Did it matter? Of course it didn't, as the make of her car didn't either. She must keep that in mind. She must aim to be more independent of what others thought of her, she told herself firmly, as she put the car in gear once more as the traffic edged towards the roundabout.

She had left home early, not wanting to be late on her first night of duty. It was as well she had. As she approached St Edith's, glancing at her watch, she saw she had only ten minutes left to park.

The automatic barrier was down at the staff car park. She could find no ticket machine. Presuming she needed a key or code to enter, she sat and waited, hoping for another member of staff to arrive so she could slip in in their wake. But no one came and now, with only five minutes to go, she would have to find a street parking space.

Not quite late, she rushed into the office to be told where she was to be placed tonight. A stony-faced Shelagh Morris was waiting for her.

'How kind of you to come finally, Sister Galloway,' she said sarcastically.

'I'm so sorry, Sister. I didn't allow enough time, the traffic was heavy – I didn't expect that.'

'You should allow enough time for any eventuality.'

'There's a pop concert out at the old holiday camp – that's why.' A staff nurse she had not noticed on the far side of the office spoke up.

'So *that's* what it was.' Chrissy smiled her thanks to the other woman, who was tall, with an enviable figure, short fair hair and an attractive strong face, her large grey eyes its best feature. 'Do I know you from somewhere?'

'I don't think so. It's probably me face – a common old one I've got.' She spoke in an exaggerated false West Country accent and grinned good-naturedly, with the confidence of one who knew full well that her good looks were far removed from being common. 'Dawn Allyson,' she said, holding out her hand to Chrissy.

'Is there any chance of any work tonight?' Shelagh sighed. 'First you're late –'

'I'm sorry – I couldn't park either. How do you get into the car park?'

'You get a permit like everyone else.' Sister Morris spoke through pursed lips, as if she had just sucked a lemon.

'I'm sorry to be so vague –' Chrissy began. 'No one told me, so there was no way I could possibly know,' she added, more assertively.

'Then apply at the office in the morning.'

'And bring your cheque for forty quid,' Dawn chipped in.

'*How much?*'

'Shocking, isn't it? The whole hospital's up in arms. It's just been brought in. Management!' The staff nurse spat out the last word with loathing.

'With your permission, Sister, may we continue?' Shelagh Morris's voice still dripped with sarcasm.

'Yes, of course, sorry.' Chrissy fiddled with the ornate silver buckle on the belt of her navy blue uniform, a sure sign that she was nervous. Shelagh looked down at her list.

'Dawn, you're on male surgical and, Sister Galloway, you take Neurology and you'll need to keep an eye on Orthopaedics – there is no senior nurse on duty. Right, any questions?'

'No,' said Dawn, picking up a large black bag.

'Thank you,' said Chrissy, and immediately wished she hadn't: it sounded to her as if she were sucking up. She picked up her own capacious bag, the strap broke and her ball of knitting wool rolled out.

'I assume you know where you're going, Sister? If so, then I suggest you go there.' Shelagh stood and turned her back dismissively.

'Is she always like that?' Chrissy asked, as she and the staff nurse walked along the long corridor from the office, their soft-soled shoes making a sibilant noise on the highly polished surface of the rubber-backed heavy-duty linoleum.

'Always. She's got problems – her husband pissed off with a staff from main theatre. And she hates dear Glynis and is waiting for her to drop dead so she can run this place herself. No doubt like Colditz.'

'Sweet,' Chrissy remarked, as she held open the door for them. 'Are you helping out during this staffing crisis, like me?'

'No. I'm a bank nurse.'

The bank nurses were the hospital's pool of staff, trained and auxiliary, set up to save the expense of fees payable to an agency. They could be called on during busy holiday periods, illness, or at any time when staffing levels were low. Some nurses worked permanently on the bank, preferring the flexibility of hours it gave them. Others, unable to secure a permanent post, joined so that, hopefully, they would be in the right place at the right time when a position was advertised nationally. More often than not, such hopes were dashed when someone from outside was appointed instead. Some of the regular staff worked on their days off to earn extra money. It was certain that a hospital like St Edith's would not be able to function without its bank of able nurses.

'I'd hate the lack of security of a nurse bank,' Chrissy shuddered. 'I mean, if you're ill you get no sick pay, isn't that so?'

'That's right, and no holiday pay, no pension scheme and no redundancy money either. All taken into account, we must save the hospital Trust a fortune.'

'Then why do it?'

'Must be bonkers.' Dawn grinned. 'Truth is, I came up here for an interview – for a job I didn't get – but I liked it and decided to stay. There were no other permanent posts so I decided to go on the bank and lurk about hoping that a position might turn up.'

'I wish you luck.' Chrissy felt uncomfortable with this conversation, wondering if the post that Dawn had failed to secure was her own. She felt sorry for her, only too aware of how insecure her job was, how with no contract she could be dropped at any time. 'This looks like Neurology.'

'Have you got your bleeper? You'll need it with two wards to look after.'

Chrissy patted her pocket. 'I picked it up on Saturday.'

'See you at the lunch break, perhaps?'

Chrissy pushed open the door of the darkened ward and walked quickly towards the office, from which light streamed.

'Anyone know anything about her?' she heard someone ask.

'No, except she's a widow,' an older voice answered.

'Sod! Then she'll be as old as the hills. Just my luck!'

Chrissy paused in the doorway. Two nurses stood at the desk. Already she recognised the colour coding of the belts, which told her that the older one with the dark red was a senior staff nurse – juniors had blue belts like Dawn Allyson's. The nurse with a black and white striped belt was a senior nursing auxiliary.

'Not quite that old,' she said, with a smile that broadened as she saw the surprised and embarrassed expressions on their faces as they swung round. 'I'm sorry I'm a little late, I'm still learning the ropes,' she said to the red-belted nurse, who she knew would be day staff and waiting to give her the report on the patients' condition before handing over the responsibility and the keys.

They sat at the desk and Senior Staff Nurse Jo Baker opened the report book. 'We're waiting for Trish Walters. She's a Project 2000 student,' she explained to Chrissy.

'More trouble than they're worth, that lot are! They're scared witless of the patients, hardly dare touch them, as if they'd bite or break,' Auxiliary Nurse Stella Gibson complained.

'Shall we get on?' Jo suggested.

'We'll wait,' Chrissy, senior to them all, said firmly.

'Do you know the area?' Jo asked, making conversation.

'I was born here –'

Her explanation was interrupted as a young woman, looking ill at ease in her uniform, as if she didn't belong in it, rushed into the room. Her cap was askew and her apron was wet. 'I'm so sorry,' she gushed.

'What happened to you, Trish?' Jo Baker asked, sounding a smidgen irritated.

'It was the bedpan thingummy,' the younger girl answered, looking mortified.

'Can't you even empty a bedpan without flooding the system?' Stella Gibson sneered. Trish Walters looked close to tears.

'Then after report I suggest you show her, Nurse Gibson,' Chrissy said sharply, quickly reading the woman's name badge. She did not like this scoring off each other. They'd all had clumsy starts once. 'I'm ready, Staff, when you are.' She sat waiting for the handover to begin. She was far more relaxed now, as the old familiar routine swung into action. A detailed report on each of the thirty-four patients on this ward – their condition, their medication, problems to watch for, treatments required and their state of mind. After that, Chrissy toured the ward with her night nurses, walking quickly, torches pointing towards the floor, used momentarily to check those asleep, chatting to those who were awake as the day staff rushed to finish their own chores. After all that, the ward and the patients would be hers for the night.

Chrissy had always enjoyed night duty. Friends had moaned and fussed but she'd look forward to it with anticipation. The wards in daytime were busy, noisy places; at night they were quieter and there was more time to care for the patients, to sit and talk to them, to listen to their worries, hopefully to set their minds at rest with thoughtful explanation. Time to hold the hands of those fearful of their future or those with no future at all. At night she always felt she was of more use. Perhaps her ability to sleep wherever and whenever she wanted had something to do with her attitude too.

This neurological ward was typical of others she'd worked on. With diseases of the nervous system dividing into medical and surgical conditions, there was a good mix. Half a dozen were post-operative, several were in for observation after accidents at sport and at work. One woman had lost the use of her legs for no apparent reason. There were some with suspected tumours; a man with a subdural haematoma, a slow bleeding in his brain. Most serious of all was a young man hideously damaged in a car crash, who had been moved from the intensive care unit to a side ward here, not, as his family hoped, because he was getting better but rather because there was nothing more that the unit could do for him: he would die, the only question left was when. In consequence his valuable bed in the unit had had to be vacated.

Chrissy and her nurses approached the side ward closest to the office, where John 'Buck' Marston lay, hooked up to the machines that were all that stood between him and death. In the next bed was another accident victim, who was also unconscious.

An agency nurse had been brought in to work exclusively with these two for they needed constant monitoring. As soon as she had finished her checks on Buck – his blood pressure, pulse, reactions, the working of the machinery, the Hickman line inserted into his chest – and had given him his medication as charted, then it was time to do the same for the other. It was a never-ending task.

Two relatives sat by Buck's bed: a woman whose worry and fear for her son had made her look elderly before her time; and a younger one, smartly dressed and carefully made-up, her bright red lipstick making a garish flash of colour in the monochrome world of this ward.

'Mrs Marston?' Chrissy asked and, as she feared, both women turned to face her.

'Yes?' they said in unison, their faces showing a glimmer of hope that here was someone new, someone who'd make their darling better.

'I'm Sister Galloway. I shall be on duty tonight. Have you everything you need? Are you warm enough? Some tea?' She ran through the list of things she could do for them, pathetically little in the face of what was coming.

'We're fine, thank you.'

'We both think he's looking a bit better, and he just squeezed my hand, I'm sure he did.' Buck's young wife, who looked too young to be married, spoke quickly, urgently.

'Really? That's good,' answered Chrissy, knowing it was of no note, that such involuntary movements – a nerve twitching in a muscle – were common.

'I've been playing him Simply Red.' Cheryl Marston pointed to the Walkman's earphones on her husband, which just added a few more wires and leads to the almost corpse.

'I expect that's what did it.' Chrissy felt a heel, half of her knowing she should not give false hope, and the other half unable to stop doing just that.

She had a word with the agency nurse, to reassure herself that the woman was competent. She'd had experiences in the past where such nurses, not belonging to the hospital and therefore lacking any feelings of loyalty, were so slap-happy they would have felt quite at home in the pages of a book by Dickens. She wondered what the situation would be over Buck's organs. Would these two agree to them being harvested? Had they already been approached? She must check. It was a situation they all dreaded, asking relatives to co-operate when they were most vulnerable. A hideous task and one that there could be no hard and fast rules about; opportunities to discuss the possibility might open up and whoever was close, doctor or a senior nurse, it was their duty to query, suggest – never to coerce. And when decisions had been made it was no easier for they were either comforting and thanking those who'd agreed – always emotional – or assuring those who'd refused that they understood when they didn't. Telling them that they must not feel guilty when they longed to tell them that they should.

Once the patients had been checked, Chrissy, without her team, checked the various rooms that were part of the ward, and thus her responsibility: the kitchen, the sterilizing room, the showers, lavatories, and finally the sluice.

Trish Walters and Stella Gibson were in the sluice. Stella, with bad grace, was demonstrating the bedpan-washing machine, slamming the heavy metal door shut and stabbing abruptly at the floor pedal that controlled the water to show her displeasure.

'But I thought in any case this was an auxiliary's work,' she heard Trish complain.

'Well, you're going to have to learn otherwise, aren't you? Hi,' Stella said, on seeing Chrissy cross the tiled floor past the large wheeled laundry bags to check the fire door.

As Chrissy turned she saw Stella's quizzical look. 'I was on a ward once where the fire door was left open. A drunk got in and terrorised the patients,' she explained.

'Nasty.'

'Could have been. But it left me with a bit of a thing about them.'

With the day staff long gone and this ward settled to her satisfaction, Chrissy left and took the lift to the next – once she'd have run up the stairs, but these days she conserved her energy whenever she could since one never knew what the night would bring, or what reserves of energy she'd need to tap.

Orthopaedics was quiet. Like Neurology, the long Nightingale-style ward had been divided into six-bed units with a special-care room – which, tonight, was empty – and was mixed-sex, women at one end, men at the other, with a shared day room. When such wards had first been introduced, Chrissy, like most staff, had found it difficult to adjust to them, but now she sometimes wondered if the presence of the other sex didn't make for faster recovery. The patients seemed to make more effort. Men, on the whole, tended not to complain as much as women – the reason Chrissy and her friends preferred nursing them – but with the mix it had been noticed that the women seemed to moan less too.

There were only two auxiliaries on this ward – the charge nurse had broken his leg playing rugby at the weekend and a replacement hadn't been found yet, and so Chrissy was in charge of both. Unfortunately for her both were young and inexperienced: they explained that they were 'testing the water' as nursing auxiliaries to see if the profession was for them before taking on the more arduous task of becoming registered nurses. But, fortunately for Chrissy, with Russell Newson away for a week and his list of operations closed for that time, and the other surgeon's operation day not until Thursday, the ward was quiet. Chrissy quickly checked the patients. All were sleeping. She made sure that the nurses felt able to cope. She made a note of the times when drugs were prescribed and when she would be needed here to check them and to supervise their being given. Returning to Neurology, and realising she'd had no supper, she made herself a cup of coffee and searched for some biscuits.

4

'Are you having breakfast here?' Dawn Allyson caught up with Chrissy, who was trudging along the central corridor of the hospital with the other bedraggled-looking night nurses. All the smartness of the night before had been erased as, with aching feet and faces grey with fatigue, they trooped along. It was half past eight. They should have finished at eight, but they never did.

'I might, but I must call my gran's first.' Chrissy had planned to go straight to Daphne's, but she needed to make friends here too. It was important to be one of the team as soon as possible.

They surged down the staircase to the basement and walked through the tunnel that led them to the nurses' home and the large canteen where the staff ate their meals.

'It's pissing down,' Dawn warned her, which was a shame for after a shift Chrissy always liked to get a belt of fresh air before doing anything else. Also she wanted to familiarise herself with the layout of the hospital outside. She had seen the posts, top-heavy with signs, pointing to the hotch-potch of Portakabins and brick buildings that housed a collection of departments and clinics. If she orientated herself in the daytime, she wouldn't blunder about so much at night.

On the telephone, her mother was short with her, but Chrissy was not put out: the morning was not Iris's best time. Reassured that her grandmother was much better she rejoined Dawn.

'How was your first night?'

'Fine. Nothing untoward. A good beginning.'

'Is that Buck Marston still alive?'

'Yes. Sad, isn't it? One almost wishes he'd die for his family's sake. His hanging on must be agony for them. I didn't at first realise his young wife was pregnant.'

'Silly sod. I was on days on A and E when he came in, pissed as a rat he was, and did you know that the bloke in the other car died? His wife was preggers too.'

'Well, he's getting punished now. Do you know why he's called Buck? It's an odd name.'

'At first I thought it was because he screwed like a rabbit, then I was told it's because of his teeth.'

They were laughing as they entered the large dining room, which was still busy despite the first day shift having eaten long before and gone to the wards. The noise of the assembled night nurses chattering was like a starlings' moot. They picked up their trays and Chrissy selected orange juice, scrambled eggs, toast and coffee. Dawn had coffee only.

'Dieting?' asked Chrissy.

'No, skint.'

'Have some of mine,' she offered.

'I might nick a slice of toast later.'

'You should eat.'

'You sound like my mother.' Dawn grinned. 'But what's a girl to do? Once I've paid for my grotty bedsit there's not a lot left over. It's food or cigs and the weed always wins.'

'You're mad.' At this Dawn grinned even wider. 'Are the rents in town that bad?'

'Yes. It's because of the computer factory – there's a shortage of accommodation. Old Victorian houses like the one I live in, are mostly converted into flats that I can't afford. I'll have to wait for my great-aunt to pop her clogs before I can think of buying.'

'If you get a permanent contract, will you live in the hospital?'

'You have to be joking – I couldn't afford to live here either. The bastards have put the rents up again.'

Chrissy felt a flush of guilt at how fortunate she was. Her grandmother had told her when she first arrived that some nurses were being threatened with eviction if they didn't pay the increase. She'd thought the old lady had been exaggerating, but it seemed that she hadn't.

'I thought they had a severe shortage of nurses here,' Chrissy said, as they made their way to an empty table.

'They have, and it'll get worse too. We just can't afford what they're asking, not unless a miracle happens and we get an increase in salary. The managers won't budge. They witter on about market forces.'

'But they won't be able to run the hospital at this rate and then there'll be no market.'

'There's talk that they'll be recruiting from Ireland, Sweden, Finland. Places like that.'

They took their seats, each placing her bulging bag, almost an appendage of the night nurse, on the floor beside her.

'But how will they be able to afford the rents?'

'They won't. I bet you they'll be given six-month contracts with low rent. Then they'll be asked to pay the same as everyone else. Then, no doubt, they'll all decamp and then they'll recruit another lot. I've seen it happen elsewhere.'

'What a way to run the system!' Chrissy said, as she took a plate and began dividing her eggs on to it.

'You don't have to,' Dawn objected.

'I want to.' She knew what she should do, she thought, as she began to eat. She had a spare room, she could take a colleague in as a lodger. She *should*, but she didn't say so. She couldn't deal with living with someone else, not for some time yet. 'Um, good eggs,' she said instead, and tried to shut out the voice of guilt inside her head. She stretched. 'God, I'm tired. I knew I was going to be but, you know how it is, I'd forgotten what it was like.'

'You haven't been nursing full-time, then?'

'Yes, I did the Back to Nursing course, but I was working at a much smaller hospital.'

'How long were you away from nursing? How long's the course – you know, if I ever escape and then want back in?'

'For six years. The changes were amazing. Thank God for that course, I can tell you. It was eight weeks long – damned hard too. And placements, of course.'

'You mean you got *out* from this hideous profession and you *chose* to return? You're certifiable!' A full mouth did not prevent Dawn from speaking, her eyes wide in mock astonishment.

'My husband died. I had to do something.'

'Sorry,' Dawn said, looking down intently at the eggs.

Chrissy regretted telling her. What she still did not know, after two years of widowhood, was how long it was going to take for these barriers of embarrassment to disappear and for normal relationships to return.

'I'm so sorry,' Dawn mumbled again. 'Tactless fool!'

'How were you to know?'

'I did know, though – everyone here does. You know these places, hospitals breed gossip like a super-bug. I just forgot.'

'Try and forget again – for me. It's all right. It was my fault for mentioning it.'

'How awful, and so young.' Dawn's eyes brimmed with concern. 'Do you want to . . . I mean . . . well . . . If it's too painful . . .' Dawn stumbled through the words in a way Chrissy had become used to.

'No. I can talk about him.'

'Was it an illness?'

'No, an accident.'

'Oh, I see.'

Chrissy had often noticed the frequency with which people said, 'I see,' when she knew full well they couldn't possibly. How could they, when frequently they had not known her or Ewan?

'Car accident, was it?'

'No.' She chose not to elaborate. Dawn, Chrissy knew full well, was longing to hear more.

'Poor you. Have you any children?'

'No – fortunately, as it turned out.'

'I'm never sure if it's easier to not have them or a comfort if you do.'

'I don't think so.' Chrissy turned her head and looked across the noisy room, as if searching for someone, purposefully putting a stop to that line of conversation. It was another subject she was not comfortable with.

'Can I join you?' A staff nurse carrying a tray of food sat down.

'Sure. Chrissy, this is Jazz Poundman – Geriatrics, only now we must remember to call it Care of the Elderly.' Dawn moved her chair to give the newcomer more room.

'It was geriatrics when I was training and it still is in my book.' Jazz sat down heavily.

'She applied for your post, didn't you, Jazz? They fell about laughing.'

'More than likely about as much as they did when you applied!' Jazz retorted.

'I'm sorry, both of you,' said Chrissy, not quite sure what was expected of her. So she had been right about Dawn applying for her job – oh, hell.

'Don't be. I only applied because I thought it was expected of me. And I didn't think I'd get it. I'd only have stood a chance if I'd been promoted to an F but then I'm pretty certain they were looking for a G.' Chrissy looked away again, not wanting to have to mention she was an F grade, but evidently the authorities had taken her past experience into account.

'It was too soon for me, too. I just thought I should show willing. Sugar, please.' Jazz proceeded to spoon some into her tea.

'That's it, Dawn. If you applied for the same post, that's when I must have seen you.' Chrissy felt quietly satisfied that that little mystery was solved. 'At the interview.'

'Probably. Sugar's bad for you, Jazz, or has no one told you?' Dawn grabbed at the bowl.

'God, I hate old people,' Jazz said, snatching it back.

'Isn't it difficult for you working with them, then?' Chrissy asked, half amused.

'There wasn't anything else.'

'It must be cataract day, Chrissy. Jazz always gets like that then, don't you, Jazz?'

'What's a cataract day? A whole group in together?'

'Yes. The eye surgeon does them in one batch.'

'That must make nursing them easier, surely?'

'I hate it. They give me the creeps. Shuffling about with dark glasses on looking like a gang of aged Al Capones.'

'Jazz. Really! That's not kind.' But Chrissy couldn't help smiling at the image. 'You never know, you might have to have cataracts removed one day. It's a wonderful op. I mean, their reaction when they can see again, it's so moving. Doesn't that make it worthwhile for you?'

'No,' Jazz said abruptly and then, as if bored with the subject, she leant forward. 'What about Russell Newson, then?'

'What about him?'

'I thought you heard everything, Dawn.'

'Well, I didn't this time. What?'

'He's been blown up by a mine in Bosnia.'

'Never! When?'

'Happened at the weekend, I'm not sure when. Ghastly business.' Jazz's face showed her eagerness to be first with the news. Chrissy quite expected to see her lick her lips with anticipation. 'Two people with him were killed, another one injured – lost a leg. And poor old Newson.'

'Is he seriously hurt?'

'Not a scratch on him, he was knocked out, though. They've done a CAT scan – nothing untoward. Odd, isn't it? Another two with them didn't have a scratch either.'

'Is he still in Bosnia?'

'Nope. He was flown into an RAF hospital. But apparently he's being moved here.' She leant forward again, beckoning the others to lean forward too, the better to hear. 'Apparently his wife went ape-shit demanding he be transferred here. She's something else, isn't she?'

'Sabine Newson is a tiny, pretty thing, like a doll, Chrissy. You'd never think she could, or would, make a fuss about anything.'

'Is he the orthopaedics surgeon?'

'The very same. He's a cold bastard, but good-looking. He gave his time to the Bosnians for nothing – you know, there were a lot of dreadful limb injuries there. Unfortunately for us he's very much married to the divine Sabine. All the men *drool* after her. Doesn't leave much for you and me.' Dawn laughed, and then stopped abruptly as if thinking she'd been tactless. She looked embarrassed instead.

'I was going to ask you what the talent was like around here,' Chrissy lied smoothly. The last thing she wanted or needed at the moment was a man complicating her life. She fibbed because she'd warmed to Dawn and didn't want her upset.

'Dire! I'm sorry ... I didn't think,' Dawn said. Jazz looked curiously from one to the other. Chrissy took Dawn's hand and squeezed it encouragingly.

'No problem. Still, I must be going.' She stood and picked up her heavy bag. 'See you tonight?' Aware of curious eyes on her as the new girl she wove her way between the tables, hurrying now for she had completely forgotten that her car was parked on the street and if it was clamped she'd never get to bed at a decent time.

'She seems nice,' Jazz said, as they watched her leave. 'She's too flaming attractive, of course. She's the merry widow, isn't she?'

'She's a widow, yes, but I'd hardly call her merry.'

'There's something odd about her husband's death. A lot of rumour, if you know what I mean.'

'No, I don't know,' Dawn said, in a bristly way, as if not interested.

'Suit yourself.' Jazz shrugged her ample shoulders.

'How would you know anything, anyway? Cornwall's miles away.'

'And my aunt lives there, works at Trelisk. Any more questions?' Jazz looked smug.

'You really can be most unpleasant without even trying, can't you?' Dawn stood.

'It wasn't me being unpleasant. Poor Ewan,' Jazz said darkly, and then refused to say another word.

5

'You took your time getting here!' was Iris's welcome. 'You're wet!'

'Is that a statement or an accusation?' Chrissy laughed, but stopped as she realised her mother was not amused. 'What's up? Is Gran all right?'

'Of course she's all right. Had a boiled egg and soldiers and then asked for another.'

'What a relief! I'll just pop and see her before I get going.'

Iris grabbed her daughter's arm and held it tight. 'You're not going anywhere. You're staying here. *I'm* going.'

'But, Mum, I'm whacked. I've got to get home and go to bed.'

'You can sleep here – there's the spare room. You won't mind my sheets, will you?'

'How can I look after Gran *and* sleep? You'll have to stay.'

'I don't *have* to do anything. Since your dad's gone, she's no longer my relation, she's yours. For years I've done my stint, put myself out. No more!'

'But, Mum, that's not fair.'

'I'd have thought you of all people would have realised that life is frequently unfair. Now, if you don't mind . . .' Iris was buttoning her coat.

Chrissy moved quickly and put herself between the door and her mother. 'We've got to sort this.'

'It's sorted. If you'd kindly move?'

'I just don't believe this. What's the hurry? What have you got to do that's more important than this?'

'What do you know about my life and what's important in it and what isn't?' Iris said sharply. 'I've masses to do, that's all there is to say,' she added, in a more conciliatory way, as if beginning to regret her original grumpiness.

'How about I go for, say, four or five hours' sleep and come back to relieve you this afternoon?' It wasn't much sleep, but she'd managed on less before now.

'No.' Iris took a great interest in pulling on her gloves.

'All right, then.' Chrissy was having to make a conscious effort to keep her annoyance under control, not easy when she was so tired. 'I'll stay this morning and you come back this afternoon and I'll kip then.'

'Are you witless this morning? Did you not understand? Then I'll have to be straight. I don't want to do this. I don't want to be here. I don't even like the old bat – I never have.' She looked satisfied with herself, as if she had just said something she'd been longing to say for some time.

'That's not true, Mum, and you know it. For heaven's sake, I didn't come back for this.'

'Then you should have thought about it, shouldn't you?'

'I don't understand –'

At that point the argument was interrupted by a sharp rat-a-tat-tat on the front door. Standing on the step was a smiling but different community nurse. Iris took the opportunity to snake past her daughter, saying a cheerful, 'Good morning,' to the nurse.

'That your car, Chrissy?' she asked over her shoulder.

'Yes, it is,' Chrissy answered, with a defiant tone. She'd had enough confrontation for one morning.

'I like it!' Iris said, to Chrissy's astonishment.

'What about tonight?'

'Sorry. No can do.' And with that Iris climbed into her sensible

Volvo.

'Hi! I'm Janis Thompson. Problems?' They shook hands. Janis was smart and morning-trim in her pink and grey uniform, which made Chrissy think of prawn cocktails. She was aware of how tired and dishevelled she looked.

'It would seem my mother is not available to sleep here tonight and I'm on nights.'

'Couldn't you phone the hospital, explain the situ and take this night off?'

'My second night? That would go down like a lead balloon.'

'Mothers! They can be such a pain. Look, let's sort Mrs Galloway out and then we'll see what we can come up with.'

Chrissy followed Janis up the stairs and realised, with relief, that for the moment someone else was in charge.

'Mrs Galloway. How are you? Had a good night?' Janis spoke with a cheerful briskness. She was a whirl of movement as she shed her raincoat, replacing it with a large waterproof apron. 'Have you eaten? Not feeling too wheezy?' she asked, while collecting towels and sheets.

'I feel an old fraud. I should be up and doing. Chrissy, my dear, how was your first night?'

'Great, and you're staying put.'

'Not when –' But Janis popped a thermometer in Daphne's mouth, putting a stop to further argument.

Fifteen minutes later Daphne was bathed, her bed and linen changed, her hair done, and she was sitting up, propped by pillows and looking very much better. She still protested she was fine but then the fatigue caused by the morning's activities caught up with her and she dozed off.

Janis entered the kitchen having made a phone call.

'I'm sorry. There's little the surgery can do to help you. You know, limited funds and all that. I'd hoped, given you were one of the profession . . .' She shrugged apologetically as she took the cup of coffee Chrissy had made her. 'Hasn't your grandmother got a friend or a neighbour who'd sleep over?'

'She keeps very much to herself, and the neighbours – well, it isn't like it used to be. Most of these cottages have been yuppified. I doubt if there's anyone left she really knows.'

'She's so much better, you know. She's probably all right to be left. After all, she's got a phone extension by her bed – I wish more of my elderly patients had them.'

'I couldn't leave her alone. I wouldn't be able to concentrate. Is there an agency where I can get someone?'

'There's nothing in Fellcar but there's one in Thorpedale. You might have to pay travelling costs too – it could be expensive. Still you don't need an RGN, do you? A nice kindly body would do.'

'How do people who can't afford to pay for professional help manage?'

'They just get on with it. If they have to leave their gran they can only hope nothing goes wrong before they can get back. The saddest to me is when it's an old couple and one has to look after the other when they can barely look after themselves. They not only feel useless but guilty too. And when there's a couple it's just presumed they can cope. And then, of course, there are the other families who don't give a tinker's cuss anyway. They probably hope the old biddy will kick the bucket so they can sell the house.'

'What do you do in cases like that?'

'Harden my heart. I could work twenty-four hours in the day and I wouldn't solve anything, only kill myself. It's like an endless tide of helplessness and then I end up feeling helpless, too, since I can't do enough.'

'Oh, but you do.' Chrissy felt concerned. Obviously, Janis's morale was low.

'It's reaching the point where I don't know which is worse – working outside like me or in a hospital like you. We all seem to be making the best of a bad job all the time.'

'Depressing.'

6

Mo, her clothes back on once more, took a seat and waited for the doctor to finish writing his notes. She looked about the smartly furnished consulting room. Dr Stratton sat behind a large partner's desk, which Mo reckoned had cost an arm and a leg. The walls were lined with shelves full of leather-bound books. The windows were double-glazed against the noise of the traffic. An imitation log fire made it even less like a surgery. And the examination table, as she'd found out, was hidden discreetly behind a lovely Victorian screen. It was all a far cry from the community medical centre with its noise, the posters, ringing bells and flashing lights. She'd been here half an hour already, unheard of at the surgery, and still the doctor did not seem in any hurry to get rid of her. Dr Stratton had asked so many questions, some she'd had difficulty in answering – how was she to know what her grandmother had died of? His examination was long too – nothing was hurried – unlike Dr Middleton's rushed five minutes with her when she'd had an almost uncontrollable compulsion to apologise for taking up his time.

'As you are aware, Mrs Fordham, you do have a lump in your left breast.' Dr Stratton looked up from his notes. 'I'd feel happier if you had a mammogram and an ultrasound done. I can arrange an appointment for you at the Beacon Hill clinic.'

'I see. The problem is, Dr Stratton – I mean, isn't the Beacon private? I don't think we could afford that. I did explain.'

'Yes, I realise. But if you could stretch to just this little extra – eighty pounds or thereabouts – it would set my mind, and yours, of course, at rest. Even if I make you a priority appointment at the hospital there's sure to be a delay, and do you want to worry longer than necessary? It's probably nothing, but better to be safe, don't you think?' He smiled kindly at her. Mo did a quick calculation, in her head, of which bills were outstanding quite apart from the expenses to come with Christmas approaching.

'When?' she asked.

'This afternoon,' he replied.

Mo felt as if the walls of the room were moving, that the bookcases were about to collapse; felt as if her guts had melted.

'So soon?' she said, almost in a whisper.

'For the best.' He looked at her questioningly.

'I'd better then, hadn't I?' She smiled, or at least she tried to, but it was as if her lips were paralysed. Her mind raced: this doctor was middle-aged, he was experienced, he wouldn't have suggested so quick an appointment unless he was already convinced of the worst.

'Then if you could make an appointment for me? Thanks,' she managed to say, and longed to burst into tears but controlled herself.

'Have you someone to go with you?'

'No. I'm fine. Really.' She blew her nose into a Kleenex. 'Hope this snuffle goes away before Christmas.' She tried a laugh. It didn't really work.

'What about your husband?'

'He's working. I couldn't disturb him.'

'You have told your husband about this little worry?' he asked kindly.

'Yes. I have. Of course I have.' Even as the words tumbled out she knew they sounded false.

'He has a right to know, Mrs Fordham. And a worry shared – you know what they say,' Dr Stratton said.

'I just told you. He knows. He's a busy man.'

Dr Stratton looked down at the notes in front of him and Mo knew he hadn't been fooled for one minute.

7

'What a day!' Lynn Petch collapsed into her favourite chair, eased off her shoes and held out her hand for the cup of tea Terry was offering her. 'You're a mind-reader.'

'Not enough to know what you want for supper.'

'No problem. I went to Marks on the way home. I got us a Tandoori chicken.'

'Brill. Your friend Chrissy phoned. Said could she call you later in the week, her gran's still ill.'

'Janis told me. She did a domiciliary this morning and met Chrissy. Bitch of a mother wouldn't look after her so she could get some proper sleep.'

'She's that stuck-up bank manager's wife who lives up on North Hill, isn't she?'

'That's her. Why people bother to try to cover their tracks in a town like this, where everybody knows everyone else's business, is beyond me. Iris Galloway's dad worked for the council and Frank Galloway's dad was a drunkard, worked on the railways – you know, the men who tap the rails, or used to. Do they still?'

'How would I know?' He chuckled. 'So, what was so bad that it made today worse than usual?'

'Where do you want me to start? I want to kill Bridget Cooper for starters. I've never known anyone capable of expending so much energy in doing so little.'

'What's the practice manager done now?' He knew all too well that the nurses' loathing of Bridget and her receptionists was ongoing.

'Two things – well, no, actually three but I'll get to the third later. I heard her giving medical advice to a patient and the only qualifications she's got are secretarial. I told her she shouldn't do that and she didn't like it.'

'What was she doling out advice on? Open heart surgery?'

'Don't be silly. Verrucas.'

'Hardly life-threatening.'

'It's the principle. If you took your car to the garage you wouldn't ask the receptionist what to do about the rattle under the bonnet, would you? It's the same thing.'

'I don't know, I might. If she was a looker, I'm sure I would, and if there was a queue.'

'Don't be so reasonable.' Playfully she threw a cushion at him. 'No, I'm going to tell Henderson about it.'

'You'll make Bridget worse.'

'I don't give a damn. And she doesn't discipline her staff. I mean, a young girl came in as quietly as possible and told the receptionist she had changed her mind about a termination and do you know what that fat moo, Enid Dodds, said – out loud, mind you – for all to hear? She said, "You can't cancel the abortion, I've done the paperwork!" I ask you, it'll be all over town by now. Did Bridget tell Enid off – no!'

'Great! And the third thing?'

'Well, it's all tied in with Middleton, who else? I was checking on his patients' notes and Bridget sails in and says, "What authority do you have to be meddling in these files?" I saw red, I can tell you. I thrust my badge under her nose. "This gives me the authority, that's what." I enjoyed that.'

'What were you doing?'

'I think he's up to no good. I loathe Giles. He's such a conceited creep, thinks he's God's gift. For one he's having an affair – *and* with a patient. And we all know where that can lead, don't we? Field day for the tabloids if he doesn't get his act together. Worse, though, I think he's nicking drugs.'

'Shit!'

'My sentiments exactly.' She smiled at him over the rim of her cup.

'Are you sure?'

'Not yet. It took me time to twig. You know I went in on Sunday to do the drug list? Well, I noticed there was a lot of temazepam used and yet we'd had a big order in not long ago. At first I thought, winter, need for tranquillisers, depressed patients, so a lot had been prescribed. Then I remembered. I went to that lecture on drug abuse at Thorpedale police station. The inspector told us of a craze for taking that particular drug mixed with alcohol. You get a high, but even better you get a second high some time later. So I was checking his files.'

'For over-ordering?'

'That, but also how. He's done it before. He finds a chronic patient on supplementary benefit who doesn't have to pay for his drugs and orders in his name then the bastard gets them for free. He's done it in the past to save money, but why not to feed a habit?'

'Quite the little Sherlock Holmes, aren't you?'

'It's the principle, Terry. I don't like the system being abused like that.'

'What are you going to do?'

'I don't know. Speak to Dr Henderson when I find out which patient he's fiddling on.'

'It could be Henderson himself.'

'No way.'

'Be careful, love. Make sure before you go crashing in with accusations. You know these doctors, they stick together.'

'I will, don't worry. But I have to sort it out. Don't forget, I've got access to the drug cabinets also. Before I know where I am I could be being accused of nicking the stuff – probably by Middleton. I wouldn't put it past him. You should have seen the way he flared up at me when I came across him in his surgery on Sunday. I wondered why at the time. Now it all makes sense. I'm pleased in a way –

anything to get rid of him. He's a bad doctor. We'll be losing patients to other surgeries at this rate.'

8

Chrissy felt as if her brain had been replaced with cotton wool. Again she had to park on the street because she had had no time to get a permit. The day had simply fled by and, unlike her, she'd hardly slept – not that Daphne had been difficult or demanding, it was that Chrissy couldn't relax. She'd got over-tired, she realised. Hopefully it would be a reasonably quiet night and she'd be able to grab an hour on the ward. At least that was one thing that had improved since her training days when to sleep on nights meant to be threatened with dismissal. Nowadays, provided the ward was quiet and adequately staffed, they could take it in turns to get some cat naps.

Chrissy walked to her allotted wards – Neurology and Orthopaedics again. Thank goodness she need not worry about her gran. Liz Boxtree, from the agency, was a kindly, middle-aged woman, who had once been an enrolled nurse but preferred the flexibility of working part-time for an agency as a care assistant. Chrissy was sure they'd found a treasure.

Lights were still on as the day staff scuttled about, trying to finish everything before the hand-over. As she passed one of the side wards a beautiful young woman, her face creased with worry, Staff Nurse Jo Baker's arm about her, walked into the corridor. Chrissy stood back to let them pass.

'You will look after him, won't you? You're sure I shouldn't stay the night?'

'No, no, Sabine. You go home, you must be exhausted.'

'I did do the right thing bringing him here, didn't I? Tell me I did.'

'Of course you did.'

'Only they made such a fuss at the other hospital.' She pouted, a bit like a little girl, Chrissy thought. 'They said they couldn't take responsibility.'

'There, there. They have to say that,' Jo cooed, making the

soothing noises of her profession. She nodded to Chrissy. 'With you in a minute, Sister,' she said, as she led away the smartly dressed woman.

In the office Chrissy glanced at the report book as she waited, and the other night staff began to arrive. She saw that Buck Marston was still hanging on.

'Sorry about that,' Jo said, coming into the room. 'Poor woman's distraught, but I wish she'd go and be distraught elsewhere. Now. The report.' She sat down opposite Chrissy whose staff – Auxiliary Nurse Stella Gibson and Student Nurse Trish Walters had gathered about her with notebooks in hand. Chrissy was pleased to see that Walters was looking a lot happier.

'Who is she?'

'Our VIP's wife. Sweet woman. Her husband's the orthopaedics consultant here – Mr Newson.'

'Ah, yes. I heard. The mine blast in Bosnia. Should he have been moved so soon?'

'His wife thought he'd be happier here. They're still running tests galore. They haven't found anything physically wrong with him. The trouble is, he's not speaking. They feel he can but won't.'

'Shock?'

'Probably.'

Chrissy did not look forward to nursing Mr Newson. If there was one thing that filled a nurse's heart with dread it was having to look after a fellow professional. The nervousness induced often made them clumsy and afraid of making mistakes. But still, she consoled herself, looking after doctors was not nearly as bad as nursing nurses: they invariably made a fuss if things weren't just so or procedures were handled differently from what happened in their own hospital. Chrissy settled back to listen to the rest of the report.

When the day staff had gone, she made her rounds of the patients, Stella Gibson and Trish Walters behind her. Once more, Chrissy made certain that the door to the fire escape was secure.

At the side ward she paused before she pushed open the door. At the sight of Russell Newson sitting in the bed, looking down at a book, which she sensed he was not reading, the greeting she had been about to make froze on her lips. For the colour of his hair, the way it flopped forward, made him look like her dead husband's double.

'Hello, I'm Chrissy Galloway. I'm new, we haven't met,' she finally managed.

He raised his head to look at her. She saw that he wasn't like Ewan at all: his face was completely different, not as handsome but stronger. He had sad, troubled dark brown eyes; Ewan's had been an untroubled blue.

She was not sure why her heart should be racing quite as quickly as it was. But as he looked at her she saw the expression in his eyes change, as if he recognised her, as if he was about to say something. She waited, but he remained silent.

9

Nights on the wards passed in one of two ways. Either with a mind-numbing slowness when every time they checked their watches only a minute had passed, or in a frenzy of activity when there was never time enough to finish everything and glances at watches merely caused rising panic. There seemed to be no middle way of a balanced night.

Consequently as she, Stella and Trish sat with a cup of coffee in the almost silent ward, Chrissy felt uneasy. Her body was tense as she waited for the inevitable chaos to begin.

'Quiet, isn't it?' Stella looked up from her knitting.

'Don't even say it!' Chrissy opened another of the patients' files which, taking advantage of this calm, she was studying.

'Have you realised they're not even snoring? They always snore,' Trish added.

'Hasn't stopped them farting, though, has it?' Stella grinned.

'The lull can't last' Chrissy chose to ignore her and stood up. 'I think I'll just go and check on Orthopaedics. Then I shall go for lunch and I suggest you two go either before or after the agency nurse takes hers.' Chrissy straightened her white apron, checked her torch and left the office.

'She's ever so nice, isn't she? Not at all how I thought a sister would be,' Trish said, as soon as Chrissy had left.

'Bit stuck up. Not very friendly, I think.'

'Stella, how can you say that?'

'I don't trust withdrawn types like her. It usually means they're hiding something.'

'What, a dodgy past?' Trish giggled.

'Something like,' Stella said enigmatically. 'Have you checked the dressing trolley?'

'I have. Though, since I'm supernumerary, you should have done it, really. But I don't mind doing the odd favour.'

'You Project 2000 lot have a nerve.'

'Not really. We're just moving with the times, Stella,' Trish said cheekily.

Before leaving the ward Chrissy paused outside Mr Newson's door. She would have liked to go in and see if she could get him to talk, unblock whatever the problem was. There was another reason too: she'd just like to see him again. She shook her head at such ideas and went to check on the agency nurse and her seriously ill patients.

'Everything under control with these two, Jolene?'

'Buck's a bit restless. The other one's fine. His obs are down to four-hourly.' Jolene Gardner looked up from the drainage bottle she was checking.

'Any idea why Buck should be like that? Have they changed his medication?' Chrissy stepped into the side ward. Over the second bed there was the faint glow of the blue light only. Buck's, however, was brightly lit and looked like a small island in the darkened room. 'Do you need all these lights? Maybe that's what's disturbing him.'

'Oh, really, Chrissy. How can the lights disturb a vegetable? In the next twenty-four hours I'd take bets he'll be —'

'Jolene, a word please,' Chrissy interrupted. 'In the corridor, now!' She held open the glass-fronted door for the other nurse to pass and closed it quietly behind them.

'I don't know where you trained, Nurse Gardner, but were you never taught not to speak like that in front of a comatose patient?'

'Like what?' Jolene asked, with a hard expression that Chrissy had not noticed before.

'You know that the hearing is the last sense to go. You do not speak of vegetative states, or death, in front of such a patient.'

'I didn't say anything about death.'

'Only because I stopped you.'

'I've looked after dozens like him – it's all tosh.'

'You think so? I once nursed a comatose woman who was not expected to live. But one day she woke up and asked me how my boyfriend was, even called him by his name. For weeks she'd heard everything we said, *and* remembered it. So, I forbid such talk on my ward.'

'Watch it.'

'No, you watch it.'

'I'm an agency nurse – you can't speak to me like this.'

'These patients are my responsibility. I'll speak as I see fit. Now, I'm going for lunch. Would you prefer to go before or after the other two?'

'It's all the same to me.' Jolene turned back into the side ward. Chrissy watched her go. She might be a competent nurse but she was hardly a sensitive one.

On Orthopaedics, Chrissy found elderly Mrs Norman in the kitchen, making herself hot chocolate.

'My, Mrs Norman, you're doing so well. Can I help you?'

'No thank you, Sister. I've got to manage when I get home.'

'Have they told you when you're leaving?'

'Tomorrow. I can't sleep I'm so excited.'

'Would you like a sleeping pill?' She smiled at the old woman, who had resolutely refused all sedatives the whole time she'd been here because, as she said, she 'didn't want to get fuzzy'. More likely she meant confused. Chrissy knew how the elderly feared that state in case it was misinterpreted and they were labelled 'senile'.

'No, thanks, the chocolate will suit me fine. But isn't it amazing what they do these days? I'd have been in a wheelchair a few years back. But, thanks to Mr Newson and his clever hip replacements, there's life in the old girl yet.' She laughed and swung her leg to emphasise her point. 'How is the dear man?'

'He's doing fine,' Chrissy said noncommittally.

'Do you think I should see him before I leave? Just so that I can thank him?'

'What a nice idea. But it's not up to me to decide if he's to receive visitors. I'll tell the day sister how you feel.' It might help him, she thought, as she made a mental note. 'Now, clever as you are, you can't manage crutches and hot chocolate. Let me help you.' Carrying the cup and saucer she walked slowly back to the side ward with Mrs Norman who, still over-excited, was telling her about the dog she missed, her garden that would need her, and her hubby who could never manage without her.

'Now try to sleep,' Chrissy said, as Mrs Norman, safely back in her bed, settled on the pillows with a contented sigh.

In the dining room Chrissy was just about to take a bite of her fish when her bleeper buzzed. Here we go, she thought, as she dialled the ward.

'Sorry, Sister, I thought I should get hold of you a.s.a.p.'

'What's happened, Stella?'

'It's Jolene. She's gone.'

'Gone? Where?'

'She said you'd no right to speak to her as you had and pissed off.' The curiosity in Stella's voice was obvious. 'I can't leave Trish alone on the ward and who's to special Buck?'

'I'll be up straight away.'

Back at the table, Chrissy took a gulp of coffee and snatched a couple of chips. 'Any chance of you keeping this warm for me?' she asked the dining-room assistant, who was wiping down the tables as if in slow motion.

'We haven't got the facilities.'

'Then I'll take the tray with me.'

'You can't do that. No crockery allowed out.'

'I don't believe it!' She pocketed her yoghurt as the assistant, suddenly activated, swooped on the tray as if Chrissy was a shoplifter. Chrissy, while regretting missing her lunch, was annoyed more by the thought that she had paid for it and would not get her money back.

'What did you say to her?' Stella, watching over Buck, was all agog when she got back to the ward. Trish was standing in the doorway, looking anxious.

'Nothing to warrant this. How irresponsible of her.'

'She's Australian,' Stella said, as if that was the solution.

'So? Some of the best nurses I've met have come from there,' Chrissy said lightly. 'Trish, you'd better go for lunch now and don't dawdle. Could you get Stella and me some sandwiches? Here.' She handed over some money. 'Be quick, we need you. Right, Stella, I'll special Buck. Have you phoned around for a replacement?'

'There isn't one available. The staff on Female Surgical said she'd see what she could do later, but she's got six post-ops of her own so they're a bit busy too.'

'Well, let's just pray nothing else turns up. Anything else to report?'

'Mr Newson woke up. Jolene left a bit noisily if you get my drift.'

'Did he need anything?'

'Peace and quiet, he said.'

'He spoke?' Chrissy said with astonishment.

'So he did! In all the drama I hadn't registered.'

'I'd better check him.' She tiptoed into his room and up to his bed. He was asleep. With the stress removed from his face he looked younger. As she watched him, her hand, of its own accord, stretched out as if to stroke his face. She stopped herself just in time. She looked down at him and knew that if she ever got the chance to know him, she would like him. She reined in that thought sharply. What on earth was getting into her?

Quickly she returned to the safety of caring for Buck, for whom she felt nothing but sympathy, and began the endless round of checks on him. Jolene had been right, he was very restless: one of his arms was twitching and at intervals he grimaced. Chrissy had seen this before in patients who, not having moved for weeks, suddenly became active as if agitated, as if they knew that death was near. She must check his wife's telephone number. How sad if he should die tonight, the first night they had managed to persuade her and his mother to go home early and get some decent sleep. Maybe that was the reason: maybe he knew that the ones who loved him were not here.

Twice Stella appeared needing medication checked for patients who had woken and were complaining.

'This is ridiculous, we need another nurse here. Are you sure there's no one?' Chrissy whispered.

'No one. I got left here once all on my own with four post-ops to look after with half-hourly obs – it was a nightmare. But *they* don't give a stuff.'

'Mrs Tomley will need turning in a few minutes.'

'Trish won't be long. She might be a bit thick but she's willing.' Stella grinned, aware that she had made a positive statement about a Project 2000 nurse, even if a shade grudgingly.

'There were no sandwiches left. Sorry.' Trish had returned.

'Help Stella with Mrs Tomley and then check in the kitchen if there's any food there – they must have some bread or porridge. And please, stop saying "sorry" when it's not your fault,' Chrissy said kindly.

Buck's blood pressure was fluctuating. Should she call the doctor? She checked the chart again: it had been like this for some time now. Why hadn't Jolene mentioned it to her? Flaming woman! Her bleeper vibrated. She picked up the phone by Buck's bed.

'Sister Galloway speaking,' she said, as quietly as she could into the receiver.

'For God's sake, can't you talk somewhere else? I'm tired. Or hadn't you noticed?' snapped the patient in the next bed and turned over noisily. She smiled at the shape which, to her imagination, seemed to be seething with disgruntlement. At least he was getting better, moaning was a sure sign of that.

'I'm sorry, I can't leave this side ward. I'll be as quiet as possible.' She returned her attention to the phone. 'Yes, what is it?'

'Sister, can you come quickly? It's Mrs Norman, she's ill.' The nurse on Orthopaedics spoke rapidly, urgently.

'How do you mean, ill?' Chrissy asked calmly.

'I don't know. Like she's having a fit. I don't know what to do!' Chrissy could hear the rising panic in the young woman's voice.

'Have you called the houseman?'

'I'm not allowed to. I'm not qualified.'

'Call him, say I told you to.'

Chrissy returned her attention to Buck. Seconds later her bleeper vibrated again.

'Yes?' she hissed into the phone.

'Lance Travers here. What's the problem? I've just had an hysterical auxiliary nurse on the phone. Something about Mrs Norman – it can't be, she's going home tomorrow. Why can't you check it out?'

'Because I'm tied up here, Doctor. Otherwise I would have.'

'This is too much.'

'Too right it is, Doctor.' But she realised she was talking into a dead phone. 'Sorry,' she said to the man in the other bed, who was now sighing in an exaggerated manner. She dialled the houseman responsible for Buck: at least this drama had resolved for her what was best to do.

'Stella,' she whispered down the corridor. Stella appeared from the darkened ward. 'We shall have to risk leaving Trish on the ward for a minute. There's a panic on Orthopaedics. I don't like the look of Buck's BP. I've called the houseman.'

Chrissy broke her new rule and ran up the stairs two at a time. Mrs Norman's screened-off bed was ablaze with light. The four other patients were sitting up, looking anxiously towards it. She parted the curtains. She was too late. Mrs Norman was dead.

10

The two inexperienced auxiliary nurses on the ward were too shocked to cope alone. Chrissy was not only annoyed but alarmed at the inadequate staffing levels in this hospital at night. It seemed that as morale lowered, sickness levels rose. Where were the nurses from the bank? Not much sign of them here! And if they were all sick where were the agency nurses? No doubt another cost-cutting. She would go to the office in the morning and lodge her complaints. Otherwise, at this rate, she was going to wear herself out racing from one ward to another, unable to give the high standard of cover her own training demanded of her.

Once the doctor had confirmed the death, she sent Carol, the most frightened of the two, to help out in Neurology. With the other auxiliary, Jane, she straightened Mrs Norman's body, closed her eyes and mouth and covered her serene face with a sheet.

An hour later, the time necessary to leave the body to settle, they returned. 'Have you laid out a patient before, Jane?' she asked the white-faced auxiliary nurse gently.

'No, I've not even seen anyone dead before, let alone die!' Jane was shaking visibly.

'There's nothing to be afraid of. Mrs Norman wouldn't have hurt you in life, would she? So she won't in death. She's gone. It's just her husk left here. Have you checked her religion?'

'Yes, she's C of E. Why?'

'Other religions have different rituals, so we must be sure we never upset anyone. Right. Let's get her nightie off so we can wash her . . .'

Together they lifted the dead woman, who groaned. The nurse stepped back abruptly from the bed, her face seeming even whiter.

'She's alive!' she exclaimed in horror.

'No, she's not. It's the air trapped in her lungs escaping, that's all. Now, you begin to wash her, I'll find her hairbrush . . .' Softly she talked to the younger woman as they worked, calming her, reassuring her. She could easily remember her first death, how upset and afraid she had been. Now all she felt was sadness – that never went . . .

The task completed, they pulled all the curtains at the foot of the beds in the ward to shield the other patients as they heard the rumble of the mortuary trolley approaching. It was a normal hospital trolley – though reserved for the dead – except that on the top was a steel frame over which was draped a purple cover. It was plain, no cross embellished it, so that no one could be offended by the wrong symbol. Chrissy and the porter checked that the plastic band on Mrs Norman's wrist tallied with the name on his docket to ensure that no muddle could ensue in the mortuary. They both helped the man lift the inert form onto the trolley: a dead body was always more awkward to handle than a living one. Mrs Norman, clean in her white hospital shroud, looked peacefully asleep as the purple cover was lowered over her and the trolley trundled past the curtained beds and out into the corridor.

'Clean up everything here. Strip, wash and remake the bed behind closed curtains. The other patients will be distressed enough,' Chrissy whispered. 'You did well, Jane.' She smiled encouragingly. Then, one by one, she checked the other patients, seeing they were all right, reassuring them. They were all subdued, a couple in tears. 'I'll get some tea.'

In the kitchen she laid a tea tray and looked up when a young doctor entered.

'I thought I heard a brew on the go. We've not been formally introduced, have we? Lance Travers, Orthopaedics houseman at your service, Sister.' He made a dramatic and hammy bow, which Chrissy was in no mood to be amused by.

'Have you any idea why Mrs Norman died? She seemed to be doing so well,' she asked briskly.

'Must have been an embolism somewhere – you know, a clot waiting to happen.' He grinned. Chrissy did not respond: she was aware that many used humour as a shield against death but she'd never been one of them and had never fully understood how it helped. The grin on Lance's face disappeared smartly, as if activated by a switch. 'How's Russell? He's not going to be too happy about this. He resents sudden death when it's one of his. And he liked the old girl.' Lance looked worried.

'I don't think he should be told. We don't want him upset.'

'Still not talking?'

'No, he isn't.' It seemed simpler and safer to lie. 'You'd better report to the registrar or the consultant he's left in overall charge.'

'That's a relief. The longer he stays mum the better, if you ask me.'

'You sound as if you don't like him.'

'I don't. He's a cold-hearted bastard, if you want to know.'

'His patients like him.'

'Because he's lovely to them. It's the people he *should* relate to, like his wife, colleagues, insignificant folk like that, that he treats abominably. I bet he can talk, he's just decided not to, to make it worse for his poor wife, Sabine. I wouldn't put it past the sadistic sod!'

Chrissy poured the tea and made no comment – how could she when she didn't know the man? She handed Lance a cup.

'Aren't you having one?'

'I don't like tea.' She finished laying the patient's tray.

'My, but you're pretty!'

'Thank you,' she managed to say, covering her embarrassment, but immediately wished she hadn't as Lance stepped towards her, his face alight with obvious interest in her, interpreting her reply as an invitation.

'When are your nights off, Chrissy?'

'Not for some time. Now, if you'll excuse me.' She faced him, holding the tray of tea in front of her like a shield.

'Not until you promise me you'll have dinner with me.'

'It's very kind of you, Lance, but I'm afraid I'm too busy at the moment.' She stepped to the right and he followed nimbly. 'I have patients waiting.' She looked straight at him with a determined expression. He tried to out-stare her, but failing, moved to one side.

'Another time, perhaps? I'll wait for ever, Chrissy.' He still grinned cheekily.

'We'll see,' she said, laughing – his effrontery was difficult to resist. 'But don't hold your breath,' she said, from the doorway.

In a way she'd enjoyed that little confrontation, even if she had no interest in him – he was too young, but worse, he was a doctor. Long ago Chrissy had vowed never to get involved with a medic: she'd seen too many broken hearts. Young doctors, without exception, seemed to think they were irresistible and God's gift. And hospital romances were thwarted by complications of difficult shifts, jealousy from others and gossip. But his interest showed she was still attractive to men, something she had not been sure of for a long time.

What a night this was proving to be, Chrissy thought, as she raced back to the neurological unit. She looked at her watch and was amazed to see it was only one thirty – it felt more like five. Buck was still twitching.

'He moaned just now,' Stella reported.

'Are you sure?'

'Yes, a bit like a whiffly snore.'

Chrissy giggled. 'There's a fine medical description.'

'Sorry, but that's what it sounded like. I think he's coming round. But the doctors said he never would.'

'It's an unwise doctor who says "never". I was going to call his family, but I think I'll leave it for the time being. You okay here? Then I'll just check the others.' Quickly she went round the ward, making sure that all was well, that procedures had taken place. Trish Walters was managing well. Sometimes, she thought, being short-staffed could turn into a good thing. The nurses simply had to manage and in doing so discovered a confidence in their ability they had not realised existed.

The light from the side ward attracted her attention. Through the door she saw that Russell Newson was sitting up in bed, reading. She tapped on the door before entering.

'Is there anything I can get you, Mr Newson?'

'Ah, it's you!'

Chrissy stood rooted to the spot. He said it as if he'd been waiting for her. He said it in a way that made her heart race ridiculously. 'It's late,' was all she could think to say.

'Bad night?' he asked, sympathetically.

'Just a bit busy. Tea or hot chocolate?'

'Why is it that whenever a nurse sees a patient awake they automatically offer tea?'

Chrissy decided she had imagined that moment of intimacy. 'What else is there?'

'Sympathy, perhaps?' He looked up at her with a slightly quizzical expression.

'We dish that out in great dollops too – goes without saying. I'm glad you're talking again. Any reason why you weren't?'

His doctors would still need to know why he'd been silent, and sometimes patients were more liable to confide in a nurse at night, when it was quiet. And, in any case, she wanted to be here talking to him.

He looked away from her, and she feared she'd been too curious too soon and that he was about to lapse into silence again. He sighed, as if too weary to speak. 'Have you ever been tired – Chrissy, isn't it? I don't mean physically but mentally?' He turned and looked at her and she had to stop herself exclaiming at his sad expression. 'So tired you just wanted to escape from everyone and everything – turn in on yourself?'

'As a matter of fact, yes, I have.' She balanced herself on the side of the bed.

'Why?'

'Oh, something happened in my life and I felt I had no reserves to deal with it.'

'And what did you do?'

'I went to the New Forest for a long weekend by myself. The only conversations I had were with waiters and the hotel receptionist, I didn't have to say anything. It was bliss.'

'Did it help?'

'It did. I sorted a lot of puzzles out, if nothing else. But it was temporary. I had to go back and found the problems had multiplied. Maybe there's never an escape.'

'Same here. Substitute hospitals for hotels!' He laughed. She liked his laugh, lighter and happier than she had expected. 'I don't know why but I just didn't want to talk to anyone. I couldn't make myself do it. But you're right. It hasn't helped. The problems still exist.'

'It must have been a dreadful experience – I mean the mine.' She spoke diffidently, needing to know professionally what had happened, but remembering that when she'd been traumatised prying was the last thing she'd wanted. She leant forward and took his hand in hers. 'Dreadful for you,' she repeated.

Russell closed his eyes as if trying to shut out a memory, but apparently only succeeded in making it sharper for he shook his head and his eyes snapped open. He pulled away his hand abruptly.

'Chrissy, I suggest you write in your report – because that's what you're snooping for, isn't it? – "The patient admitted he'd been fooling all along and just wanted some peace and quiet." How about that?' He sounded bitter.

She hid her disappointment that he seemed suddenly irritated with her. 'Maybe I will.'

'I'll be off tomorrow. Then you needn't worry about me any more.'

'But . . . I doubt it. They'll want to be sure that – well, that you've fully recovered.' He had been talking too much, she thought. One minute silence and then floods of words. It seemed, to her, as ominous as the silence had been.

'I might collapse from a sudden haemorrhage? Is that what you were reluctant to say? It's sweet of you to be so concerned, but I really am as right as I'll ever be now. I want to get back to work – that's the best solution. I feel –'

'Well, well, well, what a pretty sight. Am I interrupting? Were you just about to hop into bed with my adorable husband, Sister?'

They both swung round, surprise etched on their faces, to see Sabine leaning against the door jamb. 'Shall I go?' She smiled, and smiled even more broadly as Chrissy jumped from the bed, smoothing her uniform dress, knowing she looked guilty even though there was nothing to be guilty about.

'You're pissed.'

'And I'm pleased to see you too, dear Russell.' Sabine entered the room with a provocative, sexy walk, made sexier by the short tight dress she wore. 'Decided to talk, have we? I didn't think you'd be quiet for much longer.' She threw the shoes she was carrying on the floor and flung herself onto the bed, her hand outstretched. 'Missed me?'

'If you'll excuse me,' Chrissy said.

'Yes, go. We don't want you here, do we, Russell darling? You're dismissed.' Sabine waved vaguely in Chrissy's direction, then giggled as if she found the gesture funny.

'God, you can be such a bitch. I don't want you here.'

'But I *am* here . . .' Chrissy heard Sabine say, as she closed the door on them. She had felt such a rush of guilt a moment ago, but why should she have? She'd not done anything to be ashamed of. She began to walk towards the office. She'd felt stupidly put out that his wife had come but, after all, it was her privilege, and even if the hour was strange, Russell Newson was a senior member of staff and they were always a law unto themselves. What bothered her most of all, though, was the surge of pleasure she'd felt when he so obviously hadn't wanted to see his wife.

'No! Not that path . . .' she muttered to herself.

'Did you say something?' Trish skidded to a halt beside her, bedpan in hand.

'Nothing. Just talking to myself. I'm going mad – it must be working here.' She was aware it had sounded stilted. She walked into the office. She didn't want to feel this interest in him. Involvement with anyone, let alone a doctor, and a married doctor at that, was the last thing she needed at the moment. She settled at the desk and pulled the report book towards her. She was tired, she was imagining things, she –

'Come quick!'

Chrissy looked up to see an even more anxious Trish standing in the doorway.

'What on earth is it, Trish? Calm down.'

'It's Mrs Tomley. I'm sorry, but I think she's dead.' And Trish burst into tears.

CHAPTER FOUR

I

The exhaustion Chrissy felt came in waves, rather as she imagined morning sickness did in a pregnant woman.

By the time she had completed the paperwork involved with the patients' deaths, reported to the day staff and been to the main office, she was too late for breakfast. Even if she had finished in time she knew she wouldn't have gone. No doubt this hospital was no different from the others she had worked in – it didn't matter the size – a death was always the main talking-point in the canteen. Who the patient was, their complaint, who the doctor was, the how and the why – it rarely altered. If it was someone young the sadness was almost palpable and if it was a child, the silence was oppressive. But two deaths, both unexpected, both patients under her supervision – no, she could not have dealt with the chatter. As it was, she knew she would fret until the results of the post-mortems came through, would go over and over in her mind the care, the procedures, the drugs administered to both women, worrying about the facts for fear they had made an error, a fatal mistake.

As she approached her car she felt relieved, as if the vehicle was her refuge.

'Chrissy! Hi! I waited for you in the canteen.'

'Dawn, I'm sorry. I was held up.' She paused, car keys in hand and leant against the bodywork.

'You look done in. You must be feeling wretched. Don't let it get you down, These things happen.' Dawn placed a hand on Chrissy's arm. Chrissy wished she hadn't – she wished she'd go away. Too much sympathy and she was afraid she'd burst into tears. 'Fancy going into town and having a coffee and talking?' Dawn's large grey eyes were full of concern.

'Dawn, would you mind if I didn't? I've got my gran to check, a million things to do.' She smiled, she hoped sufficiently to show her gratitude.

'If you're sure, but if you get too fed up, give me a bell, the time doesn't matter.'

'Thanks. You're a real friend.' Finally she had the car door open and was sliding in. 'Bye,' she called, and sank back with relief as Dawn moved away. The woman was kind and meant well, but Chrissy needed a few minutes alone – like Russell, and at that thought she smiled properly.

'You're up! That's marvellous. You look so well,' Chrissy said, having found Dorothy sitting in her favourite Ercol chair in the back room, the television on and a cup of tea in hand.

'You look dreadful!'

'Thanks a bunch.' She began to unbutton her coat.

'Stop that. You're going home to get some decent sleep. I'm fine now.'

'Who said you could get up?' Chrissy asked suspiciously as she sat on a hard dining chair.

'The doctor – he came before morning surgery. Wasn't that nice? It was Dr Henderson, I'm happy to say, not that horrible Dr Middleton. The community nurse helped me dress and get downstairs and Liz is coming to put me to bed tonight – she's a lovely woman. Now, you buzz off before you fall over.'

'But what about during the day?'

'I've got the phone. The toilet's only a short step. Please, Chrissy, you look wiped out. Bad night?'

'You could call it that! Heard from Mum?'

'No,' Daphne answered, thin-lipped with disapproval.

'I don't understand her.'

'Don't you? I do. She's never liked me and that's the truth.'

'Oh, Gran, that's not so.' Chrissy was aware that she hadn't quite disguised her lie.

'And she's got a feller.'

'Mum? You're joking!' Chrissy laughed.

'I'm not. She's an attractive woman – why shouldn't your mother have a bloke?' The words sounded reasonable enough, but the expression on her face said otherwise.

'Because you don't approve, that's why.'

'I never said.'

'You didn't have to, Gran. Your look said it all. But I understand, Dad's been gone a long time now.'

'Oh, it's not that.' The old lady waved her hand dismissively, and for a fleeting second Chrissy was reminded of Sabine using the selfsame gesture. She hadn't liked that.

'It always amazed me she put up with my son as long as she did. Miserable old sod, he was.'

'Gran,' Chrissy said warningly.

'It's the truth. You can't go through life inflicting your opinions on everyone like he did. He was a little martinet.'

'He was a good dad.'

'And a strict one.'

'Only because he cared.'

'And who couldn't shake the dust of Fellcar off her shoes fast enough to escape?'

'Not from him.'

'Is that so? You do surprise me.' Daphne gave her an arch look.

'It was his house, he had a right to be fussy.'

'It's unmanly. A woman can be pernickety and house-proud, a man, no. I don't like it.'

'Who's imposing her opinions now?' Chrissy asked, with amusement.

'I'm old – I'm allowed.' Daphne chuckled.

'I thought Mum loved him,' Chrissy said sadly.

'Maybe she did once but, come the end, I don't think so.'

'I never saw them argue. Never heard him raise his voice.'

'He didn't have to. He got at her with calm reason – dripping away like a Chinese torture, poor bitch. I know how it went. "You're putting on weight." "You're too thin." "Aren't you too old for that hairstyle, that dress, that hobby?" Oh, you name it, he'd have said it. He wanted to undermine her confidence so she stayed because she thought no one else would want her. All she could do was please him in the hope he'd shut up. But he didn't – not until they put him in his coffin.'

'That's awful!' Chrissy felt her face stiffen at her grandmother's words. She could have been describing Ewan, but how could she have known that? She'd never talked about it. If her father had been like that too, even if Chrissy had not been aware of it, had some instinct made her search out someone similar? She shook her head abruptly at such a far-fetched theory.

'His father was just the same. I just ignored my silly old bugger. I don't think she could.' Daphne continued blithely, unaware of the effect her words had had on Chrissy.

'But if you understood so well why didn't you speak to her? Then maybe she'd have –' Chrissy stopped, as if a hand had been clapped over her mouth.

'Liked me? Isn't that what you were going to say? How could I? If she'd come to me it might have been different, but she didn't. In any case, I might speak ill of the dead but there is such a thing as loyalty to the living.'

'Then why do you disapprove of her having an affair now?'

'I reckon he's married, that's why. My generation has had to adjust to a lot of things – divorce, living in sin, illegitimacy, abortions – but I can't get my mind round one woman taking another's husband. Shouldn't be done. Why are you crying?'

'It's odd.' Chrissy wiped a tear from her cheek. 'Listening to you, it's like Dad's died all over again. Why is it people are so often not what they seem?' She knew the tears had come for many reasons, not just this new knowledge of her father.

'I'm sorry, I shouldn't have gone on like that. Not when you're so tired. That's what's upsetting you, probably. What's up?'

'A lousy night. No, I'm glad you told me. I mean, if you live a dream you end up looking foolish, don't you? Everyone else knowing and not you.' She looked down at her hands, not wanting Daphne to see the pain in her eyes, the memories that were flooding back.

'You're holding back on me, Chrissy. It never does any good. You can talk to me. It's about Ewan, isn't it?'

'What gave you that idea? No. I was sad about Dad, that's all.'

She stood up, wanting to get out of here quickly. 'Still, if you're sure you're okay, I'd better get going. You're right, I'm so tired.' She rebuttoned the coat she hadn't even taken off. 'You will call me if you feel funny or wobbly, won't you?'

'Promise. Now away with you and get some sleep.'

When Chrissy slept, her dreams were of Ewan and her father, and the two dead patients loomed in and out of a mist at her. She awoke feeling drained and oddly afraid.

2

'Why wasn't I told, Lance?' Russell looked angrily at his houseman.

'It was thought best not to bother you.' Lance shuffled his stethoscope from the left pocket of his white jacket to the right hand and back again. Finally he put it round his neck and played with the end of it.

'*Bother me!* For heaven's sake, Lance, a patient who shouldn't have died and you call that *bother*!' Russell could feel his anger begin to build, like bile seeping into his gullet.

'Well . . . I'm sorry.'

'Who decided? You?'

'Well . . .' The stethoscope was back to its restless swapping from pocket to pocket.

'Stop saying *well*, for God's sake. Just answer me.'

'Chrissy Galloway, the new sister. She didn't want you distressed.'

Russell, who'd been sitting on the side of the bed, stood up. 'Get me a set of theatre gear.'

'What?'

'I've got no clothes. I need –'

'You're not leaving, Mr Newson?'

'Just do it.'

Lance scuttled out of the room, his handsome face anxious, but Russell was neither concerned nor amused, he was furious. He showered and as he soaped himself his anger multiplied. How dare that woman make such decisions for him? He'd liked her too, thought he'd seen something special, different about her. He hadn't even worked out the what or the why, just an odd feeling. And he need not have bothered: she was the same as so many in her profession, bossy and interfering.

Lance, no doubt thinking it safer, had left the neat pile of theatre clothes on his bed. He quickly dressed in the pale green trousers and jacket, slipped his feet into the white clogs and left behind the cap and mask that completed the outfit.

'And where do you think you're going, Mr Newson?' In the door, barring his way, stood the large figure of the day sister. 'Get back onto that bed this instant.' She pointed sternly towards it.

'Sister, you may boss all you want. I'm leaving. Now, will you excuse me or do I have to lift you out of the way?'

'Really! Mr Newson! Whatever next!' And the twelve-stone sister giggled like a giddy girl.

'Thank you.' Russell stepped out into the corridor.

'But, really, you shouldn't be doing this. What will Fraser Ball say? Let me call him, please.' The sister trailed after him in cumbersome pursuit.

'I'm discharging myself, so you can tell Fraser Ball whatever you want. Thanks for everything,' he remembered to say, as he reached the ward door.

Two at a time he took the stairs to the orthopaedic ward. The senior doctors were not normally seen on the ward before ten so that the morning staff had time to straighten the patients and get routine dressings and medications done before the consultants swept in with their entourage for their morning rounds. It was one of the few rituals from the past that was still maintained. So the appearance of Russell at nine sent the staff into a tailspin of flapping anxiety.

'Russell, what the hell –' Sister Tina Newport came forward.

'Where's the charge nurse?'

'He's off sick. He broke his leg playing rugby last Saturday. I'm keeping an eye on here as well as my own ward.'

'Mrs Norman's notes, please.' He held out his hand.

'They're not here. They've already gone to the main office. No doubt there'll be an inquest. I mean –'

'You any ideas why she died, Tina?'

'Who knows? An embolism? You know how it is –'

'Lance said she wasn't cyanosed.'

'No, according to the night sister her colour was normal. But she went so fast that I presume –'

'Never presume, Tina. Did Phil or Milton Curtis see her?'

'Honestly, Russell, I don't know. You know this isn't my ward. I'm doubling on it and it's hell!'

'This bloody place is falling about our ears. Can you give Curtis a bell? Get him here stat? I'll just check my other patients.'

Normally this was where Russell was happiest, where he found contentment. Just chatting to his patients, reassuring them, planning procedures to be done, accepting their praise put everything else out of his mind and focused his attention. Except that today it wasn't working. He couldn't seem to concentrate, couldn't even remember some of their names – not like him – but worse, he suddenly felt a total lack of interest. He retreated to the office and sat at the desk leafing idly through notes he wasn't reading.

'Would you like a coffee, Russell? You look done in. Are you sure you should be doing this?'

'I'm fine, Tina. But a coffee would be great – no sugar.' She was an old friend of many years, but he hoped she'd go so that he could be alone to think through what was happening to him. Instead, she asked an orderly to get the drink and came back and sat opposite him.

'You should be in bed, resting.'

'Don't you start.' He managed a grin.

'Why are doctors such lousy patients?'

'Because we know best.'

'Bah!' Tina Newport snorted, with the disdain of one who knew better.

'Did you call Curtis?'

'He'll be here as soon as poss. He's a good doctor, isn't he?'

'Where was he last night?'

'Russell, don't be hard on him. The woman was dead. What would be the point in hauling him out of bed as well?'

'She complained of pain before I left for Bosnia. I thought it was nothing. I should have taken more time with her.'

'Then you'd have missed your plane. Come to think of it, perhaps that *would* have been for the best.' She laughed. He didn't. 'Oh, come on, Russell. Most patients complain. How were you to know?'

'This small voice inside me tells me I *should* have known.'

'You're not God, Russell.' Tina smiled slyly. 'Ah, Fraser. Hello! Can I help you?'

Russell looked up to see Fraser Ball, the neurologist, in the doorway. 'You needn't try to sound the innocent with me, Tina. You called him, didn't you?'

'I had to, Russell.'

'This isn't a prison, Russell. You know that. I'd have preferred you stay a day or two longer.'

'I'd rather go, Fraser. I'll rest better out of here.'

'You're not planning to come back to work?' Fraser looked relieved.

'I'm not entirely stupid, Fraser. I don't want to do anything that might harm my patients, do I? I realise I need a few days off.' He hadn't realised anything of the sort until coming here and finding himself so disorientated.

'Well, that's different. Shall I call Sabine to come and collect you?'

'No, don't do that,' he said sharply. 'I'll get a taxi, once I've seen Curtis.'

'But you've no clothes.'

'These will do.' He looked down at his theatre clothes.

'Well, if you think –'

'Can't anyone say anything but *well* in this bloody place? Ah, Curtis. A quiet word,' he said pointedly, to his senior houseman who had appeared looking more anxious than ever. Fraser and the sister took the hint and together walked out into the corridor.

'You sure he's all right to go home?' Tina asked.

'Yes. He's probably right – he'll be better out of here. There doesn't appear to be anything physically wrong with him.'

'Mentally?'

'He's got a lot to come to terms with, it would seem. But he will. I know Russell, he's a tough nut. Do you think I should give Sabine a call?'

'Better not. He didn't seem to want her here, did he? Poor Sabine, I think he gives her a bit of a hard time. She's such a sweetie too.'

It wasn't until the taxi pulled into the driveway of his house, half-way up North Hill, that Russell realised he'd no money to pay.

'Hang on a minute, would you?' He saw that the driver looked somewhat suspicious as he got out of the cab. The man had been none too happy picking him up dressed as he was: he'd asked Russell if he was sure he was a real doctor, no doubt thinking he'd escaped from the psychiatric ward.

At the door of the ultra-modern house it dawned on him that, of course, he had no key. He rang the bell impatiently. It seemed an age before the tiny figure of their daily woman appeared.

'Mr Newson! What on earth are you doing here? You're in hospital.'

'They let me out. Is Mrs Newson up?'

'She's not here. I let myself in.'

'You couldn't lend me a fiver to pay the taxi?'

'I think I can just about do that.' She rootled in the pocket of her pinafore for her purse. 'You want any breakfast? A coffee?'

'No, thanks. If you could just pay the cabbie? I'll get into some real clothes.'

'You all right?'

'As rain. Do me a favour, June, don't fuss.'

He climbed the open-tread staircase that swept in a graceful curve to the upper floor. He'd had doubts about buying this modern house, preferring the old to the new, but this stairway had clinched it. Sabine had been enthralled at the sight of it. She'd clapped her palms together with excitement in that childlike way he'd found so endearing – once. 'Oh, I shall love sweeping down that!' And, loving her and wanting to indulge her, he'd agreed to buy.

He entered the guest room, which had been his room for over a year now. Quickly he changed into casual clothes but found, to his consternation, that this activity had exhausted him. He was used to the tiredness of overwork, but this lethargic fatigue was something new to him.

He sat on the bed. He must counter this. He'd work out an exercise routine to build himself up – a surgeon had to be fit, there was no room for even the smallest deviation from that. He'd drive to the country club, do some swimming, nothing too strenuous to start with. And he'd take some long walks – the best exercise in the world, he'd told his own patients often enough.

He swung his legs up on the bed and looked at his watch. It was eleven. As an active man he was unused to such indolence. He looked about the room, tastefully decorated in white and blue. Sabine was good with colours, he'd admit that; not much good at anything else, though.

He put his arms behind his head and lay looking up at the ceiling. It wasn't just his strength he needed to sort out, there was much else he had to resolve. If last week had taught him anything, it was that he could no longer accept second best. Life was too short.

The door opened and Sabine, exquisite in a pastel Armani trouser suit, stood in the doorway. Her fine blonde hair swung loose around her beautiful face, the large blue eyes wide with surprise.

'Russell, darling, what are you doing here? No one told me. They should have done.' She pouted.

'I told them not to. I didn't want you to come and collect me like a parcel.'

'Russell, what a silly thing to say – a parcel! Whatever next?' She crossed the room to the bed.

'You'd probably have felt more emotion if it had been.' He snorted.

'Russell, don't be grumpy. You're home now. I'll look after you.' She moved until her legs were against the bed, he moved further over to the other side. 'Russell, don't look at me like that, don't shrink away from me.' She looked downcast.

'Sabine, who do you think you're conning?'

'I don't understand. What do you mean?' she asked in her breathless little-girl voice.

'You don't love me. You like what my money gives you, that's all.'

'Russell, that's not true. I begged you not to go to Bosnia. And I was right, wasn't I?'

'That was a game, Sabine. One of the many you play. Making me think you cared still. That you worried.'

'You're not well, Russell. Don't upset yourself.' She put out her hand.

'Don't touch me! Don't come near me! You reek of sex!' he hissed.

One more night and then two nights off, Chrissy thought with relief, as she inched up the steep slope of North Hill. Ahead was a dustcart and immediately in front of her was a delivery van, which was finding the steep incline too much for its engine, which, judging by the acrid smoke billowing out, was almost clapped out. Shouldn't be allowed, she thought, as the cavalcade shuddered to a halt.

Idly she looked at the house in front of which she had stopped. Set back from the road, it was all white with stark lines and large picture windows. Bet they're a pain to keep clean, she thought, tapping her steering wheel. She didn't think she'd like to live in a house like that. She imagined the interior. You would have to be tidy in a place like that – not for her! She smiled to herself. The front door, which looked as if it was made of shiny steel, opened, a woman appeared and slammed it shut behind her. She climbed into a silver Porsche, started the engine, then sounded the horn angrily at Chrissy, who was blocking her driveway. 'Sorry,' Chrissy mouthed to her, gesticulating at the traffic ahead. Still the woman hit the horn. Chrissy looked in her rear mirror and reversed sufficiently to let her out. The Porsche shot into the road, the driver making no acknowledgement. 'Charming,' said Chrissy. That was Sabine Newson! Not so sweet now, she thought, and was quite shocked at how satisfied she felt. So that was where Russell Newson lived. She leant forward to get a better look at the house, but ducked back sharply at seeing him standing at a window looking out onto the road. She felt herself blush. God, she hoped he hadn't seen her! How embarrassing. But what was he doing at home? The traffic began to move. She let in the clutch and did a messy hill start – she was still too flustered to do a good one. She wondered if her mother knew the Newsons and how she could ask without sounding too interested. And that thought shocked her too, the way it had crept up on her. Of course, it was only idle curiosity – what was more natural than that she should ask about a colleague?

She drove between the high hedge of beech, which her father had planted years ago to shield the house from prying eyes and any traffic noise, and which was now fully mature and dense. She loved this house. Built in a cottage style, earlier this century, when arts and crafts were all the rage, it had dormer windows, was thatched and had a cosiness about it that belied its size inside. She supposed at some point her mother would want to sell it. Not only must it be worth a small fortune now but with five bedrooms and four reception rooms it was far too big for her; the garden must cost an arm and a leg to maintain. She dreaded that day coming and only wished she was in a position to buy it for herself. No point in that, she reasoned, as she paused on the gravel driveway to look at it. Then, instead of Iris rattling around inside, it would be her. No, this house deserved a young family, and the noise and bustle and life that it would bring.

'It's only me!' she called out, as she let herself into the oak-panelled hall with the key she still had on her ring, left over from childhood.

'Oh!' Her mother appeared at the door of the breakfast room, which in turn led into the roomy, light, farmhouse-type kitchen. 'You could have knocked.'

'I'm sorry. I didn't think. I mean, I had the key, I just –'

'You wouldn't like it if I just walked in on you, now, would you?'

'I haven't thought about it. Probably not.'

'Pull the other one,' Iris rejoined. 'What do you want?'

Chrissy was taken aback by her mother's brisk tone. 'I thought I'd come and see you. Report on Gran.'

'How is the old bag?'

'Much better. Up and about, if a bit wobbly on her pins.'

'It'll take more than pneumonia to bump off that old girl.'

'Mum!'

'I told you how I felt.' Iris still blocked the way into the breakfast room.

'I'm still adjusting to it. It comes as a bit of a shock when you find a person doesn't much like another when you thought they were great friends.'

'Life's full of such little surprises.'

'I know,' Chrissy said, thinking about her father, but refrained from saying it. 'Any chance of a coffee? I'm beat. It was a bad night.'

'It's not actually –'

'Iris? Where've you buggered off to?' a man's voice called.

'"Convenient"? Is that what you were about to say, Mum?' Chrissy smiled broadly, wanting Iris to know she didn't mind if she'd got a bloke.

'Oh, hello. Sorry. I didn't know you'd got a visitor.' A short, but broad-shouldered, fair-haired man, with a strong, irregular-featured face, had appeared in the doorway.

'Well, you're here now. Bob, this is my daughter, Chrissy. Well . . . this is Bob.'

Awkwardly they shook hands. Chrissy knew she looked taken aback; her mother having a boyfriend was one thing – but so much younger! 'Hi!' she said lamely.

'You'd better come through.' Iris led the way. Bob stood back politely to let her pass. The kitchen was in chaos. On the floor, protected with sheets, were the chrome hob covers of the Aga and various other bits and pieces from its insides. 'You want a coffee, Bob?'

'No, I was coming to say my wrench is buggered. I'm just off to the builders' merchants. Need anything from the shops? If not, I'll get going. Leave you two to have a natter. 'Bye, love.' He kissed Iris full on the mouth, winked at Chrissy and was gone.

'He seems nice,' Chrissy said, while taking off her coat. She sat on one of the chairs at the pine table on which stood the large, wrought-iron candlesticks she'd always admired.

'Bit young for me. Was that what you were thinking?'

'No,' she lied.

'Good. Then don't. He's here to stay. So you'd better get used to the idea,' Iris said, that brisk tone returning, and busied herself with making the coffee, always a bit of a ritual.

'I didn't say a word. Good luck to you. What's happened to the Aga – being serviced?'

'Bob's a plumber.'

'Fine. You won't ever have to wait for one to come, will you?' Chrissy joked.

'I don't think that's particularly funny.'

'Sorry.' Iris might have found a bloke, but it seemed she'd lost her sense of humour – not that she'd ever had much of one, thought Chrissy, though sometimes there'd been a glimmer. 'I'd like an Aga.'

'Then have this one.'

'Don't be silly. I've nowhere to put one in my little kitchen. But you don't mean you're getting rid of it?' Chrissy asked in disbelief.

'Can't wait to. I always hated the bloody thing – you lift the lid and the temperature in the oven goes down. Only good it ever was was to lean on in winter and risk getting piles.'

'Dad loved that Aga.'

'He didn't have to cook on the damn thing. I'm replacing it with a nice built-in electric Neff with a ceramic hob. You can rely on electricity. Why are you looking so disapproving?'

'It seems sacrilegious. You know, people dream of installing one, not ripping it out.'

'There's a lot of other things coming out – those flaming rhododendrons for a start. I hate them. And I'm redoing the bathroom. I've bought a whirlpool bath and I'm putting in a power-jet shower – or, rather, Bob is.' Iris laughed at her little joke.

'I understand. A new man, new things – like you changed your hairstyle. I really am pleased for you, Mum. I think it's lovely.'

'Really? You're not pretending?' Iris placed the coffee cups on the table and sat opposite her, looking at her with suspicion.

'No. Why should I? Even if he is younger than you – why not? If it was Dad here and not you and he'd found a young girlfriend, no one would think it odd.'

'Well, that's a relief. I've been telling myself it's my business and didn't give a damn what you thought, but, of course, I suppose, I did.' She leant forward and took her daughter's hand. 'Chrissy, I can't tell you how happy he's made me. I feel reborn. I didn't know love – you know – well, the whole caboodle – could be so wonderful.' Chrissy squeezed her mother's hand, not sure what to say, never having had this type of conversation with her, but acknowledging that she'd never seen her like this before. Why, she'd shed years.

'Gran told me that Dad made you unhappy. Is that true?'

'She said what? Interfering old biddy!'

'Is it true? I really need to know, Mum.'

'I wasn't *that* unhappy, I just wasn't happy, do you know what I mean? And now, when I've found it, now I realise it was all pretty grim. It's made me angry – very angry with him. I feel sort of cheated. You probably don't understand what I'm going on about.' She laughed somewhat self-consciously.

'I do, actually.' Chrissy paused, but knew she wouldn't explain how she knew, she'd like to, had thought of doing so often, but something, she didn't know what, prevented her. 'Was he controlling?' she asked instead.

'Yes. He needed to control everything, what I wore, how I did my hair, the central-heating temperature, the bloody Aga.' Iris laughed at that.

'And he demoralised you? Made you feel unworthy?' Chrissy asked. Iris nodded. 'And I didn't know. That's what I find so difficult to grasp. He was a bit strict with me – what I wore, what time I came in – but, then, what father isn't?'

'He got far worse after you left. That's why you were unaware. I was glad you'd gone. He'd have stifled you. You know what I think?' She began to open the biscuit barrel. 'I think he knew he was seriously ill. He suddenly realised he wasn't going to outlive me and he wanted to get me to such a state that when he died I'd be too frightened to look for anyone else.'

'You mean controlling from the other side of the grave? That's twilight-zone stuff. Bizarre.' Chrissy helped herself to a chocolate digestive. 'Still, it could have been genetic – Gran said Grandad was just the same.'

'She's never said before.'

'Maybe all this explains why you've gone off her. You know, seeing her reminds you of her son and you've put up barriers.'

'Did you do a course in psychology when you did your Back to Nursing course? Sounds like it.' Iris grinned suddenly.

'No, I didn't. It was just a thought.'

'Anyway, your reasoning's too complicated. If I'm honest, I never got on with her, I just pretended for the sake of peace, and then, after Frank died, I pretended out of convention, I suppose. Then Bob came into my life, made me look at things differently, and on top of that you're back and I don't have to bother.'

'I wish you would bother. Just a bit. I can't sleep at my place for worrying if she's all right.'

'I've been selfish. I'll pop in later and check on her.' Iris refilled the biscuit plate. 'Time we started planning Christmas.'

'There's weeks to go yet.'

'No, there aren't. You know me, I like to have things organised. I presume you'll want to be eating here.'

'I'm not sure yet. I'll probably volunteer to work over Christmas – give those with husbands and families time off.'

'No one appreciates you when you make sacrifices like that.'

'Don't they? I shall feel better about it if I do.'

They sat drinking their coffee, chatting amicably. Chrissy found it strange. They'd never been friends, never close, and yet in one hour everything seemed to have changed. She liked it, she decided.

'Help. Is that the time? I must be going.' She stood up. 'Do the Newsons live down the hill – about a dozen houses away?' she asked casually, as she buttoned herself into her coat.

'Yes. We don't see a lot of him, but she's lovely. Such a sweet woman. Nobody likes him much. Most people think he doesn't deserve her. Why do you ask?'

'Oh, just nosy. I've been nursing him.'

As she passed Russell's house she couldn't stop herself taking a sneaky glance at it. But he was nowhere to be seen.

4

So many of the female population of Fellcar wanted to be a 'Friend of St Edith's' that, to give everyone a chance to help, they were divided into teams who alternated, rather like the roster of flower ladies at the local church – another popular cause.

Floss Yates could not remember how she had become the undisputed leader of her particular group of a dozen volunteers, but she had grasped the role with enthusiasm. From the start she had determined to make them the best; certainly on their days the flowers were more artistically arranged and she made sure the library trolley had an interesting selection of books, often buying and donating the latest bestsellers herself. Days when Floss was at the helm sales boomed at the shop in the entrance hall. She personally checked the trolley, laden with sweets and toiletries, which toured the wards, making sure it never had the shortages that, so often and irritatingly for the patients, were too common on other days. She had glowed with pride when she'd overheard two visitors swear that even the tea tasted better when Floss was in control.

Floss was a hands-on leader. Today as she barrelled about the hospital encouraging here, praising there, getting her team to work harder and longer than any of the others, she was, as always, in her element. Long ago she had learnt never to order or ask anyone to do anything; instead she suggested, often quite obliquely, that such and such *might* be a good idea. And invariably the others took the hint, often unaware it had been given, and even more often thinking they had thought of it themselves, especially when later they basked in Floss's fulsome praise – just as she'd planned.

Floss loved this hospital. Her involvement had begun thirty years ago when her child had died less than a day after he was born here. Instead of never wanting to see the inside of the place again, which would have been understandable, Floss had remembered the kindness and dedication of the staff. When she had learnt that the latest hi-tech incubator might have saved her son, she had been galvanised into fund-raising to buy one so that other babies might be saved. She had never wavered in her devotion. This was increased ten-fold when, ten years ago, her husband had died of a heart-attack and she was convinced that had he been nearer to St Edith's he would have survived.

Floss pottered up the basement steps that led from the small office, more like a broom cupboard, that belonged to the Friends. She turned into the ground-floor corridor towards to the administration block. She had a lot on her mind. The Friends came exclusively from the middle-aged and the middle classes. They were all of that generation when a career outside the home was a rare option. Now, widowed or with the children flown, they had time on their hands and an emptiness in their homes. Floss was fully aware that they depended on being needed here so the possibility of this hospital closing was too awful to contemplate. What would they all do? she thought, as she tapped on Glynis Tillman's office door for their weekly chin-wag.

'Everything fine?' Glynis asked, as she fussed over the tea.

'Running like clockwork,' Floss replied to her old friend. She'd spent a few sleepless nights since the day last week when her nephew Kim had told her of his worries about the hospital and she was still undecided whether to discuss the problem with Glynis.

'Thanks – two sugars,' she said, handing back her cup to Glynis.

'You shouldn't, you know, Floss. You really must lose weight.'

'Why do thin people always think they can be so personal with fat people? What if I told you you should eat more, you're too scrawny?' She said all this in a voice bubbling with laughter, a trick she had adopted to get her point of view across without giving offence. Though sometimes, like now, she despised herself for being so craven when what she wanted to do was slap Glynis's face for her impertinence.

'You know I only say it for your own good, my dear.'

'Diets don't work.' Floss helped herself to sugar since Glynis obviously had no intention of doing it for her.

'No fat people came out of concentration camps, did they?' Glynis smiled in the superior way of one who'd scored a point.

'Only someone who knows nothing about being fat ever says that. Could we talk about something you understand and not something you know nothing about?'

'Oh dear, I've offended you.' Glynis was concerned, she had few friends and she valued Floss.

'No, you're boring me.'

'What do you want to talk about, then?'

'First, I think we need to recruit more Friends.'

'But I thought we had too many already?'

'Not mixed enough. We're all middle-class and we all mean well, but I think we intimidate some patients. We need a cross-section and some younger women, too, to help with the children and teenagers. And I've been wondering if we shouldn't start self-help groups within the hospital – women who've had hysterectomies or breast cancer, say, to talk to patients in for treatment. Set their minds at rest. That sort of thing.'

'The new oncology sister suggested the very same thing – she's very keen. And parents of children with handicaps could talk to new parents. There are so many possibilities. We could get advice from the various charities.'

'I'm surprised.' Floss smiled slyly. 'I thought it might be an uphill task persuading you of all people.'

'Whatever gave you that idea?'

'You know how you medics like to keep everything close to your chests. As if only you know what's best,' Floss said, using her laughter technique, but Glynis interpreted the remark as barbed and, realising she really had offended Floss, made a note never to presume that friendship gave one permission to be too familiar.

'Funding might be difficult. We're coming in over budget.'

'What's new?' Floss snorted and picked up a digestive biscuit. She would have liked to dunk it as she always did, but knowing that that would offend Glynis, who was a mite prissy on certain matters, she refrained since Glynis was agreeing with her.

'What else did you want to raise?'

'Oh, yes.' Floss sipped her tea, aware that she was playing a game but rather enjoying being a smidgen spiteful for once. 'I've heard there's a plan afoot to privatise St Edith's. Could I have another biscuit?'

Glynis felt the blood drain from her face. She had to replace her cup and saucer on the table as her hand began to shake.

'Privatise St Edith's?' she said, sounding, Floss thought, a lot like Lady Bracknell, which made her smile. 'I don't think it's funny.'

'Of course it isn't.'

'But who told you this?'

'I can't tell you that, Glynis. I promised confidentiality. But I can assure you I learnt it from a very reliable source – as they do say.'

'No. That's ridiculous. Privatise an NHS hospital? It's not possible. It would never be allowed!'

'It wasn't to be done quite so blatantly. A group – I don't know who yet – will ensure that the hospital is not cost-effective. Its closure will, therefore, be an inevitable step. I've already heard the rumours that if it closes it will be turned into apartments. Haven't you? So, their plan is that a so-called property firm will buy it. It will remain empty for a time but not long enough for the medical infrastructure to collapse. And then, hey presto, it will be sold to a company – American, no doubt – and will reopen as a private hospital, but one willing to deal with the NHS as well as the insurance companies since Thorpedale General couldn't possibly take the overflow without massive expansion.'

'Good Lord.' Glynis slumped back into her chair, the hopelessness of her posture indicating the depth of her concern.

'It's quite clever, really. I mean, at the moment anyone in BUPA or the like has to go thirty miles at least to find a Nuffield hospital. I always said it was a mistake closing the private wing.'

'It seemed the right thing at the time, Floss. What do we do now?'

'We stop them, of course. We start a "Save Our Hospital" campaign immediately, even before they get round to talking about it officially. Nip their little scheme in the bud.'

'But who?'

'That's what we have to find out. It's crooked, Glynis – and we've got to stop their nasty, greedy little tricks.'

5

M o, sitting beside the high bed, looked about her at the long ward. Every bed was occupied by women with various gynaecological problems. It was noisy. It was drab, the radiators chipped, the bed curtains torn. Such rundown surroundings were hardly conducive to confidence. Without realising it, she grimaced.

'Pretty ghastly, isn't it?'

Mo swung round at the cutglass-voweled voice. Behind her stood a tall, blonde-haired staff nurse, a clip-board clutched to her chest.

'A little. Bit depressing, yes,' Mo said, in an apologetic way, as if she'd been caught out criticising someone's property.

'Not for much longer. The new oncology unit opens next week, hopefully. They got behind with the building. What's new?' She gave a short, sharp snort of a laugh. 'I'm Lesley Bing – one of your named nurses. What do you like to be called?' She set the clip-board on the bedside locker.

'Mo.'

'Fine. It's so much nicer than surnames, don't you think? Now, if you could pop up on the bed.'

'What's a named nurse?'

'It means that, with a junior, I'm given a specific number of patients to look after and you're my responsibility right through your treatment. It saves you having to get to know different people all the time.'

'That's nice.' Mo settled herself on the counterpane, which was cotton and scratchy and had St Edith's embossed down the centre, presumably to stop it being stolen, though who would want it she couldn't imagine.

'Now, if I could just check you in.'

Patiently Mo, for the umpteenth time it seemed to her, trotted out her details – full name, date of birth, next of kin, medical history of her family as well as herself, with a concentration of interest in those members who'd had breast problems. It seemed such a waste of time.

'Why can't the first form I filled in follow me around?'

'You went private, didn't you?'

'Yes, I did,' Mo almost whispered, feeling defensive, sensing she was being criticised. 'I couldn't deal with any waiting, you see.' Lesley did not reply and Mo wondered if she'd imagined her pursing her lips and decided she hadn't. 'It's very stressful,' she added for good measure, and then questioned why she had. Lesley began to wrap the cuff of the blood-pressure machine around her arm.

'What's oncology mean?' she asked, unable to deal with this silence.

'Open your mouth. Let me put this thermometer under your tongue.' That done the nurse began to pump the cuff. 'It comes from the Greek *onkos* meaning swelling or a mass.' She looked smugly knowledgeable as she trotted out this information, released the pressure and watched the measure fall. 'So, from that root comes oncology – the study of tumours or, in other words, cancer.' Briskly she packed away the apparatus. She flicked the watch pinned to her chest and began to take Mo's pulse.

Mo sat rigid as any statue. The plain counterpane appeared to move as if a dozen snakes were writhing beneath it. The wall of the room opposite wobbled and she felt as if the oxygen was draining from the air, making normal breathing difficult.

'Pulse is a shade fast. Otherwise everything's fine. If you could change into your night clothes and pop into bed the doctor will be round to see you.' Lesley clipped the chart to the metal hook hanging at the bottom of Mo's bed.

'Nurse. I –' Mo stopped at seeing the distracted look on Lesley's face. 'Oh, nothing,' she said, since she wasn't even sure what it was she wanted to say.

'Any questions, don't hesitate.' And Leslie swept away, stopping at a bed further along the ward. Mo looked down at the counterpane which, thankfully, was static again. Suddenly she felt lethargy swamp her so that just the thought of changing into her pyjamas was too daunting and she felt such an urge to cry that what little energy she had left was needed to fight it.

'Hi! I'm Yvonne. Want to talk?'

Mo looked up to see a woman in her forties standing by the bed in a purple dressing gown, which was not the ideal colour for her given her yellowish-grey pallor. She wore make-up which, in turn, looked garish and badly chosen against that skin. And then she wondered if, perhaps, that had been her choice of make-up before she was ill and that she hadn't realised it no longer suited her. The last thing Mo wanted was to talk, but out of courtesy she smiled.

'I'm Mo,' she said.

'Are you all right?'

'I'm fine. Really –' Mo felt the tears she had been fighting well up and distort her vision. She shook her head. 'I'm lying. I'm not fine at all. I'm so scared.' And blindly she fumbled in her locker for the Kleenex she was sure were there.

'Here.' Yvonne handed her the box. 'Brünhilde been putting the wind up you? Don't let her get you down, she does it to everyone. Evil old bitch. I've put a curse on her. We're waiting to see if it'll work!'

'Sorry? I don't understand. Brünhilde?' She blew noisily into the tissue.

'Lesley Bing. God knows why she took up medicine. She should be a prison wardress or be doing live experiments on furry little animals. She's a sadistic cow. We reckon she's got no sex life and no boobs worth speaking of so she gets a kick out of seeing ours in trouble. May I?' Yvonne sat on the side of the bed. 'Don't cry, Mo. Don't let her see she's won. Watch out, she's looking this way – give us a laugh.'

Mo tried to do as she was ordered, flung her head back and pretended to laugh.

'She looks quite disappointed,' Yvonne reported. 'What did she say?'

'It wasn't her fault, it was mine. I asked her what oncology meant and she told me.'

'The C word? You hadn't said it to yourself? Got used to all that tumour talk and it's-probably-a-cyst-or-benign crap. That it?'

'I think about it. I hadn't said it out loud. Does that sound silly? It was like if no one said it about me, then it wasn't cancer.' And unable to stop herself she shuddered at the word.

'I know they keep saying it to you but it probably *will* be all right. I've seen so many come and go here and for the majority of them it *is* just a lump. Nothing worse.'

'A friend of mine who's a nurse, she explained all that to me. The trouble is, deep down in here, I know it is – you know.' She waved her hand limply, not wanting to say *that* word again.

'Quite honestly, Mo, it's the not knowing that's the worst. That I do know. If it is cancer, at least you'll know what you're up against. You haven't talked to anyone, have you? You should. Remember the Bob Hoskins' advert? "It's good to talk."'

'My friend – I talked to her. But she's busy. And, being a nurse, she sees so much. I think they get immune to it, don't you?'

'What about your husband?'

At this Mo did laugh. 'He's the last person I'll tell. He's terrified of hospitals – always has been. It goes back to when he had his tonsils out.' She laughed weakly, plucking nervously at the counterpane. She took a deep breath. 'And, in any case, we're going through a bit of a dodgy patch. This would probably make him take to the hills.'

'Then you'd be better off without him. Mine did that. Said he was afraid of disfigurement – I ask you, how pathetic! So I said if all that kept him with me was my boobs then he could sod off.' Yvonne beamed from ear to ear as she related this to Mo. Mo looked at her closely to see if it was bravado, but hard as she looked she could see only a genuine smile. 'Oh, I meant it. I'm not lying. I mean, if the worst comes to the worst, I don't want him around when I'm dying.'

'Yvonne! Don't even say it.'

'Why not? We're all dying, it's just that some of us go sooner than others. And, in any case, there's a lot of advantages in God giving you a hint. You get a lot sorted out in your life – like useless bloody husbands.'

'Have you? I mean –' Mo floundered, unsure what she could say and what was not permitted.

'Had cancer? A mastectomy? Yes, I have. And it's not the end of the world, Mo. I like to think there's more to me than a pair of tits.'

'Oh, Yvonne.' Mo was laughing genuinely now.

'You know what you find out in hospital? There's always someone worse off than you . . . It's a comfort, if a bit bizarre. And if I get low and feeling too sorry for myself I just pop down to the kids' ward. That puts everything into perspective sharpish.'

'Will this lumpectomy hurt?'

'Nah. Bit of an ache, that's all. You'll be out of here tomorrow.'

'They told me, and then a two- to three-week wait for the results – God, that's going to be awful.'

'Keep busy. Go shopping. Got kids?'

'Two girls. They're with my sister-in-law. She thinks Robbie and I are having a couple of days away, sort things out.'

'Tell her. Lean on people. There's nothing wrong in that. You can be too brave, you know, and what does it achieve?' She stood up. 'Come along to the day room and meet the others.'

'Lesley told me to change and get into bed and wait for the doctor.'

'Don't take any notice of her. She likes us pinned down neat and tidy. The doctor won't mind. Just tell the nurses where you're going.'

'What's the doctor like?'

'Sol Brown? Vague as hell, but so clever. He's brilliant, if a bit daffy. Coming? It'll do you good.'

Mo slid off the bed. She told the young nurse at the centre table where she was going – she didn't think she had quite enough courage to face Lesley with her disobedience yet – and followed the purple-clad Yvonne to the day room, where a television was blaring, card and chess games were taking place. Yvonne introduced her to a small knot of women, clustered together by the door that led onto a balcony. Mo did not realise it but she was about to join a very select club.

6

'I hope you didn't mind me inviting myself?' Chrissy asked as, in the small hall of Lynn's house, she allowed her friend to fuss over her damp coat.

'It's lovely to see you at last. Let me put this coat over a radiator –

I'd no idea it was raining so hard,' Lynn prattled on before leading Chrissy into the L-shaped sitting room. It was simply furnished and as neat as a pin. The television was turned off sharply and Chrissy wondered if she should have called at such short notice.

'I hope I'm not interrupting . . .' She waved at the blank set.

'No. I keep it on, babbling away in the background, when Terry's not here. It's a bit of a comforter, if you know what I mean?'

Chrissy did. After Ewan had died she had left the set on and unwatched for hours at a time – but until this moment she'd forgotten that's what she'd done.

'Terry's really sorry he missed you but he's had to go to a Rotary meeting. Is a small drink out of order if you're going on duty in a couple of hours?'

Chrissy glanced at her watch. 'A weak spritzer, if you've got any white wine, would be lovely.' She'd noticed a tray with a bottle of white wine and two glasses on the dining-room table, which was set for dinner and was in the short bar of the L. 'Where are your children?'

'It was a Baker day, they've gone to my mother's. I'm lucky, she looks after them when I'm working. They like it with her, she spoils them, and they wanted to sleep over. Great, I thought. Do you remember my mum?'

'Of course – and her fairy cakes.' Chrissy thought how strange memory was – fancy *that* emerging among all the other bits and pieces cluttering up her head.

'And how's yours?' Lynn asked, as she opened the wine, not with the usual feminine fuss but deftly and efficiently.

'She's fine,' Chrissy replied noncommittally. What on earth would people think when the news leaked out about her mother and her young lover? Did it matter? 'Thanks.' She took the crystal goblet in her hand. 'What a lovely glass.' She traced the etched thistle with her finger.

'A wedding present. I only get them out for special occasions and this is one of those.'

'You didn't open the bottle just for me, did you?' Chrissy asked, realising Lynn wasn't drinking.

'I'll have some soda, just to join you.' She poured a glass. Chrissy said nothing, but wondered if Lynn had a drinking problem.

'Don't worry. I'm not an alcoholic,' Lynn said. Judging from Chrissy's expression she'd read her mind. 'I just can't drink. A glass of wine and it goes straight to my head, so I rarely do. But anyhow, welcome home, Chrissy. I hope you'll be happy here.' Lynn lifted her own glass in a toast.

'Thanks. How nice.' Chrissy smiled affectionately at her: she'd always been a thoughtful, kind girl who had evidently become a thoughtful, kind woman.

'I hope you don't mind an M and S quiche? Only I never seem to have time to do anything properly these days.'

'Lynn, I didn't invite myself for supper. How embarrassing.'

'Nonsense. I've hardly been slaving over a hot stove, have I? This family, I sometimes think, would die of starvation if it wasn't for convenience foods. I'll just go and check it's not burning to a cinder.'

Left alone Chrissy looked about her. It was a conventional room with its matching Dralon-covered three-piece suite, safe cotton corduroy curtains and beige linen-look wallpaper. The fire was coal-effect gas so that the brass fire irons, never used, gleamed as bright as gold. On the walls were a still life and two blown-up school photographs of Lynn's children, printed to look as if they were on canvas. She realised that it was so tidy because there were few possessions in the room. On this mantelpiece was a reproduction carriage clock and a soapstone ornament of a seal. She smiled at the comparison with the clutter in her own sitting room, the books, the knick-knacks, the pictures, all of which she was convinced she could not live without. Maybe she should try. Maybe living this simply would make her life simpler too. What did they call it, down sizing?

'You look deep in thought.'

'I was admiring your room – how tidy it is. I live in increasing chaos. I envy you.'

'It's laziness, really. Up in the loft I've got a box of stuff given us over the years, all dust traps. I'll get them out when I retire and need something to occupy me. The supper's ready.' She led the way to the other end of the room.

As they ate Chrissy caught up on news of their old school-friends. Lynn seemed to know where everyone in their class was, what they did, who they'd married, divorced, remarried and how their children had turned out.

'You're amazing!' Chrissy laughed.

'Not really. I've just stayed put so people contact me.'

'They'd have had a problem finding me, that's for sure.'

'You can say that again! You're one of those wretched people who make a mess of other people's address books – always flitting about. I gave you a page of your own in the end, and as soon as I decided to do that, you stayed put and I needn't have bothered.'

'You should have done it sooner. Then maybe I'd have stopped moving sooner.' She smiled. 'In Cambridge we kept changing flats, that's why. Once we got to Cornwall that's when we settled.'

'I was sorry to hear about your husband. But you must be sick to death of people saying that when they don't know what else to say.'

'Oh, Lynn, you always were different.' Chrissy sighed. 'But you're right – it *is* difficult. I still haven't worked out who's the most embarrassed – them or me.'

'Do you like to talk about him or not?' Lynn asked bluntly.

'Not.'

'Fine. Still, you're back here, that's nice. You're taking on the new oncology unit, aren't you? You must look out for Mo Fordham – she was Moira Daly, do you remember her?'

'Yes, I do. Tiny little thing with masses of dark curls. Went to do teacher-training.'

'That's right. She works at St Stephen's primary. I'm probably being unprofessional, confidentiality and all that, but since you'll be nursing her, what the hell? She's in now having a biopsy – breast. Doesn't look too good.'

'Poor Moira.'

'Don't call her that, she hates it. It's Mo now.'

'Is she married?'

Lynn pulled a face. 'If you could call it that. He's a right bastard – he's always played around. I never know why men like that bother to get married in the first place. Good-looking, though. How's your gran? You didn't say.'

'She's much better. My mother's helping out today – that's why I had this free time.'

'I'd heard you'd had a run-in with the loathsome Dr Giles Middleton.'

'Bit conceited, I thought.'

'Conceited! You can say that again. He's so in love with himself I don't know why he needs a woman. He's a lousy doctor – poor Mo, he put her through the wringer. And today he offered an abortion to a woman whose ultra-sound had shown her child *might* have a cleft palate. I ask you. The poor dear was devastated.'

'What did you do?'

'I managed to talk her into not acting too fast. I put her in touch with CLAPA, the support group that helps parents of kids with clefts. They'll get her together with a parent who knows it's not the end of the world and can be put right with an operation. It's so silly – I've lost count of the times parents are warned of handicaps and the babe pops out perfect.'

'It's a mixed blessing, isn't it, the ultra-sound? It's only as good as the person interpreting it.'

'Exactly.'

'But Middleton must know that even the most initially devastating clefts and hare-lips can be corrected.'

'Of course. It's down to funding, isn't it? A child like that will need ongoing hospital visits, operations, speech therapy. He's a right tosser, looking to the future all the time.'

'But old Dr Henderson wouldn't have any truck with this, would he? I remember him as being a sweetheart and so caring. My gran swears by him.'

'He's tired. Prefers the golf course to the surgery. It's understandable, I suppose.'

'What will you do?'

'We have a group meeting once a month. We discuss cases, finances, new equipment and existing stocks and, in theory, any grievances. I'll bring it up then.'

'Isn't that risky?'

'That's what Terry said, but they can't sack me just for speaking up – I'd take them to the industrial tribunal. And, if push comes to shove, I'll blackmail the creep . . . I'll threaten to shop him to the GMC. On top of everything else he's having an affair with a patient.' Lynn nodded as she said this as if to emphasise the truth of it.

'You'd think no doctor would ever risk it with so much at stake. Maybe he's fallen in love and can't help it.'

'Giles? You have to be joking. It's serious but not in *that* way. Do you know Russell Newson?'

'Yes. I nursed him when he came back from Bosnia.' It was ridiculous, she thought, how at just the mention of his name she felt an excited surge. Like a schoolgirl. Get your act together, she told herself sternly.

'Have you met Sabine – sweet and adored by all?'

'I've seen her around. She's very beautiful.'

'And doesn't she know it? Have you registered that she never smiles? Obviously scared she'll get wrinkles. Well, it's her.'

'Sorry?'

'Who Giles is having a ding with.'

'No!'

'Madness, isn't it? Fancy having the dishy Russell to snuggle up to at night and then risk it all for a tosser like Giles.'

To her shame Chrissy could not hear enough of this gossip. And later, driving to work, she berated herself for the pleasure she felt that Sabine was not as perfect as she seemed. Poor Russell, how awful for him. But even as she thought this she knew she smiled, and she didn't seem able to stop smiling.

7

Glynis had been reading. At least, Glynis had been trying to read, but she was unable to concentrate. Floss Yates's warning about the hospital being privatised kept racing about in her head. Logic told her that Floss was much given to drama so that any information she gave should be treated with circumspection. But logic also told her such double-dealing was possible, these days: she had weathered too many changes to be surprised by anything that might come about at St Edith's.

Glynis closed her book and stared, unseeing, at its cover. How could Floss know of such matters – a widow, only a Friend of the hospital, not one of the professionals? This doubt had been something of a comfort, seeming to prove that it was all gossip. Until, that was, she remembered the smiling face of Craig Nutting's new assistant, a keen, eager face – what was his name? Kim Henderson – and his father was a GP, whose wife was Floss's younger sister! That was where such information was coming from, undoubtedly. And, if so, then it had to be taken seriously.

Yet was the word of someone as young as Kim – as inexperienced as he in the running of the Trust – reliable? Might he not have got the wrong impression, or misinterpreted something he'd heard? Oh, she wished she had more facts at her fingertips. She wished she could talk to the young man but, then, that would compromise Floss, and she was fond of her and did not want to get her into trouble or to risk her friendship. Why did everything have to be so complex? she thought as, finally giving up all thought of reading, she placed the unfinished book on the table by the lamp.

At a ring on the doorbell she looked at her watch. Nine o'clock. Her heart lifted at the thought that it might be Matthew, but her head told her to get a grip on herself.

'Matthew!' she said, pleasure etched on her face. 'What a lovely surprise. Come in, do.' She fussed about him, seating him, pouring him a large Scotch. She had long ago abandoned the idea of ever welcoming him calmly and coolly, as if his presence was of no account to her. She was overjoyed and she no longer cared if he knew.

'You're late. You must be tired.'

'An emergency – perforated gastric ulcer. Nasty.'

'Where was your registrar?'

'In bed with flu.'

'That's becoming a problem. I was seriously short-staffed today and I dread to think how they'll be managing tonight.'

'It doesn't seem to be too serious a strain – three days out and then right as rain.'

'Hardly. I've never seen the point of asking people to go back to work until they're really back on their feet. It only leads to complications later.'

'You, my darling, are a sweet, worrying mother hen. Come here.'

Autocratic, imperious, dignified Glynis did as he bid. She knelt on the rug at his feet, looked up at him with eyes that brimmed with adoration. A surge of excitement flashed uncontrolled, unbidden, through her body as he leant forward and kissed her full on the mouth. A couple of seconds later she sank back on her ankles, struggling to disguise the disappointment that engulfed her, as he returned to his tumbler of whisky. They so rarely made love these days. He was often so tired, he worked far too hard. But knowing these matters, accepting them, did not stop the raging physical longing in her. Sometimes when she was alone she played with the idea of seducing him on such an evening as this. Asking him to come to bed. She never had, she was far too old-fashioned for that. And what if he rejected her and said, 'Not tonight'? How mortified she would feel, how utterly miserable she would be – more so than she already was.

'Another drink?'

'Just a small one. Can't risk getting breathalysed, can I?' He watched her as she got to her feet gracefully and crossed the room to the drinks cabinet. 'Thanks.' He took the refilled glass. 'You look a bit down tonight. Problems?'

That he should have noticed gave her such joy. And what luck that he had come. Who better to talk to than Matthew? He knew most things that were going on and loved St Edith's as much as she.

'Floss Yates came to see me with some alarming news . . .' And she related the whole conversation to him. 'Such a worry.'

'Where on earth did Floss get a tale like that? Bit far-fetched, don't you think?'

'Her nephew is Craig Nutting's new assistant. She didn't say, but it *has* to be him who told her.'

'He still looks as if he isn't shaving daily! What would he know? He's probably only a glorified clerk. No. Don't worry, Glyn, my darling. Closure, yes, that's always a fear, but we'll get round that, don't worry. After all, could you imagine Floss allowing any minister to close us down?' He laughed, and immediately she felt better.

Then he stood up as if to leave.

'Do you have to go yet?' she asked, the closest she could get to begging him to stay.

'Sorry, darling. Wendy's on her own, Jenna's joined an amateur dramatic society. God help us, we'll have to trot along to see her perform!' He was still guffawing at this idea as she closed the door on him. And the cottage sank back into its silent loneliness.

Everything was set for it to be a troublesome night. In the office

Chrissy was given the two wards she now began to regard as hers, but was also being asked to keep an eye on Care of the Elderly too.

'Three wards? That's impossible,' she protested.

'It will have to be possible tonight, I'm afraid. Jazz called in, she's locked herself into her flat – she'll be late,' the administrative sister in charge of delegation said dismissively.

'How late?'

'The firemen can't get to her for a couple of hours – there's a big fire on the trading estate – so she's got to sit and wait. Right, anything more? I want to get home.'

'No, I suppose not. But it's not right.'

'Not a lot is in this profession at the moment.'

Dawn Allyson commiserated with Chrissy as they walked down the long corridor towards the stairs to their wards.

'I mean, if something goes wrong who gets the blame?' Chrissy said, worriedly.

'Trust Jazz. She got locked in the lavatory here once and she's so fat she couldn't climb out. Maintenance had to break the door down. She's a walking disaster. Right, see you at first lunch?'

'I'll try.' Chrissy wheeled to the right into Ward Two and the double Care of the Elderly ward – thirty women in one ward and the same number of men in the other. Normally Chrissy would have enjoyed working here – she had always liked caring for older people. So much nursing was so hi-tech now that she sometimes felt that too much of it was pill-pushing and machine maintenance; whereas with the elderly, basic nursing was essential. It was in these wards when she felt most like a nurse.

Fortunately, since the ward was full, there was one student nurse and two auxiliaries to be supervised – even so they would have their work cut out to cope, but it could have been worse and, hopefully, Jazz wouldn't be too long in coming to relieve her.

Chrissy sped round the beds checking the patients, reassuring the confused. Most were here with fractures, chest complaints, cataract removals, and a couple were in, suffering from anaemia, for blood transfusions. It was no longer the policy to have long-stay elderly in these hospitals; instead they were sent, as soon as possible, to residential homes. Chrissy had never been able to work out if this was for the best or not. Her inspection over, she thought there shouldn't be too many dramas.

Chelsea Mottram, the Project 2000 nurse in her first placement, but who, Chrissy had learnt, seemed to know what she was doing, was waiting for Chrissy to check the medicines. These were not the dangerous drugs, which were on the scheduled list, but the cough mixtures, vitamin pills, laxatives and indigestion remedies. This done Chrissy left for her other two wards, praying that nothing untoward would happen tonight.

Russell sat in his sitting room, a television flickering in the corner of the room, mute and unwatched. Beside him was a bottle of whisky which, in his present depressed state, he regarded as half empty. On his lap and on a side table were a stack of papers, which he was working through methodically, jotting figures on a pad.

'Do you want supper?' Sabine appeared in the room. She was dressed in simple, but expensive, as he well knew, spotless white jeans and T-shirt.

'No, thank you.'

'You're sulking, aren't you?'

'No.'

'Oh, come on, Russell. We can work this out.'

He looked up at her, blankly, as if too tired for emotion. 'There's nothing but these figures to work out.'

'What are you doing?' She stepped closer. 'Oh, sums, I hate sums!' She giggled and he wondered why on earth he'd ever found her little-girl act in the least bit attractive.

'I'm deciding what is a fair distribution of our assets. I've spoken to the estate agents. They're coming tomorrow to value this house.'

'We can't sell this. I love it. I won't move out. You can forget it.' The charming innocence was quickly replaced with a determined expression. The little-girl-lost voice had disappeared.

'If you want a large cash settlement from me you'll have to agree.'

'You don't mean to go ahead with this, Russell? I've said I'm sorry. I'll never be naughty again. Promise. I want to stay with you. What else can I do?' She stood contrite – the little voice back, the big blue eyes appealing, believing the time for hard, straight talking hadn't yet arrived.

Before he answered he looked at her for some time. In a way, he had to admire how she could switch her response, her approach. She thought she could play him along as she'd done so many times before. Like so many beautiful women, she did not know the game was up, could not accept that she'd lost the power to manipulate him. He laughed, and she looked at him for a moment, triumphantly.

'Oh, Sabine! You're something else. Don't you understand? I don't want you back. You want Giles, then have Giles. I'm finished with you.'

'Russell, I love you.' She fumbled in her pocket for a handkerchief.

'Don't cry. Whatever you do, don't! You don't mean it. Stop talking about love. You don't love me, I doubt if you ever did. I'm a luxury meal ticket to you – probably that's all I ever was.'

'That's not true. I was so lonely . . . That's why . . . You *know* that's why. You were always working, I hardly ever saw you. You were more involved with your career than with me.' She tossed her head dramatically.

'Sabine, you're pathetic. How do you think the bills get paid? The Porsche bought? This house? I know you're stupid, but you're not that stupid.' He turned back to his pad and pen.

She snatched at the pen and threw it on the floor. 'Stop this! You don't mean it.'

'Oh, yes, I do, Sabine. I've suddenly woken up to what a stupid prat I've been. No more. That do in Bosnia taught me a lot, most importantly not to waste any more time – either of us. We'll get divorced. Now. No hanging around for two or five years. If you don't comply I'll name Giles as co-respondent. You understand? I'll give you money, but if you're not co-operative I'll only give you the minimum the law insists on. Now, if you'll excuse me.' He bent down and picked up the pen.

Sabine stood silent, watching him. 'Christ, you're a cold bastard, aren't you?'

Once more he looked up at her. 'Where you're concerned, yes,' he said simply.

When she was angry, as now, Sabine did not look the least bit pretty. Her mouth was set in a determined line, her eyes hooded, as if by lowering her lids she could concentrate the better. 'Pompous bastard!'

she said aloud, as she drove her silver car far too fast and noisily through the late-evening deserted streets of Fellcar. 'God, I hate this dump! Boring people, boring Russell!' she said, loudly and vehemently.

Her car screeched to a standstill outside the small block of flats down on the sea-front. She flicked on the interior light, readjusted the driving mirror to reflect herself and from her bag she took a brush and quickly tended her hair. Make-up followed – a flick of mascara, a quick pat of blusher, a slick of lip gloss. Then she got out, went to the door of the block and stabbed agitatedly several times at a bell-push.

'Who the hell's that?' The intercom came tinnily to life.

'Giles, it's me. Let me in. Please!'

The buzzer sounded, the front door clunked, and she pushed it open. Not bothering to wait for the lift she ran, two at a time, up the stairs.

Giles was waiting in his open doorway. 'Where's the fire?'

Sabine did not reply but flung her arms round him and clung to him like a pretty blonde limpet. 'Hold me, my darling. Please hold me.'

'With pleasure,' Giles said into her hair, and hugged her tight. Sabine sobbed uncontrollably as, still holding her, he led her into his apartment. Gently he prised away her arms and sat her down on the long leather sofa. He knelt in front of her, proffering a hankie. 'Poor darling. What's happened? Tell me. Shush . . .' He comforted her. Slowly the sobbing subsided. Sabine patted her eyes and looked at him, a soft little sob escaping as she did so.

'Oh, Giles, my darling, I'm so afraid . . .' She spoke softly, rapidly, breathlessly.

'Who's frightened you?'

''I can't tell you . . . You'll be so cross.' And she looked as if she was on the verge of tears again.

'I won't be. Come on, tell.'

'It's Russell. He's so angry.'

'He hasn't hit you?'

'Oh, Giles . . .'

'The bastard. How could he? A sweet little thing like you. I need a drink.'

As he poured two brandies, Sabine cried quietly.

'But why? You never said he was violent.'

'It was awful, Giles. I don't know where to start – you do love me, don't you? Tell me you do.'

'I do –' Giles looked at his drink.

'No, properly. I need to hear you say it. You never have.' Sabine sighed.

'I love you,' Giles said, looking and sounding awkward, as if such words were a foreign language.

'I love you too, Giles. Oh, so much, so very much.' She leant forward, cupping his face in her hands, looking at him intently before kissing him long and hard. His hands searched under her T-shirt for her breasts. Her sigh was different this time, soft, contented.

Then she said, 'No, darling, we must sort this out first. I must talk to you.'

'Can't it wait?' Giles's voice was muffled as his mouth searched where his hand had been. 'This is much more fun.'

'He wants a divorce.'

Giles's mouth let go of her nipple.

'He says he won't wait. He says he'll burn his money rather than give any to me.'

Giles's head appeared from under her T-shirt.

'Darling, he says he's going to name you in his petition unless I comply.'

Giles sat back on his haunches. 'He what?'

'I'm sorry.'

'Too right you're sorry. How did he find out about us?' He was on his feet.

'I told him.'

'You did *what*? You stupid cow. Oh, shit!' He thumped one hand with the balled fist of the other.

'But, Giles – you said. You just said you love me.'

'Because you told me to. It was fun, don't you remember? Right at the beginning we agreed – no strings, no sloppy romance, just good sex and *fucking fun!*' He shouted the last two words.

Sabine slumped on the sofa as if, like a balloon, she'd been deflated. This time when she cried it was real.

'Don't bloody well cry, woman. Not now. Look –' he was back on his haunches '– you've got to deny it was me. You've got to lie and say you'd made it up to make him jealous. No one else knew – he couldn't have known.'

'But why should I? Why can't we forget him? Live together, as I've dreamed.'

'Then you can dream on. If he names me, the next stop will be the GMC – you're a bloody patient! Don't you understand? I could be struck off?'

'But I love you,' she wailed.

'And I don't love you. Now, for Christ's sake, shut up and let me think!'

Matthew Kersey let himself into his house. He opened the door of the drawing room. 'Hi, my sweet ladies, I'm back.' He crossed the room and kissed his wife, Wendy, on the cheek.

'A drink?' Jenna, his sister-in-law, was quickly on her feet.

'In a moment. I've a call to make. What's for supper?'

'I cooked you *boeuf en daube*,' Jenna said, as she got out a glass.

'What a dream your sister is, Wendy. What would we do without her? Don't, whatever you do, join any clubs or societies. We need you here.' He almost laughed at his own private joke.

In his study he flicked through his address book and dialled a number.

'Craig? Matthew here. Problems,' he said, into the receiver. 'You'd better arrange a meeting. That stupid old cow Floss Yates has got wind of our plans. You'll have to sack her bloody nephew. He's obviously leaking like a tap!'

8

How anyone was supposed to sleep was a mystery to Mo as she lay in the hard uncomfortable bed. She felt hot and sticky, not helped by the waterproof mattress she was lying on. The ward had been bedded down a good two hours ago, but still the amount of noise prevented sleep. People were rustling, sighing, tossing, turning, snoring. From the sluice room the clatter of bedpans, the hiss of the sterilising machine and the giggling of the nurses was clearly audible. An emergency admission had disturbed everyone, and two post-operative patients, requiring constant attention, needed the lights above their beds to be switched on and off with irritating regularity.

Even if her lump was nothing, she'd need a rest after being in this place! Mo turned towards her locker, intending to pour some juice, not from thirst but more for something to do. Then she remembered: no more fluids were allowed until after her operation. As soon as she thought this she became immediately parched with thirst and found difficulty in swallowing.

She turned over her pillow to the cooler side to see if that would work. Somehow she was going to have to learn to deal with everything – this ward, the noise, the stress – in a far more logical way. Inside, her head felt like a race-track, with cars skidding and crashing this way and that as each worry, fear, idea churned around with no order, just generalised panic.

When the doctor had eventually turned up, he had explained to her yet again that it would be a good two weeks before she knew the results of these tests. She would keep busy – she had Christmas to concentrate on. And she'd go to the library and read up everything she could find on breast cancer. If she knew what was going on in her body maybe she wouldn't be so frightened, would be able to relax . . . maybe.

'Mrs Galloway. It's Liz.'

'Who?' Iris made no effort to hide her irritation at being interrupted while doing what, these days, she liked to do most.

'Liz Boxtree. I care at night for the older Mrs Galloway. I do hope I'm not disturbing you.'

'Of course you are! What else would you be doing at this time. It's midnight!'

'I'm sorry, Mrs Galloway. Truly. But my car's broken down. I was promised a mechanic but he hasn't turned up – obviously he's not going to get here now.'

'Obviously.'

'So, well, old Mrs Galloway's on her own.'

'Didn't you call her?'

'Yes, I did. I've phoned several times throughout the evening. She says she's all right.'

'Well, then, why are you bothering me?'

'Because I'm worried. She sounded woozy – she's taken sleeping pills, she told me. She doesn't usually. I wondered if you could go round?'

'Okay.'

'You will? Oh, that's taken a weight off my mind. Thanks –' But already the telephone was disconnected.

'Was that the woman who looks after the old girl? What's the problem?' Bob asked, as he slid across the large bed towards her.

'I've got to go round and check her.' Iris began to get up.

'Not now. We've got some unfinished business.' Bob's voice was husky with longing as he searched for her breast through the folds of her négligé. 'Give her a bell,' he whispered, as he nibbled her ear.

The phone rang. Lying on the floor of her bedroom, Daphne tried to inch towards the bedside table to pull the telephone down by its flex. But the pain in her leg was too severe. She cried out involuntarily, then slumped back on the floor, but had enough wits left to pull at the eiderdown so that it fell off the bed and across her. But she could not stop the tears, which annoyed her and which seemed to have a volition of their own.

'Can't you sleep, Mrs Fortune?' Chrissy, who'd been rechecking the patients on Care of the Elderly, stopped at the side of the bed.

'I haven't had my suppository, Sister,' Gwen said, in the tremulous voice of someone who was afraid.

'You haven't? Are you sure?' Chrissy looked at the old lady and saw her move away from her ever so slightly. She sat on the edge of the bed. 'Anything wrong, Mrs Fortune? Are you upset about something?'

'No. Nothing.' She moved further away.

'Watch out or you'll be tumbling off the bed.' Chrissy spoke in a whisper so as not to wake the others. 'Let me help you back into the middle.' The old woman was light, but her body tensed as Chrissy put her arm about her to lift her into the centre. 'Something's bothering you. Tell me.' She took hold of Gwen's hand and squeezed it gently.

'Are you afraid of going to sleep?' she asked, since often the old, she knew, were frightened of sleep, convinced that they would never wake up.

'Where's the plump nurse?'

'Nurse Jazz Poundman? She isn't here, Mrs Fortune. I'm in charge.'

Gwen Fortune's body slumped with evident relief. Chrissy frowned. 'Is it Nurse Poundman who bothers you?' The old lady lay silent. 'You can tell me. Come on, what is it?'

Mrs Fortune's lips pursed as if her mouth was preventing her from saying what her mind wanted her to.

'You've no pain? Your chest sounds lovely and clear.' Chrissy spoke reassuringly.

'They used to call it the old people's friend.'

'Pneumonia? Yes, they did, didn't they?'

'Now it's treated and I could wish it hadn't been.'

'Oh dear. I'm sorry about that. But I expect your family are pleased you were made better.' Chrissy tried not to sound as if she was talking to a child, but sometimes it was difficult not to.

'It's like I was in the waiting room and death was coming and I'd managed to get used to the idea then I got called away. Now I'm going to have to go through it all again,' Gwen said petulantly.

'Well, let's hope not for a long time. Would you like some hot chocolate or Horlicks? And I'll check about your suppository.'

Chrissy moved away from the bed.

'Sister. Thanks for calling me Mrs Fortune. It makes a nice change.'

'My pleasure.'

Chrissy found Chelsea Mottram in the linen cupboard loading a trolley with the clean linen they would need in the morning.

'Chelsea, I've just been talking to Mrs Fortune. You don't call her by her Christian name, do you?'

'No, I don't, we were taught not to. But Jazz does.'

Many of the elderly clung to formality, which made them feel more dignified. Some nurses took it upon themselves to use their Christian names, not spitefully but thoughtlessly. Chrissy decided to have a word with Jazz. 'By the way, Chelsea, she says you didn't give her her sedative.'

'I did.' Chelsea paused in loading the trolley. 'I poured her a glass of water and watched her take it – to be sure she had. She's a little confused.'

Chrissy's hand shot to her mouth to suppress a smile. 'Nurse, I think we should have a little talk. That particular sedative is given as a suppository, normally inserted at the other end of the body, so that the drug acts quickly.' Her voice was full of amusement.

'Oh, no! Have I hurt her? I wouldn't hurt her for the world.' Chelsea looked horrified.

'It'll take a bit longer to work, that's all.' She couldn't stop her laughter now.

'Oh, Sister! I thought it was a big pill too.' And Chelsea managed a little smile. 'Please, Sister. Don't tell anyone.'

'Promise. It's our secret. We've all done daft things. I'll go and tell her that the doctor decided she shouldn't have it tonight.'

With no sign of Jazz Poundman, there was no way Chrissy could go to the canteen for her lunch. She'd grab a coffee and some biscuits in the kitchen on the neurological ward instead.

Lance Travers had beaten her to the percolator. 'Hi! Long time no see.'

'Aren't you on the wrong ward, Doctor? Shouldn't you be down a floor?'

'I'm covering for Carl – neuro houseman. He's got flu. If this goes on we'll have to shut up shop, if you ask me. All getting too dodgy. Biscuit?'

'I wasn't told you'd been called.'

'Emergency. Looks like a brain haemorrhage. She's just been sent up from A and E – looks distinctly iffy to me. She'll be up in theatre within the hour, you'll see. The registrar's off with flu too, so I've had to wake the great man himself. Fraser Ball's on his way.'

'I'd better go and look at her before he gets here,' she said shortly. The more she saw of Lance the more insufferably smug she found him.

'Don't rush away – Alex Oldham's with her. Thought about my suggestion?'

'And what suggestion was that?' She turned at the door.

'Dinner?'

'Oh, that. No. I haven't.' And she moved smartly from the kitchen before he could respond.

As she made her way to the ward Mrs Marston appeared in the side-ward doorway. 'Sister. A minute. Buck's –'

'Mrs Marston, if you could wait a moment I'll be with you as soon as I can.'

'Now, Sister.'

'I'm sorry . . . Two ticks, promise.' Chrissy sped down the dimly lit corridor towards the new patient. At the bedside a young man sat watching with a tense expression as a nurse tended the very ill-looking patient. Chrissy had a quick, whispered conversation with the nurse, then did her best to reassure the husband.

'My wife's going to be all right, isn't she?'

'The consultant will be here shortly. He'll be able to give you a far clearer picture.' Chrissy had neatly sidestepped his question, to which she had no answer, but just by looking at the woman she could see how sick she was.

'She'll be in good hands. Perhaps –' But she didn't finish as the curtains were pulled back and Mrs Marston appeared.

'Mrs Marston. Really!' Taking Mrs Marston by the elbow she steered her from the young woman's bedside. 'I do have other patients, you know.'

'I don't give a fig for them. You've got to come and see our Buck, Sister.'

'Could you wait, just for a second? The consultant's due.'

'*You must come.*' Mrs Marston was pulling at her, and Buck's wife was standing in the doorway of the side ward looking wildly about her. These two women – they never seemed to sleep and were always here, or so it seemed to Chrissy.

'Cheryl, you tell Sister what you saw.'

'Sister, it was so exciting! Buck opened his eyes. He did. Honest. And it wasn't like when he did it before. When he just stared. His eyes followed me across the room. He's coming round, isn't he? Oh, God, I'm so excited!' And Cheryl Marston burst into tears. Chrissy put her arm about her just as the main ward door opened and Fraser Ball strode in.

'Doctor, you come this minute,' Mrs Marston ordered loudly.

'Mrs Marston, I told you, we've an emergency just in.'

'I can manage, Sister.' Fraser swept on. Chrissy appreciated his attitude: many were the consultants who expected the sister to drop everything the minute they appeared to attend to them.

If Buck *had* woken up he had now returned to his previous state. To all intents and purposes he was exactly the same. She took his pulse, opened his eyes – more for the benefit of his mother and wife than because she needed to examine him.

'He was awake!' said Cheryl, as if aware that Chrissy did not believe them.

'I'm sure he was,' she said reassuringly.

'You needn't sound so bloody patronising,' Mrs Marston said angrily.

'I'm sorry if that's how I sounded. I didn't mean to. Now –'

'Sister,' Fraser called from the doorway, 'about the new patient.'

'Doctor!' The older woman was on her feet in a trice.

'Mrs Marston,' he said, with weary patience. 'Lance, call theatres to prepare as quick as possible. Yes, Mrs Marston, what can I do for you?' He stepped into the side ward.

'It's Buck, he's coming round. Our Cheryl saw him – didn't you, Cheryl?'

'I did. His eyes followed me.'

Fraser looked questioningly at Chrissy. 'I wasn't here,' she said.

'He's been opening his eyes all the way through. It's not significant. I did explain to you –'

'He bloody opened his eyes and don't you bloody well say he didn't.'

'Mrs Marston –'

'Don't you Mrs Marston me. Cheryl knows what she saw!'

'Mrs –'

But Fraser got no further for Mrs Marston, with one mighty swing, hit him smack across his face. 'He's waking up. I'm telling you.'

Fraser stepped back holding his cheek, a look of surprise on his face. Chrissy moved to restrain the older Mrs Marston in case she was planning to take another swipe at the doctor.

'Cheryl. You there?' A weak voice sounded. All four swung round to face the bed. Buck, his eyes very much open, smiled, if a little vacantly. 'Where the fuck am I?'

9

Though she was pleased for his family, Chrissy could have wished that Buck had chosen another time for his reawakening.

In the small side ward all was chaos since Buck – silent now for a week – could not, it appeared, stop talking. His wife and mother were beside themselves with excitement. Chrissy had sharply to forestall any use of the telephone or else, she was certain, the whole Marston family would have been summoned, no doubt for a noisy knees-up.

'We must try to keep him quiet,' she said anxiously.

'Quiet? What do I want to be quiet for? I've been asleep a week. You sure it was a week, Cheryl? You're not having me on?'

'No, Buck, honest! Your birthday was last Thursday, and it's only just Friday. So that's a week, isn't it?'

'And you remember nothing?' Fraser asked, as he took Buck's pulse.

'Not a bean. I was in the pub – it was my birthday. Next thing I'm here. And it's now! What happened?'

'I think you should leave, Mrs Marston,' Fraser spoke quickly and kindly to Cheryl, forestalling further explanation. 'He really does need his rest. It's hard, I know. But you do want the best for him, don't you?'

'Put like that, Doc. Oh, I could hug you!' And she proceeded to do so, though Fraser had stepped back as if in alarm.

'Five minutes to say goodnight, then. Sister, a word.'

Chrissy led the way to the small office. 'I'm to call the police – night or day, they said. There was a constable on duty, I heard, for the first couple of days.'

'Leave it. They can talk to him in the morning. Meanwhile, give him fifty milligrams of chlorpromazine, IM. He should be sedated. I don't like this.'

'Too sudden?'

'Far too sudden.'

'I'll get his card.'

'Prep the other woman. I'll go and scrub up.'

'The prescription for Buck, Mr Ball –'

'I'll write it up in the morning.'

'But I can't –'

'Oh, Sister, for Christ's sake, if we don't get that young woman on the table and draining soon it'll be curtains for her.'

'It's against the law.'

'For crying out loud, get Lance to write it.' And Fraser was gone, the ward doors flapping like the wings of a frantic bird after he'd swept through them.

'Have you seen Lance Travers?' she asked Alex Oldham, who, having chaperoned Fraser Ball with the new patient, was now looking for her.

'No, he left just after you. Could you pop in and see the husband? He's in a bit of a state. He's gone to the day room.'

'Once we've prepped her maybe he can sit with her. It'll calm him down.'

Of Lance there was no sign. Nor could she raise him on the telephone. But she found the young man, head in hands, surrounded by cigarette butts ground out on the floor. She should have told him not to smoke, but she hadn't the heart. Instead she promised him tea, though he looked as if it was whisky he needed. She also promised to come and get him to sit with his wife when she was ready for theatre. She left him, filled with guilt that she was too busy to stay with him.

By now Buck was in a high state of excitement. Trying to get out of bed, pulling at the cannula in his arm.

'It's sore,' he complained.

'If you don't calm down, Buck, I shall forbid visitors for a week,' she said, in her sternest voice.

'Just you try!'

'Oh, I can, don't you worry. Now, get back into bed. And I'm sorry, but you two must go – you can see how over-excited he is.'

'At least I'll sleep tonight,' said his mother, as she picked up her bag.

'Night, my darling.' Cheryl bent to kiss him. Allowing them a few moments alone, Chrissy, back in her office, tried once again to find Lance. She dialled the theatres, only to be told that both doctors were scrubbing up. She could hear Buck laughing and shouting as she explained her problem to the theatre nurse.

'Well, if Fraser said to give the drug, I'd give it. He'll back you up. I'll tell him you called and were worried.'

Chrissy held the telephone, looking at it as if to find an answer.

'Alex,' she called out to Oldham. 'I need to check a drug that Fraser ordered but forgot to write up. It's irregular, but Buck's going to kill himself if he's not sedated.' She unlocked the scheduled drug cabinet and deftly drew up the required dose. She wrote up the dosage, which she and Alex initialled. 'We shouldn't be put in this sort of position. If anything goes wrong it's us who get it in the neck, not the flaming doctors.' Chrissy fretted, aware what she was doing was illegal and that it could cost her her job.

With Buck quietened, and the new patient in theatres, Chrissy finally had time to drink the cup of coffee she'd long ago promised herself.

On Orthopaedics the patients were all sleeping like angels. Chrissy's eyes felt the familiar heaviness which, without her even having to look at her watch, told her it was three, always her hardest time. This racing between wards wasn't helping: all she wanted was to curl up and sleep. Instead, wearily, she returned to check Buck, who was finally sleeping peacefully. She took his pulse. He didn't even wake when she took his blood pressure. The telephone's light flashed. It was the theatres' staff phoning to report that the new patient was in recovery, that everything had gone far better than they had hoped.

One of the happier tasks that night was to search out the young man and to let him know his wife had come through the operation and, although not out of the woods, was 'as well as could be expected' – she trotted out the formula, long-ago learnt. She wasn't surprised when he refused to go home to sleep, said he'd rather stay, and where were the telephones?

Almost leisurely after the night's dramas, she made her way back to Ward Two and the elderly. Even as she entered the door her bleeper sounded.

'Oh, Sister – thank heavens! It's Mrs Fortune.' Chelsea grabbed at her hand. 'She's dead!'

Chelsea was right. Mrs Fortune was most decidedly dead and looked as if she had been for some time.

'What's that draught?' Chrissy asked, as she emerged from the bedside. 'It's coming from the sluice.' Quickly she walked in that direction, the sluice door was wide open to the fire escape.

'Did you open this, Mottram?'

'No, Sister. It was locked. Don't you remember? You locked it.'

'Busy night?' a voice asked from the shadows, as she and Chelsea walked back to the nurses' station.

'Jazz, is that you? Where the hell have you been?'

'Can't manage without me?' Jazz laughed good-naturedly. 'Sorry I left you in the lurch, but my flat's on the fourth floor. Since God didn't give me wings there was no way out. But I'm here now.'

'I'm sorry I snapped – it's been a bit fraught here. Poor old Mrs Fortune's died.'

'Well, there's good news! She was a right pain. Unexpected, though. I thought she was doing well. Still, you never know with the elderly, do you? You get on. I'll do what's what here.'

'Thanks. I've called the houseman.' There seemed little point now in discussing the matter of using Christian names when patients didn't like it.

The rest of the night passed calmly. Buck slept peacefully throughout the chaos, which was any ward in the early morning with tea to be served, blanket baths, beds to strip, drugs to be given, with the nurses wanting to get on and the patients wanting only to sleep.

As Chrissy was reading though the report of the night for the day staff, Buck sat bolt upright in bed and looked wildly about him.

'What the fuck's going on?' he shouted, and collapsed back on to his pillow, his eyes rolling back in his head and his arms flailing wildly in the air as he fought unseen monsters.

10

Chrissy sluiced her face and redid her make-up to give herself courage. Earlier she had resolved that this morning she would have to brave the staff in the canteen. If she hid, every time there was a death on her shift, they would have something to gossip about. Also, and this was important and she kept forgetting it, they knew nothing about her and Ewan. She must stop being so paranoid.

She had presumed that there would be only one topic of conversation and that as soon as she appeared it would stop. But everyone was so busy gossiping when she joined the queue at the self-service counter that no one noticed her.

'Do you realise that since she joined she must have doubled the death-rate in this hospital?' a nurse in front said, loud enough for her to hear.

'If this gets out we won't have a soul who'll be willing to be a patient,' her companion replied.

'*Death Stalks the Wards*. Can't you just see it in the tabloids?' One laughed, but on seeing Chrissy standing patiently with her tray in hand blushed bright red and shoved her friend in warning. The silence that followed was almost more oppressive, Chrissy thought, as she placed coffee and toast on her tray.

'Maybe she should change her name to d'Eath.'

'Don't be ghoulish!'

'Nah, it's a real name. Honest!' she heard from one table as she passed by.

'Well, I feel sorry for her.'

'Don't be so wet!'

'Maybe she was just careless.'

She settled at an empty table by a window.

'And that Buck Marston's out like a light again. She looked after him, too,' a middle-aged nurse said, staring baldly at Chrissy. 'I heard from theatres that she'd given him drugs off her own bat – they weren't written up,' she added, for good measure.

'You're joking! She's mad. That's a dismissal offence.'

'Obviously she thinks she knows better than the docs. It's nurses like her who give us all a bad name,' the woman said pointedly. Chrissy wanted to stand and shout out her innocence, to yell at them to give her a chance. Instead she bent down, picked up her bag and quickly left the room, aware of the sudden silence as she did so and the swell of conversation as she closed the door behind her.

Chrissy sat outside Glynis Tillman's office and realised she felt sick to the pit of her stomach. She made herself take deep breaths just as she had so often instructed nauseous patients to do. Not again, she thought, with mounting panic. Once again, everything was beginning to look so bleak.

The only bright spot that morning had been Lance Travers

appearing and filling in Buck's prescription chart for Fraser so she hadn't had to confess to the day staff her stupid actions in the night. That had been worrying, especially when Buck had behaved so wildly. But he was sedated now and Chrissy had resolved *never* to do that again, no matter how much a doctor pleaded or bullied her. But that was the only thing she had going for her.

'Sister Galloway, if you'd care to come in. Some coffee? You look tired.' Glynis held the door open for her and ushered her in. 'Sister Morris said you were insistent in wanting to see me. You have a problem?'

'Yes.' Chrissy stood stiffly, awkwardly.

'Coffee?'

Chrissy shook her head as if with irritation. 'No, thank you. I need to talk.'

'Well, if you don't mind, I shall have one and I think, Sister, you need one. Now, do sit down.' She proceeded to pour the coffee and Chrissy did not even register how kindly she spoke. 'Now, tell me what's upsetting you.'

'I don't know where to begin,' Chrissy said, which was true, for she was already regretting rushing here without thinking things through. Worried now that, having done so, she might be making matters worse for herself. Finding that in this calm atmosphere her fears began to fade a little.

'I presume it's about the sudden deaths on your wards. Unfortunate, but you mustn't let it upset you. I know it's hard. One Christmas Day, when I was a student, we had six patients die that morning. Deeply distressing, but something we, as professionals, have to learn to deal with.'

'In the canteen this morning . . . they were talking . . . I heard it referred to as a *spate* of deaths. I mean, they're not just suspicious, they've decided.' And Chrissy's hands began to tremble. 'Miss Tillman, they think I killed them.'

'Sister! Really! What a thing to say! Don't you think you're overreacting?' Glynis said briskly. Chrissy looked down at her hands, one holding the other to keep them still, but she remained silent. 'You know as well as I do how gossip spreads in hospitals. The slightest thing and someone spiteful will multiply it. This is just one of those things. The post-mortems will show that and then the spiteful remarks will stop.'

'But why me? Others were on duty those nights.'

'Because you are the newest person here – an unknown quantity. Because you are the senior. Because –' Glynis stopped.

'Because what, Miss Tillman? What were you about to say?'

'If you want the truth, Sister, nothing. I had run out of causes.' Chrissy gave her a bleak look. 'Are you aware, Sister, that there has also been a spate of pilfering of patients' possessions?'

'I've heard, yes. Why? Are they accusing me of that too?'

'Oh, Sister, come, come. I only asked to ensure that you made your patients aware of the problem and told them to lock up valuables.'

'I'm sorry. I'm just so on edge.'

'You're nights off now, aren't you?'

'Yes.'

'Well, try to get some rest. It's been decided, in any case, to put you on your new ward next week. It isn't quite finished, but there's plenty of organisation to be done. We've a great need of the beds.'

Chrissy sat gazing into space. Why the sudden change of plan? Did they think it was safer to put her on that *empty* ward? The panic returned. Miss Tillman could be as calm and reassuring as she liked – what did she know? What could she understand? Chrissy stood up. 'I must be on my way.'

'Sister, a good sleep will make you see things more rationally. You're exhausted and imagining things, I'm sure.'

Chrissy stood in the middle of the room undecided: she wanted to speak, explain everything to this woman. She even opened her mouth to do so, but suddenly changed her mind.

'Is there anything else?'

'No. I'll get home now.'

'Are you sure there's nothing else you want to say?'

'No. Why should there be?' She spoke defensively, clutching at the silver buckle of her belt, playing with the filigreed end.

'Nothing. I just wondered.' Glynis looked at her as if not convinced. 'I'm always here, Sister, if you need me.'

Chrissy left without answering, and after she'd gone Glynis sat a few moments, deep in thought.

As she turned her car into Prince's Row depression swathed Chrissy. By now she was so late her gran would think she wasn't coming. At the sight of an ambulance parked further along the road, her heart plummeted. 'Oh, no!' she cried. She parked her car badly and, without locking it, ran up the road impervious to the slight drizzle which was falling. As she reached the house the ambulance, its light flashing, drove away. A worried-looking Liz Boxtree stood on the pavement.

'Chrissy, thank goodness you're here. I phoned the hospital, they said you were off duty. And –'

'Gran – what's happened?'

'She had a fall.'

'How? When?'

'Must have been in the night. Luckily she managed to cover herself with an eiderdown so there's no hypothermia. We were lucky there.'

'Hypothermia! What are you talking about? What happened?'

'Her thigh bone. I'm afraid it's broken. Poor old lady, she was in such pain. How she managed to get through the night –'

'What do you mean? Where were you? How could this happen?' Chrissy felt anger take control of fear.

'She says she got up to get herself a cuppa –'

'I repeat, where were you?' Chrissy could feel her patience slipping away. If she didn't get an answer soon she'd shake this woman.

'Didn't your mother tell you?'

'My mother? Tell me what?'

'I phoned last night when I couldn't get here. My car wouldn't start. She promised to sleep over. I couldn't settle, you see. Well, I don't want to offend, but your mother was a little sharp with me. It bothered me. So first thing this morning I phoned your gran. When she didn't answer I borrowed my sister's car and I drove straight over and I found her, and in a right state she was. Poor old dear.'

'Are you telling me my mother didn't turn up?' Chrissy's face and voice were etched with shocked disbelief.

'I'm afraid so, Chrissy. She did promise me she'd look after her. Honestly.'

'Liz, I believe you.' Chrissy put out a comforting hand. 'Forgive me for being a bit short just now – it was panic. Thank you for coming so promptly. I must go with her.'

'I'll come too.'

'Really, Liz, there's no need.'

'No, I'd like to. There are patients one gets very fond of and your gran's one of them.'

Accident and Emergency was not busy. So when first Chrissy, followed shortly by Liz, skidded through the door they popped like champagne corks into an almost deserted department. Of Daphne there was no sign.

'We're with Mrs Daphne Galloway,' Chrissy explained to the receptionist, feeling breathless from nerves.

'If you'd take a seat, please,' said the clerk.

'Could I not go through?'

'If you'd take a seat,' she repeated.

'I'm a sister at this hospital.'

'So I see.'

'Then can I –'

'If you'd take a seat,' the monotonous voice repeated.

'Come on, Chrissy. We're not going to get any co-operation here.' Liz took her by the arm and led her to the empty row of chairs. 'At least we're not going to have a long wait.'

'You'd have thought they could have employed someone with a little more compassion and charm.' Chrissy attempted to smile, but knew it wasn't working and gave up on it.

'I'll get us some coffee. Black? White? Sugar?'

God, what a day this was becoming, Chrissy thought, as she watched Liz doing battle with a recalcitrant coffee machine. If anything bad had happened to Daphne she'd kill her mother, the selfish bitch. Bad? What was she thinking? Of *course* it was bad – a broken thigh at Daphne's age was serious. If she was kept immobile too long the pneumonia could so easily return. She could die. Chrissy's stomach lurched and she felt as if she was packed with ice. Without Daphne who was there for her? Her mother was too wrapped up in herself and her new love. She'd be alone. She shivered. Why was she thinking about herself? Why wasn't she thinking of her poor grandmother?

'Here you go – it's a bit pale I'm afraid.' Liz handed her the polystyrene cup of coffee.

At the sight of the A and E sister, Chrissy jumped to her feet, slopping her coffee.

'My gran – how is she?'

'She's shocked, understandably. She has a compound fracture – we're prepping her for surgery now. You've been on nights, haven't you? Don't you think you'd be better off going home and getting some sleep? Come back here later. There's nothing you can do, you know.' Betty Greaves spoke kindly, fully aware of how helpless Chrissy felt.

'Can I see her before I go?'

'Of course. Come this way.'

Daphne looked so small in the high bed, its cot sides up, her face as pale as the white hospital gown.

'Chrissy, I'm sorry,' she said, in a croaky, parched voice.

'Don't be silly, Gran. What have you got to be sorry about? I just wish – oh, never mind. They'll patch you up here in no time. You'll soon be racing up the supermarket aisles again.' Chrissy could hear that she sounded half-witted and that Daphne would not be taken in. The situation was serious.

A nurse hovered with a small tray containing a syringe already drawn up.

'Gran, they want to give you an injection. It'll make you feel lovely and woozy and take all the pain away.' She leant over and kissed her gran goodbye. 'Liz is here too. 'Bye, Gran.'

'She's only just recovering from pneumonia,' she said to the sister, once they were outside the curtained cubicle.

'Don't worry, she told us. The anaesthetist is aware. She's a feisty old lady, isn't she?'

'The best.' Chrissy turned abruptly away. She wanted to cry. She was so afraid.

Because of the rain, which was now falling quite heavily, the lounge in the nurses' home still had a fair number of people in it. They were gossiping and drinking coffee while they waited to see if it would ease off so that they could dash home and get some sleep.

The conversation flowed back and forth over various topics, but every so often returned to Chrissy and the sudden deaths. They were like bees with pollen, unable to stay off the subject.

'What have you got against her, Jazz? You talk as if it's cut and dried and she bumped them off in some way.'

'I've got nothing against her,' Jazz said, looking affronted.

'You could have fooled me.' Dawn laughed.

'You must admit, Dawn, it does look fishy.'

'Now why on earth should a woman like Chrissy take up mass murder?'

'Perhaps she's mad.'

'Oh, come on. You know her, Alex, she's nice. She's not potty.'

'Mad people can be amazingly cunning,' Jazz explained knowledgeably. 'But, in any case, I know what I know.'

This had exactly the result Jazz wanted: immediately she was the centre of attention. She smiled enigmatically as they plied her with questions. What did she know? How did she know? What was it worth to tell them?

'What a shower you are! You're like ghouls! Oh, all right, then, I'll tell you. Her husband, Ewan – guess what he died of?'

'What?' they roared with impatience.

'Well . . .' Jazz milked the moment.

'Oh, for God's sake, get on with it, you're becoming a bore, Jazz.'

'Ewan Watson died from an overdose of insulin, that's what!' Jazz sat back with a satisfied expression at the ensuing uproar.

CHAPTER FIVE

I

The sea, far below them, sparkled as if it was scattered with silver. The wind whipped skittishly about the cliff top. The unseasonal December sunshine was, for most people, uplifting after a damp and drab November, but apparently not, judging by their expression, for the two men, shoulders hunched against the cold, who stood on the fairway.

'Is it necessary to talk out here?' Craig Nutting complained. 'I can think of better ways to spend a Saturday. It's parky enough to freeze the old proverbials off a brass monkey.' He leant nonchalantly on a golf club, which he used as if it were a walking stick. Rather belatedly, having finally grasped the many business advantages to be gained from playing golf, he was taking lessons from the Fellcar country club golf pro. So far, despite his teacher's legendary patience, his progress had been slow, not helped by his loathing of fresh air, which bordered on the paranoid.

'I deemed it safer.' Matthew Kersey lined up his ball.

'*Deemed.*' Craig snorted.

'And what's wrong with that?' Matthew looked up from addressing the ball.

'Oh, nothing. Not really. It's just that it's the sort of word you'd expect an archbishop to use. *Deemed!*' He laughed. Matthew still looked quizzical. Pompous fart, thought Craig.

Matthew's club swished through the air, somewhat angrily, Craig decided, as if he'd been able to read what he'd been thinking. In a way he wished he had: then he'd know what Craig really thought of him.

He had no liking for the man, too superior by far. Craig was aware that normally Kersey wouldn't even give him the time of day, let alone trudge round a golf course with him – but then, to be honest, Matthew was the last person *he*'d seek out.

Craig sliced his own ball, throwing a divot in the air, and watched it fall far wide of where he'd aimed. 'What I do for money!' He stowed his club away in the bag. 'You know what, Matthew, I begin to think I'm too equable for this game. I don't think I've enough of the killer instinct to succeed.' He grinned as he goaded the man, purposefully reminding Matthew of the tantrum he'd witnessed only last month. Matthew had made a right wally of himself when, having made a mess of his tee shot and in a rage, he had whammed his brand new driver into a tree and snapped it in two.

Matthew heaved his bag of clubs onto his back, scowled at Craig and set off to the next hole. Craig puffed up behind him.

'So, since we're here, let's talk.'

'We're meeting the others.'

'We're what? Well, won't that look bloody obvious, stuck out here on the course? More natural to meet up in the bar, isn't it?' Craig asked, almost hopefully.

'The others are ahead of us – they teed off a good half-hour ago. We're to meet them in Yates's copse.'

'Why is everything in this bloody town called Yates? Yates's copse, tower, park, square.'

'He was a great benefactor.'

'Bet he was on the make too.'

Matthew frowned. Craig knew that he never liked to be reminded that he might be the slightest bit bent. 'Everyone is, aren't they?' He trudged on.

'Whose idea was it – all this cloak-and-dagger malarkey?'

'Mark Fisher's. He says he's got most to lose if it comes out.'

'Oh, really! Little shit. That's the trouble with MPs, they think they're so sodding important.'

'He reckons the papers would focus on him. Tory sleaze reawakens – all that tosh. The rest of us would remain fairly anonymous.'

'And jobless!' Craig laughed at this and Matthew looked at him as if he was demented.

'What's there to laugh at?'

'Oh, nothing –' And Craig laughed even more. If jobs were to be lost it wouldn't be his, he'd make sure of that.

Two holes later they peeled off the green and disappeared down a slope into Yates's copse, where, in the centre, they found Mark Fisher, the ubiquitous MP, sitting on a log, smoking nervously while Giles Middleton leant somewhat languidly but elegantly against a tree.

'There's not much cover here,' Mark said morosely.

'Leaves fall off trees, mate, that's why.'

'I'm aware of that, Craig.'

'I've often seen groups resting here and having a natter. Just look.' Matthew pointed to the ground on which there was a fair scattering of ground-up cigarette butts.

'What's the panic?' Giles pushed himself away from the tree and sat on another handy log.

'Your partner's son, Kim Henderson, is Craig's right-hand man and he's singing like a canary. That's the panic.'

'I don't see how. Kim doesn't know anything, so what can he be telling?' Craig looked as relaxed with the situation as he felt.

'He must know something, or why would old Glynis Tillman tell me she'd heard the hospital was to be privatised?' Matthew snapped at him.

'A lucky guess, gossip – but how would she know?'

'Because Floss Yates told her.'

'Not *another* sodding Yates – I don't believe it!' Craig tittered, which only seemed to irritate the others. A right crew to be involved with, he thought, the slightest hint of trouble and they all looked suicidal. 'And who's Flossy Yates?'

'My partner Dick Henderson's sister-in-law, so your assistant's aunt. And I'd advise you not to call her Flossy, she might handbag you. It's Floss,' Giles explained. At least he was smiling, thought Craig. 'You sure he hasn't heard something? Seen a file?'

'There is no file – I'm not a berk. Even if he heard me on the phone to one of you he couldn't have twigged. *There's no way*. I don't have straight-up natters with any of you, as you well know. There's no way –'

'Have you sacked him as I suggested?'

'Oh, really, Matthew! On what grounds? That *would* put the cat among the pigeons, wouldn't it? Talk sense, man, if you're going to talk at all. And in any case, I can't sack him, he's unsackable. He's a civil servant.' Craig found this inordinately funny.

'What do you suggest we do? Forget the whole project? Yes, that's probably the safest.' Mark looked ill with tension.

'Fisher, if I'd known you were going to be such a wimp I'd never have counted you in. Of course we don't give up. We've nothing to hide, we've done nothing – as yet – but sow a few fears and alarms.' There was no humour in Craig's voice now.

'I'll start referring all my patients to the hospital, Okay? Forget Accident and Emergency for a while.'

'No way, Giles. You do that and if we're not careful the bloody hospital will start making a profit and where will that leave us?' Craig thumped him matily on the shoulder but, from Giles's pained expression, a mite too hard.

'It's only a matter of time before something's said to me – you do know that, Craig.'

'You were mentioned at the last managers' meeting.'

'There you go.'

'No, Giles. If we start acting differently in the smallest way it looks suspicious. What are you doing that a lot of GPs don't do already? You tell your patients to toddle along to A and E to circumnavigate the waiting lists. You're a good, feeling doctor with only the best interests of your patients at heart,' Craig cajoled him, but Giles looked doubtful. 'You know what, Giles? I reckon if there was ever a kerfuffle about your little activities then your patients would rise *en masse*, petitions to the fore, in your defence. Stop worrying, mate. As for you, Mark, what have you done other than to point out to the Minister that St Edith's is running at a god-awful loss and, as its MP, you wouldn't create a stir in the House of Commons if it was shut down, right?'

'Well . . .' Mark fumbled in his pocket for his crushed packet of cigarettes. He placed one in his mouth and lit it before speaking. 'Well, I might have hinted.'

'At what?'

'That if it closed there might be something in it for him.'

'You fucking moron!' Craig spat out at him. 'He's an incorruptible bloody socialist!'

'I didn't tell him the plan,' Mark whined.

'You didn't have to, did you, you useless wanker? The man's not daft – he'll put two and two together. At the first whiff of something afoot he'll stop you dead in your tracks.' Craig dug in his own pockets in the hope that he might find some chewing gum, which might help calm him down. For the first time in the four years since he'd given up smoking he felt desperate for one. 'Give us a fag, Mark.'

'Don't be such a twit, Craig. You've given up – you don't want to go through all that again,' Matthew spoke with his doctor's hat firmly in place.

'I just feel, Matthew, that if I don't have a fag I might just kill that stupid little turd.' He glared at Mark.

'Hadn't we better calm down? This'll get us nowhere. Does anybody know anything about the Minister?' Matthew asked.

'What, a spot of blackmail?' Craig perked up at this notion. 'Rumour has it that he's got a bit of skirt, lives the other side of Thorpedale – she's married, four kids and the husband's a defrocked Tory MP.'

'Brilliant! So why are we worrying?'

'That's down to you, Mark. A nice little threat if he looks the least bit iffy.'

'And the rest of us?'

'Business as usual, gents. I'm off to New York next week – a few exploratory talks, if you get my drift.'

'What if Floss starts banging her drum?'

'Deny everything, Giles, it's the only way. I should think they'll be too busy gossiping about the alleged hospital murders than worrying about this.'

'What murders?' asked Mark.

'Hardly murders, Craig,' Matthew objected.

'Bumping off three patients sounds like murder to me.'

'We're still awaiting the post-mortem results on that. Bet you it's all a storm in a tea-cup.'

'Who? What, Matthew?'

'Three patients died unexpectedly and the finger of suspicion is pointing at the poor sister who was in charge at the time,' Matthew explained, as if already bored with the subject.

'Why? What did she do?' Mark lit yet another cigarette.

'Unfortunately for her, her husband died in somewhat similar circumstances. The police hauled her in for questioning.'

'And we're employing her at St Edith's?'

'She wasn't charged, Mark. You can't not employ someone just because the police make a cock-up.'

'Makes you think, though, doesn't it?'

'Exactly,' said Craig. 'Where there's smoke . . . It couldn't have happened at a better time for us, gents. A nice handy smoke-screen which I suggest we keep pulled. Maybe a few post-mortem reports should get lost in the deluge of paperwork. Now, if you gents don't mind, I think I'm calling it a day and wending my way back to the bar. Coming?'

'I think we should split up,' Mark said.

'Suit yourself. What about you, Matthew?'

'Oh, I'll come with you. I've lost the feel of this game.'

'If it ever had one, playing with me,' Craig said good-naturedly.

'I think I'll finish. I'll amble in later, okay?' Giles picked up his golf-bag.

Matthew and Craig plodded back across the green. 'You know, I think I'm wasting my money on this golfing lark. Maybe I'd be better off taking up horse-riding.'

'If you're as bad at that as you are at golf you'll end up dead – wouldn't advise it.' Matthew laughed for the first time that morning.

'Well, there's a relief. At least you're seeing the funny side to something. That Mark's a right wally, I'm telling you.' Craig opened the boot of his car to stow away his clubs. His head reappeared just as an old and battered E-type pulled up with a screech, which made both him and Matthew step back sharply. Craig opened his car door and put his Barbour inside, aware that Matthew was talking to someone on the forecourt. By the time he emerged Matthew was alone.

'I don't think it's too bright an idea if we go into the bar for a drink, after all.'

'Oh, yeah, why not?'

Matthew pointed to a large rotund shape, scurrying towards the main door of the country club. The woman's black cape was billowing out behind her, giving her the appearance of a very fat rook.

'That's the reason. That's our Floss Yates.'

'Maybe you should talk to that sister. Bribe her with your charm and whatever other assets you've got and get her to bump that old cow off as well!' Craig laughed uproariously at this, but Matthew couldn't be sure if he was joking.

Floss Yates stood in the oak-panelled hallway of the clubhouse and looked out of place. Dressed totally in black she stood out dramatically from the golfers in their peacock-bright clothes. Overweight herself, she eyed with keen interest the number of large rear ends encased in scarlet, green and a couple of unfortunately chosen plaids. Did these people not possess mirrors? she thought, with disbelief. She winced at the shrill-voiced women, who seemed to lack a volume control, and she noted that though they wore flat golf shoes they still minced along as if teetering on stilettos.

Golf was not one of Floss's interests, nor had it ever been. She and her late husband had once rocked the community when, having been invited to put themselves up for membership, which would, they were assured, be passed on the nod, they had politely refused. Membership of the club was what many people in Fellcar dreamt of and planned and manipulated to achieve. The Yates' action confirmed in many minds the theory that they were both not only odd but mad.

'Upon my honour, it's Floss.'

Floss found a grey-haired man with a large moustache and ruddy complexion, ill matched with his orange sweater, towering above her.

'Forgive me, do I know you?' Floss looked up at him, puzzled.

'Of course you know me. I'm Stuart Rawlings-Smith – chairman of the committee – always at your command.' He bowed, hammily. 'As now. A drink that cheers, methinks?'

'So kind, but I'm meeting friends, Mr Smith-Rawlings.' Suddenly she smiled. Stuart beamed in response. But Floss looked right past him. The smile had transformed her face dramatically, changing her rather dour expression, reminiscent of Queen Victoria in mourning, to one of lightness and joy, and it was possible to see the beauty she once had been. 'Kim!' she called out, and waved excitedly. Kim, holding the hand of a pretty young woman, made his way towards her. Beside Floss, Stuart stiffened.

'You know Tiffany Lester?' he asked, in a voice brimming with surprise.

'No, I haven't had that pleasure, yet – but this young man is my nephew.'

'Tiffany's the daughter of our professional golfer, you realise,' he said, almost in a whisper.

'Really, Mr Rawlings, you needn't make it sound as if she were on the game,' Floss hooted noisily.

'Perhaps you and your nephew would care to join me for a drink, Floss?'

Floss noticed Tiffany bite her lip and blush.

'Mr Smith, you seem to be suffering under a misapprehension. I'm not your friend. I must apologise, but I have no recollection of ever meeting you. So, you must understand, I'm somewhat perplexed as to why you think you have the right to address me by my Christian name. I know I'm getting on, but I'm not so vague that I wouldn't remember giving you permission – don't you agree?' Floss smiled beatifically as she issued her rebuke in her low, attractive voice.

Stuart stood rigid and a blush he'd no idea he was capable of suffused his face making it even redder. He took a deep breath as if about to bluster.

'Now, if you'll excuse me?' And Floss swept regally towards the bar which, given her short and rotund shape, was quite an achievement.

'He asked Tiffany to leave, Aunt. Can you imagine? Just because her father's an employee. I'm resigning, I can tell you that.' Kim was steaming with indignation. Aha, thought Floss. So Kim's in love.

'You should never have joined in the first place, Kim. I did warn you. So, you're Tiffany. What a pretty name. And you, my dear, may call me Floss. Now Kim, the drinks, chop-chop!'

Finally settled at a table by a window, the niceties dispensed with, Floss folded her hands neatly in front of her. 'So. To business. Tell me all.'

'We nearly left without old Rawlings-Smith asking us to. Our boss, Craig Nutting, was on the forecourt. If he'd seen us together – phew!' Kim flicked his fingers.

'Why aren't you allowed to be out with each other?'

'Because the creep fancies Tiffany himself and he's as old as Methuselah.'

'I gather he's forty, then.' Floss chortled with delight.

'He was here with Giles Middleton.'

'Interesting. But what I need to know is how you know their plans.'

'Tiffany had better explain.'

'It was by accident, Floss. On our PC, our fax and telephone modems are –'

Floss held up her hand. 'Simply, my dear. I've just conquered the abacus.'

'In our office the computers used to be fixed to act as a telephone and fax machine as well as for e-mail.'

'A computer as a telephone, whatever next!' Floss said, wide-eyed with genuine disbelief, never once having touched one herself. 'How?'

'It *is* clever, isn't it? There's a microphone and speaker built into the casing. It could be so handy for conferences and everything on file. But anyhow, Craig decided he didn't like it, "not secure enough" I clearly remember him saying. So he ordered me to close it all down, which, of course, I did, and we returned to using ordinary telephones and fax machines. I don't know how it happened – Kim and I think it was a combination of things. A new cleaner must have seen the unused telephone jack points and known where to put them back in the machine. That wouldn't have been enough since the modems were down, but we had a bad storm the other night and Kim thinks they might have inadvertently been activated by that.

'Anyhow, I was working in the outer office and suddenly I heard Craig dialling and I could hear everything he was saying next door as it was issuing out of my computer. He was talking to the local MP about selling the hospital. Then he said he'd fax him and to stand by the machine and to destroy it immediately he'd read it. Only it came out on my fax modem as well. I shouldn't have, but I didn't like what he was saying – so, here it is.' From her handbag Tiffany took out a printout of a long fax detailing the hospital's budget and handed it to Floss. She sat back with an expression of relief at the prospect of someone else being involved and, hopefully, taking control. Floss saw, under one column headed *real*, was listed a long row of figures. Under a second, headed *massaged*, was another.

'What a clever Tiffany you are, my dear. How smart of Kim to recognise it in you.'

'That's another thing I wanted to talk about, Floss. My mother says _'

'Don't even bother to tell me. She doesn't approve of Tiffany. Stupid woman. Ignore her. You're a grown man. Do what you want, marry whom you want.' And she smiled very slyly at them.

2

Every magazine or newspaper Mo picked up seemed to have an article on breast cancer. A documentary on it was shown on TV and a dramatisation of one woman's fight against the disease was on another channel – not that she could bring herself to watch either. She could have been forgiven for thinking there was a sudden epidemic, or was the explanation that such coverage had always been there but she'd skipped it since it was of no interest to her? So there was no real need for her to go to the library to read up on it, but she went all the same and then wished she hadn't when she'd scared herself witless.

First her next-door neighbour and then a woman she barely knew, but met in the supermarket, began to talk to her about illness. Odd, when she hadn't invited or instigated the conversations. They spoke of people they knew with cancer, people who'd died – and both seemed fixated with breast tumours. And yet Mo could not remember conversations like this with them before and, since she'd said nothing about her own condition or fears, she found herself feeling the first flush of paranoia. What did they know? Who was talking?

'You haven't told anyone about me, have you?' she asked Lynn Petch, who'd popped in for coffee and to find out how she'd fared in hospital.

'Oh, really, Mo. As if I would! Whatever goes on in the surgery is totally confidential. You've no fears on that score.' But even as she spoke Lynn moved a fraction in her chair as if by moving her body she could erase the discomfort in her mind. There was, as she knew, no guarantee that Enid Dodds who, as the receptionist, had access to patients' notes, wouldn't blab – but worse, she felt uncomfortable, regretted mentioning Mo's problem to Chrissy. But in a microsecond she was reassuring herself that Chrissy was the last person to gossip and, in any case, that conversation had been on a professional level – or had it? She felt uncomfortable again.

'It seems odd to me, though,' Mo persisted.

'Well, I say everything's confidential, but you can never be a hundred per cent sure, can you? Perhaps someone at the hospital saw you and knows you,' she offered lamely. Much more likely Enid, she thought. There was no doubt, the surgery needed tightening up in more ways than one.

'It's really strange, though. It's as if the whole world, or at least the people I meet in it, are obsessed with . . .' She paused. 'With the *condition*.' She shook her head slightly, unaware that Lynn had registered it. There was still no way she could bring herself to say *that* word. 'I put that badly. It's like . . .' Mo thought for a second. 'Do you remember when you were pregnant and suddenly every other woman you saw was too? And yet you'd never noticed so many pregnancies before. Well, it's like that. And when you think I haven't confessed about myself to *anyone*. Phew!'

'You wait. When you do, you'll begin to think the whole female population is affected and your head will reel from the advice you're given. Have you told Robbie yet?'

Mo looked away.

'Oh, love, you must.' Lynn leant forward to take her hand. 'It's unfair not to. He's a right to know.'

'I'm sure he'll do a runner.' Mo freed herself to laugh.

'You don't know that. I've seen so many men who've been right wasters – not that I mean your Robbie's one,' she said, all flustered. 'The most unlikely men become towers of strength when needed,' she went on hurriedly. 'And in any case, what is there to tell? You still don't know the results of your biopsy now, do you?' she finished in a rush, knowing she'd botched up that conversation. She looked covertly at Mo, whose expression told Lynn she hadn't noticed.

'No. But *I* know. Deep down I know it is, Lynn. I just feel it. I expect you think I'm being silly.' Tears filled her eyes.

'No, Mo. I've been in this job too long for that. But don't let go of your optimism. If you're right then you'll need it in spades.' Lynn looked at Mo with concern and wished there was more she could do than pat hands and trot out platitudes.

'Are you going out, Robbie?' Mo asked, as she cleared the supper dishes from the dining table.

'I thought I would.' He looked down at the newspaper he was holding, but not before she registered the shifty expression which, she realised, she'd almost come to expect.

'Only I need to talk to you.' She folded the tablecloth.

'What about?' he asked, with a hint of suspicion.

'Katya, Kerry. Bed,' she ordered.

'It's not eight,' Katya protested. 'I go to bed at nine thirty.'

'Don't argue, Katya. Go to your room.'

'She goes to bed before me, she always does.'

'Not tonight. I want to talk to your father. In private,' she said, as Katya opened her mouth, about to continue arguing. Reluctantly, with as much huff as Katya dared muster and Kerry looking smugly triumphant, they left the room. Mo listened until she heard the angry slamming of their bedroom doors overhead.

She turned to find Robbie standing at the kitchen door about to go through it – to escape from her she found herself thinking. 'No, Robbie, please. I really do need to talk to you.' There was a hint of desperation in her voice – she knew that if she didn't tell him now maybe she never would.

'Last week when I told you I'd gone to your sister's with the kids – well, I hadn't.'

He moved back into the room at that, a suspicious expression on his face. 'Really, so where were you?' he asked. He's jealous, she thought with surprise. How strange.

'In hospital.'

'Hospital? St Edith's? What for?' He sat down.

'I found a lump in my breast. I went in for tests.'

'And –?' He half stood, his hands on the table, leaning forward.

'I'm waiting for the results. With luck, I'll get them next week.' She was amazed how calmly she spoke, how calm she felt, how prepared she was for him to walk out.

'Mo, I'm so sorry.' He was round the table and his arms were about her and he was holding her tight. 'You should have told me. You shouldn't have coped alone. Why didn't you tell me?'

'It's silly, but . . .' Her voice was muffled, held as she still was against his jumper – the blue one with a teddy bear on she'd knitted for him last year, she found herself thinking inconsequentially. Gently he pushed her slightly away so that he could hear what she was saying. 'I was silly, I suppose. I didn't want anyone to know. If I told anyone it would make it real.' He let go of her and sat down abruptly.

'Shit!' He put his head in his hands.

'Robbie, I'm sorry.' She stroked back his hair, which had flopped forward. At her touch his body tensed. 'So sorry.' Even as she said it she wondered why she had apologised – what for? It was hardly her fault. Why had he tensed? Was he afraid of her and *it*? Afraid he might catch it? He slumped in the chair. There was a despondency in his attitude that told her, far more than words could, that she'd ruined something for him. Had he made plans that this news altered? She knew from his first reaction that he felt genuine sorrow for her, but suspected that a lot of it was for himself now. She sat down too. She would have liked to hold his hand, but stopped herself, feeling it would be intrusive of her, that he must have time to come to terms with several things. As she sat and watched his shoulders heave, certain he was weeping even if she could not see his face, she marvelled at how coolly she was behaving, how strangely detached she felt. She said nothing, waiting for him to control himself, unable to tell him to stop crying since she was not sure how many of the tears were for her.

'Useless support system, aren't I?' he said eventually as he looked up, fumbling in his jeans for a hankie.

'It's the shock. I understand.' She tore off and handed him some kitchen paper from the roll on the table. He blew his nose noisily.

'You don't look ill,' he said, as if this made it not true.

'I don't feel ill. And that makes what's happening to me harder to grasp. I mean, if I have to have an operation it would be easier to face if I was in pain, longing for relief, not feeling fit as a fiddle like this.'

'It happened to a mate of mine – his wife got it. You don't expect it to happen to one of your own, do you?'

'No. Everything always happens to everyone else.' She'd registered how he was avoiding the word too. 'I've talked to doctors and nurses and some patients in the hospital. It's not a death sentence any more –

if it's cancer — and we don't know for sure, Robbie, that it's malignant. There *are* treatments. It can be beaten, you know. And nine out of ten lumps are just that, nothing ominous. I've been silly. I should have waited for the results before I even mentioned it. I'm sorry but I'd bottled it up so long, I thought I'd burst.' Now she put out a hand and took his, unaware that in reassuring him she'd used the words she hadn't been able to say before.

'You're right. There's no point in getting upset, not until the results are through, no point at all.' He sat straighter in the chair. 'It's just — I think we need a drink. Rum and Coke?'

'Lovely. Best get a couple down me in case I have to go into hospital. No drink there!' She laughed.

'God, you're brave.'

'No, I'm not. I'm scared silly. What were you about to say? "It's just —" you said. Just what?'

'Oh, nothing.' He busied himself with the bottles, but not before she'd seen a look of shame flit across his face.

'What is it, Robbie? We have to be straight with each other — especially over this.' She regretted these last words, but they had escaped before she had thought. She didn't want him to think she was getting at him. She was aware that her heart was thudding: what if he was about to confess about his bit on the side? Bet he called her crumpet, Robbie was so predictable. She found herself smiling at how oddly her mind was zigzagging about. Still, her heartbeat quickened: she knew she didn't want him to confess, not now, not more dramas. She wanted to concentrate on herself, on this terror, not on any other.

'It was just . . . I thought . . . What if —' And he circled his own chest with his hand as the words dried up and he stood looking sheepish and afraid and, she didn't think it was her imagination, guilty too.

'If I have to have a breast off? What I'd look like?' She spoke lightly, almost with relief that it was this and not the other that was bothering him — for now. 'There's no point in even thinking about it until we know what's what, is there? I wish I hadn't bothered you now. Selfish of me,' she said, briskly. And she, who normally sipped at her rum and Coke, drank greedily, for once, in need of it, wanting to obliterate this big fear from her mind. The loss of her breast she sometimes thought was an even worse prospect than death. At that, she took another gulp of her drink and told herself she was being silly. She wished she hadn't told him now, wished he'd go and leave her alone. She had her own fears to deal with, she couldn't cope with his too. And then, from somewhere, she felt a tendril of annoyance that, if she let it build, would become anger. 'If it had to happen – my breast, I mean – I'd still be me, wouldn't I?' she said firmly, looking straight at him. He shifted his gaze. In that second she knew he would not be able to cope with this; realised with a blinding certainty that she was on her own, and knew instinctively that she would manage – how, she wasn't sure, but she would.

'Right. That's out of the bag now. Thanks for listening.'

He looked up sharply, as if to check if she was being sarcastic, but she was smiling.

'If you don't mind, I promised I'd pop round to see Lynn Petch – she's got some books on the subject for me to read,' she lied, still smiling.

'Oh, I see.' He stood. 'Then you don't mind if I go to the pub?'

'Not at all, Robbie. You must do what you want.' Still she smiled.

'Fine. Then . . . I mean, if you're all right here . . . then . . . well, I think I will.'

She watched him leave. She felt sad, of course she felt sad, but at least she was not surprised.

3

Chrissy was happy to be working alone in her ward; as yet there were no patients, just empty, unmade beds, nor had she any nursing staff to help her. Jobs, Glynis Tillman had told her, had not been allotted yet. Instead she had four cleaners who, with clanking buckets and much complaining, were clearing up the mess the workmen had, unfairly, left. The windows were wide open to allow the smell of fresh paint to disperse so she worked in a thick cardigan against the chill.

She looked up from the lists on her desk in her office. The view from this ward was lovely: sea from the windows on one side and at the far end, where her office and the day room were situated, sea and what was left of the St Edith's garden. She hadn't known until she'd come to this ward that the cottage in the grounds below was Glynis Tillman's quarters. If, in the unlikely event that one day Glynis's lofty position was hers, would she want to move into it? She doubted it: she liked her own cottage; this one was too close. Glynis's life must be dominated by the hospital and its inmates. There was no escape for her. It couldn't be healthy.

She returned to her lists. There was so much to organise, with her first patients due on Monday. The linen cupboards, kitchen and sluice room were all complete and checked. She'd found, when she got here, that Glynis agreed with her on so many things: for a start, the china was pretty instead of functional, thick, institutional white. The day room was to be furnished as near to a comfortable sitting room as funds would allow. Chissy had been overjoyed to find that Floss Yates, who lived at the top of North Hill, and whom she had known all her life, was in charge of allocating funds from the Friends of St Edith's coffers. With her help she'd been able to arrange a good library of books and videos to augment the travelling one; some lovely prints to hang on the walls but, best of all, cordless headphones for each bed so that the TV in each ward could be mute and not bother those who didn't want to watch. And Floss had got the local brewery to donate an ice-making machine since patients on chemotherapy needed to drink copious amounts of water – nicer if iced.

'What I really want to get my hands on are the cancer clinic walls,' Floss had said, as they hung the pictures in the day room. 'I mean, I don't understand the psychology of the people who furnish these hospitals. Why that dreary pea-green colour? Is it necessary? And what can be more depressing or scarifying while waiting to find out if you've got the lurg than to sit in that wretched room with "Living with Cancer", "Cancer Help-line" posters looming above one. Now, a nice Matisse print or even a Van Gogh – no, maybe a bit too disturbed, better a Cézanne – on the walls to cheer the place up. There, is that straight?'

'Impeccable. Still, people have to know what's on offer, don't they?'

'Leaflets nicely and neatly arranged instead of scaring the poor souls half to death. And what's the point of that huge "SMOKING CAUSES

CANCER" monstrosity? A bit late in the day to be lecturing them, isn't it?'

'Maybe they'll have friends with them.' Chrissy had laughed reluctantly – but at least Floss had made her laugh, not much else could at the moment.

She finished her ward lists and pinned them up on the wall of her office. They gave in detail which duties were to be done, at what time and by whom. Each cleaner, auxiliary, student and qualified nurse on duty had their list and if she'd done it right the work of the ward would dovetail neatly and efficiently. Not only were there the rosters for patient care but rosters for the cleaning, checking and replenishing of every store-cupboard in the place, from the one that contained powerful drugs for use with cancers to the one that held the cleaning materials needed by the auxiliaries.

This ward would be perfect, she had resolved. She would make it as pleasant as possible. The very word 'cancer' struck fear into the soul of even the most stalwart. It was her job to try to alleviate that fear and give the treatments and thus the patients the best chance of success.

'Biscuits', she added to her list. Dry biscuits helped if nausea struck. She'd search out nice, unusual tins. Something for them to focus on and comment about. 'Plants', she scribbled. She was a great believer in nature helping to soothe. In her last hospital she'd found patients taking a quite proprietorial attitude to the pot plants. Often *their* plant was the first thing they'd check when coming back for treatment, fussing over it and watering it.

'I bet they get it in their heads that if their plant dies so will they. I don't think it's such a good idea,' the staff nurse on that ward had opined.

'It gives them a focus. Something to care for,' Chissy had countered. This was her ward, so it was up to her to decide if she had plants or not, she thought with satisfaction, and underlined the word with a flourish as if making the point.

From her eyrie she could see the arrivals and departures in the car park far below. She saw Russell Newson get out of his car and stride towards the hospital. She'd heard he was popping in occasionally to see his patients but was doing no surgery yet. She'd seen him once or twice and each time her heart had betrayed her, racing, flipping about as if it had metamorphosed into a jellyfish inside her. At night, her thoughts often turned to him. She did not understand why, she hardly knew him, and it was strange that she should think of him when she'd decided she'd no room in her life for a man. In any case, she wasn't prepared to take the risk of getting involved again – ever! And yet . . . this stupid pit-a-pat, the surge of excitement when she saw him. If she believed in love at first sight she might think that this was it, but she didn't so she had no idea why she reacted in such a juvenile way.

The clock on the wall made a grating sound. She'd noticed that as it approached the hour it made a loud noise as if winding itself up to strike. But since it had no strike it then had to unwind itself, only to do it all over again. It reminded her of herself. Winding herself up to approach the canteen or the office, coming into contact with other staff only to feel the tension slacken once they'd been confronted.

The noise of the clock also made her look up to check the time. She'd managed two relaxed hours working away contentedly. It couldn't last, of course: staff were joining this weekend. She was going to have to face them sooner or later, and then what? She rested her head in her hands and sighed with weariness. It was all getting too much for her – again. She was fully aware of the conversations that stopped at her approach. The whispers that started as soon as she'd passed by. The oblique looks people gave her when they thought she would not notice; the giggles she heard when they thought her out of earshot.

Just like it had been in Cornwall, in the village street, the shop, even when walking, alone she fondly thought, on the cliff. Worse at the hospital when she'd joined: the gossip had preceded her.

That had been a black time, a time she thought she'd never survive, never recover from, never see through. But she had. She knew she hadn't killed Ewan. That thought had finally kept her steady and able to survive.

Now again the same nightmare, but multiplied by three. Yet she'd done no wrong, she'd not killed them – she must cling to that knowledge, get a grip on herself and hold her head high. Her shoulders slumped. Easier said than done.

Only last night, when she'd visited her grandmother on her ward, she'd walked straight into a drama. She had, of course, visited her every day, but always in mufti. Last night she'd been in uniform.

'That's her! That's the one what killed poor Gwen Fortune,' an old woman in the next bed had screeched loud enough for all to hear. 'Call yourself a nurse? An angel of mercy?' She had manoeuvred to get out of the bed and get to Chrissy, and then Chrissy had stood rooted to the spot, unable to move, unable to speak and to defend herself.

'That's my granddaughter you're insulting.' Daphne hauled herself up in the bed.

'Pity for you, then, Daphne. Hope you've not got nothing put by or you'll be next. You mark my words.'

At that, Daphne, ill as she was, had tried to climb out of bed too. At least this finally galvanised Chrissy into stopping her and she was soon calming her just as the staff nurse, Jazz, lumbered up and restrained the other patient.

'Don't be silly, Thelma. That's our nice new Sister Galloway you're insulting,' Jazz's voice was bubbling with amusement. 'Now, get back into bed, you stupid old bitch,' she said in a lowered voice, but loud enough for Chrissy and Daphne to hear. Already it seemed an age since Gwen Fortune had complained about the use, by Jazz, of her Christian name. Reprimanding her now was the last thing on her mind.

'You're a disgrace, Nurse,' Daphne spoke for her.

'And what's your problem, Daphne?' Jazz grinned as if she enjoyed being told off, as if it was welcome excitement in her dull routine.

'Speaking like that. And don't call me Daphne. I'm Mrs Galloway to you.' Daphne sat upright and dignified in the bed.

'Why, I'm sorry, Mrs Galloway. I'd no idea you were so particular. I'll tell everyone, shall I? Watch out for Mrs Galloway she's a right stickler for protocol.'

'Jazz, please . . .' Chrissy began.

'What?'

'Oh, nothing,' she said, too tired and demoralised to pursue it.

She shuddered at the memory now – it had all been so unpleasant, unnecessary and worrying for Daphne, once Jazz had left, slumped back on the pillows, fighting for breath. She was glad then she hadn't rowed with Jazz who, when she called for her help, had acted swiftly and professionally and calmed her grandmother.

'In the circumstances I think we should move her into a side ward, don't you? Away from the accusations of Thelma and her ilk.'

Another sleepless night had followed. There had been too many of them lately, Chrissy thought, as she put her hands behind her head and stretched.

'I thought I'd find you here.'

'Floss, lovely to see you. Come in. Fancy some tea?' She said all this politely while groaning inside. Since last night and the scene in Care of the Elderly she'd wanted desperately to be on her own.

'No tea. I'm the senior Friend on duty and I'm up to here in tea.' Floss tapped under her ample chin, the flesh of which rippled as she did so. 'But I *had* to find you. I've just heard. I was absolutely *horrified*. And we must do something *immediately*!'

'Well, yes. I agree – even if I don't know what you're talking about.'

'Why, all the deaths, of course.'

Chrissy felt herself stiffen even as she said a noncommittal, 'Oh.'

Floss plonked herself down on the seat beside Chrissy's desk. 'Now, I'll tell you what happened.' She crossed one plump leg over the other, always a dangerous action since, because she was so fat, it stuck rigidly out in front of her for others to fall over. 'I was in the office and outside I heard two bitches gossiping about you. Absolutely appalling! I said that unless they stopped this stupid gossip you would be suing for slander. I added – and I do hope you don't mind that I did – but I added, "Just because she's a nursing sister, don't you think that she can't afford to take you to court because she can." Presumptuous of me but, *my dear*, the red mist just descended and I was *so* angry for you.'

'Floss, that was sweet of you.'

'These places need fumigating with anti-gossip gas, they really do.'

'I can't blame them – three deaths in a row like that and after Ewan's death, well, it's human nature, I suppose.'

'Don't be so infuriatingly reasonable. It's criminal of them. And it has to stop forthwith.'

'What's worrying me is that the results of the post-mortems should be through by now and they're not. It's a week since Mrs Fortune died, longer for the others. So the delay points to them being inconclusive and so they must be doing further toxicology tests. That can only mean one thing. They were murdered.'

'Oh, Chrissy, darling, don't be so melodramatic! Who'd do a thing like that here, and why?'

'That's what I can't puzzle out. I don't know anyone here, so how can anyone hold a grudge against me?'

'Maybe someone's jealous of you getting this job. Mind you that would be a bit of an extreme reaction – knocking off patients just to get at you. Don't worry, my dear, they probably all three fell off the twig quite naturally. After all, death isn't that uncommon. It happens to us all, you know.' Floss grinned but, getting no response, leapt back into the conversation with gusto. 'If they were bumped off, and note I say *if*, then it's a nutter doing it. And you're not a nutter, so what's the problem?'

'The problem would be, dear Floss, that if that was so then nobody would be safe, would they?'

'I'm going to have a word with Glynis.' Floss was on her feet.

'I'd rather you didn't, Floss. It could make matters worse for me.'

'Nonsense, how could my intervention do that? Well, at least that's making you smile. No, I'll see Glynis and tell her to tell the pathologist to pull his finger out – oh, Lor', that's a rather unfortunate choice of phrase, isn't it? Anyhow, whatever. We have to get this resolved. And that's that. I'll go and find her now.'

'There's no point, Floss. I know it's her weekend off.'

'She might still be around. That woman is so dedicated she won't mind me having a natter about you.'

'No, I saw her leave her cottage with a purposeful air a good half-hour ago. I'm like Ena Sharples up here – I can see all manner of comings and goings.'

'Seen Matthew Kersey snooping about?'

'The general surgeon?'

'The very same.'

'Why do you ask?'

Floss looked to left and right like a pantomime character. 'Secrets?' She put one podgy finger on her lips. 'Matthew and Glynis go back a long way.'

'You're joking?'

'No. Not many people know. They're very discreet, but I know. So does Shelagh Morris and a few other senior staff.'

'How sweet.'

'No, it isn't. He's a creep and she's a fool. Speaking of which, seen your mother recently?'

At the mention of Iris, Chrissy looked away, not wanting Floss to see her expression and not understanding fully what she had implied. 'We're having a little local tempest,' she said.

'What, over poor Daphne's accident? She told me.'

'My mother did?'

'No, silly. Daphne. Incensed, she was – and I don't blame her.'

'It was highly irresponsible of my mother and we had words about it.' It was a mild way to describe the full-blown row they'd had. She felt she'd never forgive her mother, not this time.

'The trouble is, when a woman of your mother's age discovers sex for the first time consideration and good manners go flying out the window.'

'You know? What don't you know, Floss?'

'Nothing that's of any importance. Oh, and by the way. Christmas Eve – I'm having a party. "Save St Edith's from Unscrupulous Creeps" the invitations will say. You're invited. Coming?'

'I'd love to,' she said, even if a large party was the last thing she wanted. All the same, she heard a small voice deep inside her wonder if Russell would be there.

4

On Saturday morning Glynis stowed her bag on the luggage rack of the 125 train. From her briefcase she took a copy of *Nursing Times* and settled to read it while the bustle and fuss swirled about the train standing at platform two, purring noisily, impatient to continue its rush to London. The reading was a ploy in case anyone who knew her got on the train – the magazine would put them off talking to her. Once the train was in motion she'd put it away and allow herself to think of the weekend. She could hardly believe her luck. Matthew had called late last night to say he was going to London and would she care to join him? She'd laughed at such a question since he already knew her answer.

An article on the post-operative treatment of children caught her attention. Genuinely interested, she was unaware of the guard's whistle or of the train moving. They were well beyond Fellcar when, countryside flashing by, the article finished, she lifted her head – to find Edna Greenbank, the senior theatre sister, sitting opposite her. As always, with Glynis's staff, Edna looked totally different out of uniform – younger and prettier.

'I didn't like to interrupt you, you seemed so engrossed.'

'I was. You might find the article instructive too.' Glynis handed her the magazine.

'Yes. I've read it. One or two points I thought we could adopt. I'd planned to raise them at the next managers' meeting.'

'Quite. Much better.' Why had the flaming woman chosen this train? Why had she read the article? Now she'd want to talk and all Glynis wanted to do was think and plan the precious days ahead.

'Going to London?'

'I'm led to believe that is the destination of this train.' She knew she sounded pompous and cool – she intended to. Freeze her out, that was the best tack.

'Me, too. I'm going to stay with my sister in Clapham. She's got tickets for *Riverdance* – it's my birthday.'

'Many happy returns.' At least they wouldn't bump into each other there. Matthew had said something about taking in a theatre, but she knew that a show like *Riverdance* would not attract him as it wouldn't her. She hoped he'd have tickets for the opera which he knew she loved.

'Shopping?'

'Sorry?'

'Christmas shopping – there's nothing to beat the London shops, is there?'

'Yes. Of course. I hope to do some present-buying.' But she smiled to herself: she hoped she wouldn't be out of bed long enough to shop!

'I like going to London, but I couldn't live there, could you?'

'No.' Keep your answers short, she told herself, then she'll get bored.

'Yet when I lived in London I thought I'd never settle anywhere else.'

'Really?'

'And when I first went to Fellcar I thought I'd last a year there – so boring! And here I am, it's my sixth anniversary at St Edith's this year.'

'Really?'

'Yes. And I must say I've been so happy there. You run a good hospital, Glynis. You care for your staff in a way a lot of managers don't.'

'Thank you.' Glynis looked down modestly, but still wished Edna would shut up.

'So, it would be such a tragedy if it were to be closed.'

'I agree.' Oh, not this old chestnut, she thought. Whenever her senior staff got together it was invariably the main topic of conversation.

'But, still, if it were privatised and we hung around long enough, I suppose we'd be taken on.'

Glynis's head jerked up as if controlled by a puppeteer. 'I beg your pardon?' She injected as much ice as she could muster into her voice, not only to stop this conversation continuing but also to cover her own shocked surprise.

'Haven't you heard? It's all over the hospital. Floss –'

'Floss Yates is a stupid, rich woman with too much time on her hands. She gossips unforgivably.'

'I thought you liked Floss.' Edna looked shocked.

'I do – within limits. I don't like it when she spreads malicious rumours.'

'But what if she were right?'

'Well, she isn't,' Glynis said firmly, and hoped *she* was right. 'And the constant repetition of such rubbish can only damage the hospital, not help it.' She pursed her lips and was rewarded by seeing Edna blush deeply and murmur that she was sorry. Good, that should do it, peace at last. Sometimes, in situations like this, Glynis could find herself having to fight to control her amusement. When she did her 'ice-maiden act', she couldn't help thinking of that other, passionate, abandoned side of her that only Matthew knew.

'I'm glad I've bumped into you in this way, Glynis.'

Well, I'm not, she thought, as she looked pointedly out of the window.

'I've a problem that I'd like to discuss with you.'

'If it's to do with the hospital, this is neither the time nor the place.' Glynis looked straight at her.

'But I think it is.'

'I'm off duty.'

'So am I.'

Again Glynis turned to watch the passing scenery feeling irritation rising inside her and wondering if she could control it. She did not know what had got into Edna, normally an easy-going woman.

'It's about Matthew Kersey.'

Glynis knew she reacted too quickly as, abruptly, she turned her head to look at Edna, eyes wide with surprise, and before she could stop herself. 'What about Matthew?' she said, anxiety in her voice. And was it her imagination, but was a sly smile playing around Edna's mouth?

'You see, I thought, well, I thought it was a godsend finding you here alone, so I could speak to you in total confidence. No prying ears – you know the hospital.'

'What about Matthew Kersey?' She managed to control her voice this time and felt confident that she just sounded curious.

'You won't tell him I spoke to you?'

'We shall have to see.' She was on more confident ground here. Whatever it was, Edna was beginning to look anxious herself. 'What?'

'I've spoken to him in a roundabout way and he was very annoyed with me. Understandable, I suppose.'

'Edna, my dear, I do wish you'd get on with it.'

'There are two things, actually.'

Glynis felt the irritation mount, if there was one thing she loathed it was people who said *actually*. 'It might help if you told me about one of them, at least.'

'He's borrowing theatre equipment to use at the Beacon clinic in his private practice and he's not paying for it.'

'I'll have a word with him.' Oh, Matthew, she thought, he could be so silly. He'd done this in the past and she'd had to reprimand him. His defence had been that everyone did it so why couldn't he, like a little boy caught out in a misdemeanour. She had told him that not all the other surgeons did it, most never borrowed, those who did declared it and were billed. It had to stop, she told him firmly, and he'd laughed and kissed her full on the mouth in her office, which was always so deliciously exciting. 'And the other?' she said, feeling almost light-headed at that particular memory.

'I found him with the anaesthetic nurse in the rest room.'

'So?'

'Well, they were in a rather compromising situation.'

Glynis said nothing, for she could not. She was aware only of the pounding of her blood through her body.

'I mean, what he gets up to in his private life is none of my business – but in the hospital, on hospital property, then I think it is.'

'Hospital property?' Glynis was aware she whispered the words.

'The bed in the rest room. They were going at it like hammer and tongs . . . I mean . . . I thought . . .'

But Glynis did not hear what Edna was saying. She felt the blood drain from her face, a dizziness seeping over her so that the table in front of her seemed to buck towards her. Suddenly she knew she was going to be sick. She stood up.

'Glynis, are you all right?' she heard Edna call after her as, buffeted from side to side by the train's motion, she struggled towards the lavatory.

5

Why was it that reality failed so often to live up to one's dreams? Chrissy thought, as she opened the small window of her sitting room. The acrid smoke, which was still the only result from the fire she had hopefully lit in the wide inglenook hearth, seemed not to notice this escape route. She flapped a newspaper to hasten it on its way, which only made matters worse. She pushed her hair back from her face in a gesture of frustration, unaware that in doing so she had smudged it with soot.

She began to cough for the smoke was pungent and thick. She put on her Barbour, changed from her suede pumps into green wellies and let herself out of the back door. She stood a moment, breathing deeply, enjoying the air like a connoisseur of fine wine. The sun was shining, even if it was bitterly cold. She'd take a walk and let the smoke clear, she decided.

Out in the lane she turned towards the cliff path and the sea. On walks like this she should have a dog to run and snuffle along beside her. That's what she'd imagined when she'd first seen the cottage – her striding along in weather like this, hair blowing, cheeks pink with health and exertion, a pack of dogs ebbing and flowing about her. Sense, once she'd got here, had told her how impractical that would be and, since she worked, how unkind to the dogs.

That idea was shelved. As was the buying of the wood-burner to solve the smoking chimney once she'd discovered the cost of its installation.

Dreams: she'd allowed herself too many of those, she saw, as she trudged along. She smiled at the silliness of her imagining herself and a man – if, in her mind's eye, only a shadow. She laughed at that particular thought. Who was she kidding? She'd seen him, and quite clearly, in her day-dreams – she knew only too well whom she wanted to have sitting by the blazing log fire before dining at a perfectly set table lit by candles, music playing softly in the background, divine food prepared by a perfectly groomed Chrissy, sipping a fine wine. Ha!

The reality? No man, and certainly not Russell – but, then, didn't she constantly tell herself she didn't want one, it was not the time, it was too great a risk? So why imagine? She strode along with more purpose, as if to put a stop to that line of thinking. And the other part of her dreams, what about them? No fire – impossible. No candles – the candlesticks hadn't yet emerged from the packing. Divine food – there was a laugh! She hadn't really shopped since she'd got here and had existed on frozen pizzas and bread and cheese. She'd decided she couldn't afford wine and once the bottles of drink she'd brought with her had gone there'd be no more. As for herself, she did not know where the hours went since she only seemed to have time to keep her uniform smart: everything else was unironed and rumpled. Her hair needed a trim and she couldn't be bothered to make herself up.

'You're going to pot, my girl,' she told herself and the wheeling gulls, as she crossed the cliff, stumbling on the tufty grass before reaching a cluster of rocks on the cliff's edge, huddled together like a large monolithic family of grey seals. She sat on a flat stone, rubbed smooth by wind and rain, and gazed down at the sparkling sea far below her in the bright sunshine.

As a child she'd often walked these cliffs with her father and for a short time with their cocker spaniel, Fluff, who had had long flopping ears, the ends of which were invariably matted. How strange to think of Fluff now, after all these years. Her mother had loathed the dog, and Chrissy in turn had hated her for that. Iris had complained that the dog was dirty, smelt, and insisted it sleep on the back porch. Her father had defended the dog, and insisted it slept in the kitchen. And it was he who had consoled her when poor Fluff, on his first birthday, had been run over by the baker's van. And had wisely decided that a replacement was not a good idea.

How old had she been? Seven, maybe eight. Had the problem with the dog been the seed that had blossomed into her clearly defined feelings towards both her parents? It was possible.

Ewan had hated dogs too – once he'd shot a stray that had wandered onto their land. She had screamed and cried and tried to revive the poor dying beast and Ewan had *laughed* at her. And that had been one of those defining moments one encountered in life, when suddenly a situation became crystal clear and actions to be taken became logical progressions.

She sat up suddenly and shivered – from cold or memories? She was aware that she wanted to cry. For the stray dog, Fluff or Ewan? For herself, probably, she thought and pulled her Barbour closer, as if being warmer might protect her from her thoughts. So many problems . . . those poor patients . . . the worry . . . the sense of isolation. Then the tears came – no longer possible to hold them back. She let them fall, made no attempt to stop them. Who was there to see? What did it matter? She raised her head and through tear-filled eyes the sea sparkled even more as if all the stars in the heavens had fallen like crystals and speckled it. And, as she silently cried, she felt a release begin inside her, deep down, way down, of happenings buried in a long gone past . . .

'Excuse me. It is Chrissy, isn't it?'

Chrissy, recognising the voice, put her hand in her pocket to search for a hankie, but did not find one. She dare not look up, not wanting anyone to see her like this.

Russell crouched down. 'I'm sorry. Do you want me to go?'

Chrissy was sure she was incapable of speech.

'Will this help?'

A neatly folded handkerchief was being offered to her. Embarrassment, confusion and excitement were playing tag in her mind. The handkerchief smelt of lemons and thyme, she noted, as she patted at her eyes and finally blew into its crisp, clean folds.

'I'm so sorry. I don't know what got into me. I'll wash the hankie.'

'No need.'

'Oh, I must.' She buried it in her pocket, but clung to it – like a heroine in a Victorian drama, she found herself thinking, which, at least, made her smile slightly.

'I'll leave you alone if you want. Or you can talk, if you want. Or I'll take you for a drink.'

Even without seeing his face she knew he was laughing at her: it was there in his voice. She raised her head and risked looking at him. He really laughed this time. 'Did you know your face is covered in what looks like soot?'

When she took out the hankie again she saw it was white and pristine no longer but streaked with black. 'My fire, it was smoking.'

'Ah, that explains everything. A bad day can be made intolerable from a smoking chimney. Can I help? I'm good with fires.'

There it was again, the amusement, which made half of her feel foolish and the other half a lot better.

'That would be very kind of you, Russell,' she said, clambering to her feet.

'I never expected to see that lovely sight here!' Chrissy said, as she entered her sitting room to see a log fire burning and Russell efficiently tidying the hearth. 'I'd virtually given up on it and planned to get a wood-burner.'

'That would be a shame. More economical, of course. Anywhere I can wash my hands?'

She pulled the coffee table forward, cleared it of books and magazines and laid two places as she waited for him.

'Are you sure soup's enough? It's from a tin,' she asked, as Russell returned to the room. He laughed. 'What's so funny?'

'Your honesty, I suppose. Tinned soup will be lovely.' He lowered himself onto the rug, his long legs stuck out in front of him, and leant his back against an armchair, as if tired. He watched Chrissy as she went back to the kitchen. Sabine would never have admitted to serving tinned soup, he thought. He'd lost count of the times she'd served guests Marks and Spencer's ready-cooked dishes and had basked in the compliments to her cooking. He'd laughed too – once, until he'd discovered that when someone could lie over something as unimportant as that, they could lie just as expertly about anything.

'Something the matter? You look so cross.' Chrissy placed steaming bowls of Heinz cream of tomato on the coffee table. 'The bread's fresh.' She pushed the basket of rolls towards him, then sat on the floor opposite him.

'I didn't mean to look glum. Sorry.' He grinned apologetically.

'What were you doing out on the cliff? I can go days and see no one, especially at this time of the year.'

'Part of my getting-fit regime. I try to walk a couple of miles a day. Today I decided to trek up here – I used to come here quite often and I always envied whoever lived in this cottage.'

'You did?' She sounded surprised. 'But your house is lovely – at least it looks it from the outside. You know, modern, different –' She floundered; now he'd know she knew where he lived and he'd think she'd been snooping. Which, of course, she had been . . . and then the thought, So what? It didn't matter what he thought of her, did it? 'I was just surprised that, living as you do, you could like my cluttered little cottage.'

'Sabine chose mine. I much prefer traditional houses. In mine you have to be too tidy – minimalism demands it. One sock out of place and the whole illusion is shattered.'

'It wouldn't do for me, then. As you can see, I'm a bit of a muddler.'

'Understandable when you have to be so organised in your work every day.'

'I hadn't thought of that. Thanks. Now I'll know what to say to my mother when she's having one of her nags. More soup?'

'No. That was lovely.'

'Coffee?'

'Nothing. Honestly.' He shifted his position so that he could throw another log on the fire. 'Why were you crying, Chrissy?' he asked quietly, as he fiddled with the fire.

'I wasn't. It was the wind – in my eyes. You know.' She was on her feet, stacking the dishes. 'Sure you don't want coffee? I'm having one.' She had to get out of the room, she didn't want sympathy – especially from him.

'If it's no trouble, then.'

She felt relieved, as if she'd escaped, as she stood in the kitchen leaning against the sink filling the coffee pot with water. She didn't want him to delve, didn't want him to be kind. If he was she knew what would happen: she'd begin to cry again, she knew she would.

He was reading when, composed now, she returned with the coffee.

'You like poetry, I see.' He looked up at her, tapping the slim volume he held in his hand.

'Some. Not all.'

'I'm afraid this stuff's a bit over my head.'

'Really?' She wasn't sure how her response sounded, bored, uninterested. All she knew was that she wanted him to put that particular book aside.

'A real doom merchant this bloke, isn't he? A bit twisted, I'd say.'

'That's the thing about poetry, isn't it? Each person can interpret it differently.'

'Not this stuff. There's only one interpretation – this was written by someone with a sick mind. E. M. Watson. I can't say I've ever heard of him.'

'You wouldn't have. It was privately printed. He was my husband.' Her hand shook and she spilled the coffee. 'Oh, look what I've done!' And she was on her feet again, but this time so was Russell.

'Chrissy, I'm so sorry. I'd no idea. I'd never have said –' He stepped towards her. She retreated from him. 'The name, it's not yours – I –'

'How were you to know? Don't be silly. Ewan would have been thrilled to bits by your opinion of him. He worked hard enough at it.' Bitterness she did not want began to seep into her voice.

'The poetry?'

'No,' she replied enigmatically, more in control now as she ran to her kitchen to fetch a cloth to mop up the coffee. 'You're fully recovered, then?' she asked briskly as she returned, putting on her professional mantle as a defence. 'No trouble sleeping?'

'What's that? Sleep, I mean.' He pulled a face.

'Didn't they give you pills?'

'Hundreds of them. I don't approve of them, though.'

'You dole them out to your patients readily enough.'

'That's different. I can't sleep because I'm plagued by nightmares. If I douse the dreams with chemicals they won't have gone away, will they? They'll still be lurking there, waiting to pop out at me again.'

'True.'

'Somehow I've got to face what happened. And beat it.'

'You'll need help.'

'I'd rather cope myself.'

'You can talk to me if you want. I won't discuss you with anyone,' she said, with her professional hat squarely on.

'And why should I tell you? You won't confide in me.' He smiled so that any hint of criticism was dispelled. 'Oh, I don't know. I fear if I talk about it then it's real. I'd prefer to pretend it's a bad dream.'

'That won't cure it.'

'You're right. So practical.' He smiled at her distantly. She said nothing, certain that he was finally going to recount the trauma. He put his head in his hands and sighed. They sat in silence. And then he shook himself slightly, as if reaching a decision. 'It's Georgie who haunts me the most. She was with me in Bosnia. I'd known her years – she was a great nurse and a wonderful woman. She'd just found out she was pregnant. She was so happy, and then *boom*.' He slapped one hand into the palm of the other. 'Some prat at the RAF hospital said to me, "At least she died a happy woman." I wanted to kill him. Instead I shut up – it seemed safer.' He looked so sad as he spoke that she leant forward and took his hand in hers. This action did not stop her wondering if he'd loved this woman Georgie, and she experienced a flash of jealousy at the thought. A totally irrational reaction but one she could do nothing about, she told herself.

'Maybe he meant well,' she said, as if to make amends for the way she was thinking.

'If so, then God save us from those who do. But I didn't mean to cause such a panic and drama back here. I just didn't want to talk. I think now I was scared I'd lose control if I did.'

'But it doesn't alter the fact that you were unconscious, does it? I mean, your silence could have been indicative of greater damage.'

'Listen . . .' He held her hand more firmly. She did not move it.

'Imagine how you'd feel if it had happened to you – people you respected and liked lying dead and wounded and you without a scratch. How would you feel?'

'Relieved and, I suppose . . . I'm not sure . . . Guilty?'

'Exactly. Why them? Why not me? That's what I have to come to terms with.'

'And are you?'

'Yes, slowly. I know I'll never resolve it, never explain it to myself, never forgive myself. So, in a manner of speaking, I've solved it. I'm beginning to understand it's something I'll have to learn to live with.'

'Perhaps, by acknowledging it like this, the memories will fade, the dreams lessen.'

'I hope you're right. Sod of a world, though, isn't it? You meet awful, grim people and nothing bad ever happens to them and then you know brilliant people who've never done anyone any harm and life hurls everything at them.'

'I think part of becoming mature is accepting just how unfair life is.'

'Have you had to accept? It's your turn now.'

Chrissy sat looking at her hands, which lay in her lap, as if seeing them for the first time.

'I'm not prying. It will help to talk. I've just learnt that.'

'I'm not used to confiding. I've always worked out things alone.'

'Maybe you should change tack – try another means.' He spoke gently, quietly, coaxing her. She looked up at him and he smiled at her, and suddenly she wanted to tell him, wanted him to understand.

'You heard about the deaths on my roster? Well, I'm being blamed for them. It got to me, that's all.' She picked up the coffee pot and had better luck in pouring this time.

'That's ridiculous. These things happen. And who's blaming you?'

'Most of the staff at the hospital.'

'You'll be saying next that they think you murdered them. Gave them a deadly overdose.' He laughed at the idea.

'They do.'

His laughter ceased abruptly as if a switch had cut it off. 'Oh, come on, Chrissy. You're not serious?'

'I am,' she said softly.

'But the post-mortems will prove otherwise. Why, look at my Mrs Norman, she had a massive stroke. And –'

'She did? No one told me.' She sounded indignant.

'Then I'm not surprised that you're annoyed. You should have been told. But then, hang on, why should they bother you when you're off duty? And if that's the case it would prove you're imagining it.'

She sighed with resigned irritation. 'I don't imagine the whispering, the looks. I think they know about my husband. Someone's been blabbing. And they're putting two and two together and coming up with five.'

'Why should they be interested in him?'

'Ewan killed himself. He stole insulin from his diabetic mother. He didn't mean to kill himself, I'm certain of that. He wanted a little coma, that was all.'

'A dangerous game – he could have been blinded, ruined his kidneys.'

'He thought he knew everything. That he could dose himself and not damage himself. He was wrong.'

'But why?'

'To punish me. He liked playing games like that.'

'What had you done?'

'Left him. It was the day after he shot the dog.'

'He did what?' Russell exclaimed.

'How stupid of me. I'd been thinking about the dog out there on the cliff and I thought I'd told you about it.' She shook her head as if to clear such confusions. 'Why did he kill it? God knows. Perhaps because I was feeding it and growing fond of it. But it galvanised me. I went to the hotel in the New Forest – remember I told you about it? – to think things through. Decide what to do. I knew I had to leave him if I was to survive intact. But he wanted me back. Of course, as soon as I heard what had happened, I came running – just as he'd planned – except he wasn't to know. He was dead. I was arrested.'

'Why, for God's sake?'

'He left a note with his mother – I suppose just in case. In it he said if anything happened to him I was to blame.'

'Charming.'

'She hated me – nothing sinister, just a mother loathing a woman who, as she saw it, stole her beloved son. She called the police and I was carted off for questioning. Something I shan't forget in a hurry.'

She laughed bitterly.

'And you think someone at the hospital knew this and let the cat out of the bag.'

'Exactly. Maybe the nutter who's going around bumping patients off.'

'Oh, come on, Chrissy, you don't know that.'

'It happens.'

'It does – but so rarely. Think it through. Who do you know at the hospital who's got such a grudge against you they'd set you up?'

'I've racked my brains. I'm not aware that I know anyone at St Edith's. Maybe they're just using me as a scapegoat. Maybe someone's fed up they didn't get my job. I don't know . . . but I'm thinking of moving on. I can't see the point of staying here.'

'And then what? Have it all happen again as the gossips in the next hospital get at you? I'm surprised. I wouldn't have thought you'd be the type to give in to scum like that.'

'How would you know? You don't know me.' She felt a flash of annoyance at his snap judgement. 'And you don't know what it's like to be misunderstood.'

'Don't I? You'd be surprised.' He knew that virtually everyone regarded Sabine as a saint and him as her tormentor. If only they knew the truth. 'Look, Chrissy. First thing on Monday, go to the office – demand to know the results. Talk to Glynis. She might seem a cold fish but, in fact, she's very kind and, more to the point, extremely fair, and this isn't a fair situation.'

'No, it isn't, is it?' She looked at him and smiled, relieved that he understood, but also because she hadn't, as she had feared she might, cried.

They dropped the subject then and talked of other things. When he left he asked if he could call again. She said yes. But her heart hadn't lifted as it would have a day or two before. As she watched him walk down the lane to where he'd parked his car she felt sad, as if by talking about Ewan ice-cold water had been poured on her heart and hopes. As if Ewan were in control again.

6

By the evening Glynis had recovered her composure. She had returned from her rush to the lavatory – white-faced, sweating slightly, apologising profusely. 'I don't normally have take-aways – last night was an exception. But never again!' she'd said, with feeling and a little laugh. 'I *am* sorry, rushing off like that.' She'd taken her seat, hoping she'd managed the incident well enough.

'I was worried. I thought it was something I'd said that had upset you.' Edna leant forward with a serious expression, which Glynis judged to be concern rather than snooping – she hoped she was right.

'What to do about Matthew? That's what you want to know. Well, my dear Edna, what Matthew chooses to do in his private life is his concern, not ours. Don't you agree? But if he chooses to misbehave, and so blatantly, on hospital property then, of course, it becomes our concern.'

'Then you'll speak to him?'

'I'd rather not – I find these matters so distasteful, don't you? Perhaps if I mention it to Fraser Ball. He's the senior physician, after all. You've spoken to the young nurse?'

'Well, no. Like you – well, it's all rather indelicate . . .'

'Let's leave it to Fraser.'

'As you think best, Glynis.' Edna looked puzzled at the other woman's apparent and uncharacteristic delegation of responsibility. And, as Edna pondered why this should be, the frown deepened. But Glynis did not see this for already she was looking out of the window at the passing scenery.

She was controlling her face muscles, forcing a calm expression, forcing a slight smile to play around her lips, forcing away the longing to cry. Her face ached from the effort, her throat ached from the dammed-up tears. Her neck and shoulders throbbed with tension. Inside her there was no silence; inside her she screamed with anguish, pain and desolation.

Glynis had planned to shop, then visit her London hairdresser. Afterwards, if she had time, she had wanted to go to an exhibition at the Tate that had attracted her attention. Instead she took a cab straight to the hotel.

Once she was safely in her room, the porter departed, she stood motionless for a second. Then, rippling through her body her muscles felt as if they were softening. Her head and shoulders slumped, she bent double at the waist, her knees buckled, her legs gave way and she fell to the floor in a heaving, weeping heap.

She had no idea how long her emotions gushed from her in an apparently unstoppable torrent. She rode the storm, spirit battered, feeling emptiness engulf her but unable to do anything about it. Never in her life had she given way to her feelings in this way. She had no idea where it would lead or when it would end.

Eventually the crying stopped as if she'd drained the source of the tears. She sat up and felt despair and exhaustion. She got to her feet and stumbled across to the bathroom. Seeing her face in the mirror, red, swollen, ravaged with tears, she felt self-loathing begin to build. She leant on the basin for support, since suddenly the floor felt unstable, and studied her face. No beauty there now, just ugliness. Her pulse was racing and she was breathing far too fast. Rapidly she ran the cold tap and sluiced her face with water, she held a soaking flannel against her eyes. She took deep, regular breaths. The dizziness began to subside, she felt herself slipping back into control as if putting on a familiar well-worn coat.

She went back into the bedroom, crossed to the telephone and ordered room service. While she waited for her sandwich and double whisky to arrive she tidied herself, repaired her make-up and brushed her hair. She sat waiting, a strange calmness cloaking her. The storm had passed and, methodically, she began to think, to wonder and to plan.

Why, was the easiest question to deal with. Men were notoriously attracted to young women. She did not need to be married or living with Matthew to know that. The newspapers were full of prominent men risking all for sex with a young body. She'd thought about it often over the years, expecting that one day it would happen. Maybe she had become smugly confident when it hadn't. But then, and here she smiled slightly, maybe it had. Maybe the past was littered with young women he'd had and discarded – how could she know?

If he'd had an army of lovers she should have been comforted, for if he'd left them for her then it meant she was more important to him. But this theory depressed her. She'd never needed anyone else, had never even thought of cheating on him. Her love for him had always consumed her.

Of course, the answer could be that men were different from women, that their sexual needs were stronger, uncontrollable. At that she shivered: intellectually she could understand, emotionally she found it all too distasteful.

She had been shocked all those years ago when she had learnt that Matthew's wife was pregnant. She'd accepted his explanation; she knew now she'd never really believed him. But the idea of his body entwined with Wendy's had disgusted her – and that had been his wife!

The whisky and sandwich arrived. She needed the drink even if she could have done without the interruption to her thinking. She settled back in the armchair taking the glass, ignoring the sandwich, knowing she'd only ordered it out of propriety.

All her past, her sacrifices, for what? She sat in the lonely room, in the large London hotel, unaware of the traffic in the street far below, unaware of the whirring of the vacuum cleaner in the corridor outside. And she contemplated the wreckage of her hopes and longings.

How often, when friends had been suffering from trauma, had she trotted out the old cliché that nothing was ever a waste? All experience was valuable – she'd said that so many times too. Now she shivered. Time, life, love, devotion – what had they made her? Nothing! What advantage had they given her? None!

She was as she was because of him. But what was that? Contained, distant, cold, even. She'd had to be, so that no one would know, so that she never let out the secret. And why? To protect Matthew. And what had it done to her? Isolated her, given her a life of snatched hours of happiness that punctuated the loneliness.

Why had she bothered? He hadn't. He hadn't thought of security, or Wendy's feelings, or hers when he'd been rutting and panting over the nurse in the rest room! She shuddered again.

'Oh, really!' she said aloud. Purposefully she drained the whisky.

Five hours on, running late as usual, Matthew Kingston arrived at reception. 'My name is Tillman. I've a room booked. Has my wife arrived?'

The receptionist's fingers flew over the computer keyboard. She paused and read the screen. Again she keyed in a list of instructions.

'Mrs Tillman has checked out, sir.'

'Checked out?'

'Early this afternoon.'

'Are you sure?'

'Yes, sir.'

'You mean she checked in and then out?'

'Yes, sir.'

'Where did she go?'

'I wouldn't know, sir. Do you still want the room?'

'Yes. No. Hang on – I've got to think.'

Matthew swung round towards the bar and, fortunately, didn't see the smirk on the receptionist's face. He ordered a large gin and tonic. Where was the stupid woman? She was so reliable normally. What could have happened? He didn't like this at all – he needed to talk to her, to try to counteract the gossip of that stupid woman Floss Yates. Should he phone her cottage? He'd certainly better phone Craig Nutting. Shit, he hated these complications. He ordered another drink. What had he done recently that might annoy? Of course, there had been the incident of the nurse in theatres when Edna Greenbank had barged in. But he'd sorted that, even if it had cost him an expensive dinner and an even more expensive suite in a ludicrously expensive country-house hotel. He thought he'd banged some loyalty and forgiveness into Edna!

Glynis sat at the small table in the dining room of a hotel north of Fellcar. She'd come by train and car, and had chosen this hotel since it held no memories of Matthew for her as so many other places did. She had booked in for several days. She needed time to reappraise how she felt and how she was to deal with *her* future.

7

Mo looked around the empty ward. She was the only patient to have been admitted so far. The staff nurse had explained that the other patients would be coming up from the gynaecology ward where they'd been housed before this special unit

215

had opened. Even then it wasn't officially open – the nurse had told her they hoped to get a Royal to do that some day soon.

Mo had wandered around the ward on the top floor of the hospital. The views were sensational, one side looking out at the sea and the other looking down on the town with a glimpse of the moors in the background. It was light and airy, thanks to the long casement windows: Mo had become accustomed to the ubiquitous sludgy green paint that dominated most of the hospital. Here, however, the green was banned and replaced with cream and pale yellow. The bed curtains were primrose and white check. Nice paintings hung on the walls. In the day room, at the far end of the ward, the furniture was comfortable and arranged more like a hotel lounge than a hospital room. Someone had gone to a lot of trouble to make this a cheerful place to be in remarkably uncheerful circumstances.

Mo had been able to choose her bed and had opted for one that overlooked the sea. Perhaps she was hoping that the stiff sea breeze would blow away what ailed her. She returned to her bed and unpacked her overnight bag into the light ash-wood locker. She sat on the easy chair by the window, opened her *OK* magazine – and read nothing.

Everything was moving too fast. It was as if she wasn't to be given time to adjust to one lot of bad news before she was hurtled into the next bleak scenario.

She had attended the clinic last week. She'd hated that clinic the first time she'd been, and she hated it even more now. The posters on the wall had offended her with their aggressive tone – *don't do this, eat this, don't drink that, exercise more, no smoking* – as if everything was her fault. She wondered, if she'd followed all the advice, would she have been here in the first place? She saw the blank expressions of the other patients as they waited their turn. Like dumb animals at an abattoir, she had found herself thinking, until, with a shudder, she wondered if she had the same resigned expression and forced herself to look alert. There were people who looked not only fitter than she but fitter than the staff tending them so solicitously. But there were others who looked as if they were about to die at any moment. Some were bald and others wore sadly obvious wigs. She began to play with her own hair, but stopped when it dawned on her that that smacked of 'Look at me, I've still got my crowning glory.' It hadn't been, she had been playing with it to reassure herself that it was there and she wanted to touch it in case it all fell out too. She kept moving her place as others came in, not wanting to sit too close to the obviously ill; she was not sure if it was from fear of catching what they had or that she just did not want to be near those who looked as she might one day. They were a motley group, from children to the elderly, men and women, fat and thin and, judging by the clothes and accents, from every social class. So what was the common link that had felled them when others weren't? She longed to be anywhere but here, and found it quite easy to persuade herself that probably it was all a ghastly mistake and she shouldn't be here in the first place.

When it was her turn, the young doctor was pleasant enough, she couldn't complain. She felt a fleeting annoyance that since he was so young he could not possibly be the consultant, as if her illness was not important enough for him to attend. To her it was the most important illness in the world. While he was speaking to her, his manner was odd, detached, which had made her feel as if she wasn't a person to him. He didn't seem to grasp how shocking his words were to her, how devastated he was making her feel. And as he spoke she sensed that just by being here she was no longer in control of her own life and future – that from now on things would be decided for her. But afterwards she had thought that maybe some of it had been her fault. Hadn't she sat with a silly smile on her face as he'd told her she was to come into hospital for *her* lump – though he had said *the* lump – to be investigated further. This lump was to be removed and tested to see if it was malignant or not and her lymphatic system was to be checked too, and if that was involved, though he'd said compromised, then she would need a course of chemotherapy. However, he'd ploughed on, she was most fortunate: normally she'd have had to wait for a bed, but since the new oncology unit was opening she could go in on Monday. She'd found herself gushing her thanks at her good luck!

It wasn't until afterwards that she had realised she hadn't asked him anything. What did the chemotherapy involve? Would the operation hurt? Where were her lymph glands and what did they do? That's what she needed to know. Why was it that the minute she entered a doctor's surgery all sense deserted her and she became an empty-headed idiot?

'Hi! Hit the jackpot, have you?'

Mo looked up to see Yvonne Clarke in a wheelchair, a potted plant on her lap and carrier bags crammed either side of her gaunt frame. Her colour was even worse, Mo saw.

'Sorry? I don't understand?'

'Further tests? Aren't you the lucky one!' Yvonne laughed and Mo saw that her tongue was furry and discoloured, while her breath smelt. Mo had to force herself not to reel back.

'Oh, yes, my lump's coming out. Do you know where my lymph glands are?'

Yvonne raised one scrawny arm and pointed to her armpit. 'Those are the ones they mean. They're everywhere and they're all interlinked. So, it's not a good idea, if you've got the lurg, for them to be involved. They're a generous lot and will spread it around to any other handy organs who might feel like being diseased. That's called metastasis – it's a handy word to listen out for when the bastards are talking over your head as if you have no brain and don't exist.'

'So it's serious?'

'You could say that.'

'And you?'

'Mine were compromised – bloody stupid way of putting it, isn't it? As if I'd been caught out with someone else's husband!' She laughed again and Mo wished she wouldn't. 'Did you tell your old man?'

'I did. It wasn't easy. He was very sweet but frightened.'

'So, he didn't do a runner?'

'No. But I have this sneaky idea he wished he could.' She laughed even if she found the subject far from amusing. 'I'm not expecting him to visit me here, that's for sure. He loathes hospitals.'

'And the kids?'

'At my sister-in-law's. She's being a brick. She's even doing my Christmas shopping for me. She's bought me all these books on alternative healing. I said, "Hang on, let's find out if I've got it first," but she wouldn't listen. She rushed out to the bookshop and says she's ordered another load.'

'Burn the lot!' Yvonne said, with a dismissive wave.

'Oh, I couldn't do that. There might be something in one of them – you never know. At least I'd feel I was doing something for myself.'

'There's no harm in the diets and all, I'll give you that. If you can stick to them, that is. No, it's all the positive-thinking crap that gets on my left *and* right – if I had them, that is!' Yvonne again laughed uproariously at her joke, which Mo thought was no joke at all.

'But all the research shows that people with a positive, happy attitude to life have less chance of getting cancer. So it must do some good,' Mo persisted.

'*Less chance of getting* is the operative phrase. What if you've *got it*? In any case, no doubt some bright spark will bring out another load of statistics and prove the opposite. They always do.' Yvonne looked out of the window behind Mo as if at something a long way off, though from her position in the wheelchair it was likely that all she could see was sky.

'Yvonne, you sound so bitter. What's up?'

'Me? Bitter? Never! I thank God every day for my luck and that I'm still around. No, what gets at me is giving people false hope. So you read the books and you meditate and you visualise your malignant cells until you're crackling with positive thoughts. And still it spreads. So what then? Did you fail? Did you not think positively enough? Is it your fault you're bloody well dying?' And to Mo's horror Yvonne burst into tears. She sat in her chair rigid with shock. Yvonne was a positive, cheerful person: why was she like this? And what was she thinking of, inflicting her behaviour on Mo like this?

At this thought Mo's hand shot to her mouth. She looked at Yvonne wide-eyed with horror at her own self-obsession, her own selfishness. 'Oh, Yvonne. What is it? What's happened?' And she was on her feet and putting her arm round the sobbing woman's shoulders with no thought of fetid breath or contamination. The plant slid from Yvonne's lap and its pot shattered on the floor. Mo looked about her for help just as Chrissy Galloway appeared in the doorway.

'Oh dear. What seems to be the problem? Yvonne, it's me, Chrissy, your new sister. Are you in pain? Can I help?' Chrissy looked questioningly at Mo.

'We were talking about positive attitudes to cancer and she suddenly burst into tears.'

'I think you'd better come with me, Yvonne. Let's find that bed you chose. Maybe a little rest. It's been a busy day with all the moving about. I expect you're tired.'

'Why do nurses have to be so sodding patronizing? I'm not a child.

I'm a fully grown woman with no tits! So treat me with some respect, okay? Or are you too dumb to understand?'

'I'm sorry, Yvonne. I didn't mean to sound like that. If you want to be angry, then go ahead. It's your privilege. Come on, let's get you back to bed.'

Mo watched as Chrissy pushed the wheelchair out of the ward. How awful it must feel to be spoken to like that when she was only trying to help. And sadly she realised Chrissy hadn't even recognised her, though she had known her immediately. Why was that? Had she changed so much, or had this lump made her look older and iller than she thought? She shivered and returned to *OK*, forced herself to shut out the incident and to read.

8

It was rapidly turning into one of *those* days, Chrissy thought, as she pushed Yvonne back to her own bed in the ward at the far end closest to her office.

'I went OTT just then, didn't I?'

'Understandably,' Chrissy answered, as she turned back the bed covers and smoothed the bottom sheet. 'You're tired.'

'Too right I'm tired,' Yvonne said as, with difficulty, she hoisted herself out of the chair.

'Hang on, I'll give you a hand,' Chrissy said, from the far side of the bed.

'I can manage.' Yvonne was unaware of how deeply she frowned as she edged her way to the side of the bed. She stood a second as if studying it, perhaps deciding the best way to climb in, thought Chrissy, as she busied herself arranging the carafe and glasses on the bedside table, making sure Yvonne did not guess she was watching her.

'You're like me, too short in the leg for these beds. How about using this stool?'

'You can't fool me, Chrissy, my love. You've got legs like a Bluebell girl. I know you want to help but I want to do this myself. I have to, don't you see? Otherwise I might just as well give up – now, this minute.'

'No, you won't, you're not the sort.'

'How the bloody hell would you know? We've only just met.'

'I've read your notes. But in any case experience and instinct tell me you're not a quitter.'

'I bloody well am. I've had enough. I don't want any more treatment, is that understood? I'm sick to death of feeling grim.' She'd got herself onto the bed and collapsed onto the pillows. At seeing her shoulders heaving Chrissy thought she was crying. She wasn't, she was laughing.

'What's the joke?'

'Did you just hear me?' Yvonne spluttered. 'I said I was *sick to death*. Well, I am, aren't I? Sick . . . and going to die.' Now she was crying. Chrissy hitched herself up beside her and put an arm round her and held her. She said nothing, this was not the time. She stroked Yvonne's hair – at least she'd kept that, she thought, even if it was thinner than once it had been. She felt the old sensations of uselessness as she cradled the woman. What was there to say? What words of comfort were there? It was impossible to picture the degree of anger and fear this woman was experiencing.

'It's not bloody fair!' she wailed. 'Why me?' She sobbed. 'Why me?' She repeated the mantra of the terminally ill, stricken long before their due time.

'I know, Yvonne. It's not easy.'

'Easy? Of course it's not sodding easy! What crap you women talk!' She glared. 'What can you possibly know about it?'

'I know enough to know that nothing I say can help you at this moment. I understand your frustration and your anger. All I can do is be here and hold you and let you swear and curse at me if it helps.'

Yvonne looked up and peered at her through tear-filled eyes. 'Am I being a pain?'

'Not really.' Chrissy smiled, aware that the storm was passing.

'Sod it. I wanted to be. Now you've spoilt it . . .' She was laughing again, that exhausting swinging from one mood to another, neither being how she felt. But the words did not exist for that.

'Are you feeling sick? I'll get you something for it. Have you had a digestive biscuit?'

'If I have to eat another of those flaming things I'll scream.'

'Have a peppermint.'

'You're risking turning into a pain yourself, Chrissy. I don't want anything except my clothes. I'm going home.'

'But, Yvonne —'

'No buts, Chrissy. What's the point? The doctor this morning was straight with me. I could wish he hadn't been. No, that's not fair — I asked him. Told him no bullshit. So, if I've got only weeks I want to go home and cuddle my dog and not feel sick any more.'

'Stay tonight. Talk it out with Sol tomorrow. Maybe he'll change the treatment.'

'No. I'm off. Even in this sodding contraption.' She pointed at the wheelchair. 'Do you know, Sister? People ignore you in that thing. Talk over the top of you. I was waiting for a lift last week and some people barged in front of me, got on and didn't hold the doors for me. Didn't even see me.'

'And you said nothing? Doesn't sound like you.' Chrissy smiled at the woman whose courage had moved everyone who'd dealt with her over the years. Now she'd given in to what ailed her and Chrissy couldn't help but think good luck to her. If their situations were reversed she doubted if she'd have lasted half as long. 'I'll give Sol a bell.'

'I don't want him trying to change my mind. Promise?'

'I promise. But he'll want to discuss medication and ancillary help for you.'

'One thing, Chrissy. I shouldn't have carried on like that in front of the new patient. Don't tell her, will you? Say I was suddenly discharged. I was shameless in there, totally selfish. Mo might be one of the lucky ones, after all.'

'Mo? Did you say Mo? Not Mo Fordham? I know her. Hell, what must she be thinking of me?'

Yvonne calmed as well as could be expected. Sol contacted. Half a dozen phone calls dealt with. An influx of patients sent up from Gynaecology and settled in their beds. Three new patients welcomed and admitted. A belligerent husband reassured. Finally Chrissy had a chance to phone the office to make an appointment to see Glynis only to be told she had taken a few days' leave but that Chrissy could be fitted in on Friday. Only then was she free to get back to Mo.

'Mo, I'm sorry. I was so involved with Yvonne.'

'Don't worry. I thought I'd aged so much you didn't recognize me,' Mo said, as if she was apologizing for herself.

'Flapping, that's what I was doing. It's the ward's first day up and running and I want everything to be perfect. And then I behave in this fine way – not welcoming an old friend who's a new patient.' She sat on the edge of the bed. 'Are these your girls? They're so pretty.' And for a while they talked of Kerry and Katya, just like the old school-friends they were, not like patient and nurse, thought Mo. As they chatted Chrissy was fretting about all she had to do. She really hadn't time to chat like this. That was the trouble with this job – there was never enough time.

'Now, did Nurse Bing explain things to you satisfactorily?' She finally got back to the business in hand.

'No, she didn't,' Mo said baldly, thinking, what the hell? 'She was busy,' she added – apologizing again, Chrissy thought.

'I'd better explain it for you then. Everything is done under a general anaesthetic so you'll feel nothing. In fact, everyone looks forward to their pre-med – the drug we give you to relax you before the op. As you know, the lump will come out. Lumpectomy – a grand name, isn't it? And the surgeon will also remove tissue in the immediate area as a precaution. If, and I only say if, it's malignant then your lymph glands, here,' she indicated on her body 'will be checked to make sure nothing has spread.'

'They can take it round the body. Cause metastasis, Yvonne called it.'

'That's right.'

'I like to know what's what.'

'If you do then we'll tell you. People vary in what they want or need to know.'

'I don't like being kept in the dark.' Mo said this with a marked lack of conviction, which she was unaware that Chrissy picked up.

'If it's just the lump involved then you'll have six weeks of radiotherapy. You come into Outpatients for that. However, if the lymph glands are affected – and it doesn't follow that they are – then you will need chemotherapy as well as the radiotherapy. A simple lumpectomy and you'll be out before you know it. With the lymph system involved you'll be in longer.'

'How long?' Mo's mind was already racing over whether the children would be all right with her sister-in-law; how much food was in the freezer; would Robbie remember to feed the guinea pig, and what about his shirts?

'It varies. We have to insert draining tubes and until the drainage stops you'll have to be here. You'll also need physio on your arm to stop it stiffening up. It all sounds grimmer than it is.' She smiled, hopefully confidently.

'Will it hurt?'

'Probably a little soreness at the wound site.'

'If I need chemotherapy where do I go?'

'You'll come here to this ward. That's part of my job . . .' And Chrissy explained the possible courses the doctors might take, although even as she spoke, she knew that Mo was absorbing only a fraction of what she was telling her.

'Will I lose my hair?' Mo asked the question that all women asked.

'Not necessarily. It will depend on which drug the doctors decide to use.'

'I won't wake up and find my breast has been removed, will I?'

'Mastectomy is a treatment that's still used, but it's getting less and less, and certainly in this hospital our doctor prefers to use chemotherapy and radiation only, when possible.'

'I never liked my breasts much, I always thought they were too small. But for all that I'd rather hang on to them.' She laughed in an embarrassed way.

'I don't blame you. Let's just worry about one thing at a time, shall we?'

'Just now, Yvonne – she said trying other things was a waste of time.'

'Nothing is ever that. You mean alternative therapies? Some patients are helped enormously, others aren't. But please let us know what you intend to do and never stop your medication for an alternative. If you feel something is doing you good, then it's certain it is.' Chrissy heard herself trotting out the careful line, encouraging as much as possible, but not really promising anything that might jeopardise the hospital's position.

'So why was Yvonne so angry?'

'Yvonne was fed up. We all get fed up, don't we?'

'You talking about me? I heard!'

Chrissy and me turned to see Yvonne walking tall and straight towards Mo's bed. When she reached it she leant against it. 'I've come to say goodbye and good luck.'

'Are you off? But I thought –'

'Nah. Just seen the doc. He was surprised I was so much better – said he didn't want me cluttering up a bed.'

'And the wheelchair?'

'Taken away. He told me I was being a lazy cow. Now, Mo, my love, don't let these buggers get you down. And, if you'll take my advice, get some cannabis – it'll do you more good than all the crap they'll want to give you. Right. I'm off before they change their minds.' She bent down and kissed Mo goodbye on the cheek.

'I'll see you off.' Chrissy walked beside Yvonne, wary that she might stumble and fall, but not touching her. They got to the ward door. Yvonne waved through the window at Mo. As soon as she passed out of sight her legs buckled. Chrissy caught her and supported her, calling out to a passing nurse to push the wheelchair closer.

'That was very brave of you, Yvonne. Walking in there unaided must have been so painful.'

'Nah. Nothing to it. I had to make amends, didn't I?' Even as she began to smile, it failed and converted into a grimace.

9

'Do you think you'll stay?' Dawn appeared in the kitchen doorway, a glass of wine in her hand.

'What? Here or at St Edith's?' Chrissy looked up at her. She was checking the food in the oven. 'It's only a chicken and mushroom pie, courtesy of Sainsbury's, and a salad – I hope you don't mind?' She was unaware she'd changed the subject.

'Mind? After the hospital slop I shall think I'm in heaven. Would you like me to lay the table?'

'Bless you. Here.' Chrissy handed her a tray with cutlery, glasses and napkins, which she'd got ready before leaving for work. All that was needed was to wash the ready-bagged salad. Her father would have had a fit at such extravagance. She swirled the lettuce in the salad spinner. 'If you'll excuse me, I'll just get changed,' she called into the sitting room, where Dawn – who, since it was her day off, was already in mufti – was setting the table.

In the bathroom she washed quickly – she'd have liked to bath, as she always did to get rid of the feel and smell of the hospital, but with Dawn here she hadn't time. She made do with clean jeans, a baggy jumper and a quick flick of the hairbrush.

'It's kind of you to invite me,' Dawn said, as she returned.

'My pleasure. It can't be much fun in a bedsit.'

'You can say that again! This is a lovely cottage. Mind if I snoop?'

'Be my guest.'

'I love looking at people's possessions, seeing what they're really like,' Dawn added.

Chrissy fussed over the table realigning knives and forks, changing the position of the glasses. 'Sorry, there was nothing wrong – it's living alone, you know, you get set in your ways.' She was flustered at her fussy actions, which could easily have been misinterpreted, but Dawn, studying a small watercolour, didn't seem to have noticed.

'None of your husband's paintings are on display.'

'Well, no. I –' Chrissy paused, about to explain that they were at Ewan's mother's house since she could not stand to be in the same house as them. 'But how did you know Ewan was an artist? I never told you,' she said instead.

'Everyone at the hospital knows. Jazz Poundman's the oracle where you and your husband are concerned. Her aunt's a nurse in Cornwall.'

'Oh, that Jazz woman. She haunts me.'

'She's not too bad when you get to know her.'

'Her patients wouldn't agree with you. Right, you ready? The pie must be done by now.'

In the kitchen Chrissy clattered about as if the noise of crockery and oven doors slamming could obliterate talk of Ewan and Jazz. Already she was regretting that she had felt sorry for Dawn and invited her to supper. She hadn't remembered, when she invited her that, of course, Dawn had no transport so she'd either have to run her back to her digs or Dawn would have to stay the night. She'd opted for the latter, but if she was going to go on about those two all evening she'd live to regret it. *Stop it*, Chrissy's inner voice said sharply. She leant against the sink and forced herself to calm down. She must stop getting in a state like this when Ewan was mentioned. Of course Dawn was curious – everyone was. She must stop this type of reaction: it made her seem guilty in her own eyes so goodness knows what others thought.

'Here we go. Sainsbury's finest.' She held the pie in front of her, all smiles as she returned to the room. They settled to their meal, sitting opposite each other at the small gate-legged oak table.

'Such a pretty table. You *are* lucky.' Dawn stroked the polished surface. Chrissy poured their wine and they began to talk about the different personalities at the hospital – though, fortunately, not Jazz.

'Shall I do the honours?' Dawn picked up the wine bottle and replenished their glasses.

It was an age since Chrissy had spent time alone with a woman friend, and she found she was enjoying the inconsequential chatter, the light-hearted gossip, the talk of clothes and make-up and men. Dawn made her laugh with anecdotes of the creeps in her life. 'There's something about me, I always attract the bastards!'

'Join the club!' Chrissy raised her glass, giggling. 'Oops, it's empty. How sad. Fancy another bottle?'

'Do bears crap in the woods?'

As Chrissy got another bottle from the fridge she discovered she'd already had too much to drink and was weaving slightly. What the hell? she thought. She hadn't had fun talk like this in years. She concentrated hard on walking in a straight line back into the sitting room where they were now ensconced in armchairs either side of the inglenook.

'I love a fire like this.'

'Russell Newson fixed it for me – or, rather, showed me how to light it without dying of smoke inhalation.'

'I didn't know you knew him – socially, that is.'

'Oh, I don't. He was on the cliff, out for a walk. He rescued me from the smoke.'

'You look like the cat who had the cream.'

'Well, he is rather dishy, isn't he?'

'He's married. Married men mean only one thing – disaster.'

'Can't I look?'

'All right, then. You can look but not touch!' And they both shrieked with laughter.

'It must be awful losing the love of your life as you did. Just awful.' Dawn shook her head in sympathy at the thought.

'Well . . . it wasn't quite like that. I hated my husband,' she said suddenly.

'Chrissy, I'm so sorry. I didn't mean –'

'No. I've never really told anyone – not everything. Not how, come the end, I hated him and was trying to get away.'

'Why did you marry him, if you don't mind my asking?' Dawn said practically.

'I loved him in the beginning – he was so alive, so good-looking, so attentive. He made me feel alive, gave me the confidence I was lacking. I'd have done anything for him, but then . . .' She stopped and sat gazing into the fire. Quietly Dawn rose, topped up their glasses and sat on the rug at her feet. She took Chrissy's hand.

'Talk, Chrissy, love. It'll help you. You've got to let it all out. You can trust me.'

Chrissy's shoulders slumped. 'Trust? What an innocent little word.' She laughed – at least, the sound was of a laugh but it contained no joy. 'I *trusted* him with my life and love, and he shattered it all. He'd given me all that love and tenderness just to take it all away again. But why?' She looked down at Dawn, her eyes brimming with tears.

'Some men are control freaks if they're with the wrong woman.'

'Oh, I was the wrong one. But who'd be right for someone like him?'

'Someone who knew how to handle him, but you're not explaining yourself. What was he like?'

'Jealous, possessive.'

'Some women like that.'

'Oh, in moderation, I agree, it can be flattering, but not when you can't make a move. I couldn't go to the shops, take a phone call without a grilling afterwards that could go on for hours and hours. He opened my mail. Then he began following me. I thought I was going mad as well.

'Then he killed a dog one day, and I suddenly saw everything so clearly. I looked at the dead dog and I knew I had to get out or one day he'd kill me. So I ran away – I didn't know what I was doing, but I had to be on my own to think.' She sighed deeply.

'And that was when he killed himself?'

'Yes. How clever of you to guess.'

'It must have made the guilt intolerable.'

'Unbelievable – but I think I'm getting out of it now.'

'Will you ever?'

'Oh, God, I hope so. You see, I'm sure he didn't mean to do it. I think he must have miscalculated the dose. He didn't mean to die.'

'Why do you say that?' Dawn was still holding her hand, which was comforting.

'Because we had a fishmonger who always called on Tuesdays. If I wasn't there he made himself a cup of coffee – we were half-way on his rounds. I think Ewan planned for Ted to find him – not unconscious, just acting strangely, and then rush him to hospital. I'd be contacted and rush back to him full of contrition. Only he chose the day Ted's van broke down and he was three hours late – far too late for Ewan, who was dead when Ted got there.'

'How dreadful for you.'

'I couldn't grieve, you see. I just felt enormous relief. I didn't have to be frightened any more. I realised then that I'd wanted him dead for some time without really knowing it – that's where the guilt lies.'

'I'm sorry, Chrissy.'

'I shouldn't be loading all this on you.'

'Why not? I'd like to think I was your friend.'

'I've never told anyone, except the police, the whole story.'

'Then I'm honoured.'

'Bless you, Dawn, you're a true mate. Oh, really, this is silly. Let's round the evening off with a brandy. Just talking I feel better already.' Chrissy was on her feet and finding the bottle. She felt exhausted now and longed for bed and sleep, but she also felt strangely light, as if the talking had removed something – bitterness or guilt, she hoped.

'I've set the alarm for seven. Would you like tea or coffee first thing?' she asked later, as she showed Dawn to her room.

'Tea, please. Oh, look – the cat your father won for you.' Dawn swooped on the gaudy flower-encrusted ornament.

'How on earth did you know?'

'Because my daddy won one for me too. Only a daddy would give you something so ghastly.' She laughed gaily. 'See? We've a lot in common, you and me!'

CHAPTER SIX

I

Lynn could not fail to notice the frigid atmosphere in the surgery as she went about her work. While she was involved with the women attending her family planning clinic it did not matter – she was otherwise occupied. She wasn't too bothered when Enid had virtually hurled the patients' notes at her – she was far too used to the woman's rudeness. Only the doctors, who could do no wrong, and the practice manager, who was her immediate boss, were exempt from Enid's surliness. But the unfriendly feeling in the air got to Lynn at the coffee breaks and at the end of the day, when normally they chatted and the medical teams conferred. For nearly a week now she'd been left out of conversations, no one offered to pour her coffee and people left the staff room promptly when she walked in.

'I felt I had to say something,' Lynn said to Ella Thompson, the other practice nurse, when she found her alone in the kitchen one day. She had stood in the doorway so that Ella couldn't escape. 'This thing is just dragging on.'

'I think accusations with no proof are snide.'

'The pharmaceutical orders show there's something amiss,' Lynn said defensively.

'Oh, that could easily be a clerical error,' Ella said, looking uncomfortable.

'Come off it, Ella. You know that's not so.'

'It could be anyone, not necessarily Giles. Why pick on him?' Ella looked indignant now. Lynn was aware she had a soft spot for Giles and lived in hope that one day he might notice her – not that he'd given any indication of it.

'Anyone? Who? Me, you mean?'

'Did I say that?'

'No, but who does the pharmacy lists? Yours truly. Don't you see that's why I had to speak up? Otherwise I just knew I'd end up being accused.'

'But you've no proof. You said that at the meeting.'

'I hoped Giles would explain it away. Say he'd made an error or maybe had over-ordered to help someone out – you know how sometimes they do that if they think they can't afford to pay their prescription charges.' She'd thrown that in to try to placate Ella – old Dr Henderson might, but she'd never known Giles Middleton help anyone, least of all a patient.

'You should have checked it out more thoroughly, Lynn. You could have checked on the computer.'

'I did. It wasn't down to any of the likely patients.'

'There you are, then.'

'No. Computer files can be altered.'

'Then the date, when it had last been altered, would show.'

'None of the dates is different from the consultations.'

'There you are, then.' Ella repeated, insufferably smug now.

'It could mean that the date on the document was changed too, to match the automatic dating on the machine.'

'Then you'll have to check with the appointment book. Make sure everything tallies.'

'That'll take for ever.' Lynn looked aghast.

'Then you shouldn't have started all this, should you? Not if you weren't willing to see it through.'

'It's not that. It's down to time. I really thought you'd understand, Ella. That you'd care.'

'I do care. I hate to see a good, dedicated doctor accused like that. You're lucky he's as nice as he is and isn't suing you for defamation of character. And when you sounded off about the woman and her foetus having a cleft palate. Well!'

'That isn't right and you damn well know it isn't.'

'But, Lynn, you heard him. He told us he never said any such thing. That the woman had got the wrong end of the stick.'

'I don't think she had. You didn't listen to her or hear her crying. You weren't the one who comforted her.'

'Come on, Lynn. You know how ignorant some people can be about their bodies – half of them don't even know where their uterus is, let alone grasp what the doctor's telling them.'

'That's so patronising, Ella!'

'You needn't get ratty with me just because you've made a mess of things. I still can't believe it. You, of all people. You were always so professional. Now, if you'll excuse me, I've got a diabetics clinic to run.'

Lynn had stood transfixed in the kitchen. She was hurt. She and Ella had always worked well together and had respected each other. Now here they were sniping and calling into doubt their abilities. Perhaps Ella was right: maybe she had been a fool.

'Sod that!' she said aloud to the empty kitchen. She'd stay after work. Ella was right. She'd have to check the appointments book against the computer entries. There was a discrepancy in there and she was determined to find it.

It was quiet in the surgery, except for the clicking of computer keys and the rustling of paper as Lynn leafed through the large appointments book, checking each patient's notes on the computer to match their attendance. She'd been at work on this task for nearly two hours and had only just got started on the Gs. Her neck ached, she was hungry and she was tired.

'Lynn?'

Her head jerked up, she clutched at her chest. 'Giles! You gave me such a start.' She laughed nervously and felt embarrassed at being caught out.

'It's late for you still to be here. What are you doing?'

'It's your day off.'

'I needed a book. You still checking me out?' He grinned expansively.

'Not necessarily, but there has to be a discrepancy somewhere. I've got to find it, Giles.'

'I understand that. After all, because the pharmacy list is your responsibility you're under a cloud, aren't you?'

'Giles, I'm so pleased you understand that. No one else seems to.'

She leant back in the chair and brushed her hair off her face in a gesture of relief.

'I don't want us falling out, do you? The atmosphere here this past week has been pretty grim, hasn't it?'

'I'd agree with that. But at least it's shown you how popular you are. Me? No one wants to know.' Lynn laughed ironically, but looked sad.

'Honestly, Lynn, it's not down to me. I don't know what's gone on or who's buggering about, but I promise you I've done nothing wrong.' Giles perched on the edge of the desk, his face serious.

'Then there's all the more reason for me to check these records out, isn't that so?'

Giles looked thoughtful and eased himself off the desk. 'Fancy a drink?'

'I don't drink.'

'What, never? Come on, just this once. Show we're friends again.'

'Just a little one, then.' Lynn didn't want a drink, but if Giles was willing to make the peace it would be churlish of her to refuse.

'I've only got whisky.'

'Couldn't be better,' she said, and began to close down the computer. He might be being friendly, but she wondered if he was putting up a smoke-screen. After all, he was still denying that he was involved and she was convinced he was.

Giles reappeared with two glasses of whisky. 'Sorry. I can't get the ice tray out so I've added a smidgen of water – we don't want to drown it, do we?' They clinked glasses. 'Here's to a speedy resolution,' he said, smiling smoothly.

'I'll drink to that,' she said, with feeling.

Half an hour later Lynn was in her car, driving home and going over and over the problem in her mind. The trouble with Giles was that, in his presence, everything he said seemed right. It was when she was away from him that the doubts crept in. She peered through the windscreen, The lights at the side of the dark road seemed to be moving. The trouble with Giles – She shook her head. She'd just thought that, hadn't she? She felt hot and quickly wound down her window. The car veered across the road. Lynn slammed on the brakes just as a car with a flashing blue light screeched to a halt beside her.

2

Ever since her evening with Dawn, Chrissy had felt an easiness about the past she had not felt before. It was odd that, never having told anyone the whole story of herself and Ewan, merely bits and pieces, she should have chosen someone she barely knew. She'd heard people say often enough that it was easier to unburden yourself to a stranger, so this looked like the proof. More likely too much wine, she thought, and pushed open the door of her grandmother's ward.

'How are you, Gran?'

'You look tired,' Daphne said, peering accusingly at Chrissy.

'We're not discussing me.'

'I'm fine.'

'You don't look it.'

'No need to be personal.' Daphne laughed, but disintegrated into coughing. Chrissy picked up her water jug, and saw that it was empty.

'I'll pop along to the kitchen and fill this up.'

'Bless you. I've been dying for a drink.'

'You should have asked.'

'What? This lot? What would be the point? There isn't a nurse on duty in this ward on this shift who isn't deaf.'

Jazz and an assistant nurse were in the kitchen, drinking coffee and eating sandwiches.

'Come to see Daphne?' Jazz asked.

'Mrs Galloway? Yes.' Chrissy ran the cold-water tap. Judging from the suppressed giggles behind her she could guess that Jazz was pulling a face at her or something equally childish. 'Some old ladies like to be addressed formally, I'd have thought you knew that, Jazz.' She spoke calmly as she rinsed out the jug.

'And most prefer we use Christian names,' Jazz defended herself.

'But not my grandmother. Why didn't you ask her? Why presume?'

'I wasn't aware you'd been posted to this ward, Chrissy.' Jazz was studying her fingernails archly.

'Don't like the criticism, Jazz? Well, I'm sorry, but while my grandmother's a patient here, I'll be taking an interest. And while I'm about it, don't you think the water jugs should be checked?' She turned back from the sink just in time to see Jazz poking her tongue out at her. 'Oh, Jazz, really. Why don't you grow up?'

'I should watch it, if I were you, Chrissy. You've only just joined us and your track record hasn't been *that* impressive so far, has it?' Jazz smiled sweetly. 'And I'm sure you don't need me to spell out what I mean.'

Chrissy wiped drips of water from the side of the jug. She could feel anger growing, but forced herself to control it and not answer back: this tit-for-tat was undignified and would get her nowhere. As she walked out of the kitchen, they did not bother to restrain their laughter.

Nurses like Jazz made her mad, she thought, as she returned to Daphne's bed. There were always one or two like her and it was a constant mystery why they had become nurses in the first place: they resented the work; they were invariably idle but used much energy to avoid tasks; they complained all the time of their lot and loathed the patients. She'd seen how they manipulated their charges, playing off one against the other, confusing them by being nice one day, a bitch the next. They had favourites so that there was always someone on the ward they could guarantee would speak up for them, if trouble arose, in glowing terms. She supposed they liked the power they felt they had. The poor public, naïvely thinking that all nurses were angels could never quite adjust to having a rogue one around.

'There you go, Gran.' Back at Daphne's bed she poured a glass of water.

Daphne gulped thirstily at the water. 'Oh, that's bliss. Better than a gin and tonic any day.'

'Gran, are you often without water?'

'Too often. They're idle cows. And that Jazz is a bully. You have to pee to order too. You can't get a bedpan when you need one. See that old lady two beds along? Poor old cow had rung and rung her bell and called out. Then, when inevitably she wet her bed, oh, the fuss they made! Call themselves nurses – they're a disgrace to your profession.' Daphne snorted with indignation, but Chrissy noted she was plucking at the top sheet of her bed with agitation.

'I had a word with Jazz about the water.'

'Oh, Chrissy, you never did!' Her fingers clutched at the linen. 'Now she'll have it in for me, you can bet on that.'

'Gran, I'm sorry. I don't want to cause you any trouble.' She smoothed the crumpled sheet and, with a shock, understood that her grandmother was scared. She'd blithely thought that no one could put the wind up Daphne. 'Gran, are you frightened about something or someone?'

'Me? Frightened?' Daphne looked away from Chrissy, biting her bottom lip as she did.

'If you are you must tell me, so I can help,' Chrissy coaxed her.

Daphne sat silent, gazing stolidly at the wall opposite. For a moment, Chrissy thought she was not going to speak but eventually she took a deep breath, as if the extra oxygen would give her courage. 'Only of that Jazz. The ward's lovely when Sister's on duty. But that bitch – she gives me the willies!' And Daphne shuddered.

'Gran, I'm going to have to do something about this.'

'Are you sure you have to? Who will you speak to? Sister? That won't do you any good. She's so sweet she wouldn't believe you – she wouldn't be able to grasp that someone on her ward could be so awful.'

'Then I'll talk to Glynis Tillman. She'll sort it out. If you let someone like Jazz get away with it she'll get worse.' She glanced at her watch. 'Heavens, look at the time – I'm setting up a self-help group this evening.'

'What for? Those with breast problems?'

'That's right.'

'I hope they're paying you overtime.'

'How is it, Gran, that you always hit the nail on the head? No, I volunteered. There's not enough funds in the coffers.'

'You let people put on you, Chrissy. It's not right. Never undersell yourself.'

'That wouldn't help my ladies, though, would it?' She moved the chair she'd been using back against the wall.

'Have you had those post-mortem reports on those patients you were worried about?'

'Not yet.'

'Then what's the delay? Who's playing silly buggers with your sanity?'

3

It was cold and raining when Chrissy left the hospital and made for her car. She was feeling pleased with herself: the first meeting of her support group had gone well. Her main worry had been that too few would turn up. In fact, there had been twelve, ten rustled up by Lesley Bing and two from the ward. She was only sorry that Mo had been too groggy from her anaesthetic to attend.

She started her car and switched on the windscreen wipers. It was always sticky getting a new group up and running. English restraint and years of not discussing personal matters were so ingrained that it normally took time for them to loosen up. Tonight they'd been lucky: one extrovert, that was all it needed, saying exactly how she felt – angry, scared – and they were away. The reward she looked for was the relief on their faces as they realised they were not alone; that here was a group who understood exactly what they were going through, the helter-skelter of emotions they felt.

Chrissy swung out of the car park. Of course she was the first to acknowledge that such discussion groups weren't for everyone. There would always be those for whom confessing their problems made matters worse. But no one was coerced or tricked into taking part – that would negate everything she was trying to do for them. Still, she thought, it was famously mean of the managers not to pay her and her nurses' for their time.

Along Hursty Avenue, the road ahead was blocked by a badly parked car and a police car, its lights flashing. With the rain allowing her such poor visibility, Chrissy decided it would be safer if she waited until the police waved her on. She was about to change the cassette when, in the headlights, she saw a wet and wan-looking Lynn Petch. She was out of her car in a trice.

'Lynn, are you all right? Have you had an accident?'

'Who's that? Who are you?'

'Officer, what's happened?'

'Are you a friend of this young woman?'

'I am. Is she hurt?'

'No, she's lucky. But she's coming to the station. She won't give us her address.'

'I would – I can't remember it, honest.' Lynn was slurring her words. She was obviously drunk. Despite her longing to get home, Chrissy felt she could not leave her friend in this state.

'She lives in Timber Lane, Officer. Number forty-two. I'll come to the station with you, if you want, Lynn?'

'Please.'

It was one of those decisions that, the minute she made it, Chrissy knew she would regret. And so it was. By the time they arrived Lynn was even more incoherent. It wasn't a case of she wouldn't give them a sample, it was that she couldn't. As the police became more irritated with her, the more confused and noisy Lynn became. She must have had a tankful to be in this state, thought Chrissy, who decided to telephone for Terry, since Lynn was incapable.

'Lynn? Drunk? I don't believe it,' he said, his voice a mixture of disbelief and indignation.

'I'm sorry but she's in a rare old state, Terry. I think you should get down here.'

'But Lynn rarely drinks – a glass of wine, maybe, but that's all and that's usually when she's safe at home.'

'Yes, Terry. I understand.' She felt sorry for the man. Maybe Lynn was a secret drinker despite her protestations that she didn't touch the stuff.

Even with Terry on his way, Chrissy felt a heel as she slipped out of the police station. But, she had reasoned with herself, there was nothing she could do to help, not now that Lynn had been led away to be examined by the police surgeon. And the last thing she wanted was to be part of Terry's embarrassment; the presence of a friend might make it harder for him.

Sabine stood in the heavy rain in the middle of the driveway.

'I know you're in there, you bastard!' she yelled, as she bent and picked up a handful of gravel and hurled it at the window of the second-floor flat. But she was small and had never been sporty; consequently most of it missed and rattled the panes of the flat below.

'What the hell?' The window was flung open. 'What the bloody hell do you think you're doing?' An irate man's head appeared. 'Stop that or I'll call the police.'

'It's all right, Trev. I'll deal with this.' The front door had opened, and Giles appeared. 'Sorry about the racket. Any damage?'

'No, but it gave me a start. You never know these days, do you?'

'Won't happen again. Say sorry to the nice man, Sabine.' Giles held her upper arm and squeezed it. When she did not respond, he squeezed it again.

'Sorry. I shouldn't have done that,' she said, in a disgruntled tone.

Giles led her through the glass door of the apartment block, across the hallway and up the stairs, along the landing and through his front door. He did not let go, nor did he speak until the door was shut firmly behind him.

'Don't ever do that to me again,' he said, ominously quiet.

'But you didn't answer. And I knew you were here,' Sabine whined.

'I told you on the telephone I couldn't see you. Don't you understand English?'

'Why couldn't you see me? I know it's your day off.'

'I had other things to do.'

'You've got another woman.'

At this Giles threw back his head and laughed. 'Of course I haven't. I just told you, I'm busy. You'll have to be patient.'

'But I hate being patient.'

'Then you'll have to try. Now, please will you leave? I've had a difficult day.'

'Don't make me, Giles. Please let me stay with you. Russell's at home and I can't deal with the atmosphere. You know what it's like.'

'No, I don't know.'

'I want to move in with you – get away from him.'

'Are you crazy? And have me struck off?'

'I wouldn't do anything like that. I'd never report you to the GMC.'

'No, but he might. Don't be so bloody stupid.' Giles stepped back, putting distance between them.

'Giles – please, I –'

'Sabine, be a good girl. Just go home. I'll give you a bell.'

'But you won't. You're tired of me, aren't you?' She pouted, but this time she was not play-acting: the pout held her hurt as her lovely eyes filled with tears.

'I think we should see less of each other – just for the time being. I don't want any fuss – or trouble.'

'Giles. What's up? Need any help?'

Sabine swung round to see a man she didn't know in the doorway of Giles's sitting room.

'No thanks, Craig. Just a little local difficulty.'

'You shit!' Sabine kicked out and landed a sharp blow on Giles's shin, which made him yelp.

Craig laughed. 'Well, you're a little fire-cracker, aren't you?' He grinned at Sabine.

'Oh, oh!' She stamped her foot. 'Go boil your heads!' she snapped, and was mortified at the gale of merriment she heard as she banged the front door behind her.

Terry held the steering wheel so tightly that his knuckles showed white. His mouth was set in a thin line. Easy-going, tolerant Terry was angry. Lynn, beside him in the passenger seat, was crying quietly.

'Oh, for goodness sake, shut up sniffling.' He spoke in an uncharacteristically brisk manner.

'I can't stop.'

'Of course you can. Just pull yourself together.'

'Speaking to me like that isn't helping.'

'How else do you expect me to be? If there's one thing I loathe and despise it's drunk drivers.'

'I'm not drunk! How many times do I have to say it?' Lynn slumped back in the seat. It was difficult to talk: the words emerged muffled and slurred and the effort required seemed to have exhausted her.

'Can't you hear yourself? You're as pissed as a rat. And arguing the toss with the sergeant, as you did back at the station, didn't help.' Terry drove onto the hard standing outside their house. He turned to her. '*You*, of all people. I never expected to see you in this state.' And, switching off the engine, he climbed out of the car, slammed the door and without a backward glance marched across his cosseted lawn and into the house, slamming the front door with equal ferocity.

Lynn sat in the car, shocked and horrified at everything that had happened to her and with such alarming speed. She was puzzled. She knew she was not drunk, but if she wasn't what had happened to her? It was all too difficult to work out, especially with her mind in such a muddle – as if she and her brain were on a carousel going round and round in a thick fog. She had a lot to work out, but for the time being she did not know how or where to begin. She'd stopped crying now – there didn't seem to be much point in it – and suddenly she felt so tired and all she wanted to do was curl up and sleep. So she did.

As she sat in her cottage and waited for the doorbell to ring Glynis was quite calm. She felt rested after her few days away in the hotel and, to her surprise, after the huge storm of emotion, she felt almost detached, as if this drama was happening to someone else and she was just an interested bystander.

It amused her when at the first trill of the bell she checked her watch and saw that he was punctual, to the second – that must be the first time in the whole of their relationship.

'Good evening, Matthew.' She held open the door for him as she had on so many occasions, smiled pleasantly as she had times without number.

'Darling – where were you? I waited and waited at the hotel. Were you taken ill suddenly, to leave like that?'

'No, Matthew, I wasn't ill. If anything I would say I'd begun to recover. A drink?'

'A large Scotch, please.'

'Is that wise when you're operating tomorrow?'

'You've never queried my drinking before.' He sounded offended.

'As I've not queried many things. But as you wish.' She poured a generous measure of *Highland Park* whisky, but nothing for herself. He looked at her quizzically as she handed him the tumbler.

'You're acting a bit strange, Glyn, my love.'

'Am I your love, Matthew? Truly?'

'Of course you are, my sweet. What a thing to say after all these years!'

'Yes, it has been a long time. Maybe too long. Is that why you were discovered in a compromising position with a young theatre nurse last week?' She really was surprising herself at how calm and rational she sounded.

'My darling, what *are* you going on about? Me? With whom, what, when?' He laughed confidently, as if at a good joke.

'I travelled up to London with Edna Greenbank. She confided in me the circumstances she'd found you in – "going at it hammer and tongs" was the somewhat unoriginal way in which she described your actions. She asked my advice, what to do. No doubt you find that amusing too?' Glynis thought how smoothly she had trotted out the words that had led to the breaking of her heart.

'Oh, really! Edna, of all people. Is that all? You had me worried for a minute – so serious, so on your dignity with me.' He sat himself down in an easy chair and stretched contentedly. 'Come here. You haven't kissed me yet.' He patted the arm of the chair. She took a step back, unaware that she had done so. He leant forward. 'Oh, my darling, you're not telling me that you listened to – let alone believed – Edna's ramblings, are you?'

'She said she'd seen you.'

'Darling, I've never told you this before because I didn't want to upset you or cause problems between colleagues. But Edna has had, well, I suppose you'd call it a *crush* on me ever since she joined the hospital staff. I'm forever fending her off. Dearest, it's all in her imagination, nothing more.'

'If, as you say, she had a crush on you then why would she tell me? What good would that do her – to lie about you with another woman?'

'God knows what goes on in Edna's inscrutable mind. To make you jealous, perhaps. To get you to kick me out of your life. I don't know.' He shrugged easily, as if the whole incident was of no importance. 'Any more whisky going?'

Like an automaton Glynis took his glass and returned with it to the drinks tray. As she refilled it she was unaware of how intently Matthew watched her.

'But, if that were the case,' she turned to face him, 'that would mean she knew about us? How could she possibly know?' She frowned deeply.

'Dear Glynis. I know you like to think this is our secret but, if truth be told, I reckon half the hospital knows.'

Glynis sat down suddenly. 'Surely not? Oh, how dreadful,' she said, with genuine distress.

'Why? What's dreadful about it? I'd like the whole world to know about us and our great love for each other. It saddens me – and it always has – that because of Wendy we have to live as we do.' He leant forward and took her hand in his. 'I'm proud of your love for me. Truly proud.'

At his words the calmness and control deserted Glynis and to his horror, as well as her own, she began to cry. It was not a noisy crying, not a wailing, not a shriek of pain, but rather a silent, sibilant weeping that shook Glynis to the core and was all the more heartrending for its silence. After the initial shock of seeing Glynis in tears, something he had never witnessed in all the years he had known her, Matthew was on his feet and kneeling at her feet. 'Oh, my poor, sad darling, don't cry. Please don't spoil your pretty face – not for me.' And he held her tight to allay her fears . . .

Later, as they lay curled in each other's arms in her bed, he stroked her hair gently. 'It's got to be said, Glynis, but I'll only say this once. I really am disappointed, not only that you listened to that madwoman Edna but, most shocking of all, that you believed her.'

Glynis muttered an apology. She said it quietly for she was not convinced. She wanted to believe him but feared she never would. Strangely, she knew that, if this was not the end of their affair, the end was not far away. Sad, sorry and apparently contrite as she was, she knew that her trust in him had been destroyed and that it could never be mended.

4

It was late when Russell drove back from the country club where he had been for a swim. He was pleased with his progress, each day managing to swim and walk further without the dreadful fatigue of last week returning. In fact, as he drove along, he was feeling pleased with himself on several counts. He had never liked to be in a muddle, and now that he had made resolutions about his life and marriage and was putting them into motion, he felt a new burst of mental energy too.

There was excitement to be enjoyed too, in the knowledge that a new future beckoned. When he thought this, as so often happened, he thought of Chrissy too. It was strange the effect she had on him. He hardly knew her and yet knew that he wanted to; that when he did get to know her he would like what he found. But Sabine and the mess that was their marriage had to be sorted out first – he did not want to take to Chrissy the baggage from his past mistakes. She had to know that he was sincere, that he wasn't playing adulterer's games.

He laughed at his presumption. What made him think she would want him? Maybe she had not felt the same spark he had. No, he told himself, that wasn't so – they had been so relaxed last Saturday in her little cottage, more like old friends, comfortable with each other, than new acquaintances.

He had reached the outskirts of Fellcar and slowed down. Nothing was as straightforward as he had anticipated, though. Having made up his mind that his marriage was dead, he had thought that the worst was over, that everything would be plain sailing now and that he could get on with his life. He'd had no way of knowing how disturbing it would be to have to continue to share his home with Sabine. He'd presumed that this affair of hers, which had lasted longer than most, and in which she had thrown discretion to the wind, meant that she'd wanted the end of their marriage as much as he now did. That she loved Giles and had decided, like Russell, that they could not go on like this, that the charade must end.

Instead, he was learning that Sabine, faced with the end of their marriage, was clinging on to it, almost with desperation. Her mood-swings and emotional outbursts were as exhausting for him as they were for her. She could be contrite one moment, pathetically trying to make amends, yet hurling a glass vase at him two minutes later. From not wanting him to touch her she was trying to seduce him at every opportunity – with glances, négligés and endless innuendoes. He was finding it distasteful and embarrassing. It was as if she were a stranger to him and one he didn't particularly want to know.

He'd reached the reluctant conclusion that things with her lover were probably not running smoothly – why else would she want Russell? And that made him feel sad for her but there was nothing he could do to help. She'd destroyed any love he'd ever had for her and love, once lost, could never be retrieved, he was certain.

On the last stretch of his journey up North Hill he wondered what his next move should be. As he pulled into his drive he saw with irritation that every light in the house was burning – one of those petty little things Sabine did these days just to annoy him.

Inside, he stood in the sitting room doorway and looked about him with disbelief. The room was a shambles and his first reaction was that they had been burgled. But when he entered Sabine's room and saw it neat and immaculate while his was devastated he knew that no criminal had been involved – just his wife.

His clothes were ripped, his books torn, paintings he'd loved were defaced, his precious LPs were scratched, his CDs dented, his photo albums scattered, his aftershave and toiletries split everywhere. Little of what he owned remained intact.

He turned on his heel, ran down the stairs and hurtled out into the night, into his car and drove like a demon to get away from the hatred and the loathing. He resented this anger, as with racing pulse and quickened heart, the bile of rage threatened to choke him and the furies of outrage raced in him. This was not what he wanted his life to be. He had no idea where he was going or where he wanted to go. He brushed his face with a weary gesture. He wanted peace and quiet. God, how he longed for that.

He drove through the pouring rain. He'd planned an aimless drive, just something to do to tire himself out so that he could sleep and tomorrow face the chaos of what had once been home.

The road he was on petered out. He stopped the car and looked about him. If he hadn't known what he wanted, his car seemed to have worked it out for him. He had had no intention of coming here and no recall of how he'd got here!

He hunched up, ran through the falling rain and knocked on the door.

'Hi!' He tried to smile but he was too tense to manage it. 'I hope you meant it – that I could call again?'

'Of course I did. You're welcome. Come in.' And Chrissy, who had been peering nervously out of the door, unsure who could be calling this late, held the door open wider.

'Is it too late?'

'Yes, it is.' She laughed. 'But come in all the same.'

'I'm sorry. I decided to go for a drive and my car just seemed to head this way. I hope you don't mind. And then I saw your light still on –'

'I was late back,' she answered, not pointing out that the lane outside her house didn't go anywhere. He stood stock still in the rain, which he did not even seem to notice. 'Are you all right, Russell? You look very pale.'

'Me? Yes, fine.'

He did not look it, she thought. 'Well, you won't be "fine" for long if you stand out there – you'll catch your death. Please, come in. I was just getting a bite to eat. Do you want some? It's only an omelette and salad.' She led the way into the kitchen.

Russell began to say no when he suddenly realised he was hungry. 'Heavens! I haven't eaten all day. An omelette sounds great.'

'You're hardly going to recover your strength if you don't eat.'

'Yes, Nurse,' he said obediently, as he followed. He sat at the small pine table and watched her as she added extra eggs to the bowl and beat them into the mixture.

'I wish you wouldn't look at me like that, you make me nervous,' she said, half laughing with embarrassment as she splattered the worktop with egg.

'I didn't know I was.'

'Would you care for a drink – or is that wise on an empty stomach? Mind you, you look as if you could do with one.' He said nothing. 'There's a bottle of wine or some beer in the fridge.'

'Wine sounds great.' He was glad to have something to do. While Chrissy cooked he uncorked and poured the wine. Sitting in the warm, his glass in his hand, surreptitiously watching her at the stove, he felt the tension begin to peel from him like layers of skin. By the time she placed their supper on the table he felt relaxed, the storm of anger spent, as if the chaos at his house hadn't happened.

'Why did you forget to eat?'

'I don't know. Preoccupied, I suppose,' he answered. He had no intention of burdening her with his problems – hadn't she enough of her own? And, in a strange way, he felt ashamed of what had happened. Something had pushed Sabine to the edge. He hoped it had been Giles and not something he had said or done – he had no room for any more guilt, not yet. It struck him that that was an odd thing to think, but it was true. He had failed her in some way, hadn't given her the happiness she yearned for. But it didn't look as if she had found it with Giles either. Despite everything, he could feel sorry for her: she'd thoughtlessly thrown away one relationship only to find that the substitute was worthless. Still, she need not have destroyed the things he loved. It had been an exhibition of mindless, childish tantrum and successfully quashed any sympathy he might have felt for her. At that he realised that his thoughts, his moods, were beginning to swing as alarmingly as Sabine's, and sighed mightily.

'Gracious, you sound as if all the world's problems are on your shoulders. What a sigh.'

'Did I?'

'Then it's a deep-rooted problem.'

'Not for much longer.' He looked down at his plate. That was the way he must go – stop the guilt, the who did what to whom. Sabine hated him. Then get out, he told himself. Suddenly he smiled. 'It might have been once, but no more.'

'That sounds like you've come to some resolution. And you look happy about it.'

'Oh, I am,' he said, but with no smile this time. Chrissy wondered what had happened to make him as moody as this. He looked so sad and she wished she could lean over and hug him, make him feel better. He had a lost look as though he had had a shock, and there was a detachment about him as if he was distracted and only half here. She longed to know why and what, and if she could help in some way.

'Would you like some music?' she asked. At least that would fill yet another silence that had descended – she was at a loss to know what to say.

'Only if you would,' he said unhelpfully, but at least he seemed to come back to the present and remember that he had social obligations for suddenly he was talking about the novel he was reading. Soon they were away, chattering about music and books they liked, the safe exploration of each other's interests and concerns. They kept off the subject of poetry, she was pleased to note, and touched upon nothing personal.

She suggested they move into the sitting room where it would be more comfortable. She refused to allow him to clear up – 'I'm on late shift tomorrow.' She served coffee and the last of her brandy, and he settled by her fire once again. They sat back on the comfortable chairs but a silence came and again she couldn't think of a thing to say. Russell looked as if he was miles away and she wished they'd stayed in the kitchen, where conversation had been so easy and this embarrassing lull need not have happened.

'I like talking to you. I find it easy,' he said out of the blue, almost shyly she thought.

'You could have fooled me for the last ten minutes.' She laughed, and immediately wished she hadn't for his face changed, became expressionless as if he were retreating from her. 'Only joking!' she lied, hurriedly.

'Were you? I thought – oh, it doesn't matter.' He drained his coffee.

'What did you think, Russell? Please tell me. I'm sorry if I offended you – I didn't mean to.'

'No, I'm sorry. I'm being over-sensitive. It was just – the other night we seemed to get to know each other and I felt we were comfortable together. And I thought tonight would be easy too. And I hoped . . . But really –' He stood up. 'It's really not important.'

Chrissy stood too. She wanted to put out her hand and stop him leaving. She wanted to explain things to him. She wanted to get close to him – only she was afraid to. And how to explain that?

'Your coat,' she said, to cover her confusion. Fetching it she clutched it to her as if she were holding him. Then it dawned on her what she was doing, how fatuous it was, and she handed it to him. 'Here.'

'Thanks.' He put it on quickly and stepped out into the hall. The front door was soon half open.

'Russell.'

'Yes?' He turned to face her.

'Please come again.' She knew she blushed.

'Is that what you want?'

'I do . . . It's difficult to explain, but when you've been trampled on it takes time to get up again,' she said, and hoped he understood.

'I'll see you, then,' he replied, and she presumed he hadn't.

The light from her small hallway cut a bright swathe across the garden but was not strong enough to reach the rough grassland of the cliff top beyond so neither of them saw the figure, crouching behind a gorse bush, lie flat on the ground.

After he had gone, Chrissy did the washing up she had promised she would leave. He had reacted so strangely, as if he was hurt, as if she had hurt him. Something had happened that had so rocked his equilibrium that he wasn't thinking straight. Something had ripped away his defences. What else could she have done? He wasn't letting on, so how was she to help him? And yet she wanted to, desperately. She should have come out in the open and asked him. She should have but she knew she never could. What if he rejected her or laughed at her?

'Oh, Russell,' she said aloud to the empty kitchen, 'if only we could forget the past, you and me, and trust again.'

Russell felt confused as he drove back to Fellcar. He'd always found it difficult to get on with people when he first met them, yet he hadn't felt that with Chrissy. His shyness, which most people presumed was coolness, hadn't been there with her. And he'd allowed himself to think her different – but he'd done that one time before too. Why couldn't he just accept that he was wrong about her, that he was imagining something that wasn't there?

Then he remembered her face just as he left and he knew, he just knew, that something awful had happened to her and she was afraid of committing herself to him, or anyone.

He must be patient – he who was always so impatient, he thought, as he parked his car. He noticed that Sabine's car was not there, which did not surprise him. When she drove up five minutes later and they met in the hall, they passed each other without speaking.

5

Lynn Petch was having difficulty in making out who was speaking on the telephone to her, so muffled was the voice. 'I'm sorry, I can barely hear you. Would you mind speaking up?' she said, loudly but amused: she wasn't afraid that this was a heavy breather, there was something familiar about the voice she couldn't quite pin down. There was a noisy harrumphing along the line. 'Oh, it's *you*, Dr Henderson. You sounded as if you were down a mine-shaft.' She laughed, but as she listened the laugh was not repeated. She sat down with a bump on the chair beside the telephone table, clasping the receiver. 'Yes, I'm still here,' she said. And then, urgently, 'No, I don't understand. You can't do this –' But she spoke to herself, the telephone was silent and Lynn was left with the frustration of one who'd been cut off. She'd been sacked. She exhaled slowly. Not that old Henderson had said that, 'termination of contract', he'd called it, but whatever it was labelled it was still the sack.

'Who was that?' Terry looked up from his bowl of Weetabix – three in number, his customary breakfast.

'Dr Henderson. My P45's in the post.'

'You what? He can't do that.'

'He can, apparently. He read me a clause in my contract. Apparently he can terminate it immediately for unprofessional conduct. Getting breathalysed is sufficient.' Lynn sat at the table, picked up the teapot and poured herself a cup.

'You seem quite calm about it.'

'I'm stunned. I'm still taking it in.'

'Well, I see their point.' Terry pushed his cereal bowl aside and picked up his tea.

'Thank you so much for your support, Terry Petch. I just knew I could count on you,' she said bitterly.

'I'm sorry, Lynn. You know how I feel about drunk drivers. Ever since –' He didn't finish the sentence, but closed his eyes. Lynn knew why: the flash memory from years ago of a white Mercedes smashing into the side of the Ford Fiesta he had been driving, killing his best friend, Nick, on his twentieth birthday.

'I respect that, Terry. I know the drunk bastard who killed Nick is still out there swanning around in his big gas guzzlers. There's one slight difference. *I – was – not – drunk.*'

'Lynn, it's a rare drunk who admits to it. I saw you, remember? You could barely speak. You were pissed out of your skull!'

Lynn wanted to scream at him, lash out at his obduracy. Instead she methodically poured herself another cup of tea, then traced with her finger the raised embroidery on the immaculate tablecloth. 'I won't go on about it, Terry. I understand how you feel and why you should think it. But I promise you I wasn't drunk. I'd had less than half a whisky. I think it was spiked. And I really would appreciate you believing me.' She looked down at the sugar bowl, wondering inconsequentially how many grains there were in a pound and with a spoon began to play with it.

'I wish I could, Lynn. But I can't. I just keep thinking you could be dead – and in my book that just shows how little you must think of us. Now, if you'll excuse me.' Terry was on his feet, his chair pushed back, and he left the room. She heard the front door close. In thirteen years of marriage that was the first time he had left without kissing her goodbye.

She could have slumped there at the table, bewailing her fate and the unfairness of it all. Instead, Lynn stood up, collected the blood sample the police had given her, put on her coat and picked up her car keys.

Her first stop was in Thorpedale where she delivered the phial to an independent laboratory to be analysed. She didn't like the knowing way in which the receptionist smiled when she had asked for it to be done as soon as possible – no doubt what everyone asked.

She drove back far too fast to Fellcar, she knew she did, but she needed to speed for then she had to concentrate and could momentarily control the confused, angry thoughts whirling about in her mind like trapped birds.

Enid's face was such a picture of shocked horror that it had certainly been worth coming here, thought Lynn, as she swept through the door.

'Morning, Enid,' she said breezily. 'Got a problem?'

'No – I – What are *you* doing here?' Every line of Enid's comfortable frame was tense.

'What a charming welcome. I've come to pick up my things. You've evidently been told I've been kicked out.'

'Dr Henderson mentioned – still, if that's all you want.' And, like a balloon slowly deflating, Enid's ample curves relaxed.

'Is he here? I want a word.' And Lynn looked amused as the folds of Enid's flesh tightened again. 'Doing aerobics, are you? Good.'

'Sorry? I don't understand,' Enid gabbled, but Lynn was through the door and into her own office, where she saw Giles Middleton bent over the drawers of her desk. Even through her anger and worry she could still admire his rear end, and she could smile at her own contrariness.

'Lynn!' he said, as he swung round to see her standing in the doorway. 'Hi.'

She was glad to see that at least he looked embarrassed. 'Giles.' She nodded slightly. 'Are you looking for something? Can I help you?' she said, with heavy irony.

'I've always liked your desk. I was just checking to see if it was empty yet.' He stood up straight and leant against it.

'My, my, you're behaving like a rapacious relative when the corpse is still warm.' She began to take off her coat.

Giles laughed. 'Put like that –'

'As far as I can recall your desk is identical to mine. Not much point in swapping, is there? Come on, Giles, you were snooping, weren't you? Frightened I'd solved how you fiddled the drugs ordering?'

'Watch it, Lynn.' He wagged a finger at her, an action she hated and which always annoyed her.

'No, Giles. You've got it wrong. It's you who is going to have to watch it. I'm not threatening, I'm promising you.'

The door opened and Dick Henderson bustled in with dough-faced Enid lurking close behind.

'Lynn, there was no need for you to come here. We could have parcelled up your possessions.'

'I needed to come, Dick. I have some property here I don't want others to see.'

'Anything pertaining to the patients like computer printouts is practice property and covered by confidentiality. Nothing can be removed.' Giles stepped forward bossily.

'Did I say they were, Giles? Aren't you jumping to premature conclusions? Why would I be interested in patients' files if I'm not going to be working here any more? Didn't they tell you I've been sacked?' She was unaware that her voice was raised.

'Now, come on, Lynn, there's no need to be like this.'

'Dick, there's every need. Are you concerned I'm taking computer data with me?'

'Well, no –'

'So why's he so worried? Don't you see? He's running scared that I've found something out about the temazepam he's been nicking. And that's the reason why he spiked my drink last night – to ensure I got the push.'

'That's slanderous. Did you hear all that, Enid?'

'I did, Dr Middleton.' Enid glowed with self-importance.

'It might help, Lynn, if you could tell us what it is you want from your desk,' Dick Henderson said, calmly enough, with the distressed but resigned expression of one who loathed scenes.

Lynn crossed the room, opened a lower drawer and took out a small jeweller's package, which she snapped open. 'Cuff links for Terry's birthday.' She waved the box in front of them. She bent down, opened another drawer and fished out a folder. 'My bank statements, so Terry wouldn't see them and spoil the surprise. Satisfied?'

'There. You see, Giles? Nothing wrong there.' He smiled happily. 'I do think you've all caught some paranoia bug, accusing each other in this way. It's unpleasant.'

'Dick, honestly, you're blind! I'm telling you, Giles is crooked. You've sacked the wrong person and I shall prove it to you.'

'If you do, then of course I shall apologise and you'll be welcome back here. But I shan't be holding my breath.' He smiled indulgently at her.

'I wouldn't come back here, not if you doubled my salary. I've given you years of loyal, hard work and you don't even have the decency to come and see me and hear my side of the story. No, you'd rather listen to *this* creature, who's been here – how long? A year? Dick, you couldn't even spell the word loyalty!' She picked up her bank statements and the jewellery box, crammed them into her bag and flung her coat around her shoulders.

'But, Lynn, don't go like this. Let's talk.'

'Oh, Dick! I've just been talking, but you won't listen. Now, if you'll excuse me?' she asked Enid, whose bulk was blocking the door.

'Lynn –'

'Oh, stuff yourselves! I'm glad to be out of here and shot of the lot of you.' She stumbled through the door and rushed across the reception area to the main entrance. She didn't want them to see she was crying, did not want them to know how hurt she was, how sad to be leaving the clinic she'd set up, deserting the women who attended it and who trusted and liked her.

Safe in her car she had to sit for a second, controlling her emotions until she was safe to drive. Chocolate. She needed a whole block of it, she thought, as she put the car into gear.

At the local Tesco she decided to do a shop as well as buy the chocolate. She trundled the trolley up and down the aisles, hurling stuff into it that attracted her attention.

'Lynn, hello!'

Hell, she thought, put her head down and pushed the trolley swiftly away from the voice.

'Lynn? What's the matter? It's me.'

'Oh, Chrissy. I'm sorry. I thought you were a patient. Rather, an ex-patient.' And her eyes filled with tears, which she hastily wiped away with the back of her hand.

'Lynn, love. What's the problem?' Chrissy glanced furtively at her watch – she was already running late. 'Do you fancy some lunch?'

'That would be nice. Yes, that's just what I need. And a large gin and tonic.'

'Do you think you should?' The words were out before Chrissy could stop herself.

'Probably not, but I want to explain to you about the other night.'

'Right. See you in the Fox and Fiddle in twenty minutes'.'

Chrissy pulled into the windswept car park of the public house just as, with a throaty roar and spray of gravel, Floss Yates's ancient but loved E-type Jaguar followed her.

Perhaps asking Lynn to join her had not been such a good idea when she was meeting Floss for lunch. She well knew that the older woman was not for everyone: she was loved and loathed in equal parts. But Lynn had had such a desperate, almost manic, look about her that Chrissy felt she should do something. And maybe Floss was a good idea. She was the type who, if she set her mind to it, could chivvy her along.

'An old friend who's in a bit of a state is joining us, if you don't mind,' Chrissy said, as the pub landlord led them to their reserved table in the somewhat over-chintzed and horsebrassed dining room.

'Why should I? I like talking to you young people. And I adore solving others' problems. Could we have another place setting, Les?'

'For you, Floss, anything. This do you?' He gestured with pride at the window table.

'I'd never have thought of coming here. It used to be a real spit and sawdust place,' Chrissy said, as they settled with the menus.

'Still is in the public. Les has been quite cunning. Nice bit of posh in here with silver service – people set great store by silver service, you know – but he's kept the public noisy and they do a wonderful karaoke evening.'

'Ah Floss! Will you ever grow up?'

'I certainly hope not.' She settled her ample frame on the red velvet banquette. 'The steak and kidney pie is to die for. And the main reason I suggested coming here.'

'Lynn!' Chrissy half stood and waved at her friend, who was standing looking uncertain in the doorway. Diffidently for her, she moved across the crowded room towards them. 'Do you know Mrs Yates, Lynn?'

'Not really, though I've seen you around. I thought –' She turned to Chrissy, about to explain that she'd assumed they'd be alone. 'I really don't think I've time –'

'Lynn, please join us, you look done in.'

Lynn looked downcast as if the concern in Chrissy's voice might be the last straw.

'You sit by me, my dear.' And Floss manoeuvred her bulk along the seat to make room for Lynn. 'Before we sort out what's ailing you, let's order. A problem on a full stomach is virtually solved, I always say. The pie and a burgundy, or would you rather have claret?'

Floss insisted on doing the ordering, even though Lynn protested she couldn't eat a thing and didn't drink, at which she glanced quickly at Chrissy as if to gauge her reaction. Chrissy meanwhile would have preferred the fish and had to refuse the wine since she was on duty in just over an hour. But both were resigned to letting Floss, who was a bit like a tank when she'd decided something, order the food for them.

'Now, my dear Lynn, what's the problem? Tell Floss. I'm the soul of discretion if I want to be and we might be able to help you. In fact, I'm sure we can.' She smiled expansively at Lynn, took her slim hand in her podgy one and squeezed it firmly. Lynn returned the smile as she felt a great safety blanket of kindness and reliability enfold her.

'Well, you see, I was breathalysed. But . . .' Lynn relayed her sorry tale. 'And I'd bet everything was down to Giles spiking my whisky,' she finished.

'Lynn, I'm so sorry. How awful for you. I must apologise. I jumped to the conclusion that you were blotto too.'

'You believe me?' Lynn sounded surprised.

'Of course. If you say you hadn't been drinking excessively I believe you.'

'I'm so happy someone does.'

'I'd believe anything of that Giles Middleton – you realise his partner is my brother-in-law? I didn't like Middleton and I told Dick so. Too full of himself by far, and of the school that thought just because he'd passed his exams to be a quack he was a superior being. But would Dick listen? No. Men always know it all, don't they?'

Lynn picked up her handbag from the floor. 'At least I've got these.' She pulled out the bank-statement folder she'd taken from her desk. 'It's dreadfully illegal, but what else can I do? They're copies of the computer pharmaceutical files on the last few patients of Giles that I didn't have time to check.'

'Clever girl.' Floss beamed approval.

'Has it crossed your mind, Lynn, that that stretch of road you were on – it's residential, isn't it? How often do you see huge police cars there? The odd Panda car maybe, but the full jam sandwich?'

'What do you mean, Chrissy?'

'I was just wondering if they'd been tipped off – by Giles presumably. You know "I'd like to report that there's a drunk woman driving towards Timber Lane". It's just an idea.'

'Then we must find out for certain.'

'But how?' Lynn looked pleased and doubtful at the same time.

'Leave that to me, my dear. I've excellent contacts in the local constabulary. Ah – the pies. Now, tuck into that and tell me I'm wrong.'

Lynn suddenly found she was ravenous and Chrissy quickly forgot the fish.

'There's something else . . . I overheard Dr Henderson and Giles Middleton having one hell of a row one night when I was working late. I didn't really understand what he meant – I'm still not sure. So it might not mean anything.'

'What was it, my dear?' Floss asked gently.

'Well, I heard Dr Henderson shout, "You do that, I'll report you to the GMC." I naturally thought he meant his affair with Sabine Newson, but he didn't because when Giles yelled back, "You wouldn't dare. If you do I'll kill you," the old man said, "I'm warning you, Giles. You go ahead with this hospital plan, I'll bury you." Aren't men over-dramatic sometimes?'

There was a clatter of a knife and fork as Floss, of all people, suddenly lost interest in her food.

6

As the doctor, Sol Brown, spoke to her, his voice seemed to be coming from a long way away. Mo could hear him, she understood what he was saying, but she felt oddly detached, almost as if he was talking about someone else. He sketched diagrams for her to help his explanation – except it didn't since she found she couldn't concentrate on them either. Her hand was being squeezed in a gesture of comfort. She looked up and smiled brightly at Chrissy, who was sitting with her beside the bed while Dr Brown stood opposite. He was fiddling with her water jug, then the counterpane and finally with his tie.

'Do you understand, Mrs Fordham?'

'Please call me Mo. I asked to be called Mo – it's less clinical isn't it? I need things to be less clinical.'

Sol looked across at Chrissy, one eyebrow very slightly raised, his expression one of concern.

'Mo, Dr Brown needs to know if you've taken in everything he's said.' Chrissy still held her hand and spoke quietly.

'Oh, yes, sorry. I feel a bit strange. It's not every day you get news like this. No, I understand I'm to have radiotherapy for six weeks and, because my lymph glands were involved, chemotherapy too. How long will I have to stay here?'

'You can go in a few days once your wound has drained, and then your treatment can be conducted as an outpatient. I'd like you to have some physio so that your arm and shoulder don't get too stiff.' He was making notes rapidly as he spoke. Mo registered his handwriting: spiky and neat, not at all like a doctor's. It was legible, even if she couldn't understand the words.

'But I'll be here with you on this ward, Chrissy?'

'Of course. You don't think I'm going to let anyone else look after you, do you? And you're not feeling too bad?'

'No. My arm's sore, otherwise I'm in absolutely top form!' She laughed at this but the other two frowned, and she realised they were afraid that she was tipping over into hysterics. She was sorry she was worrying them so.

'You know, Mo, from my experience it's best to talk freely about all this and how you feel. Try not to bottle things up – it doesn't help,' the doctor advised.

'I shall become the local breast-cancer bore, don't worry.' And the laugh rang out again. She wished it hadn't but she couldn't stop it and knew that if she didn't laugh she risked bursting into tears.

'Is there anything else you need explained, Mo? If not, I'll be on my way.'

'Just –' These words would be difficult to form. Even as she thought what to say she felt as if her stomach had turned to liquid, felt the now familiar helter-skelter of nerve endings connecting with each other. 'I was wondering – if – well – perhaps – how long –' Somehow she forced the words out.

Sol took her hand. 'You know what I always tell patients who ask me that? The prognosis depends on what sort of patient the disease has.' He smiled kindly at her and she smiled back, if puzzled by what he meant.

'Thank you, Doctor,' she said. 'You've been very kind.'

'I just wish –' He shrugged, not finishing the sentence as if he couldn't think what it was he wanted to say. He nodded, Mo wondered at what, until it dawned on her that it was a nervous tic.

'It's not your fault, Doc.'

'Well, if you'll excuse me?' Even as he moved away, he was straightening his tie again.

Chrissy and Mo watched him leave the ward, tall, gangly, edgy, and Mo wondered if he'd be less tense in a different job.

'Poor man. It can't be pleasant having to give patients doomy news all the time. I hope it doesn't get him down too much. He looks a bundle of nerves and far too thin.'

'Don't you worry about him, he's fine. I bet he was born hyper like that. More to the point, are *you* all right? Anything I can get you?'

'Nothing. I'm fine.' Mo swung her legs to the side of the bed, careful of her arm, which was attached to the drip, and holding her drainage tube. 'It's really odd, in the circumstances, but in fact I'm more than fine. I was a bit wimpy just now but, Chrissy, do you know? It's like a great weight has gone. I haven't got to worry whether I've got cancer or not. I have, and it's almost a relief to know. Now I'm aware what I'm up against, what's to be done. I've got a focus, something to fight.'

'That's the spirit. You'll do fine. See what the doctor meant? Your illness chose a fighter.'

'So that's what he meant. Will I be fine? Is that a promise?'

'It is.' Chrissy paused imperceptibly. 'Fancy a cuppa?'

In the ward kitchen Chrissy put the kettle on. She could have bitten off her tongue just then. It had been foolish of her to say that Mo would be fine and get caught into making it a promise. This was a field in which promises should not be made. She should have been vaguer. She leant against the counter and gazed out over the stunning view of the sea.

Women like Mo never ceased to amaze her. Their courage was humbling, and yet at the same time inspiring. She often wondered how she would be if faced with the same situation – nothing like as brave as Mo, she was certain of that. No doubt she'd be like those patients who, given bad news, collapsed in a sobbing heap, turned their faces to the wall, and endlessly asked, 'Why me?'

She began to lay the tea tray. Certainly for the staff it was a relief when a patient reacted as Mo had. It made things easier, and there was no doubt in Chrissy's mind that the treatment often worked better with an attitude like Mo's. But, for all that, Mo must be watched in case a delayed and adverse emotional reaction kicked in – as it often did.

'Hi, Chrissy.'

She turned to see Dawn Allyson standing in the doorway of the kitchen.

'Hello.'

'Reporting for duty, Sister.' Dawn grinned broadly. 'I'm your new staff.'

'Dawn, that's wonderful news! I called the office earlier today and they said I had to wait for a replacement.'

'I was summoned by La Tillman. She said that as I was the only bank staff nurse available she was sending me to you – sweet of her! I could have hugged her. Then I asked if they were advertising this as a permanent post – if so I fancied applying. She went all po-faced – she's in a right old crabby mood today.'

'There's to be no recruitment until further notice, that's probably why. It must be galling to be in her position and controlled by the suits at Thorpedale.'

'That would explain it. Though she needn't have been quite so sniffy with me. "Nurse Allyson, when that time comes we shall be looking for someone with extra training in oncology." She didn't even let me finish. Old bitch!'

'Have you done oncology as a speciality?'

'Well, not exactly. I started, but never finished . . . Something got in the way, you know how it is,' Dawn said. 'Yes, a feller!' And she grinned even wider.

'Where were you?'

'Plymouth.'

'I worked in Truro.'

'I know.'

'Well, we need you and how. This ward, being part residential and part outpatients, takes some getting used to. Lesley Bing is going on maternity leave next week. That's why I wanted someone now so she can settle you in before she leaves.'

'That old moo? Unbelievable. I'm amazed any man found her attractive enough to impregnate.'

'Hi, Lesley,' said Chrissy, towards the door. Dawn swung round – no one was there.

'You monster! I nearly had a heart-attack!' Dawn was laughing. 'Serves me right, though. My big mouth – it's always getting me into trouble.'

'Better look behind you next time.' Chrissy poured the boiling water into the teapot.

'Lesley doesn't look pregnant.'

'She's only just. Apparently she had a miscarriage last year and doesn't want to take any risks this time. Can't say I blame her.' Chrissy swirled the tea. 'I do hope they won't move you again. I need you permanently. I think I'll have a word with Glynis about it. Tell you what, when she *can* recruit again, apply for the post. I'll be involved with the selection, after all.'

'Would you do that? You're a brick.'

'Depends on your nursing.'

'Of course. But that doesn't worry me, I'm one of the best.'

'Can you hold the fort here? There's nothing dramatic going on. I've got an appointment with Glynis in five minutes.'

'Good luck, then. I told you she's got a right moody on – no doubt been ditched by her precious Matthew Kersey. Serves her right if he has ditched her – he's a married man. I don't think you should meddle with other people's husbands, do you? It can only lead to complications.'

Chrissy felt uncomfortable with the direction the conversation had taken – she would have liked to ignore the question, it was a little too close to home. But there was something in the way Dawn asked, a mite eagerly, that made her wonder if she herself was embroiled, or was about to be, in an adulterous relationship. 'It's difficult to say, isn't it? I mean, who knows what goes on in a marriage, the reason people stray?'

'That's true. I hadn't looked at it quite like that. You know me – everything's black and white in my world.'

'It would certainly make things simpler. The greys complicate everything. I'll just give this to the patient.' Chrissy picked up the tray.

'Do you always make the tea, Sister?' Dawn quipped. 'You'll be swabbing the floors next.'

'We're so short-staffed that on this ward everyone mucks in,' Chrissy replied. 'When I get back from Glynis we'll have a talk and I'll show you around.' Dawn, with her natural cheerfulness, was going to be an asset on this ward, she thought. She'd be good for the patients, better than Lesley. She was aware that Lesley's brusqueness was a defence mechanism to cover up her true feelings of pity and frustration – the problem was that it was a rare patient who understood this. Dawn was far less complicated.

When she reached Mo, a short, stocky, blond-haired man was sitting on her bed and holding her hand, a look of utter bleakness on his face. As quietly as she could she placed the tray on the bedside table. They both looked up at her.

'Your tea, Mo. Would you like a cup, Mr Fordham?'

'No thanks,' the man replied.

'I'll leave you two, then.' Sharply she turned and walked away, puzzled by the laughter that followed her.

'Oh, Ash! She thought you were Robbie.'

'Wish I was,' Ash said seriously.

'Dear Ash. Best not even to think it.' And it was Mo's turn to squeeze his hand comfortingly.

'Yes, Sister Galloway, what can I do for you?' Glynis ushered Chrissy into her study and indicated the seat she should take. Chrissy sat down, aware that once again she felt like a schoolgirl in the headmistress's study – convinced she'd done something wrong when she knew she hadn't. She told herself to pull herself together: as a patient's granddaughter she had every right to complain about Jazz.

'It's about Staff Nurse Poundman.'

'Your grandmother's on her ward?'

'Yes, that's right. I'm afraid I've come to complain about her, Miss Tillman.'

'Oh, really?' One slender eyebrow was raised questioningly.

'You realise I'm not happy doing this?'

'If you're not happy with it, then why do it?' Glynis asked sharply.

Chrissy felt herself involuntarily move back in the chair as if she had been slapped. She had known this was going to be difficult but she hadn't expected quite such a bald reaction. 'Because I feel I should. I owe it to the patients.'

'So?' Glynis looked irritated.

'If you're going to be this dismissive there doesn't seem any point in my continuing.' Chrissy half rose.

'I apologise,' Glynis said easily – she had never found an apology difficult if it smoothed the way. 'Please continue.'

Chrissy sat down again but looked even less sure of herself. 'My grandmother is afraid of Jazz and she says the other patients are too. She calls the patients by their Christian names, which a lot of the elderly do not like. And standards are sloppy.'

'For example?'

'Empty water jugs. Bedpans reluctantly given.'

'Did you speak to the sister in charge?'

'No.'

'Why not?'

'My grandmother says she wouldn't believe me.' Chrissy shifted uncomfortably in the armchair.

'Then why should I?'

'Don't you want to know when things aren't right?'

'Of course. But there are procedures to be followed. You should have complained to the sister and, if matters weren't rectified, then to me.'

'I'm sorry. I thought this was the best way.'

'Be that as it may, we have never had any complaints about the care of the elderly before. Jazz Poundman has been a hard-working, dedicated nurse – and she has been here some time.'

'What are you saying? That I haven't, and so therefore my word is less reliable?'

'I said no such thing.'

'You implied it.'

'I wasn't aware that I had, but you must, of course, interpret things as you wish,' Glynis said coldly. 'Anything untoward in my hospital is of concern to me. I just wish that certain channels of communication were respected. Otherwise confusion may set in.'

'Then I'm sorry. I'll be sure to observe them in future.' She hoped she sounded sufficiently sarcastic. 'So am I to go back and report to the sister?'

'No, that won't be necessary. It's too late now. I shall investigate personally. I shall let you know my findings.' Glynis stood, a sign of dismissal. 'You should be warned, Sister, that your actions are quite likely to lead to bad feelings. Sister Fleming is a particularly popular and senior member of staff. And since you're –' She turned away.

'I didn't hear what you said, Miss Tillman.'

'I said no more.'

'What were you going to say? That I was already unpopular

264

enough, what with all the gossip about me swirling around this hospital?'

'I never listen to gossip, Sister. I'm interested only in facts,' she said coldly.

Chrissy stood and faced Glynis, puzzled. This wasn't the reception she'd expected. She'd thought Glynis a fair woman, if a rigid one, but today she appeared to be vindictive. She squared her shoulders. She was here now, she might as well get everything sorted one.

'Are the post-mortem reports on my patients in?' she asked.

'I've seen nothing. They must still be with the pathologist.' Glynis returned to her desk.

'Aren't they taking a long time over them?'

'Are you complaining about that too?' Glynis responded, her face a mask of detachment.

'Thanks for nothing!' Chrissy said, exasperated, and slammed the door after her. Once she was on the other side she realised she'd forgotten to mention Dawn – which was just as well: at the moment, with Miss Tillman in that mood, no doubt anyone she recommended would get the sack!

Glynis slumped at her desk. She pushed her hand through her immaculate hair and sighed. She'd handled that so badly, so unreasonably. There had been several complaints about Jazz Poundman and it was a problem she was going to have to resolve. Such behaviour was so unlike her – she didn't know what was happening to her – but then she did. She despised herself for her behaviour last night with Matthew: she had been like a stupid teenager with him. But she felt so on edge, with a premonition that everything was about to collapse about her. Logically, such a feeling should be ignored, only Glynis found it would not go away.

7

When she'd lived alone in Cornwall, working at the local hospital, Chrissy had thought herself rushed off her feet. She could laugh at that notion now. Life then had been one long holiday compared with her workload here! She never seemed to stop rushing – organising herself and her own life, getting the ward started and arranging her group meetings. Visiting her gran, doing her shopping, checking out the local nursing homes for the old lady, and not sleeping too well from worry. And she'd toyed with the idea of finding a fella! When would she have time to fit him in? If she did find someone, it would have to be love by appointment. No, she was better off alone. She began to snort with laughter at these thoughts but stopped herself. For someone who kept saying she had no need of a man, she seemed to spend an inordinate time telling herself so. As usually happened these days, when she was thinking about this subject, an image of Russell flashed into her mind and she had to push it away quickly. She concentrated on changing gear, just like an L-driver, she thought, as she prepared to drive up the steep North Hill to her mother's house.

'I thought you'd fallen off the edge of the world,' Iris said sharply in greeting.

'I'm sorry. I've been so rushed recently I haven't even finished unpacking,' she replied. She could have pointed out that her mother could just as well have contacted her, but she didn't. She didn't want any falling out with anyone over anything – she was too tired for that.

'Any news on those odd deaths you were fretting about?'

'Nothing,' said Chrissy, feeling her face tauten in a nervous reaction, which it always did if she'd managed to forget, even for a few minutes, the cloud of fear that hovered over her. She hung her coat on the hat-stand.

'Then there's something amiss, wouldn't you say?' Iris led the way.

'Why?' She tried to make the one little word sound genuinely curious and, yes, dismissive, wanting to hear what her mother thought without asking her outright.

'When your father died we had the results in a day. How long's this been? A week? Two?' Iris opened the sitting-room door.

'Maybe the results weren't conclusive and they're having to do more tests.'

'Or maybe someone did bump them off. Wasn't you by any chance?' Iris chortled, but Chrissy did not join in. 'You needn't look so po-faced with me.'

'Mum, it's hardly a joking matter, is it? The gossip in the hospital is like a plague. I hear people whispering behind me, avoiding me. It's getting me down.' She was unaware that she was moving her hands, one inside the other, as if she was washing them.

'Well, you must expect that after Ewan.' Iris poked the fire.

'I don't see why. I did nothing wrong.'

'Suspicion clings. It'll never leave you. You know what people are like, where there's smoke . . .'

'You mean that for the rest of my life people are going to say I killed my husband?' she said.

'If you haven't worked that out then you're stupid and I never thought that of you. G and T? Sherry?'

'Nothing, thanks.'

'Well, I will, if you don't mind.'

'If that's the case, and people are going to think that, then I'm in the wrong job. In fact, I couldn't be in a worse one. People die in my care – I can't change that, I can't work miracles.'

'But what else could you do?' Iris said bluntly, as she sat down opposite Chrissy, who was huddled in what had once been her father's wing chair.

'I can administer,' she said eventually.

'What? You?' Iris was dumbfounded. 'You're too disorganised for that, wouldn't you say? No, you toughen up and see it through.' She took a sip of her drink, apparently blissfully unaware of having chipped away at Chrissy's self-confidence. 'Poor Ewan,' she added suddenly, and her face softened at the words. Then she changed the subject. 'Do you want that chair?'

'This one? Dad's?' Chrissy fingered the dark blue cut velvet. 'I don't know where I'd put it.'

'Then I'll sell it.'

'No. No, don't do that. I'll find room somehow. Perhaps you know someone with a van who'd drive it out to the cottage for me?'

'Are you getting at me?' Iris demanded.

'No, heavens, what have I said?' Chrissy looked astonished.

'Well, *of course* I know someone with a van – Bob's got a van, hasn't he?'

'I didn't think.'

'You often don't.'

'What's the matter, Mum? You're so edgy, these days.'

'I'm not. You're the edgy one, not me.'

'Whatever you say,'

'See, there you go again, acting all sarky.'

'Shall we start again, Mum? Pax?' She smiled at her mother. 'Honestly, it was an innocent question, and I wondered why you were selling it.' She felt she was being two-faced as she spoke, but the last thing she wanted was a further falling-out with her mother, despite her failure to look after Daphne the other night.

'I'm getting shot of everything – furniture, house, the lot.'

'You can't do that! Not this house. Oh, Mum.' Chrissy was appalled.

'New start. You said yourself the other day what a good idea it was.'

'But I meant the Aga. If you didn't like it, then –'

'Oh, I've put that back. The estate agent advised it. He said it was a good selling point.'

'Where will you go? Something smaller?'

'No, I'm buying a boat and I'm sailing the world. It's what I've always wanted to do.'

'I'd no idea you liked sailing or that you'd ever done any.'

'You don't know everything. I never told you many things that I would like to do. How could I? I'd have been laughed at – me, the bank manager's wife, dreaming of a hippie seafaring life.'

'Still, if it's what you want,' Chrissy said unconvincingly. 'But how will you manage? I mean, what do you know about sailing?'

'Bob's coming with me. Sailing's his hobby. Didn't I say?' she added, with wide-eyed innocence.

'No, you didn't. It's a relief to know you aren't planning to go solo.' Chrissy forced a laugh. She was upset, and doubly so when she realised that she was far more perturbed at the thought of her family home being sold than of her mother leaving.

'So why are you here? You must have a reason since you so rarely come to see me. I might have felt differently about going if you had. I might have found it difficult to cut my ties.'

Chrissy smiled. 'I doubt it, Mum. But yes, I'm here on a mission. Gran.' There seemed no point in prevaricating.

'What about her?'

'She hates the hospital. She's frightened of one of the nurses. I want to get her into a nursing home – she's up and about now on her Zimmer frame. She'd be happier.'

'So, do it, if that's what she wants.'

'Yes, but they cost an arm and a leg and her pension won't cover it. I can help a bit, but I'm pretty stretched. I was wondering –'

'No, is the answer.'

'You don't know what I was about to say.'

'Yes, I do. You want a contribution from me. And I can't afford it.'

'But if you sell this house, surely you can?'

'I shall need every penny I can raise. Boats – good ones – don't come cheap and I'll have to invest to give me an income. You must see that, otherwise a day might come when you'd have to cough up to rescue me from some hideous fate in some far-off place.' Iris seemed to find this funny.

'Gran needs our help now. She's old and infirm.'

'Probably does, but she shouldn't have banked on me. I told you I've never liked her and she's never liked me. Why should I do anything?'

'For the very good reason that she's Dad's mother, and Dad worked hard to buy this place. And he got where he did because of the sacrifices she made when he was a boy. You wouldn't even be going around the world if it weren't for Gran.'

'You do things in this life you want to, not because you're expected to.'

'That's not right, Mum, and you damn well know it.'

'She helped your father because she loved him. She got pleasure from his success. In my book that's that. That's all she's entitled to.'

'But Dad wouldn't have felt like this. He'd never have left you everything if he thought you wouldn't look after Gran.'

'Just as well he doesn't know, then, isn't it?'

'I can't believe I'm hearing this. What on earth has got into you, Mum?'

'I'm doing what thousands of women would like to do. I'm grabbing at happiness and freedom before it's too late. I've paid my dues a thousand times over. Now I'm reaping the reward. And don't even think of lecturing me. My mind's made up.'

Chrissy stood up. 'No. I won't waste my breath. I guess you

wouldn't be listening,' she said, her weariness etching the words. They both heard a key turn in the front door.

'Going already?' said Bob, as he entered the room, a large case in his hand.

'Stay and have a drink, Chrissy, do. She's been disapproving, Bob. Haven't you, Chrissy? Not sure she wants her mummy running off to sea with you.'

'Bit of a shock, I expect.' Bob grinned sheepishly at her.

'No, you must do as you want.' She looked pointedly at the case.

'Bob's moving in. We've decided to hell with the neighbours. Haven't we, Bob?'

'Sure have.' Bob twined his arm around Iris's shoulder protectively. He looked lovingly at her as she snuggled into the curve of his body. They looked so happy, so together, that Chrissy, despite her disappointment and anger with her mother's selfishness, found herself smiling at them – and envying their closeness.

'Don't forget to pack your life-jackets – that's all the advice I've got to give,' she said, as she picked up her bag from the floor. 'I'll leave you two in peace.'

She was still smiling as she left them, but outside, away from their happiness, the smile left her. The changes in her mother had taken place too swiftly for Chrissy to accept easily. How could she be so blatantly egocentric? Perhaps she'd always been so but Chrissy had blanketed her with the child's cloak of unquestioning love for a parent, and she'd been too young when she'd left Fellcar to have reached the point at which she could see her parents as they really were.

'Drat!' she said, at dropping her keys. She bent to search for them in the road as a car approached and picked out her bending form in its headlights.

'Chrissy, hello!' she heard Russell call as he slammed his car door shut. He walked speedily up the hill towards her. 'What are you doing here?'

'This is my mother's house.'

'I didn't know that. I've just been to your place.'

'I haven't been home yet.'

'Fancy dinner?'

'Oh, I don't know. I'm tired and –'

'Please, Chrissy.' He took her hand in his. 'I want to apologise about the other night. I was stupid, bloody stupid.'

She grinned at him. 'Yes, you were rather.'

'I was tired. It had been an awful day. Can we try again?' Silently he prayed she'd say yes. 'What do you say?'

'Okay. But I've got nothing in the house.'

'No, I meant may I take you out? Have you eaten at Chez Sylvie? It's a little French restaurant down on the front.'

'I'll have to go and shower and change.'

'What if I come and pick you up in an hour?'

'Lovely,' she said. To her surprise he bent forward and kissed her cheek. 'Actually, it'll be better if I meet you at the restaurant.' And then, knowing she had sounded a little tense, she added lamely, 'I'll be less flustered.' They were standing under a street-lamp and clearly visible to Iris who was watching from an upstairs window. Two doors further down so was Sabine.

8

A serious staffing crisis was looming, there was no doubt of that, Glynis thought, as she worked on her ward allocation charts, on which she was prepared to spend as much time as necessary. The flu epidemic was almost over, but several of the nurses hadn't returned to work – when morale was as low as this, though, she was not in the least surprised. Also, persistent rumours of the hospital closing were always harmful to staffing levels. Too much work had been expected of them for too little return and it was understandable that if a more attractive job was offered they would go for it, not that any other work could give the sense of achievement that nursing did. Of that she was convinced.

With Christmas fast approaching, Glynis expected further resignations. The part-time nurses would be aware of catastrophe looming, and those with young families would not be prepared to work over the holiday. Accident and Emergency was most vulnerable, and they would have to pray that no major incidents would stretch the department to its limits or, worse, lead to its collapse.

There were times when Glynis could quite happily have throttled the Craig Nuttings of this world. If he hadn't banned further recruitment last month she would still have a problem, but perhaps not quite as acute as this was becoming. She pulled out her list of bank nurses to see if there was any juggling she could do there.

She shouldn't have moved Dawn Allyson over to Oncology when she had. It had been stupid of her, she couldn't have been concentrating, but she so wanted the new department to succeed. What if she moved Dawn back to A and E, perhaps on a permanent basis? But that would leave Oncology short, and how could Chrissy Galloway cope with Lesley Bing on maternity leave and on a ward where they liked to arrange the treatments so that the patients could enjoy Christmas at home? Perhaps if she asked Dawn to work on A and E just over the Christmas period. Though she had seemed very pleased with her new posting. Oh dear. Glynis sighed. Dawn was a good nurse and one whom she was not prepared to upset.

Perhaps Chrissy, single and alone, wouldn't mind working through the holidays, and could help out in other departments where needed. That was a situation she didn't like, but what other choice had she, with a staffing emergency on the cards? In which case, her unreasonableness at their last interview, which still worried Glynis, was unlikely to help the problem. She should never have been so short with her: the woman had every right to be concerned for her grandmother's well-being. Jazz reminded Glynis of a girl at her school – oh, so long ago, too long – who'd had the same stocky build and was a bully, which was a wrong and illogical approach to the problem, she knew. But how weary she felt, how low such problems made her feel. Maybe she should make an appointment to see someone in Occupational Health. She was working under par, she couldn't sleep, she was . . . 'Oh, really, Glynis, pull yourself together and don't be such a wimp!' she said aloud, as she often did when she was reprimanding herself.

Staffing levels! She pulled a writing pad towards her. She would send a memo to all senior members of staff, requesting that they be on call throughout the Christmas period should a major emergency present itself. It was the best she could do.

'Come,' she said, to a rap at her door, glancing with irritation at her watch. She wanted to get away early tonight: she was dining with

Floss Yates, something she'd looked forward to all week. 'Problems?' she asked, in an almost resigned way at the sight of an anxious-faced Edna Greenbank.

'You could say that. Remember the nurse I told you about – the one I found bonking with Matthew Kersey?'

'Of course.' Glynis winced inwardly at Edna's choice of words.

'Well, she's honking away and useless to me. How can I run a theatre when one of my best instrument nurses keeps having to rush out to throw up?'

'Has she seen a doctor? What does he say is wrong with her?'

'She's pregnant, of course – by *him*.'

'By whom? The GP?'

Edna sighed. 'No, of course not. By Matthew.'

Glynis paused, almost imperceptibly, as she assimilated this news. 'How would you know that for sure? It could easily be someone else.'

'No, she says it's him and I believe her. She also tells me you haven't had a word with her. Does that mean you haven't had a go at Matthew either? Or got Fraser to talk to him?'

'It's easy enough to accuse a man. But DNA testing will sort that out.' Just recently, no doubt due to her age, Glynis frequently felt insufferably hot when she was stressed, so she was surprised to find she felt quite cool. 'And I did speak to Matthew.'

'And?'

'He denies the incident.'

'You're having me on!'

'No. That is what he told me and I have no reason to disbelieve him.'

'Glynis, when will you wake up? The man is a serial adulterer. No woman's safe when he's around. He's making you the laughing stock of the whole hospital.'

'How could that be? Don't be so silly.' She loosened her collar, in preparation for a flash of heat, which did not appear.

'I'm not the silly one, it's you. You swan around as Madame Purity – but everyone knows about you and Matthew. He laughs about you behind your back. Did you know that?'

Glynis was hot now, but from anger, not hormones. She stood up. 'I'll tell you what I do know, Edna, that you are infatuated with Matthew and, as is so often the case, such an infatuation has distorted your judgement. I can only guess at what has motivated these accusations of yours – an obsessive jealousy, no doubt.' Having made this speech with extraordinary self-control, she sat down again. To her consternation Edna threw back her head and laughed as if she could not stop.

'And what cock-and-bull story has he been telling you?' she asked, dabbing away tears of mirth a tissue. 'Look, Glynis, I'm not jealous. I'm sorry for you. You obviously love Matthew and he doesn't deserve you. You're an attractive woman. Stop wasting your time and your life on a creep like him.'

'Quite honestly, Edna, I don't know what you mean.' Glynis knew she spoke in a clichéd way, but it was difficult to find any other words – and she clung to the old, well-used ones as if they were a life-raft.

'Then I'll tell you. Oh, like a lot of others I fancied Matthew – he's a good-looking bloke, rich, successful, and he can be fun when he isn't ditching you and covering his own back. Not that I wanted an involvement – no way, I've more sense than that. But when I found him with the nurse and read the Riot Act I wasn't surprised that he turned his amorous attentions to me. I knew what he was about, that he wanted to buy my silence. To stop me running to you. But I'll admit I was flattered for all that. So when he suggested a weekend away in the country at a super hotel I thought, Why not? We had a ball, food was great, sex so-so, but I knew what I was supposed to do in return. Shut up about the nurse in theatres.'

'Then why didn't you?'

'I doubt if you'll believe me, but it was because I like and respect you, Glynis. I didn't want to see you humiliated, but even more I didn't want to see you hurt.'

'I'm supposed to believe that? Oh, Edna, what do you take me for? If I had any interest in Matthew Kersey – note I say *if* – then by telling me all that rubbish you'd be certain of hurting me, wouldn't you? As it is, I haven't. I like the man as a colleague and as a friend. After all, I've known him for many years. Now, if you wouldn't mind, I've work to do and a dinner appointment. Goodnight, Edna. I'll see what I can do about a replacement nurse for you but she'll have to come from the bank. Craig Nutting, as you know, has banned new recruitment.'

Edna stood. She looked down at Glynis for a second. 'Suit

yourself,' she said, before she walked to the door. 'Mind you, I'd like to know what it is you've got on him to keep him on a leash this long – must be something quite juicy.'

Glynis pretended to ignore the remark, studying her charts with an intense expression. Only when the door had closed did she raise her head. She sat still, gazing into space. And then, like a clinician of the soul, she began to take stock.

In a strange way, what Edna had told her had come as no surprise. She found she was even sorry for the young pregnant nurse, and found herself wondering what the girl would do about the baby and, from that, what she would have done if she'd ever found herself in the same position. It would not have been a difficult decision, she was sure: she'd have kept it.

She wasn't even surprised by Edna's claim of a weekend affair: she wasn't angry – rather, she found the idea distasteful. Or that he had lied to her the other night – she felt almost as if she'd known it at the time.

The most surprising discovery of all was that she was calm. She wasn't, for the moment, hurt. Instead, she found that she was disappointed in Matthew. *Disappointed.* What a lame word for the ending of such a passionate affair. For it was the end, she knew. Now she understood that the love, the passion, the romance had died inside her that dreadful afternoon in the London hotel. As she'd wept and ranted she'd undoubtedly killed it. She was relieved to find that there was no hate within her, only a void, which somehow she would fill. She had to. Of one thing she was sure: there was no going back.

9

The interior of Chez Sylvie was warm and welcoming on such a bitterly cold night. It was a restaurant caught in a time-warp of nearly thirty years ago. Red and white checked tablecloths matched the frilled curtains at the windows. On each table stood a wine bottle heavily encrusted with years of dripped candlewax. Strings of obviously artificial garlic and onions hung from the ceiling. No nouvelle cuisine was served here: instead there were generous portions of the food of the French countryside – thick, nourishing soups, hearty casseroles and stews. Accordion music issued from an eight-track stereo system, which was obviously on its last legs and constantly stalled, usually remedied by a hefty whack from *la patronne*.

Sylvie, like her establishment, was also rooted in the past. False lashes and black liner ringed her eyes, and her pale pink lipstick seeped into the vertical lines of age around her mouth, making her look as if someone had shoved her from behind while she was eating candy-floss. Her tight black leather skirt was a mite too short for one of her age, but not for her still elegant legs. Her platform-soled shoes were the height of fashion, but by accident. Since she'd never been known to throw anything away, fashion had gone full circle and such shoes were back in vogue again.

Sylvie preferred to remain anchored in the early seventies, a time when she'd been young and happy and had arrived in Fellcar. Her clothes, music, décor, food were all of that time. Even her accent had stayed as thick and impenetrable as it had been then.

The restaurant had always been popular but just recently, with the swing back in fashion, it looked chic again.

'Can you imagine? One has to book a table. Sylvie's doing so well.' Floss flicked her generously proportioned napkin onto her lap and eagerly picked up the menu.

'They deserve it. The food is so consistently good.' Glynis poured herself a glass of water from a carafe.

'You look a bit peaky, Glynis, are you all right?'

'I'm fine.'

'You'll say that on your death-bed, no doubt. What's up?'

'Staffing levels are bad. I think we're approaching crisis level.'

'Again! What's new? You should be used to that particular worry, my dear. So what is it?'

Glynis, who would never normally have confided her shopping list to anyone, let alone the problems of her heart, did something completely out of character: she looked at Floss, her kind face, her warm brown eyes, and suddenly felt such weariness and a need to unburden herself. And so, quite calmly and coolly, Glynis confided in Floss her conversation with Edna. As her sad story unfolded, she found it rather comforting to share it.

'You don't seem too put out, if you don't mind my saying so,' Floss said as Glynis, came to the end.

'I'm not. It was as if I'd been expecting it to happen. I was completely unsurprised. I'm wondering if a reaction will set in later.'

'Lor', what a cool customer you are! Well, at least it makes it easier for me to talk to you about a rather distressing matter. I've found out more about the proposed hospital closure and who's involved. I've been given a fax – and it's certain that Matthew is one of the conspirators.'

'Floss, nothing surprises me any more,' Glynis said, with a sad weary smile . . . and Floss leant over and urgently, quietly, told Glynis of her plans.

'Do you see who's sitting over there?' Russell leant across the table towards Chrissy. 'Our beloved Clinical Services Manager with Floss Yates.'

'I hope they don't see us.'

'They seem too engrossed. But does it matter if Glynis notices us?'

'She doesn't like me. I don't think she approves of me.'

'Glynis? What makes you think that? No, don't tell me, you think she's listened to the gossip too. I wouldn't believe it of her. She's always struck me as a very fair person.'

'Maybe, but not to me. Maybe she's found out something about Ewan and me and the police. If I've learnt anything, it's that the past always catches up with you even if it's an untruth.' She played with her napkin. As always, any thought of Ewan and a pleasant mood could disappear in a trice. Not tonight, she resolved. 'I'm being silly. Let's change the subject. Tell me, how are you feeling? You look so much better, less strained and tired.' She smiled tenderly at him.

'I'd forgotten what it's like to be smiled at like that. As if you really care.'

'Of course I care – what an odd thing to say.'

'You wouldn't think that if you were me.'

'Gracious, I can almost hear the violins!' She laughed lightly. 'What's got into you? You're handsome, successful, your patients adore you. Half the nurses drool over you – doesn't seem too bad to me.' And you've got the most beautiful woman in Fellcar for a wife, she thought, but of course she didn't say that.

'I wasn't talking about them. I was meaning someone special in my life.' He put his hand across the table and covered hers. Quickly she removed it and placed it in her lap, as if to keep it out of harm's way. 'Why is it that whenever I get close to you you shy away as if I burn you?'

'Do I?'

'You know you do. As soon as I think it's safe to get close to you – like just now when you smiled so sweetly at me – you react as if I'm Jack the Ripper. It's confusing.'

'I'm sorry, I don't mean to. It's . . .' She shook her head almost defiantly. 'No. That's not true. What's the point of pretending? The truth is that I'm scared to let us go any further.'

'Scared? Of me? What have I done?'

'Nothing.' She looked miserably at her plate. She longed to tell him that she wanted him, ached to be held by him, kissed, loved by him – but she knew herself, knew that her brain would not permit her body to do what she wanted. Too much pain, too much humiliation, too much mental abuse stood in the way. She shook her head again, not in defiance this time, but in an effort to erase those memories that seemed to refuse to be gone. 'That apart,' she said, not realising she had not explained how she felt, only thought it, 'I don't think it's right to be involved with a married man. I shouldn't really be here now.' She sounded prim and precious, and knew she did, but didn't know how else to explain herself: how she feared he'd return to his wife, and if she gave herself to him she'd be hurt and disillusioned, and she knew that she couldn't deal with any of it. But she couldn't bring herself to explain. He said nothing, as if he was waiting for her to continue.

'I'm getting divorced,' he said abruptly, when she didn't.

'But you still live in the same house as Sabine.'

'If that's what's bothering you then I'll move out tomorrow. Will that solve it? Will you accept me then?' he asked eagerly. Chrissy didn't answer but looked frightened, her large brown eyes startled. 'It isn't just that, is it? There's more. It goes further back. You need to talk, my darling. Who better than me? I promised myself I'd be patient and not rush you, but I've got to say it – I'm falling in love with you, I'd never hurt you. All I want is to care for you, protect you.'

'*Bonsoir*, Russell. 'Ow lovely to see you.' Sylvie's heavily accented English interrupted him. 'Ze special tonight . . .' And she listed the dishes of the day. Chrissy relaxed in her seat, as if some danger had passed. Russell sighed, aware that a moment had slipped away and he was unsure if he would be able to recapture it.

Certainly that evening it did not return. Chrissy, it seemed to him, had erected a barrier around herself, which tonight, at least, he would be unable to scale. They ate their meal with enjoyment, drank the wine with pleasure. They talked of many things, Russell having made a conscious decision that he must not move too fast with Chrissy or he would lose her.

'And you say you spoke to Glynis about the post-mortem reports and she's heard nothing? This is ridiculous. It's not fair. If you want, I'll sort it out tomorrow.'

'Would you? Would you have time?'

'Time is what I have a lot of at the moment. The pathologist is a mate of mine. He'll sort it out. Thank God for that! You're actually smiling again.'

'If you could find out something for me it would be such a weight off my mind. I wake up in the morning and I feel fine for a second and then I remember and all the worry floods back. It's awful!'

'Poor darling. If it makes you happier –' He caught himself – he'd called her darling again.

Sylvie served their coffee and petit fours.

'Do you really understand what she says?'

'About fifty per cent. The rest sounds like Serbo-Croat to me. But I think it's all an act. The longer she stays the thicker her accent becomes. Floss, Glynis! I didn't realise you were here.' He stood up as he fibbed.

'Lovely nosh, isn't it, Chrissy?' said Floss, and kissed her on both cheeks. 'When in France –' She grinned.

'Good evening, Miss Tillman.'

'Won't she let you call her Glynis? Really, you can be such a stuffy old crow sometimes, Glynis.'

Glynis looked embarrassed and spoke so softly that no one heard what she said.

'I think Miss Tillman is happier with formality,' Chrissy said, not looking at her.

'Trouble with Glynis is she hasn't worked out yet that it's the end of the century and not the beginning. She'd have been happier working under Flo Nightingale, wouldn't you?'

'Really, Floss. You're the most appalling bully at times,' Glynis laughed good-naturedly enough, but Chrissy was aware that she still looked uncomfortable.

'You're both coming to my party?' Floss looked at Russell and Chrissy. 'It should be quite an interesting night.'

'We'll be there,' said Russell.

'If I'm not on duty,' added Chrissy.

Once the goodbye kissing ritual was completed the two older women were ushered away by a fussing Sylvie.

'I think I should be going too.' Chrissy began to feel for her handbag on the floor.

'Already?' He sounded disappointed.

'I'm on early shift.'

'How's it going?' he asked, as he signalled for the bill.

'Fine. It's quite a challenge – such a senior post combined with setting up a new unit, but I'm enjoying it, or at least I will when I get rid of all the accusing glances and whispering.' She smiled, but Russell felt it was a sad smile, which he longed to alter.

Russell paid the bill and they walked to where their cars were parked. She wished he'd take her hand in his, but he didn't. She couldn't blame him, not after the way she kept reacting when he made the mildest of advances. Russell tucked his hands in his pockets, he could not rely on himself not to grab hold of her and frighten her even further away.

'That was a lovely meal, Russell. Thank you,' she said, as she stood by Rommel, her car.

'I'm glad you enjoyed it. We must do it again.'

'I'd love to.' She opened the car door. She wanted to invite him back for nightcap, but after she'd obviously rejected him how could she? Not that she'd wanted to put him off. It had happened before and it seemed she could not stop herself doing it. She climbed in and put the key in the ignition. He closed the door behind her and bent down as the window slid down.

'I was wondering –' He stopped.

'Yes?' she asked, expectantly.

'Oh, nothing,' he replied. 'See you.' He stood up. He'd been about to ask if he could follow her car home and congratulated himself on the self-control he'd exerted. He waved and walked across to his own car.

Chrissy drove out quickly into the street. All the way home she berated herself for her stupidity. She had somehow to erase Ewan's damage from her mind. Logic told her that much of what he'd said to her in the past was lies. The same logic could acknowledge what his game had been: to make her feel so demoralised that no one else would ever want her. She knew she wasn't fat; the mirror told her she wasn't ugly; her skin was unblemished and smooth; her birth certificate showed she was still young; she ran a demanding ward so she was not stupid; Russell enjoyed her company so she could not be boring. When she thought like this, the list appalled her. And her stupidity in the past, in believing Ewan, angered her. Oh, yes, she could think it through sensibly, logically. Then why?

Why was she afraid to let Russell near her – to touch her skin, to see her naked? She knew the answer only too well; given an endless diet of criticism, enough sneering looks, sufficient derisory laughs, the most beautiful, the most confident woman would end up as she had.

She turned into her gateway. She paused a second, enjoying the smell of the wind, heavy with ozone from the sea – her own personal tonic. She unlocked the back door, entered her kitchen and stood stock still.

The room was exactly as she had left it, with the lights on for her return. Nothing was out of place. And yet Chrissy had the feeling, no, more than that, she was certain – that someone had been here while she was out.

CHAPTER SEVEN

I

'Sorry, Russell, I can't help you. I finished my reports several days ago. It's all gone to Thorpedale.'

'Thorpedale? Why? Why not here?' Russell asked into the telephone.

'It's normal for a copy of any post-mortem we perform to be sent to them, but I'll tell you, Russell, I was surprised when they requested that *all* copies be sent and none to go to Fellcar.' And he thought, but didn't add, that the instructions that the pathologist at Thorpedale would handle everything from then on were the oddest of all.

'Any idea why that should be?'

'Well . . .' There was silence. Jim, the pathologist, patted his pockets for the cigarettes he'd long ago given up. Habits died hard, however. 'I'd rather not say.' The telephone finally came to life again.

'So you did find something untoward. Which patient?'

'Look, Russell, don't push me, please. I really don't want any hassle. Ask Craig Nutting what's up. He's the one sitting on them.'

'But, Jim, it's me – we go back a long way.'

'Not far enough, Russell,' he said, and hung up.

Russell sat at his desk, picking at the raised edge of the black-leather blotter tooled in gold, part of a desk set Sabine had given him years ago when they still bothered to search out expensive presents for each other. Jim was edgy and hiding something, he was sure of that.

He swivelled the black-leather chair, picked up the telephone and punched in the necessary buttons for Fellcar hospital and asked to speak to Fraser Ball, the neurologist.

'Fraser, it's Russell. Your Mrs Tomley, the sudden death, have you heard the post-mortem result?'

'Now you mention it, I haven't. I've been away at a conference for a few days. I must chase it up – not a good thing to have hanging over the department.'

'Was it totally unexpected? I mean, anything you were concerned about?'

'In neurology we're always prepared for the unexpected.' Fraser laughed. 'But I was surprised. I thought she'd made a good recovery. The worry is, if one made a mistake or didn't pick up on something that shouldn't have been there but should have been spotted. You know how it is. What about yours?'

'Mrs Norman? Natural causes – I heard last week.'

'Lucky you. Why are you asking?'

'Oh, nothing, just curious.'

The Care of the Elderly consultant could shed no light either. 'Old people, Russell, you can never tell. But thank you for reminding me.'

Russell replaced the receiver, made a few notes and quickly tore them up. He was getting paranoid himself. Just because the system was working differently why should he immediately jump to the conclusion that there had been foul play? But what shocked him more was the way his thoughts had followed from that to thinking of Chrissy and her dead husband, Ewan. 'No,' he said, aloud and emphatically.

'No what?' Sabine asked from the doorway. 'You know what they say about talking to yourself.' She giggled nervously.

'Been doing it a long time,' he said, more to cover his confusion at being overheard than as a gesture of friendship. Sabine interpreted it as the latter and stepped further into the room, smiling less tentatively.

'Russell, can we talk?'

'If it's about selling up and dividing our things, well, what's left of mine, yes.' He glanced round the room at the possessions he'd hastily gathered into piles. 'If it's about our relationship, I've nothing further to say.' He swivelled his chair, put his legs up on his desk and his hands behind his head.

'It's both.'

'I've just said that I'll only discuss the division of spoils.'

'Russell, why are you so hard on me?'

'I assumed you understood why.'

'Why can't we try again? We were happy once, weren't we?' she pleaded.

'I thought so, but I know now it was a sad illusion. Sabine, this is a conversation that will get us nowhere and I have to go out.' He swung his legs down.

'There's someone else, isn't there?'

'What if there is?'

'You're so cruel.' Sabine lunged at him, hand raised as if to strike him. Russell was quickly on his feet, he grabbed hold of her arm to restrain her. 'You're hurting me,' she whined.

'No, I'm not.' He let go of her arm. 'You're the one who's done the hurting. What's all this about? Does Giles not want you? Is that why you're back here sniffing about me? You sicken me, Sabine. There's no going back. Why don't you just leave? Pack and go?'

'My lawyer said –'

'Stay put. Yes, so did mine. But they don't have to live like this, do they?' He was on his feet moving to the door.

'Where are you going?'

'Out.'

Lynn slapped the letter from the laboratory down on the table in front of Terry.

'Now what have you got to say?' she asked, hands on hips, her stance aggressive, but the effect spoilt by the wide grin on her face.

Terry read the single sheet report. He looked up at her. 'I'm sorry,' he said.

'Say it in full.'

'I'm sorry I accused you of being drunk.'

'And are you sorry you didn't believe me?'

'Yes.'

Lynn sat down at the table. 'I was shattered you didn't believe me, that you didn't trust me.'

'I said I'm sorry. I can't undo what I said. But I hope you're not going to keep banging on about it.'

'Me? And sound like my mother?' Lynn was unable to stay cross for long. 'No way!'

'For all that this report says you were well below the limit, you acted as pissed as a lord – or is it a newt?' He stabbed at the paper.

'I think this proves my point. Giles put something in my drink. You know me, I've never been able to take alcohol – one gin and I'm anybody's! But at least it takes a whole drink to do that. Yet a couple of sips of whisky and I'm falling down drunk? There had to be something else in that whisky – and have you thought what might have happened if I'd drunk the lot? I reckon I'd be dead!'

'Lynn, don't even say it.' Hurriedly Terry touched wood. 'But if there *was* something else, wouldn't they have picked it up in the blood test?'

'Not if they weren't looking for it or if it was only a trace.'

'But if it was so little, why did it make you like that?'

'My low tolerance.'

'Bloody mystery to me. What are you going to do now?'

'I've two options. I've spoken to Glynis Tillman about joining their nursing bank.'

'You've always said you'd hate to be a bank nurse, moving from pillar to post.'

'No. She asked me how I felt about caring for the elderly – staffing those wards is always a problem. If I go there, I reckon I'll be made permanent as soon as they recruit again. She's had a stop put on. I'll get in by the back door, so to speak.'

'And the other? You said you'd two options.'

'I've got an interview today at the Mimosa Home. And I'll pop along to the hospital and suss out the situ there.'

'Isn't the Mimosa an old people's home? Would you like that?'

'No, it's a nursing home, not residential. It's quite a good post, pay's not too bad. Loads of responsibility. The hospital is a staffing job on Care of the Elderly proper – usual NHS rip-off paywise.'

'Why work? You don't need to. Stay at home.'

'What, and look after you lot exclusively? No, ta. I'd go mad cooped up in these four walls.'

'Why not try to get your old job back?'

'I wouldn't work there if they paid me double. But I'll get an apology from Dick Henderson before I'm finished.'

'What do you think's got into him?'

'He should retire, only I don't think he can face spending his days with his wife. He's tired and I don't think he cares any more. I think he loads too much of the work on Giles and so he's stuck. He can't control him any more and Giles can do whatever he wants. If he's going to keep a better eye on Giles he'll have to get off his bottom and work harder and, as I said, he's weary and doesn't want to any more.'

'But apart from the drugs what's so sinister?'

'Giles is permanently on the fiddle. I couldn't prove it, but I bet he takes bribes from the pharmaceutical companies. Certainly the reps spend longer with him than they do with Dick.'

'But that business about sending patients to the accident department, if he can enable people to jump the queue that's a good thing, isn't it? And he's saving the practice money.'

'I agree. It's great for the patients, but I doubt if the hospital sees it that way. But the savings?' Here Lynn laughed. 'Any savings made at the practice should be ploughed back into it. In this case I'm certain they aren't. Henderson has to know about them – after all, he's the senior partner – so what's the game? I reckon they share it and put it in their pockets. Maybe that's another reason why Henderson lets Giles get away with murder – one, he's got used to the extra cash, and two, he knows Giles could blackmail him with what he knows.'

'Have you proof of this?'

'No. I've worked it out.' She tapped her skull.

'Then keep mum or you could land up in serious trouble. Promise?'

'I promise,' she said, but under the table she crossed her fingers. She wasn't about to tell him that she'd already told Floss Yates her theories.

'Mr Newson, isn't it? Can I help you? Kim Henderson.' Kim held his hand out in greeting. 'You operated on my aunt.'

'Did I?' Russell said warily, hoping he remembered who the patient was. In his experience relatives were easily offended if he didn't remember names – he normally remembered faces, whatever his workload and the number of patients he saw.

'Mrs Yates.'

'Ah, Floss. What a character. I reckon St Edith's would collapse without her and her Friends. Is she well?'

'Blooming. She's . . .' Kim paused, wondering if he had the nerve to arrange a meeting with Russell, confide in him his concerns, or if he should leave it to his aunt. 'Well, you know my aunt.' Perhaps better not. After all, Russell was here to see Craig – and why? Was he in on the scam? Kim sighed inwardly at how difficult it was to know whom to trust. 'Mr Nutting will be free in just a moment.'

The connecting door opened, as if on cue, and Craig appeared. 'Russell Newson, well, this is an honour. Come in and take a pew.' He indicated a deep leather chair opposite his large but tidy desk. 'Now, what can I do for you, Russell?'

'I'm told you have the post-mortem reports here on Mrs Tomley and Mrs Fortune, two patients who suffered sudden and unexpected deaths a couple of weeks back at Fellcar.'

'Are they patients – or should I say late patients – of yours?' Craig asked, cockily.

'No, but –'

'Well, then, I can't tell you anything, can I?'

'Why not?'

'You wouldn't want me to divulge confidential information, would you? That would be unprofessional in the extreme. But, then, you know all there is to know about being professional – an important doctor like you. There's nothing I could tell you about all that, is there?' He spoke pleasantly enough, and the cockiness had gone, but for all that, Russell felt he was sniping at him – though for what reason he had no idea.

'Good God, man. I'm a consultant there. Once the results are sent over I shall know all about it, whether they're my patients or not.' He knew he was blustering, and that he was pulling rank in an unpleasant manner. Normally, he wouldn't do that, but there was something about this weasely man that made him act like this, despite himself.

'Of course you'll know when they get theirs. But now? Sorry, no can do.' Craig was enjoying this. What had started as a delaying tactic had all the makings of a great drama – and bad publicity for the hospital. It couldn't be better.

'But why the delay?'

'Is there?'

'You know there is.'

'Wheels within wheels, Russell old boy, you know how it is. They must have been important patients. Everyone wants to know about them – even good old Glynis.'

'Of course she does. This delay isn't fair on the staff.'

Craig's eyes lit up with immediate interest. 'Got an interest in the staff? One member in particular? One of the little nurses? Don't those black stockings make your heart go pit-a-pat? Better than any electric-shock treatment, wouldn't you say?'

'If there's a problem, members of staff should be told. I think there is and I'm demanding that the reports are released forthwith. And if there's something untoward why are the police not involved?' Russell could hear how pompous he sounded, but in the presence of this man he seemed to have lost the ability to speak normally.

'My, my. You *are* getting agitated, Russell. Who is it? Tell old Craig here. Is it that pretty little new sister I've heard about? The one whose husband died in rather odd circumstances? Bit dodgy. Are you sure you're safe there, Russell?'

Russell longed to hit him, to wipe off that supercilious grin. He stood up. He knew he had to get out of this room before he lost his self-control.

'Going?' Craig looked artificially surprised.

'There seems little point in continuing this conversation.' He turned and walked to the door.

'One little snippet, Russell, for old time's sake. Tell that little sister she'd better start looking for a lawyer. Just in case, you know . . .'

As he shut the door, his face rigid to disguise his shock, Russell heard Craig laugh as if he'd just cracked the best joke ever.

2

As Chrissy came out of the front door of the Mimosa Nursing Home, Lynn was approaching.

'We do keep meeting in odd places!' Lynn began to laugh, then stopped and put her hand on Chrissy's arm. 'Love, what is it? You look so tired.'

Chrissy shrugged, as if pushing away inessentials. 'Overworked and not enough sleep, and I've just had an interview here and heard their costs.' She, too, laughed, but Lynn thought it sounded hollow.

'Want to talk? I'm early for an interview. I've got a good fifteen minutes.'

'Mmm.' In truth, Chrissy didn't want to talk to anyone, but Lynn was always kind so she followed her.

'Why aren't you sleeping?' Lynn asked, once they were settled in the front of her car.

'Have you got all day?'

'Long enough.'

'Oh, I don't know. I'm worried about so many things. One, I could deal with, but they've all piled onto each other and I feel almost punch-drunk. I'm enjoying my work, but I'd no idea of the amount of tedious paper-pushing that would be involved in setting up a new unit. So I get tired and then I'm so afraid I'll start making stupid mistakes because of everything else.'

'And what's everything else?' Lynn coaxed.

'There's my grandmother . . .' And she related her worry about Daphne being afraid in the ward and her own mother's refusal to help her move her, and now the realisation that there was no way she could afford the nursing-home fees herself.

'St Edith's have named teams of carers, haven't they? Can't you ask for your grandmother to be transferred to another team?'

'That would be fine – if it worked. You need full staffing for that and we don't have it. So that ward's a bit like the old days – in theory they have a number of allocated patients, in practice everyone mucks in.'

'Is it just her leg and the aftermath of the pneumonia? So she's not poorly enough for continuing care in hospital?'

'They'd never keep her in.'

'Yet she's too crocked to be considered for care in the community – such as it is. Poor you, what a worry.'

'Then there's my mother . . .' And without mentioning Bob she told Lynn how Iris had changed, so much so that she barely knew her any longer. 'And she's selling my old home and I just hate the idea. On top of that there's been a spate of sudden deaths at the hospital and I know the finger of suspicion is pointing at me . . .' And she had of necessity to explain about Ewan and his death and the gossip and the guilt, even though she had no reason to feel guilty. She realised as she talked that, since her session with Dawn – even though she'd had too much to drink – it had been easier to discuss Ewan. By talking to Dawn, she'd unblocked something inside herself. She would like to have discussed Russell and her mixed emotions – wanting him and yet fearing involvement and, the biggest stumbling block of all, Sabine. But she didn't, she couldn't go that far. It wouldn't be fair, not when someone else was involved. It was a silly idea, it was early days and she hardly knew him. She sighed deeply.

'What else is there? That sigh says it all.'

'It's probably my imagination, but – oh, hell, I feel stupid just saying it. I think someone has been snooping about in my cottage.'

'You're not joking, are you? Good heavens! Have you been to the police?'

'And say what? That I've got this *feeling*? They'd laugh me out of the station.'

'With your responsibilities you need to have some help through all this, or something will give. But you're probably right about Jazz. About six months ago she was carpeted for rudeness and roughness with a patient – one from our surgery, that's how I know. But who did the lay board believe? The "angel of mercy" or the poor old OAP? Jazz, of course, and the patient was deemed demented.'

'You wouldn't think someone like Glynis Tillman would be taken in, would you?'

'Word is that she had a go at Jazz, but what's she to do? Care of the Elderly has always been notoriously difficult to staff. It's hard, physical work, as you know, and it lacks the drama of elsewhere.'

'I always enjoyed working there.'

'Me too. But, then, we love nursing, don't we?'

'What worsens the nightmare is that, knowing this about Jazz, I find I have to leave my gran there at their mercy because I can't afford to put her anywhere else.'

'And you're sure your mum won't help out?'

'No way. She's only thinking of herself these days.'

'A lot of widows do that, don't they? Kick over the traces. She'll be taking a toy boy next.'

'She already has,' Chrissy said bleakly.

'Oh, Chrissy, I'm sorry.'

'No, it's her life, and he seems a nice enough bloke. He's her plumber.' She burst out laughing. 'That always makes me laugh, especially when she's such a snob. I mean, if I'd gone out with someone like Bob she'd have hit the roof. Double standards aren't in it!'

'You say Glynis bit your head off over the post-mortem reports? Strange – maybe she's worrying too. Still, you're probably fretting unnecessarily. Deaths often come in clusters like that. And after the Ewan thing, well, maybe you're being just a bit sensitive about what people are saying, don't you think?'

'No. The gossip is real – I'm not imagining that.'

'What about Floss? Why not talk to her about it? She knows absolutely everyone.'

'I might do that.'

'I would. And get yourself a fellow – that's what you need, someone to snuggle up to and confide in.'

'You reckon?' Chrissy laughed genuinely for the first time. She looked at her watch. 'Oh, my God, Lynn, we've been here half an hour. Your interview – you're hopelessly late.'

'Oh, forget it.' Lynn waved her hand. 'You've made my mind up for me. I'll take the bank job on Care of the Elderly at St Edith's. I'll keep an eye open for your gran, so that's one less worry for you.'

'That's wonderful news! But I thought they weren't taking on any more staff for the time being?'

'Glynis said something about that but I reckon she's decided it didn't cover bank nurses.'

'Bless her. And you, Lynn, really are an angel!' Chrissy turned in the car seat and hugged her friend.

Mo was up and about on the ward, pushing the trolley to which her intravenous infusion was strapped, like an appendage in front of her.

'I hear you're feeling less sore,' Chrissy said to her, on meeting her *en route* to the day room.

'Much better, thanks. I looked out for you this morning.'

'We work a shift system. I'm on now until ten.'

'It's very confusing.'

'I'll give you my rota, then you'll know when to expect me. Was it anything in particular?' she asked. Mo nodded bleakly. 'Come into my office and we'll talk it through.' She had a dozen jobs to do and, as always, was running late, but Mo and any worries had to come first. 'Now, what's bothering you?'

'A friend came to visit me last night. I told her about me having chemotherapy and she said I was mad to agree to it, that her mother had had it and it made her feel worse and it didn't work – and she died anyway.' Mo looked doleful and close to tears.

'It's so easy to dish out advice when it's not you who's ill, isn't it? You'll have to get used to this sort of thing, Mo. The world is full of people who know better than the doctors. They have no end of pills, potions and alternative remedies to offer you, and they mean well, but I think it just confuses you more.'

'But she said when they give you chemo it's the last resort.'

'Well, that's a load of rubbish to start with. Times have moved on and that's just not true. We get amazing results these days. And, in any case, this course of drugs is preventive. No one can be a hundred per cent sure that when you had your operation all the cancer cells were removed. These drugs and the radiation treatment are to be given to you to mop up anything that's left which, in any case, might not be there. You see?'

Mo relaxed visibly. 'But . . .' And she stiffened again. 'She said I'd feel so sick I'd want to die.'

'Some people feel nausea, others don't. Some get indigestion, others don't. You can't make sweeping statements like that. And if, unfortunately, you do feel sick, we have drugs that can help you.'

'She said cannabis was good for it. And do you remember Yvonne said the same?'

'So I've heard. Unfortunately we don't give it!' Chrissy giggled at the idea.

'I think I'd be too scared to try it. Though my husband occasionally smokes it.'

'I could never inhale, that was my problem. But some people swear by mint or ginger. But what are we doing jumping the gun? Let's sort that out *if* it occurs.'

'Okay.' Mo still sounded doubtful.

'Mo, do you remember when you were pregnant all you heard were horror stories? You'd have thought that no one had ever had a normal birth. Well, having cancer is a bit like that – everyone you meet has a gory tale to tell. Try to ignore them and talk to us who know.'

'I find I'm listening to my body all the time, expecting something else to go wrong.'

'Everyone does. You've taken your body for granted for so long, then this happens and suddenly you're aware of it.'

'You understand so much.'

'It's my job to.'

'I'm so glad it was you on this ward.'

'So am I! Still, you're lucky, you've got a supportive husband – that helps immeasurably.'

'Me? He hasn't even been to visit me. He's too scared of hospitals.'

'But the other night –'

'That was a friend, Ash. He's my husband's partner.'

'Oh, I'm sorry. Only, the way he was looking at you – well, I thought . . .'

Mo blushed. 'I think he's got a soft spot for me.'

'I'd put it stronger than that.'

'Still, what you said about being pregnant . . .' Mo changed the subject to cover her embarrassment. 'It's so like that. I was talking to a woman yesterday – she's got the same thing. And it was odd but I felt such a bond with her, just like with the other new mothers when the girls were born.'

'That's good. Anything else?'

'I just wish you'd talk to the doctors, teach them.'

'Me? What?' Chrissy chuckled at the idea.

'They're so detached. I suppose they're so used to dealing with patients that what they say has become automatic. It's like you're on a conveyor belt.'

'It's different for the nurses. We know you all better than they do. Sometimes I think the doctors appear remote because it's a sort of defence mechanism.'

'You reckon?' Mo snorted her disbelief. 'Still, I'm keeping you from your work.' She stood up. 'You've helped a lot. Thanks.'

The phone rang. It was an irate theatre nurse complaining that the patient whom Chrissy had sent up earlier hadn't had her notes and X-ray with her.

'I'm so sorry. I forgot,' Chrissy said, but she was appalled that she could forget something so simple and so routine.

Dawn appeared in the doorway. 'We've got a bit of a problem, Chrissy. Pharmacy say they haven't had the ward order, it's due today and where is it? You know what fuss-pots they are.'

Chrissy looked at her desk. There, on the top, was the list. 'Oh, hell! Look, there it is.'

'And Mr Hobbs says he told you he was a diabetic but he didn't get a special diet meal.'

Chrissy's shoulders slumped. Dawn approached her, bent down and put her arm around her. 'Don't worry, Chrissy. You've got too much on your plate at the moment. Look, it's quiet here. Why don't you go home early? I can cover for you.'

'Would you, Dawn? I could do with an early night. You're a treasure.'

'No problem. You can do the same for me one day.'

3

Chrissy had been a nurse long enough to know that it was wisest always to cover one's back. Something she hadn't done that night when she had given Buck Marston a drug that the doctor had only verbally ordered. That action had been illegal and she had been stupid – she'd put her career on the line that night. But she'd been lucky, that time: Fraser Ball hadn't let her down and the dose had been written up in Buck's notes. Miraculously, no one had found out. Ever since she'd often wondered if Fraser would have stood up for her if he'd forgotten to have the prescription done. He was a nice man, but if that had been the case he'd have risked getting into trouble himself. Never again, she'd resolved then and she meant to keep to that – so, rather than just leave Dawn in control, she was on her way to the office to report that she was leaving early.

'Sister Galloway! Cooee! Sister!' a voice called.

Chrissy stopped at the next flight of steps down. 'Mrs Marston. Good gracious, how strange! I was just thinking about Buck. How is your son doing?'

Mrs Marston puffed up to the landing. 'He's a blooming walking miracle, Sister. He always was a tough nut. I said at the time it would take more than a bang on the head to finish the little blighter off.'

'He's obviously doing well, then?'

'Well? He's zapping about like a racing driver. Can't wait to get out of here.' Mrs Marston giggled. 'No offence meant, you understand.'

'And his head?'

'Well, there never was much in there to start with, but he's had no more fits. His memory's a bit wobbly but Mr Ball says that'll probably clear up – he's very pleased with him.'

'And your daughter-in-law?'

'A little boy, two nights ago, Liam – lovely name, isn't it? I'm like a yo-yo visiting her then Buck. Back and forth, no time for anything else.'

'Do give her my congratulations, won't you?'

'I will. We're hoping that they'll both be home for Christmas. They'll have to come to me – it'd be too much for Cheryl to manage, so soon after the baby and all.'

'I shouldn't make plans . . . I mean, it's early days for Buck.'

'Oh, he says he'll discharge himself if needs be. You'd have to tie him down if he's made his mind up to go.'

'Let's hope it will be a happy Christmas for you.' She paused, remembering the other family that, because of Buck, would most certainly not be having a jolly time. 'And the police?' She pulled a face as she spoke, but she had asked on purpose, not wanting the other driver to be forgotten.

'Ah, well, that's a blight to be sure. But then, as I said to Buck, he was drunk, he should never have been driving, so he must take the consequences. We hope, because of his injuries, they'll be lenient. You know – that he's suffered enough.'

'I see.' Chrissy edged towards the stairs. Once she had started Mrs Marston was difficult to stop. 'If you'll excuse me . . .' She had a foot on the step.

'Now you mind, Sister. If you ever need a good lawyer, our Buck's man is the best. Goodnight now.'

Chrissy clutched at the brass banister, her heart lurching sickeningly. Why had the woman said that? Good God, were the patients involved too now? She ran down the stairs towards Miss Tillman's office to explain why she was leaving her shift three hours early.

'You're not going down with anything?' Glynis asked kindly, in contrast to her tone at their last interview.

'No, I don't think so. I'm very tired. I haven't been sleeping well.'

'Because of the post-mortem reports? I've chased them up. We shall receive them tomorrow.'

'Thank goodness.'

'Chrissy, I think I should tell you. They're not being sent over from Thorpedale, the police are bringing them. I think you should sit down. You look very pale.'

Chrissy exhaled. 'I didn't want to hear anything like that,' she said, as she groped for a chair.

'I'm sure it's all a misunderstanding. That we'll find a plausible explanation and that they're only involved in a routine capacity.'

'I hope you're right,' Chrissy said, though she doubted it.

'Chrissy, there's something else I wanted to talk to you about.'

Chrissy looked up at her expectantly.

'It's none of my business, but . . . well, no point beating about the bush. I was worried when I saw you with Russell Newson the other night.'

Chrissy stiffened in the chair, unaware that she was holding its arms as if for support. 'So?' she said, trying to sound defiant and failing.

'Mr Newson is a married man.'

Chrissy got to her feet. 'You're right, it's none of your business.'

'Please, Chrissy. I'm not having this conversation to sound censorious, it's because I'm concerned for you. Please sit down.' Reluctantly Chrissy did as she was asked. 'I'm speaking up because I don't want to see you waste your life or be hurt by a married man.'

'He's just a friend.'

'Then I hope he stays one.'

'I'm sorry, Miss Tillman, but I really –'

It was Glynis's turn to breathe deeply, preparing to take a step, hardly believing what she was about to do. 'I speak from experience, Chrissy. I did the same thing. Years ago I became involved with a married consultant. For sixteen years I believed he would leave his wife for me. I've been a fool and I've been duped.' She spoke hesitantly, as if she were having to force the words out.

'It's costing you dear to talk to me like this, isn't it?'

'It's not in my nature to discuss my affairs.'

'I appreciate your concern, I really do. But please don't worry on my account. I've no intention of getting involved with Russell. I've too much else to worry me, I can assure you.' Chrissy was touched to see Glynis relax at her words. 'And you? Have you recovered from your liaison?'

'Does one ever?' Glynis smiled a somewhat lopsided smile, and Chrissy, seeing a woman hurt and damaged, not the ice-cold distant figure she normally was, wanted to jump to her feet, take Glynis into her arms and cuddle her tight – but, of course, she didn't. She could not presume too much.

After her session with Glynis, Chrissy popped in to say goodnight to her grandmother and to tell her that Lynn Petch was joining the staff and would keep an eye on her. She had, with difficulty, avoided telling Daphne what was bothering her – not an easy task with a mind-reader like her gran. Despite leaving her shift early, once she had driven home, it was almost the time she would normally have got back. So much for an early night, she thought, as she parked her car outside the cottage. There was a high wind and she clutched at her coat as she walked quickly to her back door.

'Mrs Galloway, might I have a word?'

'Heavens!' Chrissy stopped dead in her tracks, her heart pumping with fear. 'Gracious, you made me jump!'

'I'm sorry, but I need to talk to you.'

Chrissy sighed audibly as she put the key into the lock. The last thing she wanted or needed now was a confrontation with Russell's wife. 'You'd better come in. You'll catch your death of cold in this wind.' She paused and wondered why. 'Have you been waiting long?' she wittered, and realised she was doing it because she was nervous. Why? What had she done wrong? Not much. A couple of evenings together here and one dinner out and stupid dreams worthy of a teenager – hardly earth-shattering adultery. 'Right, just let me put an electric fire in here. Do you want a coffee or something stronger?'

'Nothing. I'm not cold. I wish you'd just sit down and listen to what I have to say.'

'Right. I'm sorry.' Chrissy, flustered, removed her coat and sat down obediently, not even registering how rude Sabine had sounded, thinking only of how beautiful she was and how effortlessly elegant. Such thoughts made her smooth her dark uniform dress and place her feet, shod in the black lace-ups she found most comfortable, neatly together and wished she'd redone her make-up and brushed her hair.

'I love my husband.' Sabine stood on the hearth rug and leaned forward defiantly. She swayed slightly and Chrissy wondered if she was drunk. 'So? You hear?'

She *was* drunk, Chrissy thought.

'I said, I *love* my husband.'

'That's very nice for you,' said Chrissy, unsure what else she was supposed to say.

'There's no need for sarcasm.'

'I'm not being sarcastic.'

'Then leave him alone. He's mine. You're ruining everything.'

'Look, I think you're under some misapprehension here.'

'You've been seen with him.'

'Yes. He took me out to dinner the other night.'

'There you are, then!' Sabine tossed her head triumphantly.

'I was told you were separated. In which case –'

'That's a bloody lie. Did Russell tell you that? The bastard.' She was swaying distinctly now.

'Don't you think you should sit down? Would you like some coffee?'

'Are you implying I'm drunk?'

'No ... I just thought you'd be more comfortable,' Chrissy flannelled.

'I want you out of my husband's life. You understand?'

'I'm hardly in it. He's a friend, that's all.' This was so silly, thought Chrissy, and, in a distorted way, it was even funny.

'I thought you'd say that. They all do. You know about all the others, do you? All the other bits on the side he's had.'

'No, I don't.' Chrissy was not finding this interview so amusing now.

'Oh, you poor dear. You didn't know, did you? Didn't know he's St Edith's own Casanova.' Sabine finally sat down. She crossed her long legs, smoothed her hair, leant forward and took Chrissy's hand. 'I'm *so* sorry. If only I could have got to you earlier and warned you.'

Her lovely eyes filled with tears. 'I can't tell you the number of times he's pulled this little trick – that I don't understand him, that he's lonely, that he needs you. Is that what he said to you?'

'If he does this, then why do you stay with him?' Chrissy sat rigid, disappointment, betrayal, anger playing tag in her mind.

'Because I love him . . . What can I do? It's the tender trap, isn't it? Have you a Kleenex? I seem to have lost my hankie,' she said, between deep, heart-rending sobs. She patted the pocket of her trousers. Tears were rolling from her large blue eyes and down her cheeks. Chrissy fetched the Kleenex box from the dresser and handed it to her, at the same time wondering how Sabine managed to cry and still look attractive. If Chrissy cried she always ended up looking a red, bloated mess.

Chrissy stood beside the chair while Sabine sobbed, feeling ineffectual, not knowing what to do or say, thinking she should make the coffee.

'He's destroying me and he'll destroy you too, if you let him.'

'Look. I'm sorry about this, but you seem to have got the wrong end of the stick. I'm not having an affair with your husband. I've problems of my own to sort out – I don't have room for a man.'

'But that's when you need one. To support you, help you. I know.' She dabbed at her eyes and Chrissy wished she could ask her what make of mascara she wore, but that would be too unfeeling in the face of such misery.

'How long have you been married?'

'Six blissful years.' Sabine sobbed.

'But you just said –'

'I know what I said!' Sabine snapped. 'You see, Chrissy, I may call you that, may I? It's like an illness with him. It's difficult for him to resist. You know how it is – an important consultant, a busy hospital jammed full of frustrated nurses desperate to get into bed with him.'

'Oh really?' In Chrissy's experience nurses had a marked degree of cynicism where doctors were concerned and, in any case, were often too exhausted to leap into bed with anyone. The man Sabine talked about didn't sound like the Russell she knew. Was she such a hopeless judge of character? She smiled to herself. Why did she need to ask herself that after making such a huge mistake over Ewan?

'Will you promise?'

'Sorry?' Chrissy collected herself. 'I didn't hear what you said.'

'I asked you to promise to drop my husband and give my marriage a chance.'

'Look, Sabine. I'm sorry you're unhappy, I really am. But I don't know what to say to you. Nothing has happened between Russell and myself. If you won't believe me . . .' She shrugged her shoulders.

'Oh, I do. If that's what you say.' Sabine was on her feet again, looking quite cheered and no longer tearful. 'I'm sorry to have bothered you,' she said, with dignity, picked up her shoulder-bag and allowed Chrissy to show her to the door.

After she'd gone, and Chrissy had checked and locked the house, she made herself a cup of hot chocolate in the hope that it would help her sleep better, though she doubted it. As she sat at the pine table she mulled over the scene. It had all been unreal. Had Sabine been drunk or playing at it? Or had Chrissy mistaken an attempt to appear vulnerable and weak from grief as a session with a bottle?

Whatever. She sighed, as she looked at the chocolate swirling in her mug. She jumped visibly at a noise from outside. Tentatively she pulled back the curtain and peered out at the darkness. She was edgy. The feeling that someone had been here snooping wouldn't go away.

Still, she thought, as she sat down again, maybe it had been Sabine trying to find out more about her, her sadness and grief for her marriage making her act crazily and like a criminal.

'Oh hell!' she said aloud. What was the point? She couldn't deal with these dramas. She'd be better off not seeing Russell again.

4

When Chrissy awoke a slight breeze lifted the flowered curtains of her bedroom window. She heard the soft, sibilant murmur of a calm sea after last night's high winds. She stretched contentedly. And then –

Her hands shot to her face and covered her eyes as if they were trying to blot out the thoughts that came flooding in. A bleakness descended as she remembered.

It was far from being a good day. It was far more likely to become an awful day. She remembered that the police were coming, which could only mean the post-mortem findings were suspicious. No doubt the gossip, bad enough as it was, would move up a gear, and the sly glances, the whispering would intensify. At Fellcar she had hoped for a new start, a stab at happiness. Yet now she had this new nightmare to contend with. She felt so afraid and dreadfully alone.

If only she could see Russell, she thought. If she talked to him, he would calm her in his logical way. But she also wanted him to hold her, kiss her, make love to her, say all the silly things that lovers say — there was no point in denying it. She knew she yearned for him and her body ached for him . . . but she also knew she must not think this way. What had she virtually decided last night? She was wasting her time dreaming of him and what might have been. He was married, he'd lied about his wife, his marriage, Sabine had said. He was like so many men, he was not to be trusted. And yet . . . Chrissy believed in him, sensed he had told her the truth. It was difficult to switch that off and make herself distrust him. But even if she wanted him she was probably better off without him. Still. She turned in the bed, buried her face in the pillows. Deciding things was easy, seeing them through might be a different matter. She longed to cry for her lost dreams, but sense told her that that would solve nothing.

'Fancy a quick coffee, Chrissy? We've got time,' Dawn Allyson called to her in the car park as Chrissy parked and Dawn locked her bicycle.

'I don't think so. Better get straight up to the ward.' Chrissy looked about her, searching almost shiftily for people who were talking about her, lying about her.

'Chrissy, you've got to face them sooner or later.'

'Hell, am I that obvious? But, Dawn, it's so hard. I can't.'

'Yes, you can. I'll be with you. If I hear one whisper against you I'll belt them.' She raised her fists like a shadow boxer.

'You are kind.'

'Not at all. You'd do the same for me, I know you would. All you've got to hold on to is that you've done nothing to be ashamed of. Come on, hold up your head and sod the miserable cows.'

'You're on.' And arm in arm they walked into the hospital, down the stairs and into the tunnel that linked it with the nursing home and the canteen.

There was a perceptible drop in the noise level in the room as they entered. 'Morning, all,' Dawn said loudly and, with a broad grin, led the way to the servery.

Once they had their trays they looked about them for a space. 'Over there.' Dawn pointed.

'I'd rather not,' said Chrissy, seeing that the gaps were on a table where Jazz Poundman was holding court.

'Nonsense. Jazz is a bully. Get her on your side and you're home and dry.'

'I don't need her "on my side" as you say. There's no side to take!' She spoke sharply and regretted it. Dawn meant well. But she need not have fretted for she was talking to herself, Dawn was already forging ahead towards the table.

'Don't often see you in here, Chrissy,' Jazz said, moving her chair with a scraping noise to make room for the two newcomers.

'You know how it is. I'm always in a rush, Jazz.'

'Checking out other people's wards, no doubt.'

Chrissy ignored the remark.

'Have you seen the fuzz? One of them's to die for. The inspector's a bit long in the tooth, but the sergeant – wow!' Jazz fanned herself with a napkin.

'Are they here already?' Dawn asked.

'Been in with the saintly Tillman for a good hour now. Exciting, isn't it?' Jazz boomed.

'An excitement I could do without,' Chrissy said quietly.

'I expect so, Chrissy dear. But, then, you've got more to worry about than the rest of us, haven't you?'

'What are you implying, Jazz? Out with it.' Dawn swung round in her chair to face her.

'*Moi*? Nothing, Dawn. What makes you think that?' Jazz batted her eyelashes in a parody of wide-eyed innocence.

'Because you are a stirrer, Jazz. That's why. If nothing exists then you make it.'

'Honestly, Dawn, what an almost existentialist statement that was. Clever girl.'

'Watch it, Jazz.'

'Watch what, Dawn?'

'Come on, Dawn, let's go.' Chrissy put her hand on Dawn's arm.

'No, Chrissy, I want to know what she's getting at.' Dawn shook away Chrissy's touch.

'I'm not saying anything that other people aren't saying. Mrs Fortune died in iffy circumstances, that's all. Very similar to a certain someone's husband, that's *all*.'

Chrissy pushed back her chair noisily. On her feet she grabbed her bucket bag. She mumbled apologies to those who hadn't been saying anything and made quickly for the door.

Half-way to the hospital Dawn caught up with her. 'You shouldn't have left like that.'

'Why not? I didn't want to hear any more snide remarks.' They entered the building.

'It's just – oh, nothing.' They began to climb the stairs, the lift, as always in daytime, in use.

'What? Finish what you were going to say, please.'

'Well, it looked as if you had something to hide, that's all. It would have been better if you'd faced them out.'

'That's a matter of opinion. But thanks, anyway, for your help. You're a brick and I appreciate it,' she said, as they pushed open the swing doors of the ward. Half-way down the corridor she saw Russell.

'Sister, might I have a word?' he asked formally.

'I've yet to hear the night staff's report.'

'Just a minute. In private.' He looked hard at Dawn.

Her office would be full of staff, the kitchen busy with maids washing up.

'The linen cupboard will be quiet.' Chrissy led the way, held open the door for Russell and left it open.

'God, this takes me back to my youth – trysts in the cupboard!' He grinned at her, but when she did not respond he became serious. 'What is it, Chrissy?' he asked, concerned.

'I've only a minute. What did you want?' she said coldly, when what she wanted was to fling herself into his arms.

'I thought I should see you as quickly as possible. I called several times last night, but your phone was constantly engaged.'

'I was tired. I took it off the hook.'

'Oh, I see. Only I went to see Craig Nutting yesterday. There is a problem with –'

'I know. Mrs Fortune. Or that's the buzz in the canteen.'

'How do they find these things out? Craig said something odd and it's kept me awake all night. He suggested you get a good lawyer.'

Chrissy felt as if the floor would give way under her.

'I took the liberty, when I couldn't contact you, of phoning a friend of mine, Henry Yates. He's a good lawyer. I just thought, since you were new to the area, that you wouldn't know who to turn to.'

Chrissy glanced at the piece of paper. 'I know him. His father was our family solicitor.'

'Of course, I'd forgotten you were born here. You see the state I was in? I'd have come round, only I didn't like to. I didn't want to appear to be pushing myself on you.' He looked all ways but at her.

'Just as well. I was asleep,' she lied.

'Chrissy – I –' He put out his hand, as if longing to touch her.

'I've work to do, Russell. If you'll –'

'Chrissy, what is it? You're backing off again. Why? What's happened?'

'Nothing, of course. Nothing has happened at all between us, has it? And nothing will. It's best that way, Russell.' And she turned away from him and was in the corridor, so did not see him hit the shelf labelled *shrouds* angrily.

'Tea or coffee, Inspector Webster?' Glynis asked politely, of the thickset, grey-haired man who sat opposite her. The grey hair, she decided, made him look distinctly older than he was. The lack of lines on his face, his clear brown eyes, put him a good ten years younger than it implied. 'Coffee or tea?' she repeated, flustered at her unexpected interest in him.

'Either. In this job you take whatever's on offer.' He laughed, and she noted how small crows' feet appeared at the corners of his eyes.

'Well, I usually have coffee at this time.' She picked up the internal phone on her desk and ordered it. 'It's strange that we haven't met – Fellcar is quite a small place.'

'I'm stationed in Thorpedale, but I'm new. I worked in the Met,' he patted his chest, 'but it all got a bit much for me. My choices were taking early retirement or moving to a quiet backwater.'

'It must seem like that to you, but you should be in our A and E on a weekend night. You wouldn't call us a backwater then. And now all this.'

'It must be distressing for you. It'll make your patients edgy, to say the least, until we catch the culprit.'

'I just can't believe it could be a member of staff. There's no doubt?'

'The poor woman had well in excess of two hundred units of insulin in her blood. That's a massive overdose, isn't it? And I'm afraid it's not unknown for a serial killer to be in a hospital.'

'Of course, that dreadful case with the children – one likes to forget. But St Edith's?' Glynis frowned and George Webster longed to tell her not to worry, but didn't like to.

'I'll need everyone's personnel notes. Everyone, from sisters to cleaners, consultants to gardeners.'

'This will be so unpleasant.'

'We'll be as quick as we can. Sergeant Townley, who is working with me, will set up an office here at the hospital, if we may?'

'The boardroom would probably be best – it's quiet and only used for meetings so you won't be interrupted.'

'There are two things I'd like to discuss in confidence, Miss Tillman. You have a Sister Galloway working here?'

'Yes. And before we go further, I feel I must say that there was gossip about the poor woman right from the start. I gather her husband killed himself using insulin. But she was investigated by the police in that area and found innocent. Once the gossip started I checked for myself. It's most unfortunate.'

'How do you regard her?'

'She's a highly competent sister, conscientious and hard-working. She has a very responsible position here and shows all the signs of becoming a dedicated sister. And I, for one, do not believe that she could have been involved in poor Mrs Fortune's death. In any case, why did you mention her first? It hardly seems fair.'

'We've been doing a bit of homework ourselves,' he said, not mentioning the anonymous phone call that they'd received accusing Chrissy of murder. 'I'd like to start with interviewing the staff on that ward.'

'You said there were a couple of things you wanted clarified?'

'Yes. Do you know why the notes were sent from the pathologist to Thorpedale – to the desk of Mr Craig Nutting?' He glanced at his notepad to check he'd got the name right.

'I've no idea. We had to chase them up ourselves. Normally a report goes to them at the same time we receive ours. Maybe because of the circumstances . . . But, then, you, the police, should have been notified immediately.' Glynis tutted her disapproval.

'Mr Nutting apologised, said that it had been a mistake and that the papers got stacked, unnoticed, with a pile of others. But tell me, Miss Tillman, who chased them?'

'I did, and the consultants – Mr Ball, Mr Green, oh, and yes, Mr Newson.'

'Mr Ball is the neurologist and would be involved with, ah . . .' He glanced at his notes again. 'A Mrs Tomley? Right? Who suffered an embolism – anyway, natural causes. And Mr Green's patient would be the unfortunate Mrs Fortune? So why did Mr Newson find it necessary to chase them up? I gather he was informed last week that there was nothing suspicious in the death of his patient, Mrs Norman.'

Another frown flickered across Glynis's face. 'I've really no idea,' she said firmly. But George Webster had seen the frown and made a mental note that the beautiful, calm-looking Glynis Tillman was probably lying.

5

The day dragged. Every time Chrissy looked at her watch minutes only had passed. The ward was busy, which normally made time fly, but not today.

There were five outpatients in for chemotherapy. She'd spent the morning settling them and explaining to Dawn the various doses of the forceful drugs, which they mixed in a special pharmaceutical room, where either they were added to bottles of saline solution for intravenous infusion or into injections to be given intravenously too. Once the drugs had been administered, the patients needed constant monitoring for their physical well-being, and their spirits needed careful checking too.

Two patients were having doses of radiotherapy for the first time and, afraid of the unknown, had to be reassured and their worries listened to patiently. It was imperative that they were not made aware of her own anxiety.

Today she knew she was working at half her usual level of efficiency. Half of her could concentrate on the patients and allay their fears, wipe the tears, treat the nausea as well as comfort them. She reassured Mo for the umpteenth time about her stitches. But the rest of her was in tumult, worrying about herself. It was pointless to tell herself she had nothing to fear since she had done nothing wrong. What did that matter if everyone else thought she had?

The phone call she dreaded, and yet longed for, finally came. She left Dawn in charge of the ward. In the outer office she found Student Nurse Chelsea Mottram sitting and staring at nothing in particular.

'What do you think happened, Sister?' she asked, turning her stare on her.

'I've no idea, Chelsea. How's the course going?'

'Fine. I'm doing Care in the Community. I think I like that better.'

'It's a worthwhile branch.'

They both looked up as the door to the boardroom opened and Jazz bounced out. 'Well, that was a doddle. I don't know why they bothered talking to me. I wasn't even here when the old trout's number came up. Coming, Chelsea?'

Chelsea jumped to her feet.

'Oh, I thought you were next in line.' Chrissy's heart plummeted at the prospect that she was now next.

'No, they've done me. I was waiting for Jazz. Don't look so worried, Sister. They're ever so nice.'

'But poor Sister's got her own worries, haven't you?' Jazz grinned, but before she could answer Chrissy's name was called by the sergeant.

The police had set up their papers at the far end of the long room at one curved end of the massive table, so Chrissy had to walk the length of the room, aware that the inspector was watching every step she took. She wondered if it was intentional, that he'd given himself time to observe them as they approached. She forced herself to smile at him as if she hadn't a care, while her heart thudded alarmingly.

'Take a seat, Sister Galloway. Do you fancy a cup of coffee?' Inspector Webster indicated the tray.

'No thanks,' she said. Her hand wasn't steady enough to lift a cup to her mouth. She immediately wished she had said yes, since the inspector looked disappointed. Maybe he was hoping to take a break. 'I've just had a cup, thanks,' she added, knowing she was trying to ingratiate herself with him.

'Right. I think the best thing is if you tell us about the night Mrs Fortune died and what, if anything, you noticed.' With a coffee cup in one hand and a pen in the other, he waited for Chrissy to begin.

'Well, that night –' She had to stop and cough, since her voice sounded husky, as if she had a cold. 'I had three wards to supervise on that particular night.'

'Three?' He looked at her in disbelief. 'How can you look after three wards? Were they on different floors?

'You learn to walk fast,' she said, with a tentative smile, and was rewarded with one in return, which helped her feel a little bit better.

'Is this normal?'

'No, but the staffing levels are very low here – there's been a flu epidemic and I heard a rumour that no new staff were to be recruited. So everyone has to do more.'

'Whose order was it that no new staff were to be taken on?'

'I don't know, you'd have to ask Miss Tillman that.'

'So what happened that night?'

She told him that Mrs Fortune had been agitated, but said she did not know why, that the elderly often were.

'Had she any complaints?'

'She didn't like her Christian name being used. Many patients don't.'

'You weren't on the ward when she died?'

'No. Neurology was disturbed that night – we had a problem with one patient and an emergency admission. Once they were settled I returned to Care of the Elderly. Nurse Mottram met me and told me Mrs Fortune had died.'

'Who was on the ward apart from her?'

'A couple of auxiliaries. Staff Nurse Poundman was late on duty. She arrived just moments after me. And then she took over from me, even though the death had happened while I was in charge – she knew I was rushed.'

'She was locked in her flat, I hear?'

'Yes. She'd had to wait for the firemen.'

'You're sure she was locked in? It's common enough to be locked out, but *in*?'

'I think so. I mean, that's what I was told.' She was puzzled. 'I suppose . . .' Her voice trailed off.

'What do you suppose, Sister Galloway?'

'Oh, nothing.'

'But I'd like to hear your *nothing*.' He smiled kindly at her.

'I, well . . . I don't want to get anyone into trouble . . .'

'Yes?' He leant forward eagerly.

'I suppose she could have been skiving and made up the story about the fire brigade – but that's only my idea.' She looked uncomfortable.

He sat back, his face mirroring his disappointment. He made notes in a rapid but unreadable hand and added an asterisk beside his note to check with the Fellcar Fire Brigade.

'And nothing else was untoward?' He looked up from his pad.

'Yes. I felt a draught. The fire-escape door was open, and I knew I'd locked it. I always check – it's a phobia with me. Years ago, at another hospital, an intruder had got in that way. That was all.'

'Was this before or after Nurse Poundman arrived?'

Chrissy thought. 'I'm sorry, I can't remember.' Which was true. She couldn't remember the sequence of events that night in such detail.

'You've no theories as to how this tragedy happened? Any suspicions?'

'None,' she replied simply. It was not fair to mention the complaints about Jazz, she knew only too well the damage that could be inflicted by thoughtless gossip based on nothing but spite.

There was silence as Inspector Webster wrote some more. Strange, he thought, as he made his notes, that she hadn't mentioned Mrs Fortune was afraid of Jasmine Poundman – everyone else had.

'Would you say Nurse Poundman was a good nurse?'

'I don't know her work well enough. She can be a little brusque with the patients,' was the only criticism Chrissy allowed herself.

Inspector Webster scribbled some more, deciding he liked this woman, she was fair, unlike some of her colleagues who had almost tripped over their tongues in their haste to accuse her. She *might* be the culprit, but he'd bet a year's pay she wasn't.

'Thanks for your help, Sister.' He smiled up at her.

'Is that all?' She looked astonished.

'For the moment.' He began to pack up his books and pencils. 'Time for a spot of lunch, I think.'

He escorted Chrissy back along the room. Glynis Tillman was waiting in the outer office.

'I was wondering about your lunch, Inspector?'

'Very kind of you, Miss Tillman, but I've a lunch appointment with Mrs Yates.'

'You know Floss?'

'Why, yes. Floss and I go back a long way.' He smiled, and Glynis smiled too, but without much success. However, she hoped it hid her disappointment that the inspector would not enjoy the sandwiches she'd had prepared and sent to her office.

The shortness of her interview had confused Chrissy, and she made her way back to the ward deep in thought. Did it mean she was off the hook? Or did *for the moment* mean that she was going to be hauled back? She wished she could feel optimistic and rid herself of this wretched fear, which followed her like an ephemeral stalker.

'Chrissy Galloway! Where have you been hiding?' Lance Travers, stethoscope doubled up around his neck, the collar of his white coat turned up, blocked her way.

'Good morning, Doctor.' She attempted to walk round him. He moved in front thus preventing her.

'Why are you so formal with me? Me Lance, you Chrissy.' He pointed his finger at his chest then at Chrissy's.

'Fine, Lance. Now if you'd let me pass I've a ward to attend to.'

'Not until you promise to have dinner with me. Please?' He placed his hands together in supplication.

'Fine. Tonight? Eight?'

Lance acted a parody of fainting.

'Great! Chez Sylvie?'

'No, not there,' she said sharply. She wanted somewhere she had not been with Russell.

'Fine. The Grand? How about that? They do a good steak. I'll come and pick you up.'

'No, I'd prefer to meet you there.'

'As you wish. Eight. The Grand. Great!' Lance was grinning from ear to ear and still looked as if he didn't really believe he'd heard right.

But he let her pass.

As she continued towards her ward she already began to regret agreeing to see him. What had got into her? She didn't even particularly like him. And yet – she had to get Russell out of her mind. She must begin to look at him as forbidden fruit. She had to fill the inevitable space that not dreaming of being involved with him would leave in her mind.

She heard someone running up behind her.

'Chrissy, how did it go?' Russell had caught up with her. She stopped dead, her body, her face rigid from self-control.

'Fine, thanks.' She did not look at him and began to walk again.

'Chrissy, what is it?'

'Nothing.'

'When a woman says that a man is a fool to believe it!'

Chrissy stopped walking and turned to face him, this time she looked straight at him. 'Your wife came to see me, Russell. She had an entirely different slant on your marriage. I think it's best if we don't see each other, other than professionally.'

'But, Chrissy, whatever she told you –'

'She told me she loved you and wanted her marriage to work. That's good enough for me.'

'But it's all lies, Chrissy! Please.'

'Look, Russell, the state of your marriage has nothing to do with me. If we continue to see each other we might do something we'd regret. We haven't, so let's make sure we don't.'

'I don't believe this! That woman is evil. She –'

Chrissy held up her hand as if she was a traffic policeman. 'Russell, I don't want to be involved with a married man. Okay? It's not my style. Now, if you'll excuse me, I've a ward to run.'

6

His lunch with Floss had been very productive, thought George Webster as he got into his car. Things were obviously awry at St Edith's – not only the possible murder of Mrs Fortune, but the plans to close it. He'd have to make a point of seeing this Craig Nutting. He paused as he got into his car and looked across the town at the hospital perched on top of the opposite hill. George was a lover of Victorian architecture and St Edith's was a fine example. He liked the way the building stood like a giant guardian over the town. He liked Fellcar: it was the sort of small town he'd once dreamed of retiring to with Penny, his wife, the type of place where everyone knew everyone else, much like the small town he'd grown up in. Except that Penny had died ten years ago and he'd shelved that particular dream. But now?

He was more than interested in the news he'd gleaned from Floss that Glynis was single. It had been a long time since he'd been so attracted to a woman and he wondered if it was conceit on his part that he'd sensed a spark of interest in her too.

As he climbed into his car he resolved to take matters a step further and ask her out to dinner.

Floss had given him a lot to go on. He'd hardly got a foot in the door before she was telling him in no uncertain terms not to listen to the gossip surrounding Chrissy Galloway – it was all lies. And so he hadn't even had to bring the subject up and subtly find out if Floss knew her or what she felt about her.

Then there was the interesting matter of Dr Middleton, Matthew Kersey, Craig Nutting and their nefarious schemes. It was looking certain that this investigation had been deliberately delayed by Nutting. No doubt out of mischief – he must have had one hell of a shock when he found out that someone had died of an overdose. And Giles Middleton had a lot to answer about a certain Lynn Petch and a spiked drink.

It always intrigued him how often one investigation invariably led him into various other dubious actions. Circles within circles, ripples upon ripples, he thought, as he parked his car outside the hospital.

As he crossed the car park he saw Glynis Tillman approaching. 'Ah! Miss Tillman, the very person.'

'Your investigation is advancing, Inspector?'

'Slowly. But it wasn't about that I wanted to talk to you, Miss Tillman.'

'Please, my name is Glynis,' she said, and felt ridiculously skittish as she did so.

'George,' he replied, with a slight bow. 'What I wanted to ask is if we might have dinner together tonight?'

'Why, George, how kind. I should love to.' She smiled, amazed at how easy it was to accept.

'I don't know Fellcar. Do you have any suggestions?'

'Chez Sylvie is excellent – and not too expensive.'

'Right, Chez Sylvie it is,' he said, deciding, with such consideration for his pocket, he liked her even more.

As a favour to Glynis, Lynn Petch had started work earlier than planned. She'd forgotten just how hard working on a ward was. By lunch-time she felt as if her feet were about to fall off and her calves had begun to ache. Tomorrow her muscles would be agony. Lifting patients in, out and up the bed was straining her back. She knew the correct way to lift but she was out of practice.

Because she was new to the ward she had to make twice as many trips looking for things that the other staff could lay their hands on in a trice. As soon as the thirty beds were made it seemed time to start again, let alone the odd incontinence in between, which necessitated, if not a complete change, at least a clean draw-sheet. And the bedridden patients had to be rolled first one way, then the other, and pressure areas treated. Feeding the weak and badly confused should have been a time to sit and rest, but instead she was flustered, aware that four other patients were waiting, like cuckoos, to be fed. Working on this ward, she felt today, was like being in a nursery, only the babies were giants – sweet giants, she told herself hurriedly.

It was finally time for her tea and, with weary relief, she made her way to the canteen. She stood, her tray in her hands, looking about for a familiar face – not easy on her first day and knowing no one. Her face lit up as she saw the large, butch Jazz Poundman at a far table.

'Mind if I join you?' she asked.

'Of course not. This, everyone, is Lynn who, mad thing that she is, has joined us on female geriatrics.' Jazz introduced her expansively.

'How are you doing?' a senior staff nurse asked her.

'My feet are killing me. I'd forgotten how hard it was. And the smell! Why, in this day and age, do hospitals still have to smell of boiled cabbage and disinfectant?'

'If you could solve that you'd make a fortune.' Someone laughed.

'Jazz says you're a great friend of the resident murderess?'

'I'm what?' Lynn looked shocked.

'I told them you knew Chrissy.'

'She's no murderess. Whatever next?'

'If it's not her, then who is it? Someone bumped the old woman off.' Jazz bridled.

'Well, it isn't Chrissy. She's a lovely woman, and in any case –'

'In any case what?' Jazz was smiling at her.

'Nothing.'

'Were you just about to tell us about Ewan? We know. And, if you ask me, that makes it look dead dodgy.'

'Nothing like this had happened until she came. You have to acknowledge that,' one of the others argued.

'Have none of you heard of that great old British custom that no one is guilty until proved?'

'And what about "no smoke without fire", then?' piped up one.

'She's not the only person working here, for goodness sake,' Lynn said shortly.

'No, but it was her ward that night.'

'And where were you, Jazz?'

'Stuck four floors up in my flat, waiting for the fire brigade, that's where.'

'And has anyone checked? Excuse me, I can't stand this spite,' Lynn said. She stood up, picked up her tray and moved to another table leaving the others puffing with indignation, and Jazz sitting in shock with her mouth agape.

As she dressed to go out Glynis felt elated – and foolish. 'I've only just met the man,' she said to her image in her dressing-table mirror, but even as she said it she could not control the mischievous smile that flickered about her mouth. Why was she so confident that this evening was to be one of significance? Stupid, when she thought of her track record and how easily she had been fooled by Matthew. Acknowledging her past weakness did nothing to quell this feeling that would not be controlled. She double-checked that she had her bleeper with her – she was the manager on call tonight. Chez Sylvie was close enough to the hospital for her to get there within a couple of minutes in the unlikely event of disaster striking. Shame she wouldn't be able to enjoy any wine – she liked good wine.

As she dressed Chrissy wished she could shake off the feeling of unease this cottage now gave her. It was so stupid of her to give in to such inconsequential amorphous sensations. She had no proof that anyone had been here: nothing had been taken or touched. She was just certain that her space had been invaded.

Why the hell she'd even agreed to this date beat her. It was one thing to decide to do the right thing and not get involved with Russell, but it had been completely mad to agree to dine with Lance, of all people.

As she buttoned up the smart black dress, which she thought suitable for the lofty, chandeliered pomp of the Grand Hotel – even if it was somewhat faded these days – she wished she'd suggested a pizza and then she could have worn jeans.

Lance was waiting for her in the bar. As usual, seeing people away from their environment, and Lance in his own clothes rather than his hospital whites, was a shock, as if they did not quite belong in the new setting.

'Punctual – I approve of that. And looking so pretty!' he said, making to kiss her cheek, but with a swift move of her head she made sure he found himself kissing the air in the region of her right ear. And she wished she'd been late, since she had no desire for his approval in any shape or form. She should never have come. It wasn't fair on him.

'Look, Lance, before we go into the dining room I'd like to make it clear that I want to pay my share.' She felt remarkably better for saying that.

'Let's see how the evening goes,' he said, with such a leer that she found it hard not to laugh. She noticed that he seemed to be talking to her breasts and not to her.

'I insist,' she said as, with his arm under her elbow, he steered her towards the cavernous dining room. Everything the poor man did seemed destined to annoy her. She longed to say she was capable of finding the way, but generations of female submission in her genes stopped her from saying anything for fear of appearing rude – another lot of genes to blame, she thought, with a wry smile.

The meal was good, she'd no complaints there, and once she'd got over her initial irritation with Lance she began to enjoy his company. He was a natural joker, who made her laugh with his fund of hospital stories.

They were at the coffee stage and Chrissy felt quite relaxed. She shouldn't have worried, he was like a little boy, really, and hardly a threat. She'd expected him to come on heavy with her and he hadn't even tried.

'What about this news about zinc?'

'What news about zinc?' she innocently asked.

'Haven't you heard? It's good for the prostate, the memory, the immune system, it reduces cold symptoms *and* tooth decay.'

'Really? That's interesting.'

'It prevents damage to the retina and helps the sperm count.'

'Good gracious, so much!'

'It's more than interesting, it's brilliant. I can see you while I'm screwing you, remember your name, bite you without sneezing, get you pregnant without catching Aids. All in one go – a bloody miracle, wouldn't you say?' And he flung back his head and laughed so that she could see the fillings in his teeth and his furry tongue.

'I should save your zinc capsules for someone else. I can assure you, you won't be screwing me. Goodnight, Lance. This should cover my share.' And with a sweeping gesture she threw a pile of banknotes onto the table.

As she left the dining room she could hear him calling her name almost in a wail.

'Without doubt that's one of the nicest meals I've had in a long time,' said George, as he helped Glynis on with her coat.

'Sorry?' she said, for the bistro was crowded now with an influx of late diners and she could barely hear him.

'I'll tell you outside,' he yelled.

Sylvie escorted them to the door. They thanked her for the meal.

'Tell me, Sylvie, there's the most lovely smell in your restaurant tonight. What is it?' Glynis asked.

'Ees zee jasmine, zee joss-sticks for zee garz –'

Before she had finished the almost incomprehensible sentence there was a mighty roar of thunder. But this was no thunder for the roar was accompanied by a blinding flash of light as an explosion ripped mercilessly through the restaurant and the diners inside.

7

The explosion ricocheted against the opposite houses, shattering glass in its rush to be free. There was a momentary silence and then the screaming and shouting began.

Glynis sat up, puzzled. Why should she be sitting on the pavement, covered in rubble, dust and bits of glass? Instinctively she ran her hands over her face, head and down her body. She felt shaky, but otherwise unhurt. She had been deafened briefly by the blast so at first she did not hear the screaming. She winced as a man, racing from the building, stumbled over her, kicking her in the ribs.

She got to her feet then realised she'd moved too quickly and swayed. She bent her head, controlled her breathing and remembered. With a rushing roar her hearing returned and she heard the cries of the hurt.

'George!' she called out. 'George!' With increasing panic.

'Glynis, over here.' Despite the pandemonium he'd heard her and she him. She was by his side in a millisecond.

'George, are you hurt?'

'I think – my – leg –' he said, with difficulty and in obvious pain.

She knelt down and gingerly felt both his legs. A warm patch on the right one alerted her, and the awkward angle of his trousers gave a warning. 'Don't move, George.' She stood upright, took off her overcoat and rolled it into up, like a bolster, and wedged it against his leg, then did the same with her jacket. From her handbag she took the nail scissors she always carried and quickly ripped open his trousers.

'Those are new.'

'Then you'll have to buy newer,' she said promptly. 'Ah. That's a relief.' She slumped back on her ankles. 'No arterial blood. Stay as you are. Don't move that leg. I'll see if I can help. The ambulances must be on their way.'

'You'll catch cold.'

'I'll be too busy to be cold,' she said briskly, looking about her at the number of people lying on the ground and at others stumbling about the road. 'Don't move,' she ordered.

'I wouldn't dare.' He grinned at her through the pain.

'Oh, really!' She laughed gaily before assessing the first of the wounded.

Chrissy was just about to turn into her lane when she heard a news flash on the local radio station about an explosion in town. She reversed into a gateway and sped off in the direction of St Edith's.

When she arrived it was to find organised chaos in the A and E department as a fleet of ambulances disgorged the first, and therefore the worst, of the wounded.

'What happened?' she asked the first nurse she saw.

'I'm not sure, but they've put in motion the Major Incident Plan. I heard someone say there'd been a bomb at Chez Sylvie.' Nurse Margaret Harper looked as shocked as some of the patients being checked in.

'A bomb? In Fellcar? How many injured?'

'I don't know, but everyone on call has been pulled in. Are you on call? Then you're to report to Sister.' She fiddled nervously with her belt.

The waiting area was heaving. Margaret was having little success in trying to persuade patients who were already in attendance before this influx to leave if their problems were not acute.

'I was here before them. I'm staying put.'

'Don't you mess about with me, bitch!' A drunk spat at her, then let loose a stream of invective. A mild-looking young man sitting beside him jumped to her defence.

'Don't you dare speak to this young woman in this way! I think –' But he got no further for the drunk swiped him on the jaw and he crumpled to the floor.

'Oh dear,' said Margaret, flummoxed and close to tears.

Dawn Allyson appeared at her side. 'Over here. Get rid of this creep,' she ordered one of the porters.

'You! Out.' The porter grabbed the drunk by the collar and hauled him away.

'I'll sue you. I'll sue this fucking hospital,' he yelled.

'Sue who for what? I saw what happened. Here's a nice policeman – tell him.' But the drunk twisted from his grasp and was out of the door in a flash.

'It's all right, Margaret, don't cry. We've too much to do here for tears.'

'Yes, Nurse Allyson.' Margaret blinked. She was scared, convinced she'd never get through the night.

'Now see to the poor bloke who got hit. Defending you, was he? That's nice,' said Dawn, before speeding off to report to Sister.

Margaret turned her attention to the man, who had by now hauled himself back onto the chair and was rubbing his chin.

'That was very kind of you. Does your jaw hurt badly?'

'No, just sore. It was worth it to get your attention!' He grinned bashfully, and Margaret Harper blushed to the roots of her hair and blinked behind her round spectacles.

Already patients' relatives, alerted to the accident by a television news flash, were beginning to pour in. This added to the overcrowding so that the ambulance crews were having difficulty in getting their trolleys through the milling, noisy throng.

'Everybody. Listen. Per-l-e-a-s-e!' Freddie Favour, the A and E consultant, had jumped on to the receptionists' counter and was clapping his hands for silence. He achieved a modicum. 'Look, everyone, I know you're concerned, but we need some order to treat the patients. All relatives to follow this nurse.' He pointed to the staff nurse. 'You'll be asked to wait in a room next door, where the police will take your details. You will be informed of any developments here. Those patients with non-urgent conditions, please go. If you're worried, contact your GP. If you stay I promise you that you will not be seen in order. We have to treat the badly injured first. If you insist on staying you might have to wait all night. The choice is yours. Right. Thank you.' He jumped down, resigned to even worse confusion as everyone milled about the department sorting themselves out.

'Where the hell's the manager on call? There's no organisation, no central office set-up. What in God's name is going on?' Freddie looked angry.

'The manager on call is Miss Tillman. She's not answering her bleeper,' Sister Betty Greaves explained patiently, 'but we've contacted the next in line. I've had the switchboard alert all staff on standby. We're managing.'

'Glynis? Not responding? It's not like her.' Freddie bent down over one patient. 'Orthopaedics needed here.'

'Sister, I'm sorry, I was delayed.'

'Glynis, are you all right? You're covered in dust.' Betty turned to see a dishevelled Glynis behind her.

'I'm sorry. I was there, you see. Right.' Glynis stood upright, as if bracing herself. 'Have all senior staff been notified? Social workers? The Friends? The chaplain?'

'Being done, Glynis love. Don't you think you should sit down and take it easy, you've had a shock.'

'I'm right as rain, don't worry. Any press here yet? I'd better set up a press information desk before they distort everything.'

'Freddie, will you persuade this woman to sit down?' Betty said with a bemused smile.

'What, me? Stop Miss Tillman in her tracks? I'm not man enough for that.'

'Mr Favour, you are a tease!' To everyone's astonishment, Glynis almost giggled.

Nurses trained in triage were able to assess patients the minute they were wheeled in. The more seriously wounded were weeded out for the doctors' immediate attention in the resuscitation rooms, others, less damaged, were wheeled into side cubicles. The dead were put in a side ward for their identity to be confirmed.

Chrissy found Betty Greaves.

'Chrissy, bless you, how's your gran?' Betty asked, ice calm in the chaos.

'She's mending fine,' Chrissy said, amused that in the midst of all this drama Betty could remember Daphne. 'What can I do?'

Betty glanced at a list. 'Take Cubicles Three, Four, Five. There's an emergency buzzer to alert us if you need assistance.'

In Cubicle Three, Chrissy found a young girl lying patiently, looking up at the ceiling. Chrissy checked the notes clipped to the board at the bottom of the trolley. All it contained was her name and age, eighteen. No checks had been done on her.

'Hello, Amber. How are you feeling?' she asked, while noting the girl's extreme pallor, the thin film of sweat on her face.

'Afraid. Otherwise I'm fine. There's others . . .' She closed her eyes and shuddered. 'Some were hurt.' A tear slipped out from under an eyelid.

'I know, but they're being looked after. Now, does it hurt anywhere?'

'Nowhere. I said, I'm fine. I shouldn't be taking up this space. It's my birthday. Dad took me out. Mum wouldn't come – they'd had a row.' She bit her lip as if this memory disturbed her too.

'I'm sorry. But happy birthday anyway. Now, you just lie back. I'll take your blood pressure, if you don't mind.' Chrissy did not like the girl's colour. She wound the cuff around Amber's arm: her blood pressure was alarmingly low. She took her pulse, which was racing wildly. Chrissy feared she might be bleeding internally. Then she saw the bed covers at her feet move and ripple, like an incoming tide, as Amber began to shake, her eyes rolling. Holding her head for fear of neck injury, Chrissy removed the pillow. She hit the emergency buzzer. She heard the alarm's high-pitched, continuous wail. In a trice she was at the end of the trolley activating the hydraulics, which raised Amber's feet higher than her head.

'She's gone into shock,' she said, in a clipped voice to the young houseman who appeared.

'Porter,' he yelled, as with Chrissy he began to push the trolley out of the cubicle towards the resuscitation room. A nurse took Chrissy's place and she returned to the cubicles she'd been allocated.

'Nurse. Are you a nurse?' A woman in her late forties grabbed Chrissy's arm as she passed. 'My daughter! Have you seen my daughter?'

'All relatives are to go –'

'I've been there. They tell you nothing.'

'Your daughter's name?'

'Amber Nicholls. It was her birthday. We'd had a row.' At this point the woman burst into tears. 'I can't find my husband,' she said, in an ugly, gruff voice through her sobs. Chrissy looked wildly about her. This woman needed help, too.

'Floss!' she called with relief at the sight of her and several of her kindly Friends of St Edith's. 'Could you?'

'Certainly. Now, you come with me, my dear. I'll see what I can do for you.' And taking the woman's hand Floss led her away.

In Cubicle Four Chrissy stood transfixed. On the trolley, his eyes looking blankly at the ceiling, was the police inspector. She clutched her throat and knew she was being silly. Why should she feel guilty at seeing him? Pull yourself together, she told herself.

'Hello, Inspector. What's the problem?'

'I've broken my leg – compound fracture, lacerations, no arterial involvement.'

'My, you sound as if you know what you're talking about.'

'Not me. My friend Glynis told me. If you've got patients worse off –'

'A compound fracture is nasty enough, Inspector,' she said gently, as she collected together equipment to clean his wound. 'Have you had a recent anti-tetanus injection?'

'Yes.'

'Good. Do you know what it was? I heard a bomb.'

'Gas explosion more or less, I reckon. Sylvie, we think, said something about a smell before the whole kybosh went up. But her accent's so thick.' He smiled.

'I know what you mean. Now I'll try not to hurt you.'

'So, what have we here? My name's Newson, orthopaedic surgeon.'

Chrissy felt her heart flip at the sight of him and looked down, knowing that she was blushing, that she was glad to see him.

'Sister.' He nodded formally.

'Mr Newson,' she said politely.

Together, efficiently, as a team, they set to work on the Inspector's broken leg.

The screams, when they came, were appalling. They curdled the blood of all who heard.

'What the hell? Sister, go and see if you can calm whoever it is,' Russell said, looking up from the new patient they were attending.

Chrissy pushed back the curtain. Mrs Nicholls, with Floss in puffing pursuit, was racing down the corridor towards the resuscitation room.

'Oh, no,' Chrissy said aloud, as she followed her. When she reached the room Amber was lying as if she was asleep. Her mother scooped her off the trolley and held her in her arms, rocking her, screaming her name, screaming her denial, screaming how sorry she was. The nurses in the room looked at the scene with horror.

'Her husband died too,' Floss said quietly, behind Chrissy.

'It was Amber's birthday,' Chrissy said, but to no one in particular.

'How sad. She looks so young.'

And she'll never look older, Chrissy thought, feeling the lump harden in her throat, and leaving the others to sedate and try to calm the mother, but knowing she would hear the screams for a long time to come. Just as she remembered the screams of Ewan's mother over his corpse when she couldn't even cry.

8

It was three in the morning. The staff room was crowded as the exhausted doctors and nurses had a quick cup of coffee before dispersing and leaving the regular staff to cope with the rest of the night.

'Thanks, everyone who came in – we'd never have managed without you.' Freddie Favour lifted his coffee mug, emblazoned with the words The Boss, in salute to them.

'At least we showed that our Major Incident Plan worked. Comforting after all those dry runs,' Betty Greaves said, satisfied.

'Bit of a kerfuffle at the start, Betty. I know this isn't my department, but I think when the next major incident happens the first thing we do is have someone on the door controlling where people should go, leaving the main area free,' Matthew Kersey pointed out. 'I had to fight my way in.'

'The problem there, Matthew, was that the manager on call was delayed,' Betty explained.

'Well, he or she damn well shouldn't be *delayed*. What sort of excuse did they have?' Matthew said irascibly.

'It was Glynis. She was at the restaurant.'

'She should have been here, not living it up at Chez Sylvie.'

'Oh, come on, Matthew. Glynis isn't like that. I bet she didn't have a drop. She'd hardly have known she was about to get involved in an incident of this magnitude. And if she hadn't been there, we'd have had a couple more deaths, I bet. By all accounts she was magnificent,' Freddie said stalwartly.

'What else would you expect from Glynis? She's of the old school. I bet she could set up for a triple heart bypass in the Borneo jungle with a tin can and her sewing kit,' Betty butted in, aware of Glynis's relationship with Matthew – a man she could not stand.

'That little hiccup apart, everything went swimmingly. And getting back to Glynis – what a relief we had her here to deal with the press. Those monkeys would have been teeming about, searching for patients waiting on trolleys in corridors to make a song and dance about, but not with Glynis to deal with. She had them corralled and totally under her control. No hysterical false info in the papers today, that's for sure. I think we can congratulate ourselves that we handled that emergency brilliantly.' Freddie stretched with the contentment of a man who knows that a job has been well done.

'And they threaten us with closing this department? It doesn't make sense,' said Russell, from his position on top of a small filing cabinet. 'It would have been a lot worse if they'd had to be transported to Thorpedale.'

'Too right,' several agreed.

'What was the final tally?' Lance Travers asked from his position squashed between the filing cabinet and the washbasin.

'Four dead – two here, two at the site apparently. Two in Intensive Care. Two helicoptered to the Burns Unit. Eight admitted. Fourteen walking wounded sent home.'

'Is Sylvie in Intensive Care? Will she make it?'

'Fifty-fifty. She doesn't know her husband's dead – could set her right back.'

'Did you hear Glynis's extraordinary tale? Apparently she was standing beside Sylvie, yet didn't have a scratch on her,' Betty said.

'Blast does funny things,' Russell said quietly. Chrissy looked across the room at him and wished that she was beside him and could hold him, knowing that he was returning in his mind to his own personal horror.

'Was it gas?' Dawn Allyson asked.

'Looks like it. That inspector said he thinks Sylvie said so just before –'

'Anyone seen Glynis?'

'She went up to the orthopaedic ward with the police inspector.' Betty told them and was rewarded by a suggestive *wow* from the group. 'Holding his hand!' The next *wow* was deafening. Slyly she glanced across at Matthew and was content to see that he looked very put out.

For ten more minutes the group analysed the night: recalling patients and how they'd been treated, any complaints, any suggestions for improvements in the system.

'Right, folks, I suggest we meet in a couple of days' time. We'll notify you, then we can have a proper debriefing. Mull over what has happened in case we can make any improvements. That said, I think we try and get some sleep while we can.' Freddie effectively broke up the meeting, which risked going on indefinitely as they worried back and forth about whether they could have done better.

Chrissy walked across the car park with Betty and Dawn, and wished she was on her own, just in case Russell should be leaving too and catch her up.

'Well, thanks for your help. Hope we didn't mess up any plans.'

'No, I was only going home to a hot bath and bed, which is what I'm going to do now.' Chrissy reached her car.

'And I was packing – any excuse was a blessing.' Dawn laughed.

'You've moved? Did you say? I'd forgotten.' Chrissy put the key in her car door.

'No. An aunt died. Left me enough to put down a deposit on a flat – one of those in the old Victoria Hotel. And I promise you that's the truth. You must come over when I'm settled.'

'Why shouldn't it be the truth?' asked Betty.

'With all the pilfering going on I don't want anyone to think it's me!'

Over Dawn's shoulder Chrissy saw Russell approaching, she willed the women to move on. But they lingered.

'Good night, ladies,' Russell called over. She would like to have thought he looked straight at her, but she knew he didn't.

On the way home she thought over the night. They'd worked well together, smoothly, professionally. But that was all. She'd be lying to herself if she thought there had been a look, a touch, a message from him. But what did she expect? It was she who'd told him she didn't want to be involved. What right had she to expect any interest from him now? She was the one who'd rejected him, told him so, been firm about it. She banged the steering wheel. Only it wasn't so! She wanted him, she wanted to be with him, to talk to him, to be free to love him. The car swerved. Love? She'd thought the word. It was true. She was falling, had fallen, in love. Now it was too late. She'd thrown it all away. She wanted to cry, and her throat ached from the restriction she imposed on it, trying to stop the tears. Oh, if only Sabine would leave, run away, disappear . . . If only.

As she entered the ward Chrissy could not stop herself yawning: sleep had been a rare commodity last night.

'Chrissy, what happened? You look washed out,' Mo asked from her position on top of her bed.

'There was an emergency, we worked most of the night. I'm whacked.'

'We heard the bang. It shook the windows. Join me.' Mo grinned as she shifted on her bed making room for Chrissy.

'I wish I could. So, you're off?'

'Until the next time. Still, the doctor says I can wait to start my treatment until after Christmas. At least we'll have a good one this year, I'm determined on that.'

'You've earned it. Are you being picked up or do you need transport?'

'No thanks. My husband's coming to collect me.'

'Gracious. He's taking the risk of entering a dreaded hospital? I'll see you before you go.'

Chrissy returned to her duties, even though she felt as if she was in a heavy diving suit of fatigue as she walked to her office. She must watch herself today and double check everything. At least with the run-up to Christmas they were not as busy as usual. She envied Dawn who, if she had any sense, was still curled up in bed. She pulled her order book towards her. It was hardly surprising she felt like this – she'd enough on her plate to last most people a lifetime. One thing she knew: she had to keep busy. Last night on A and E she hadn't once thought of the police and Mrs Fortune. Now, in daylight, sitting here alone it was all flooding back. She pushed away the book. It would have to wait: she needed physical activity. She pulled a large plastic apron over her uniform and went to find some nursing to do.

'Mrs Fordham's ready to leave, Sister.' An auxiliary popped her head round the door of the side ward where Chrissy was changing a patient's dressing.

'I'll be right along. Ask if she can hang on a minute.'

Her task completed, she pushed the equipment trolley back into the dressings room, washed her hands, pulled off the plastic apron, brushed back her hair and went to say goodbye to Mo.

'We'll miss you, Mo,' she said cheerfully, as she entered Mo's ward. 'Hello, Bob. What a surprise to see you here.' She smiled across the bed at her mother's lover.

'I didn't know you knew my husband. This is Robbie,' said Mo.

Chrissy looked up sharply. 'Your husband?' Bob looked trapped.

'How do you know Robbie?' Mo asked brightly.

Chrissy's mind raced, trying to find words to say. The pause seemed to go on for ever. Bob looked everywhere in the room but at her.

'I met him at my mother's . . . He's been doing some work for her.' From the corner of her eye she saw Bob, or Robbie, or whatever his name was, relax.

'You never said, Robbie.'

'It was only a little job,' he muttered.

'Taking an Aga out and then putting it back again, wasn't it, Bob? As my mother kept changing her plans. She's going round the world in a boat, Mo.' She stood rigid, aware she sounded false, but normal speech had deserted her.

'Lucky her. I wish I could do that, don't you, Robbie?' Robbie did not answer. 'Oh, Chrissy, I must go. Look at the poor man, he looks green. He's so terrified of hospitals, aren't you, Robbie?' She pushed him playfully. 'Good job he wasn't born a woman, isn't it?' She walked around the bed and kissed Chrissy goodbye. 'Try and pop in for a drink over Christmas.'

'Yes . . . Yes, I'll do that,' said Chrissy, motionless with shock.

Mo hadn't expected to feel so exhausted. As Robbie helped her from the car she suddenly felt a hundred years old and had to hang on to the car door for support.

'You all right, love?' Robbie hurried round to her side.

'Just a bit dizzy. It's the excitement of coming home. Oh, just look at that.' She pointed to the front door where Katya and Kerry had stuck gold and silver letters. 'Welcome home, Mum', she read. 'Isn't that sweet of them? Where are they?'

'They're still at my sister's.'

'Oh, I'd hoped they'd be here.'

'I thought it was best.'

'I'm not going to be an invalid, Robbie. I've decided that. I'm going to start as I mean to go on. This business is not about to beat Mo Fordham.'

'Jeez, you're something else,' he said, as he took her arm and, carrying her small case, walked her up the short garden path.

'No, not really. Like others before me, I'm just having to come to terms with this – thing.' Out of deference to him, she refrained from saying 'cancer': she'd seen him wince once or twice at the word in the hospital. She must be patient with him. She wasn't the only one with adjustments to make.

'Tea?' he asked, as he settled her in a chair. She smiled up at him, unused to him fussing over her. It looked as if some things were changing here. This, she was certain, was the first time he'd ever waited on her. She looked about the sitting room as he disappeared into the kitchen; it was tidy and he'd made an effort, but it wasn't quite up to her exacting standards. She smiled at herself – well, there was something that hadn't changed, she was still as fussy as ever. She made herself more comfortable in the chair. Her shoulder was still sore, but she'd have her tea first, then do some exercises. She leant back. The house was so quiet without the girls, unnaturally so . . . She wished he'd collected them from his sister. She wanted them all to be together this first day home. She closed her eyes for a moment.

Maybe, she thought, what had seemed to be such a catastrophe might turn out to be a blessing in disguise; might bring them all back together again as a family should be. No one could tell her how long she might have, or if she would be one of the lucky ones, so she'd like to make every second count, make every day a special one.

A sound made her open her eyes. Robbie was standing in front of her, staring at her. It was an intense stare and made her feel uncomfortable.

'Can't find the tea-bags?' She smiled up at him.

'There's no easy way –'

'Yes, there is – just make sure you boil the water.'

'I'm leaving.'

Mo stared back, a smile in place. He looked like a little boy standing there, hands at his side, head bowed, guilt written all over his face.

'I'm sorry,' he added, when she said nothing. 'I wish it could be different.'

'When?' she asked, after a pause that seemed to hang in the air between them.

'I moved my stuff out last week.'

'You'll be staying in Fellcar?'

'No, Portsmouth.'

'Alone?'

'No.'

'I see.'

Mo felt as if she were viewing this scene, as if it was happening to someone else – not to her. In a bizarre way she found she was quite fascinated at how she was assimilating the news. She wasn't surprised, that was evident. But was she hurt? She wasn't sure.

'Are you all right?' She noted he asked quite anxiously.

'I'm absorbing the news.'

'You seem to be calm about it,' he said suspiciously, as if she was acting and would suddenly erupt and catch him unawares.

'There's not much I can say or do, if you've decided.'

'It wasn't an easy decision.'

'No, it couldn't have been.'

'There's no need to be sarky.'

'Oh, Robbie, I wasn't. It must have been hard. We haven't been getting on, I was aware of that, we both were . . . It's just . . .'

'What?'

'Well, I can't exactly congratulate you on your timing.'

'I know everyone will think me a shit, but would you want me to stay with you out of pity?'

She flinched at the word. 'No.'

'So, I'd almost made my mind up before you found the lump. It all got a bit delayed – my plans, I mean.'

'Sorry to be an encumbrance.'

'There you go again, being sarcastic.'

'How am I to manage?'

'You said you didn't want pity.'

'I did – but a bit of loyalty might have helped.'

'I'm sorry for you – I mean I am – Shit, this isn't easy for me, Mo. I feel a bastard. I really do.'

'And the kids?'

A frown came over on his face. 'I've told them. They cried.'

'You what? You told *them* before *me*? How dare you? I suppose your sister knows too,' she shouted, angry now in a way she hadn't been initially. His not answering confirmed her suspicions. 'And your mother, our friends, the whole sodding world, I suppose? Thanks, Robbie, oh, thanks a bunch.'

'I'm sorry.'

'You keep saying that. If you really were you wouldn't be doing this, would you? When I'm in the hospital who'll –'

'Look after the kids?' he interrupted. 'My sister says she will. Until you're back on your feet. She says she'll move in.' He looked pleased, as if he expected her to congratulate him on his forethought.

'And money?'

'Ash has bought me out. You can have all of that.'

'And when that's gone?'

'You'll have the house and your job.'

'And what if my treatment doesn't work and I can't teach, what then?'

'I'm sure it will. You'll be all right, Mo. You know you will.'

'I know one thing. It would almost be worth dying just to cock up your plans.' She laughed.

'There's no need to get hysterical.'

'I'm not. I think it's funny. I honestly do. And I know something else.' She stood up, forcing herself not to show any pain. She faced him. 'You're a creep, a waste of space – especially my space. I shall be glad to see the back of you.' She turned away her face.

'I'd hoped we could be friends.'

Her laugh this time was even louder. 'Friends! You and me? Hell will freeze over.'

'I'm sorry –' He turned, and she wanted to scream at him not to keep saying sorry, but she didn't.

'Who is she?' she asked, as he got to the door.

'Iris Galloway. Your ward sister's mum.'

At that the room rocked for Mo.

'Did she know? Did Chrissy know about you two?' Her hands were clenched: that would be one betrayal too many.

'No,' he said, from the doorway. 'She thought I was just the plumber.'

Mo heard the front door slam, his feet on the path, heard him start the car, heard it drive away. She stood alone in a capsule of expectation. She waited for the grief, for fear, for tears. Nothing came. She felt herself in a vacuum, knew instinctively that whatever she decided now would affect the rest of her life.

'I don't need him,' she said aloud, to the empty room. She had two things to survive now: her illness and his abandonment. She looked at herself in the mirror over the fireplace, saw the determined set of her chin. 'I'll surprise everyone! I'll do it alone!' she said, in a voice tinged with triumph.

9

'He's married, Mum.' Chrissy stood, her coat half on half off, in the centre of the kitchen, her expression serious with concern for her mother.

'Oh, don't be silly, I knew that!' Iris retorted.

'You knew? Do you also know he's got young children?' She sounded shocked.

'So? Then he won't mind me being past having any for him – thank God!'

'His wife's in hospital.'

'I'm aware of that.'

'She's a patient of mine.'

'Yes.'

'She's got cancer.'

'So Bob said.'

Chrissy sat down. 'Mum, I don't believe I'm hearing this. What's got into you?'

'Nothing. It's not my fault she's got cancer.' Iris lifted her chin in a defiant gesture.

'But don't you realise that the stress of finding out about this could make her worse?'

'She didn't have it when we started this relationship. It's too late. What's happened has happened. Drink?' Iris shrugged her shoulders as if without a care.

'Mum, please listen to me. Mo is a sweet woman, brave, devoted to her children, ill. This just isn't fair.'

'Life has a habit of not being fair. I keep having to remind you of that.'

'But don't you see the sort of bastard this shows Bob is? To even contemplate leaving her at a time like this?'

'He's not a bastard and don't you dare say he is.' Iris wheeled round to face her, her face distorted with anger. 'It's not his fault all this has happened. We fell in love . . . His marriage was over, finished. They were planning to split.'

'I wonder if he thought to tell his wife that?'

Noisily Iris poured herself a drink, the bottle clanking against the glass as if her hand were shaking, but Chrissy could not see for her body masked what she was doing. She paused a second, squaring her shoulders as if controlling herself.

'I've got a buyer for the house,' she said calmly, turning from the drinks tray to face her daughter, sounding as if she was bored with the previous conversation.

'So you're still off?' Chrissy looked away. 'I don't believe all this.'

'It's quite simple. I told you what I was doing. When I make my mind up I don't change it. You know that.' She sat down at the table, her drink in front of her. She played with the glass, twirling it, making the ice clink.

'When?'

'In the spring.'

'So at least they'll have that time.'

'No. We're leaving. Going south down to Hampshire to look for our boat.'

'But it's Christmas!'

'Sometimes, Chrissy, you sound as if you've never grown up. Christmas, Easter, summer, it makes no difference to me.'

'God, Mum, you're so selfish. Don't you see?'

'I'm fed up with being bloody unselfish.' Iris's voice exploded with anger. 'Always thinking of others, putting them first, doing what they wanted and not what I wanted. Now it's *my* time – at long last. I spent my youth living with your boring father, bringing you up, knowing you loved him more than me – don't bother to deny it, I always knew. I was nothing but a skivvy to him.' As she listed her grievances her voice became shriller and uglier.

'Don't talk such rot,' Chrissy yelled back, her own voice staccato with her mixed emotions.

'It's not. It's the truth. I've always been truthful. At least I'm not a hypocrite like you.'

'I beg your pardon?'

'*You* lecture *me*.' Iris pointed a finger at her breast. 'How you have the nerve to talk to me like this. Your lover's married.'

'I haven't got a lover!'

'No? What about Russell? He's married. His wife's heart is broken – by you. You're a two-faced bitch.' Iris spat out the words. Chrissy felt her face stiffen as if her mother had slapped her.

'I've seen him, yes. But I –'

'And what about Sabine?'

'How do you know all this?'

'Poor Sabine came to see me. Begged me to ask you to leave her husband alone and give her marriage a chance. But I'm different from you, I'm loyal and, what's more, I don't stand in judgement on others as you so evidently do. I told her it was none of my business, as Bob and I aren't yours.'

Chrissy stood up, knocking the chair over on the tiled floor behind her. Neither woman noticed. 'Now, just hang on here. I've told Russell I'm not seeing him any more, that he's married and I don't think it's right.'

'Oh, aren't we the pious one?' Iris smirked.

'I've never slept with him.'

'Well, you make a habit of that, don't you?' Iris got to her feet.

'What does that mean?'

'You know.'

'I *don't*. Tell me. I insist.' The two women glowered at each other.

'Ewan.'

'What the hell has Ewan got to do with all this?' she said, with noticeable exasperation.

'You didn't sleep with him either, did you? Made his life hell with separate rooms. No wonder –'

'No wonder what?' She stepped towards her mother, anger plain in her face, aware that she was about to be accused of causing his suicide, once again. 'What is it you long to say, Mother, just like everybody else? Join the band, why not? And while you're about it don't you dare lecture me about loyalty!' She could feel a mounting hysteria that matched her voice.

'Very well then, since you insist. That he turned to others for comfort, of course,' Iris shouted.

'Oh, yes. Since you claim to know so much about my marriage who in particular? You've got quite a choice.' Chrissy half laughed, surprised by her mother's words when she had expected her to say something else.

'Well, me for a start.' Complete silence attended this remark until it was broken by Iris sniggering. 'I thought that might wipe the smile off your face.'

A flash of memory of Iris's extreme grief at Ewan's funeral seared Chrissy's mind. Surely not. No. Not this – this was too much.

'How interesting,' Chrissy said coldly. 'And when did this little ding of yours happen? We hardly ever saw you.'

'On a rare visit to Cornwall – the invitations weren't that copious, were they? It was easy. You liked your long walks with your father so we'd take the opportunity to snuggle up together in your bed!'

'How very strange when Ewan didn't even like you.'

'What a spiteful bitch you are, Chrissy.' And at last Iris slapped her hard across her face.

Chrissy did not flinch. 'What I find odder is that he didn't tell me – he always did, you know, he liked to give me all the details. He wouldn't have missed the joy of telling me he was having it away with my own mother!'

Iris hit her again, harder, as if it was Chrissy who had sinned. 'Sorry, Mum, you'll have to do better than that. I don't believe you.' Chrissy twisted on her heel and fled from the room, from her childhood home and, she was sure, from her mother's life.

'Chrissy, if you don't calm down you're going to have a breakdown. Now, get a hold of yourself.' Daphne, sitting in an easy chair beside her bed, grasped Chrissy's hand and squeezed it as if trying to transfer her own strength to her granddaughter.

'It's everything. It's all getting on top of me.'

'Any news about the police investigation?'

'Pst!' Chrissy made a dismissive noise. 'They don't seem to be doing anything. And now the inspector is laid up from that explosion last night I suppose they'll do even less.'

'What a racket! We all thought it was the end of the world – just like the blitz. Mind you, it meant we got a nice cuppa and – Chrissy, what is it? Why are you crying?'

Chrissy looked down at her smooth hand held by her grandmother's lined and gnarled one. The contrast upset her even more. Her gran had always been there for her: what would she do without her? Who would she turn to? Without her, who would cry for her?

'There was a girl last night, she looked fine, she said she was fine, but an artery ruptured and she died – she died so quickly. I felt so helpless. I –'

'Listen, Chrissy. You're doing what you told me that as a professional nurse you could never allow – you've let her death get to you. Blaming yourself. You've lost your detachment. Why?'

'I don't know. It's everything. I just said. And she was so sweet, and her mother – oh, God, her poor mother.'

'Are you sure you're not grieving for this girl because of something else? Has something else happened? You can tell me. I'll try and make it better. Do you remember how Gran always kissed the pain away?'

She looked across at the old woman, blinking through her tears. 'I'm being silly. This isn't like me.'

'Exactly. So tell me.'

'It's a long story.'

'I've got the time. Where else is there for me to go?' Daphne asked.

'He's called Russell. He's married.'

'Ah, well, I'm all ears.'

She started diffidently, knowing how intransigent her grandmother was about adulterers. But, as she talked, her confidence grew and finally she declared that she thought she was in love. 'No, that's wrong. I *am* in love,' she stated, more than said.

'Do you think he's an honest man?'

'Yes.'

'Then if he says his marriage is over, why don't you believe him?'

'His wife came to see me and begged me to get out of his life.'

'Wives tend to do that. I should see him, have it out with him. Don't look so surprised. Did you think I wouldn't approve? If a marriage is over there's no patching up will put it back together again.'

'But Mum called me a hypocrite. You see . . .' And she told Daphne about Iris and Bob and Mo and Robbie, and how could she do one thing while disapproving of her mother doing the same?

'It's a rather different set of circumstances, isn't it? I know you. If it were Sabine who was ill you'd fade into the background.'

'But Mum said –' And then she told her grandmother the last of what was bothering her.

'What upsets you the most? That she claims she slept with Ewan? Or that she disapproves of you and this Russell? Or that you think she's lying?'

'It's finding out things like this. It shakes the foundations of my life. It's like being in a mental earthquake. How can I ever believe anything or anyone ever again? I've had to adjust to Dad not being what I thought he was. Now this, my own mother.'

'Phew, her and Ewan? In her dreams! Don't you love that expression? I do. You're too naive, Chrissy. You always believe what people say. Just because you're truthful, it doesn't mean everyone else is. She's lying to you to annoy you.'

'But why?'

'God knows with Iris. Maybe she's jealous – you're young and she's middle-aged. You've done something with your life, she's done nothing with hers.'

'But she's got Bob.'

'Oh, yes, and how long for? When she gets a bit longer in the tooth he'll be off, mark my words.'

'Oh, Gran, I'm so confused.'

'My advice is simple. Talk to Russell, but keep a little bit of cynicism in store, just in case.'

Chrissy laughed, her tears forgotten now. 'What would I do without you, Gran? And you seem a lot happier.'

'I am. That Jazz Poundman stopped being such a tyrant – did you have a word?'

'No,' she lied, so as not to worry her.

'If anyone's guilty of bumping off patients she'd be my first choice, even if she's trying to be nicer. I wouldn't trust her further than I could throw her – and at her weight that wouldn't be far.'

'She was locked in her flat that night. She's got a foolproof alibi.'

'So she says,' Daphne said enigmatically.

10

As soon as she got home and had changed, Chrissy checked Russell's number in the telephone directory. She sat for some time studying the phone before she picked it up then replaced it as if it was burning her. Several times she went through this ritual. But finally, with a determined expression, she dialled, praying that Sabine would not answer, and holding the receiver with both hands as if to stop herself replacing it on the cradle. 'It's me,' she said when, with relief, she heard his voice. 'I need to talk.'

While she waited for him to arrive, she wandered about the cottage, straightening pictures, pulling curtains, adjusting the lighting, moving ornaments. In the guest bedroom her hand stayed over the fairground cat her father had won for her. That's odd, she thought. It had moved from its position – not much, a couple of inches, but she knew she'd not put it so far to the right of the shelf. Such niggling worries were halted by the ring of her doorbell.

One last look in the mirror, one last pat of her hair, a dab more perfume and, with a dry mouth and a pounding heart, she ran down the short flight of stairs.

'Thanks for coming,' she said, holding the front door open for him. 'It sounded important. What's up?'

She stood in the middle of her sitting room, certain he could hear the banging of her heart, knowing that this was a moment she would never forget – a moment that held her whole future. She turned and faced him. He looked so tense, a worried frown on his face.

'The other night at the restaurant – you said – only I wasn't sure if you meant it – and then . . . None of this is sounding as I planned it to be.' She stood twisting her hands as he waited patiently. 'I think I've fallen in love with you,' she blurted out. She'd been holding her hands nervously in front of her, now she let them drop to her sides as if they were weighted. She smiled nervously as still he stood watching her. She licked her lips. 'Sorry,' she said.

His laugh was a short burst of relief. 'I thought you'd got me here to say you never wanted to see me again, that you were moving away. Why do you say sorry when you're making me so happy?' He stepped towards her, but she took one step back.

'I think I'm apologising for my inconsistency. I thought you must be fed up with me. One minute I'm obviously longing for you and the next pushing you away.'

'It's been a tad confusing – but, then, how could I blame you? The circumstances have hardly been ideal.'

'I think we should talk about that, if you don't mind,' Chrissy said. He took her hand in his, lifted it to his lips and gently kissed it. The kiss flummoxed her. 'That's why I asked you here – I've got to know where I stand. I didn't mean to tell you I love you. It just sort of came out.'

He still held her hand. 'I'm glad you did,' he said softly.

'It's so silly. We've only known each other a few weeks.' She pulled away her hand.

'A few days, a few weeks. What's the difference? I knew in the first *minutes* of meeting you that this, that you, were something different.'

'That makes it even madder – *how* could you know? Please don't make pretty speeches, it doesn't help.'

'Chrissy, my father saw my mother pass by on a bus and he knew. He raced after the bus on his motorbike until she got off. They've been together forty years. It runs in the family.' He smiled.

'But you're married. Don't you see? Your marriage, I mean, I'm not prying, I need to know.' She knew her apology sounded limp but what else could she say?

'You've every right to know.' He sat down on one side of the inglenook. She sat opposite him. She'd like to have been closer, but she did not dare, not until she had heard everything he had to say. 'I've been so miserable. I couldn't get you out of my mind. And when you said that Sabine had been to see you. Lying to you!' He shuddered. 'My darling, my marriage has been well and truly over for more than a year. It was just my pig-headedness, hoping things might change, and of course they never do. We've had separate rooms all that time. I know that's what married men say – it's quite a cliché, isn't it? But in my case it's true. I've nothing I can swear it on to reassure you. You've only my word for it.'

'So, whose fault was it?' she asked. She knew it was a sneaky question, that marriages fell apart for a thousand reasons, not one, but she had to know whom he would blame. His answer would tell her so much.

'You can't apportion blame. It was my fault as much as Sabine's. If I had been the husband she wanted and needed, she wouldn't have strayed. Her need for lovers is partly my fault too.' Chrissy relaxed against the cushions in her chair at the apparent honesty of his answer and she wanted to cheer that Sabine was not the wronged victim.

'We should never have married in the first place. Still, how many people say that? I'd been engaged to someone else and had been badly let down. Then one day I was talking to a friend, a car drew up and these wonderful legs appeared. I suppose you could say I fell in love with her legs.'

'The rest of her is fairly wondrous too.' Chrissy felt a small frisson of jealousy at talk of Sabine's beauty.

'Yes, but falling for someone physically isn't the best grounds, is it? It wasn't fair of me to marry her. There was so little we had in common. I bored her, I was soon aware of that. She liked dances and discos. I preferred home and a good book. She only ever read magazines – oh, you know, the usual. I pretended, even to my friends, that all was well with us. And Sabine is a great actress – that's what she should have been – so everyone thought we were perfect for each other. When I could no longer live the lie, I knew I would get all the blame. And I didn't mind until you appeared and I longed to tell you the truth, but by then I found it almost impossible to do so.'

'So why did Sabine choose you?'

'She'd had a hard life. Her father deserted them, mother liked to drink – who could blame her? She's got four brothers and sisters, and there was little money. She wanted all the nice things. I was rich, I was security for her.'

'How sad.'

'It is, isn't it? I felt guilty, I suppose, that I wasn't what she had dreamt of. The loss of one's dreams, that's one of the saddest things of all.'

'When did she start playing about?'

'Three months after we were married. I found a letter from a lover under her pillow. They were planning to run away. She didn't go, of course, he'd no money. But I suppose I just wasn't good enough in bed for her.'

She loved him for that admission and what it must have cost him to make it.

'So, why does she want to hang on now?'

'I fear this lover has begun to tire of her. She's afraid of losing everything I can give her. I told her she's in love with my wallet, not me.' He laughed a short, bitter little laugh.

'But you wouldn't leave her short?'

'Oh, no. I've given her the house and she can sell it for a tidy sum. I was packing to move out when you called – against my solicitor's advice. But I thought, What's the point? It's over, it's best to get on now as quickly as possible. I can buy another, smaller house.'

Or move in with me, she thought, but sense told her not to say it, not yet. But, oh, she hugged the thought to her.

'Thank you for telling me, Russell.'

'Been my pleasure.' He laughed ironically. 'Now, I need to know about Ewan and what happened to make you so afraid of love.'

Chrissy looked into the fire, collecting her thoughts, wondering how to explain the inexplicable. 'Ewan liked playing games with me. Cruel games. He had a reason, he was a possessively jealous man and he set out to demoralise me so that I'd think no one else would ever want me.'

'He didn't succeed, then?' He grinned, leant forward across the space that separated them and stroked her cheek gently.

'Looks like it.' She chuckled – a precious moment to preserve. 'He was handsome, a brilliant artist, charming. Everyone thought how lucky I was.' She gave a gentle snuffly snort.

'You've none of his paintings here?'

'No, they were too warped, like his poems – well received, but not by me. Looking back, I don't understand why I put up with it but I did. Other women – he loved to tell me about them and what they'd do in bed, unlike me! He said I was a failure there. The possessiveness became intolerable. Then he shot the dog and I ran and the rest you know.'

He stood up and moved towards her, put out his hands, clasped hers and pulled her to her feet. 'So we're both lousy in bed?'

'It sounds like it,' and she laughed, but not for long for his mouth was on hers, his arms about her and she clung to him and returned his kiss fervently. He felt just as she'd thought he would; he smelt, close to, just as she'd wanted; and he kissed her full and hard on her mouth in just the way she'd imagined in her dreams.

Somehow, she could not remember when or how, they had climbed the stairs. Now she lay in her bed naked and she waited for him to return to her as, across the room, he removed his own clothes.

Effortlessly he lifted the covers and slid in beside her and she felt the hardness of his body against the softness of hers. He lifted himself on one elbow, resting his head in his hand and looked down at her with such gentleness and love in his face that she almost cried out with joy.

'Chrissy, I'll never hurt you – never,' he said.

'I know, my darling. I know.' And she put her arms up to him.

Chrissy had had no idea how much her body had longed for this physical release. Her awkwardness, her fear of not pleasing him, lasted only seconds before her body seemed to melt into his as he caressed, kissed, licked, nibbled and loved every part of her. Nerves that had been dormant so long were thrillingly activated.

He wanted only to please her, to satisfy her. And when, finally, he climbed upon her and entered her, and she felt the warm hardness of him, her body rose in rhythm with his as they rocked and thrust, and together climbed the levels of pleasure to climax, and then again and again.

Satiated, twined in each other's arms, their sweat and their breath mingling, they fell asleep.

Once in the night Chrissy woke with a start and sat bolt upright, suddenly afraid, as if someone was in the room. Then she heard his gentle breathing, laughed at herself, at some already forgotten bad dream, snuggled back into his arms and was quickly and contentedly asleep.

The sun woke her – they had overslept. She lay, watching his face, for several minutes. She felt so happy, so complete, so unafraid and relaxed.

Gently, so as not to wake him, she slipped from the bed. In dressing-gown and bare-footed she ran down the stairs and into the kitchen. She filled the kettle and, while it boiled, looked out of the window at the sea beyond. She took two cups from the dresser and spooned the coffee into the cafetière . . . Her heart lurched. On the worktop stood a teapot. Gingerly she put out her hand and touched it. It was warm.

Her screams woke him and he thundered down the stairs wrapped in a sheet. He found her wide-eyed with terror pointing at the teapot.

'Oh, Russell. Who is it? I never drink tea!'

CHAPTER EIGHT

I

They sat in Russell's Mercedes outside the police station.

'They didn't believe me. You do realise that?' Chrissy turned in the seat and faced him.

'I think they were fairly useless. Less that they didn't believe you than that they thought it a joke. I mean, when that sergeant asked you if you walked in your sleep!' He started the car, then swung it into the road.

'Where are we going?'

'Henry Yates — my lawyer.'

'Oh, Russell! Do you think I should?'

'Yes, I do.'

'But it'll look as if I'm guilty when I'm not. I've done nothing, so why should I need the advice of a lawyer?'

'A precaution, that's all.'

'How much will it cost?' she asked, with the anxiety of one with bills to pay.

'You needn't worry, I'll see to that.'

'You damn well won't.' She was so annoyed she sat up rigidly in the seat, but had to change position when the seat-belt cut into her. 'I pay my own way.'

'Okay, okay.' He took his hand off the wheel and mockingly fended her off. 'I was only trying to help.'

'Well, thanks, but no thanks.' Everything was ruined, she thought miserably. Last night she'd been so happy and content with him. But then, upon finding the teapot, all that had collapsed like a flimsy house of cards. And all the old anxieties and worries had rushed back led by distrust. What if he was playing games with her? What if he'd got up in the night and made the tea – just to scare her? She looked at him from the corner of her eye. It had been such a shock, and then having to face the police and be laughed at. Yet he didn't look particularly serious. In fact, he was smiling – she was sure he was. A small, fluttery smile played around his mouth and made her stuff one hand to her own mouth to stop her from crying out. Ewan had smiled like that when he'd had a private joke; Ewan would have thought it highly amusing to frighten her witless as she had been this morning.

'What's funny?' she asked, and hoped her voice did not sound as squeaky to him as it did to her.

He glanced across at her. 'Funny? Nothing.' He looked back to the road. 'I'm happy, that's all. Well, actually, that's everything! I can't believe you wanted me.' He lifted his left hand and placed it on her thigh. 'You've made me the happiest man in the world – I know that sounds like a cliché but I didn't know what else to say. The words haven't evolved to say what I mean, what you've become to me in such a short space of time.'

'Russell, if only –' He couldn't be lying. He sounded sincere, but then –

'It's a bad time for you, Chrissy. But don't worry, it'll get sorted. And then we'll have the rest of our lives together.'

'To find the words?'

'Yes, and to live them too!'

She wanted to believe him, needed to love him, to have someone to rely on, to care for. She couldn't be duped a second time – surely God would not be *that* cruel.

Mo woke and lay in the bed, their bed, looking at the ceiling yet not seeing it. This was the beginning, the challenge, she thought. She'd expected not to sleep but she had and felt refreshed by it. She wondered where he was.

She sat up. There was nothing to be gained lying here wittering to herself. She had things to do and, given her new circumstances, she had to find ways round doing them. She was going to have to learn to pace herself intelligently, conserving her energy, being mean with it, if necessary. She must list the priorities. The first adjustment she would have to make would be with her home. She'd always been so house-proud; now she was going to have to learn to let things slide. Once out of the bath she put on her dressing-gown. She'd always been so particular about the food she'd put into her family: no convenience food for them – even with a full-time job she'd made sure of that. But now her days of standing in the kitchen for hours at a time were over too. She'd have to take short cuts, stock up the freezer and get some tins in – still, that would be easier without a man around hogging everything. She smiled at that thought as she crossed the small landing and looked into Kerry's room – it was neat as a pin and always was. But, as she pushed open Katya's door, she knew she'd see the opposite. She did, the room looked as if the January sales had taken place in there. Not one drawer was shut, all were half open, their contents spewing out. Clothes lay on the floor where Katya had taken them off and let them drop. Mugs with the congealed remains of coffee littered the floor. Poor Katya, she was going to have to grow up fast, she was going to have to learn to help.

Downstairs, over a cup of tea, Mo made a list of people she needed to talk to. She'd phone the bank and ask the manager if he could call round – no point in wasting energy going there when for the first time in her life she'd be in funds and needing advice; she wondered if managers did that sort of thing or not. Ah, well, she'd soon find out. She added Ash's name: she had to know what the true state of the business was. Maybe she'd like to reinvest in it – after all, she'd lived with their heating enterprises since day one, and she knew she could work with Ash. Maybe she could do the paperwork. Such an idea cheered her up. Robbie giving her all that money meant the Galloway woman must be rich – or had he given it all to her? And was it his decision or had his mistress had a hand in this? She didn't want to have to feel any gratitude to her. She'd ask Ash how much money was involved. She made a note. And what about poor Chrissy? No doubt Chrissy had presumed that the money her mother was spending would come to her one day. She added Chrissy's name to the list. Those two, with their selfishness, had put Chrissy in an intolerable position – they must have known Mo was Chrissy's patient. She needed to talk to her, reassure her that she was fine and harboured no hard feelings.

She'd phone the school she taught at, too: she had to find out her entitlements. Knowing what kind of budget she could look forward to was a priority.

Mo pulled the phone towards her and dialled her sister-in-law's number. She could hear the embarrassment in Sue's voice. So he hadn't been lying, he really had told her. Great! Why was the wife always the last to twig? she wondered.

'If you could bring the girls back, Sue. I'm a bit sore to drive.'

'Do you think that's a good idea? I'm happy to have them.'

'I need them here.'

'Yes, of course. But how will you manage?'

'We'll manage fine.' And, as she said it, she knew she would.

'What's up? Why are you so grumpy?' Iris pushed a cup of coffee towards Bob.

'I'm not.'

'Well, you could have fooled me! I lived for years with a bastard who hated the mornings. I hope I haven't ended up with another one,' she said tartly.

'Haven't you got any instant coffee? I hate this muck.'

'That, young man, is best Kenya blend.'

'I haven't come here to be educated. Get some instant in.'

'I wouldn't be seen dead buying it.'

'Then I will.'

'If you must.'

A silence descended over the breakfast table, a simmering silence in which real anger could so easily take hold. Iris leafed through *Vogue*, the glossy paper crackling as she turned the pages. Bob was half hidden by *The Times* which, judging from the speed at which he was reading, he was not terribly enjoying.

'I'll get you the *Telegraph*, if you prefer.'

'Thanks.' He grinned at her across the table. 'Sorry. You're right, I'm a bit bearish.'

'Do you want to talk about whatever's bothering you?'

'I'd have thought it was fairly obvious what the problem is.'

'Hardly, unless you choose to tell me,' she replied as, neatly and precisely, she buttered her toast.

He watched her with an irritated expression. 'I've only junked my bloody wife when she needs me most. What am I supposed to do? Split my sides laughing?'

'Really, Bob. You needn't take this out on me. It was your choice. If you feel guilty about it and don't think you can cope with it, perhaps you've made the wrong choice.' Delicately she scraped a sliver of marmalade on to the toast and nibbled daintily at it.

'You can be a cold bitch, can't you?'

'Not always.' She leant forward and the front of her dressing gown gaped open showing her breasts. She smiled suggestively at him.

'Witch!' He was grinning again, and the angry mood subsided.

Sabine was not having a good morning. Russell had not come home last night and, checking his room, she saw he'd begun to pack his belongings. So he'd meant it. She was scared – of a future alone, of having to manage her own affairs, of not having a man to rely on. She crossed the hall to answer the ring on the doorbell. 'Giles!' she exclaimed with relief. 'Come in.'

'You evil bitch!' he shouted, waving a piece of paper at her. 'I could kill you!'

'Giles! Whatever do you mean?' She stepped back in hurt surprise.

'The GMC – you reported me, unprofessional conduct with a patient! That's what you've done.'

'Giles, I never did. And please keep your voice down.' She looked anxiously over her shoulder towards the kitchen. 'My cleaning lady's here. We have to talk.'

'Too right.' He stepped into the hall.

She showed him into the drawing room. 'Do you want some coffee, Giles?'

'A whisky.'

'At this time of day?'

'With this to contend with – any time.'

She poured him a large malt. 'Giles, you must believe me, I didn't do this. I wouldn't hurt you, you know that.' She would like to have added that she loved him, but refrained, sensing that it was not exactly what he wanted to hear.

'If it wasn't you, then who was it? Russell?'

'I doubt it. He wouldn't do anything mean like that. He's not a petty man.'

'Maybe he doesn't see having his wife stolen as inconsequential. I wouldn't.'

'But you would love your wife. He doesn't love me.'

'Well, if it's not one of you, who was it?'

She looked downcast at his answer to the opening she'd given him.

'Someone at the surgery – another woman, perhaps?' she added suspiciously.

Giles looked thoughtful. 'One of the nurses might have. She'd have cause.'

'Then shout at her.' She looked close to tears which, for once in her life, were genuine.

Giles laughed. 'I'm sorry. I panicked when I picked up the letter. I saw my whole career in ruins. And after the other night, well, I just jumped to conclusions. I apologise.' He looked contrite, she noted, so she let him take her hand.

'You're not serious? That would be awful! A wonderful doctor like you. Is there anything I can do to make it easier for you?'

'Get divorced in double quick time and marry me – they might see things differently then.'

'Oh, yes, my darling. Of course I will,' she said, in an unseemly rush. 'I'd be so happy to be your wife.'

Giles looked somewhat taken aback at the speed of her reply. She saw a look of uncertainty cross his face and moved quickly to sit on his lap. 'I'll make you the happiest doctor in the world.'

'I couldn't give you a home like this – ever.' She did not like the doubt in his voice. 'I don't earn the sort of money your *consultant* husband screws out of the patients,' he sneered.

'But, my darling, with you I wouldn't need any of this,' Sabine said breathlessly, and for the time being she meant what she said.

2

Fiona Henderson replaced the telephone receiver on its cradle with a thoughtful look. Her hand rested on it as she stood deep in thought. Looking up, she saw herself reflected in the ornate gilt mirror hanging over the table and, never able to resist her own image, she practised a few gracious expressions and patted her stiffly styled hair.

'Who was that?' Dick Henderson asked, as he ambled into the hall looking for his medical bag.

'I'm still in shock! You'll never believe this, but that was my sister, inviting us to her Christmas party.'

'Floss? Good heavens! What's afoot? We've not been asked for years – ever since she accused you of exerting undue influence on your mother and her will!' He smiled with quiet satisfaction: he didn't often get the chance to best his wife and so never let the opportunity pass him by.

'Why must you repeat that slander?' she snapped.

'Because it's true,' he muttered.

'What was that?'

'Nothing,' he blustered. 'Maybe now that she's getting on she wants to make friends again. You know, "time's winged chariot", and all that guff.'

'Bah! Floss will go on for ever, just to annoy me. She's the one person who will never accept that she's getting old – just look at those ridiculous clothes she wears for a start. That woman's incapable of dignity.' She sniffed disdainfully. 'I know my sister – a perpetual Tinkerbell.'

'Bit on the stout side for flying, isn't she?' Dick snorted happily. He was rather fond of Floss and regretted not seeing much of her. She was always such fun, and long ago he had concluded he'd pursued the wrong sister.

'She wants something,' Fiona said.

'So we're not going?'

'On the contrary, we must go. I accepted. I have to find out what she's up to. She was particularly insistent that you were there. What have you been up to?' she asked, in an accusing tone, honed by years of despising her husband.

'Not a thing.' He held up his hand as if swearing an oath. 'Honest.'

'You're late.'

'I can't find my bag.'

Fiona crossed the hall, opened the stair-cupboard door and, with a know-all look, handed him his case. 'It was where it always is!'

'I couldn't see it.'

'You never see anything. You'd rather wear me out looking for it.' She sighed exaggeratedly. 'So what are you waiting for? Why are you lurking?' she demanded.

'Oh, I don't know. I don't want to go to work, I suppose. This Lynn Petch business has upset me more than I'd thought. I wish she'd never left.'

'Left? She was sacked by you, or don't you remember?' she said tartly. 'Get her back. Offer her her old job. You've not replaced her – or have you, and have you *forgotten* to tell me?'

'I tried. She won't come back. She's got a new job at the hospital.'

'I can't say I blame her – leaping to wrong conclusions, it's so typical of you, Dick. It's that Giles Middleton you should have got rid of. I never liked that young man, I never trusted him. Now he's sniffing about that poor Sabine Newson.' Her face, as she spoke, showed her disapproval and abhorrence of all matters sexual. 'I do hope you won't have to get involved in this GMC hearing.'

'Oh, I'm sure I will. But if you felt so strongly about him why on earth didn't you say?'

'I did. Frequently. But the trouble with you, Dick, is that you only hear what you want and not what you should.'

'Yes, dear.' He began to put on his coat. Why on earth he'd thought he'd rather be here than at work when Fiona was in one of her moods, as now, he couldn't imagine.

'What happened about the missing drugs? Did you solve it?'

'I fear Lynn might have been right and that Giles has been nicking them. I suppose I'm going to have to have a word with him.' He sighed deeply as if the prospect had tired him already.

'Report him to the GMC.'

'What? A fellow doctor? I couldn't do that – he's a colleague.'

'Don't talk such prattish rubbish, Dick. You'd be advised to. Cover your back or he'll take you down with him,' she said ominously. 'Mark my words,' she shouted after him as, rather like a startled hare, he bolted out of the front door.

In his car he relaxed and grinned broadly. He was enjoying his own secret and had no intention of telling a living soul that it was he who'd tipped off the GMC about Giles and his goings-on. That way, he'd not have to sack him and put up with all the legal complications that might bring. And he'd come through still regarded as good old Dick! 'Serve the bugger right,' he said to himself, as he bowled down the hill.

Daphne Galloway sat in the chair beside her bed, conscientiously doing the exercises the physiotherapist had taught her.

'My, you're working hard.'

'I want to get out of here, Lynn. Nothing personal, though! It must be so hurtful for you nurses when you care for us and then we thank you by saying we want out!'

'Perfectly normal – something we look for in a patient. When they want to stay here we tend to say, "Eh oop! What's gone wrong?"'

'That makes me feel better.' Daphne gritted her teeth as she lifted her leg.

'Don't push yourself too hard, will you?' Lynn smiled fondly at the old lady. 'Do you know where you're going after here?'

As soon as she had asked she wished she hadn't, for Daphne's whole body slumped dejectedly. 'No. I'd hoped . . . Well, I wanted to go to somewhere like the Mimosa but . . .' She rubbed thumb and first finger together.

'Have you heard of the Escalls Trust? No? It might be worth getting in touch with them. They take your house and sell it, and invest the money for your fees.'

'But I don't want to move permanently. Oh, no, I couldn't leave my little home. It's only till I'm back on my feet.'

'You could will them the house, then they'll look after you when you want, but you stay in your own home.'

'But I wanted to leave it to Chrissy – I've little else to leave her. It's all wrong, isn't it? I've paid my taxes all my life, now when I need help I can't get it.'

'If it's a choice between inheriting a house or your well-being I know which Chrissy would go for. Talk to her about it.'

'Poor Chrissy, I don't want to give her any more worry.'

'I wish I could help her. The atmosphere in this hospital is dreadful! Everyone here is being interviewed, you know? Not just Chrissy.'

'It's Chrissy they think did it, though.'

'Gossip – it's the only reason. Still, it looks as if she and Mr Newson are becoming an item, as they say,' she said, forcing jollity into her voice.

'What's he like?'

'Bit brisk, but lots of surgeons are. Perhaps it's the responsibility.'

'One of the nurses was saying how lovely his wife is.' Daphne frowned from worry.

'Stunning, but a cold bitch. She's been having an affair with one of the GPs I used to work with. In fact, they're both grim and deserve each other.' She laughed.

'Nurse Petch, are we going to be gossiping all day?' Jazz Poundman appeared suddenly in the doorway. 'There's work to do or haven't you noticed?'

'She wouldn't see work if it was shoved in her face,' Daphne said quietly.

'Just coming, Staff,' Lynn called, suppressing a laugh. 'Now, Mrs Galloway, you stop worrying. Everything will work out just fine.' She straightened the counterpane on Daphne bed, checked her water jug and that her book and bag of knitting were within easy reach before she left the side ward.

'Well, thanks for ambling along,' Jazz said unpleasantly, and the auxiliary nurse beside her giggled. 'When I say jump, you jump, Petch, understood?'

'No, Poundman, I don't understand and I jump for no one. I was reassuring a patient – part of my job description, I'd have thought.'

'What? Telling the old girl that her precious granddaughter isn't about to be arrested? Was that kind?' Jazz smirked and the auxiliary giggled even louder.

'I think, Jazz Poundman, you should watch your mouth. You could get into serious trouble saying things like that.'

'Me? That's a laugh. I'll tell you this just once, Petch. Watch it! You're new here and it won't do you any favours to be sucking up to dear Chrissy. You'll end up getting tarred by the same brush. Meanwhile, if it doesn't interfere with your social life, Mrs Bantam needs her pre-med. She's due in theatres to have her femur pinned. If you don't mind?'

Lynn decided not to pursue this tit-for-tat. She turned on her heel and went with another nurse to check out the pre-medication drug.

They dressed Mrs Bantam in her theatre robe, then Lynn took the woman's engagement ring, gold cross and chain and placed them in a large manilla envelope. 'We'll put these in the safe, then you won't have to worry about them being stolen. You'd be surprised what goes walkabout in these places. Now, are you sure you've no other valuables?' Mrs Bantam said she hadn't. They then signed the envelope, which Lynn sealed. She checked for false teeth or if she wore contact lenses, and if Mrs Bantam had sneaked something to eat or drink. For the umpteenth time she explained the operation procedure to the poor, frightened woman and explained the injection she was about to give. Slowly, patiently, there was nothing worse for an anaesthetist than a tense, terrified patient.

'Will you stay with me, Nurse?'

'I'll go with you and I'll be here when you wake up. I promise. Now, if you'll let me –' She prepped her patient's arm, gently injected the drug.

'Tell me when you're going to do it, Nurse.'

'I already have, Mrs Bantam. Now, you just go to sleep. I'll hold your paw until you do.' She nodded to the auxiliary to go, sat by the bed and did as she promised. With Christmas coming they weren't overly busy. Jazz would have to lump it.

Lynn kept her promise and was with Mrs Bantam until her general anaesthetic had been administered. As she left the main theatres she looked at her watch, it was time for her lunch break, but she'd go back to the ward and make up a post-operative bed for the patient first. Lynn liked to go off duty leaving straight everything for which she was responsible.

On her crêpe-soled shoes, she made barely any noise as she turned into Mrs Bantam's ward, where she was the only patient. Jazz Poundman's large bottom was in the air as, noisily, she rootled in Mrs Bantam's locker.

'What are you doing?' Lynn asked.

'Do you have to creep up on people like that? You nearly gave me a heart-attack!' Jazz laughed, and as she did she stuffed a hand under her apron, but not fast enough. Lynn had seen the roll of notes in her hand.

'What's that?'

'What's what?'

'You know. That money. Whose is it?'

'Oh, this money?' Jazz said, wide-eyed with innocent surprise. 'Really, Lynn, you were very sloppy. You should have checked. The old get confused and there must be a good hundred quid here that the stupid old bat had stowed away in her locker. Someone could have stolen that. Now, if you don't mind, I've work to –'

'Stay there,' Lynn ordered as she crossed to one of the empty beds where, taking up the bell pull, she pressed it. 'Get Sister,' she ordered the nurse who appeared.

'No, don't. Don't bother Sister,' Jazz interjected.

'Get Sister. Tell her I've just found Nurse Poundman stealing from a patient's locker.'

'You bitch!' Jazz hissed.

'No, Jazz. You've got it wrong. You're the bitch.'

3

If there was one time when Floss was in her element it was when she was organising her annual parties. The electricians were wiring the huge pine tree in the garden with the fairy-lights that were always a feature, both of her summer garden party and, as now, at Christmas.

'I hope it doesn't rain. Then no one will see. Nothing sadder than fairy-lights in the pouring rain,' the electrician said doomily.

'It won't rain. It never rains at my parties – it wouldn't dare. Ah! The champagne.' Floss turned as fast as her frame would allow to the delivery van in the forecourt. 'I've filled two baths with ice, let me show you.' And she was off to supervise the man as he unloaded the bottles.

Next polished glasses and cutlery were inspected for shine. The buffet tables were taken down and replaced in a different position, only to be put back in their original place. A damask tablecloth had a crease that did not please so had to be re-ironed, as did twenty of the hundred matching napkins.

The flower arrangements were admired, but Floss had to interfere, and two huge vases were redone while three more were touched and fiddled with, to the attendant florist's agony.

Each gaudily wrapped present was checked for the correct name tag. The tinsel and ribbon wrappings were tweaked and fussed over – as Floss made a soft cooing noise of approval, for she loved a vulgar wrapping.

The champagne had to be sampled as, of course, did the food, which had been delivered by the caterers. Floss never left anything to chance, nor did she ever rely on others to check things for her. Her parties were famous for their high standards, which she saw as her duty to maintain.

Only when all this checking was done did Floss, much to the relief of her staff, disappear into her library to make telephone calls.

'But I said I'd be there, Floss.'

'Yes, Jake, but I'm just reassuring myself. I'd be so devastated if you didn't appear.' She fluttered her eyelashes and pursed her lips, even though there was no one to see as she spoke in a low, sexy voice, full of chuckles, which she knew no one at the other end of the line had ever been able to resist. The Minister of Health's name was ticked with a flourish and another number dialled.

'But I said I'd be there, Floss.'

'Yes, Angus, but I'm reassuring myself.' And she repeated the previous dialogue before ticking the name of the chairman of the Fellcar NHS trust, who also happened to be the Lord Lieutenant of the County.

Then she checked that her favourite police inspector and newspaper editor were still coming. And finally that Craig Nutting, Matthew Kersey, Giles Middleton and Mark Fisher, the local MP, had not made other arrangements, which might have spoilt everything.

'Now!' she said aloud, clapping her hands with happy anticipation. Her watch told her that her hairdresser and manicurist were due in five minutes. Then, and only then, would she decide which of the sequin-spangled dresses she would wear – 'The red, the green or the yellow,' she trilled the old folk song happily.

'Buck, don't go out. Stay with us.' Cheryl Marston begged her husband.

'I told Wayne I'd meet up with him.'

'But you're still weak – you're not totally recovered. You know what Mr Ball said – that you were to be quiet, no rushing around.'

'I know what Fraser Ball said and I don't have to listen to a dead head like him. He should operate on his own noddle – give himself a brain transplant.'

'I wish you hadn't discharged yourself.'

'Another day in that place and I'd be in the loony bin.'

'You won't drink anything?'

'Nah.'

'You promise – on Liam's life?' She cuddled the baby close to her, and he, smelling her milk, nuzzled her.

'Nah. Don't worry. Wish I had an optic like that.' He pointed at her full breast.

'Don't be silly, Buck.' Cheryl giggled and lowered her head with embarrassment. 'Promise? You know what Mr Ball said about drinking when you're on them pills.'

'Oh, for Christ's sake, Cheryl. I'm meeting Wayne for a coffee. We're not even going to the sodding pub.'

'All right – keep your hair on. It's just that I love you.'

'And I love you too, Cheryl. Honest.' And Buck shuffled his feet. Sloppy talk always made him feel a right tosser.

'Do you feel happier now you've got a lawyer?' Russell asked Chrissy, as they stood on the steps of the fine Georgian house that was the office of Henry Yates.

'He's very pleasant. And he seems to know what he's talking about. He certainly made me feel more confident.'

'Don't find him too pleasant, will you?' Russell put his arm possessively round her shoulder. 'I wouldn't like that.'

'Don't crowd me, Russell, please.' She shuddered.

'What the hell?' He dropped his arm.

'I'm sorry,' she said, confused.

Russell took her gently by the shoulders and sat her down on the steps leading to his solicitor's office. 'Now, you listen to me,' he said sternly, looming over her. 'Ewan is dead. Gone. I'm here. I'm not Ewan, I'll never be him. I'm in love with you and I adore you and I'll want to kill any other man who touches you. It's called jealousy. Where you have love you have the other. Understand?' She nodded sheepishly. 'Because I'm jealous, and I want to guard you and what we have, does not mean I'm going to turn into a nutty monster, twisted and cruel. Got it?' She nodded again. 'I shall not open your mail, listen to your phone calls, snoop in your life, *crowd you*, interrogate you. I will trust you with this love, with my soul. Anything else?'

'No, Russell.' She smiled up at him. 'I'm becoming neurotic, aren't I?'

'You are.'

'I do love you. I don't want the past to hurt us.'

'It won't, if you'll let go of it.'

'I don't hold on to it − or him.'

'Don't you?' He bent down, crouching in front of her, oblivious to the odd looks they were getting from passers-by. 'When we made love the other night you were tense. You were expecting me to become sadistic, cruel − to hurt you. The bastard was in our bed. Now, Chrissy, I understand the why and how but it's time to stop being afraid. It's time to allow yourself to be loved and to live − with me, preferably.' He grinned.

'God, I'm so lucky to have found you.'

'Then loosen the guilt. That's what's anchoring Ewan in your life. It was not your fault he died. Get that straight and then we can move on.'

'I'll try. I will. I need you.'

'And I need you.' He pulled her to her feet and hugged her hard. They started walking down the street.

'The solicitor wasn't too happy with you moving out of your house.'

'He didn't have to live with Sabine. And he doesn't have this neurotic woman I've fallen in love with who needs to be reassured.'

'You shouldn't have done it for me.'

'Oh, no? I disagree. If you were living but not living with a husband, I'd be crawling up the wall. I didn't want you to suffer that.'

'Where will you stay?' she asked, wishing she had the confidence to invite him to move in with her, but feeling that would be too pushy and might frighten him away.

'With you I was rather hoping.'

'I didn't like to ask you.'

'Why?'

'In case you said no.'

'And pigs would fly! You sure you don't mind?'

'Me? Now I know you won't snoop into my letters.' She laughed gaily.

'And, in any case, I don't think you should be on your own – not with all that's going on and your poltergeist.'

Chrissy, who'd been smiling, stopped. She'd been happy, truly happy, for a few precious moments. But, as kept happening, reality rushed back in with her fears in hot pursuit.

4

Glynis was efficiently supervising George Webster's discharge from the orthopaedic ward.

'I don't understand why I had to stay in for three nights.'

'Shock from the explosion – people don't understand how dangerous it can be. And they were a bit worried about a possible wound infection.'

'But I'm a tough old nut. What do you think of my plaster?'

'It's fine, but you're having a wheelchair.'

'I've got crutches.'

'Wheelchair,' Glynis said firmly, and George grinned broadly, knowing that the owner of such a voice was used to being obeyed.

'This is very kind of you, Glynis. I could easily go back to the hotel.'

'Nonsense. I wouldn't hear of it. Your nice sergeant has collected your baggage.' She began to push the wheelchair along the ward corridor towards the lift, which a nurse was holding open for them.

'Why do hospitals always smell the same the world over? Tons of boiled cabbage mixed with disinfectant and an overlay of treacle.'

'George, you are silly. I can't smell any such thing.' The lift clanged to a halt.

'That's because you're so used to it you probably don't notice it any more. Hang on.' He put up his hand. 'Why are you aiming for the front door? My temporary office is thataway.' He pointed in the direction of the boardroom.

'I thought you should rest today.'

'Then you thought wrong. I've an investigation to conduct. Either push me there or I'll get out and hobble.'

'You are a most intransigent man.'

'Since you are the female version, my dear Glynis, you can easily recognise it in me. Good morning, Sergeant,' he said, as she wheeled him through the large mahogany double doors.

'Boss! I'd expected you to be laid up for days.' The sergeant stood, flustered, looking anxiously at the top of the long table, which he'd covered with papers.

'Having a sort-out, I see. Anything of interest?'

'Quite a development, sir. Yesterday a staff nurse on Care of the Elderly was seen behaving oddly with a roll of fivers from a patient's locker – the patient was being operated on at the time.'

'No! When will they learn not to keep their valuables with them? The nurse's name, Sergeant?' Glynis asked.

The policeman looked questioningly at George, who nodded. 'A Jasmine Poundman.'

'Oh, no!'

'You know something about this nurse, Glynis?'

'I had a complaint about her from Sister Galloway – you know, the poor woman who's been so victimised. But we were short-staffed. I spoke to Jazz but fairly ineffectually – I couldn't risk her storming out. I fear I should have been sterner, but . . . it was not a good day.' She finished lamely.

'What was the complaint about?'

'Bullying. It's rare, but it does happen, I'd be a fool to deny it. But stealing!'

'We don't know that yet, Miss Tillman. Of course, Miss Poundman denies everything and says she was collecting the money to put in the safe.'

'Which she could have been, of course.' Glynis sat down at the table, feeling suddenly weary from anxiety.

'Hang on. *Poundman.* Wasn't that the nurse who was locked in her flat the night of the murder? Was that checked out with the fire brigade?'

The sergeant began to shuffle papers about again.

'You didn't do it, did you?' George asked, resignedly. 'Then I suggest you do it now, immediately.' He barked the order and the officer dived for the telephone as if his life depended upon it.

Glynis did not know whether or not she should leave, but something kept her rooted to the spot. George was furiously making notes. Glynis watched him and realised how much she wanted to push his reading specs, which were sliding down his nose, back into position and to look after him. But she reined in such ideas, firmly telling herself not to be stupid. Hadn't she been fooled enough for one life? She sat up straight in her chair, as if the rigidity of her posture would control her idiotic thoughts.

'The fire brigade have no record of helping a Miss Poundman that night, sir.'

'Right,' said George, trying to stand, but remembering that he couldn't move very easily. 'Where is she?'

'At her flat. It's her day off . . .'

'She might have a reasonable explanation for the money, but she'll have one hell of a job explaining away the Fellcar fire brigade. Looks like we've got her.' George rubbed his hands in glee, enjoying the surge of adrenaline that the prospect of an arrest always gave him.

Each day Mo felt better. The scar had healed well, so movement no longer hurt her. She was able to plan her Christmas which, she was determined, was going to be a day to remember for Kerry and Katya.

She was making her shopping list when she was interrupted by the doorbell ringing.

'Ash! What a lovely surprise. I've telephoned you a couple of times but you're always out.' She held open the door for him.

'Sorry, but I've been so busy, what with –' He stopped as they entered the kitchen.

'With Robbie having done a runner. Is that what you wanted to say but didn't like to?' She put the kettle on. 'It's all right, Ash. I can talk about him. I won't collapse in hysterics.'

'Mo, you're something else. I'd like to strangle the bastard.'

'Ash, don't get in a state – it's really not worth it. Or maybe I'm saying *he's* not worth it.'

'The girls, how have they taken it?'

'Kerry's upset – she loves her dad. Katya's angry with him, but she's older and understands more. Don't worry, they'll be fine. I'll see to that. Now sit down, do, you're tiring me out.' She patted the kitchen chair beside her.

'I don't understand how he could leave you now, what with . . .'

'The cancer? Really, Ash, you're going to have to learn to finish your sentences,' she teased, but then she became serious. 'Look, Ash, he didn't plan this. It happened. We'd been heading towards a break-up for years. I don't know why it wasn't working, but it wasn't. It takes two to make a marriage and two to break it. Should he have stayed with me when I was ill? At first I felt sorry for myself, let down, but then I thought, Why should he? He'd have been around out of pity – as he told me – and that would have been humiliating. No, I can make it, and that's a promise.' She stood up to attend to the coffee.

Ash sat with the expression of a man who did not know what to say. He coughed awkwardly. 'About the business.'

'Yes?' She placed the coffee cups on the table.

'I didn't know what to do. When Robbie put the proposition to me – well, I said yes.' Ash looked shifty.

'Perhaps it would have been better if you'd waited until you'd talked to me,' she chided gently. 'I might have wanted to be in partnership with you. Then I could have taken Robbie's shares and saved you a lot of hassle finding the money. It's what I wanted to talk to you about. I don't know anything about installing systems but I could do the accounts and type the estimates – as your partner.'

'Mo, that would be marvellous. You mean it?'

'If you're in agreement.'

'You need to ask?' Ash was grinning from ear to ear. 'It won't be too much for you?'

'There'll be days when I'm on my chemotherapy when it probably will, but I reckon that having a goal, having a part in a business which is mine, might help me keep my mind occupied.'

'Mo, it's no good. I've a confession to make. I don't know how to tell you . . .'

Mo tensed, afraid of what he was about to say.

'I persuaded Robbie to take the money. It was me who suggested buying him out. I thought if he's going to go he will, and if I arranged the loot for him he'd go further. That's it.' He sat back, relieved the truth was out, but anxious at her reaction.

'But why?' she asked.

'Because I've been in love with you for years, Mo. And I want to be there for you and care for you and the girls.'

Mo exhaled gently. 'Ash, you're the sweetest man in the world. But, Ash, please don't rush me. Not now. It's not the time,' she said quietly.

'Does that mean you're not interested in me?'

'No, Ash. I like you more than I can say, but with everything so uncertain – what if you were saying this just because you felt sorry for me? Where would that leave me?'

'I've always felt like this. I want to be there for you.'

'Give me time, Ash. Give it for both our sakes.'

Without doubt, despite everything, Chrissy felt young again, vital and alive. Last night had been like that first one – an endless making love and exploring their feelings for each other. She wanted to be home and to see him, not here. As she went about her duties she kept glancing at her watch, the hands of which did not appear to move. She was under-occupied, that was half the problem. There was only a handful of patients to care for since as many as possible had been sent home for Christmas. Those who remained were seriously ill and two, she knew, were unlikely to be here in the New Year.

She checked her dress for the party which, in its bag, was hanging behind the door in the linen cupboard. The plan was to shower and change here so that there'd be no need to go home. Russell would go ahead of her, but even though she wasn't getting off duty until ten, there would still be a party to go to.

'Dawn, you go off. I can manage here,' she'd said earlier to her staff nurse. 'You must have Christmas shopping to do. If you're quick, you'll catch the shops.'

'You sure? I don't object to staying on. After all, you've got this party to get ready for.'

'It's no problem.' Floss Yates's parties always went on into the small hours.

'Well, I have got one or two things to do.'

'Shoo . . . before I change my mind.'

Five minutes later Dawn popped back.

'Guess what? They've arrested Jazz Poundman.'

'Jazz? What for?'

'Murder! Isn't it exciting?'

Chrissy sat down with sigh. 'Thank God for that,' she said, with feeling.

Everyone and everything was working for her, Chrissy thought, as at ten past ten she began to take her shower. The report for the night staff had taken only five minutes.

Once she was dry she made up her face carefully, clipped on her earrings, smoothed her gossamer stockings, slipped on her grosgrain stiletto heels and finally, gingerly, so as not to mess up her hair, she put on the stiff black taffeta dress she'd bought specially for the occasion. She twisted her arm behind her back to do up the zip, which jammed.

Twenty minutes later, despite the night staff's efforts to mend the zip, Chrissy, flustered, was back in her uniform dress and driving hell-for-leather to her cottage.

Leaving the car with its headlights on she ran up the path, fumbled her key into the lock, hurtled up the stairs to her bedroom and flung open the door of her wardrobe, riffling through her clothes searching for a long-skirted black suit that should be there.

As she grabbed the hanger and pulled the suit towards her, her hand froze. She raised her head, held her breath and listened. What was that noise? She strained her ears. Suddenly she gasped, clutching the suit to her as if it was a baby's comforter. She could hear someone breathing – on her stairs!

5

If noise was any indication then this party of Floss's was an enormous success. The decibel level was deafening. There were no complaints and no police appeared on the doorstep for the simple expedient that all Floss's neighbours were merrily quaffing her champagne and adding to the din. And, since virtually all the senior police officers from the area were here as guests, what junior policeman would dare to show his face?

Floss, resplendent in a scarlet sequinned trouser suit, emblazoned with a huge silver eagle, which did nothing for her figure but much to raise the festive spirit, wafted about introducing here, interrupting there, joking and teasing, laughing uproariously. She moved like a glowing red spirit – a spirit of enjoyment and jollity. In her hand she held a large glass of clear liquid. Most presumed it was gin, but they were wrong. It was Highland Spring: one of Floss's stringent rules was that she never touched alcohol at her own parties – never!

Tonight she'd taken particular joy in insisting that her stuck-up sister meet, and be pleasant to, sweet Tiffany and her equally pleasant parents. She enjoyed dropping a judicious hint that it would please her if Kim and Tiffany were to marry and produce another generation of heirs for her fortune. She did not say it so baldly – she didn't need to: Fiona understood, and when she saw the greedy glitter in Fiona's eyes, she knew that wedding invitations would soon be winging their way. Why, she'd even begun to wonder if the reception couldn't be held here – or would Tiffany's mother mind? She'd give her a call in the morning.

'Russell. You came. What have you done with Sabine?'

'She's with her lover.'

'Ah. Yes. Well.' Floss laughed nervously, for once rendered speechless.

'Giles Middleton.'

'You *are* joking, Russell? So the rumours were true. Interesting.'

Floss was slightly put out when Sabine arrived with Giles. Though a true description would have been that Sabine made an entrance, pausing dramatically in the doorway, swirling a scarlet-lined cape around her. Unfortunately too many noses were in the trough for anyone to notice her. Floss was put out not because she feared a confrontation between Sabine and Chrissy – she would probably quite enjoy that. No, she hadn't invited Sabine, and Floss was a stickler about such social niceties. So she proceeded to ignore the woman, as if she wasn't there. This was a new experience for Sabine and put her in a sulk, which was noted by many: she did not look nearly as attractive with such a face. 'Don't forget, library at eleven, Giles,' Floss ordered.

Iris Galloway swept in with her new lover in tow. Floss could quite see why she'd called and asked if she might bring him – if Floss had a muscular young man like him she'd have wanted to show him off to the world. Dream on, Floss said to herself, but with amusement.

Floss had always liked George and was pleased to see Glynis arrive with him. Now, that's the sort she should have been involved with all these years – strong, dependable, with a sense of humour and widowed – highly suitable. Floss would be the first to admit that she took an inordinate pleasure in introducing him to Matthew Kersey, who blustered his annoyance away. Wendy kissed Glynis with obvious pleasure – Floss had often wondered how much Wendy knew and how much she chose to ignore. Floss was quite cool when she greeted Wendy's sister, Jenna, a supercilious woman she'd never taken to and who – she'd always kept this to herself – for at least two years now, had been having an affair with Matthew. What a two-timing creep he was, she thought angrily.

'Oh, Matthew, darling. I'm so sorry, clumsy me. Have I ruined your suit?' Floss fussed, apparently distraught at the damage she'd caused when she'd purposely jogged his elbow.

Craig Nutting strode around with obviously satisfied pleasure. He thought he'd cracked it, had finally been accepted by nobs like Floss. We'll see, Floss thought, as she waylaid Mark Fisher, and reminded him she'd like a 'little talk' in the library.

The party motored on, creating its own momentum.

'Floss, might I phone Chrissy? She should be here by now.'

'Be my guest, Russell.'

The night staff told him that Chrissy had left half an hour ago, and Floss's was ten minutes at most from the hospital. He dialled her cottage, but the phone rang and rang.

Chrissy felt frozen to the spot. The phone on her bedside table jangled. She wanted to answer it but was too scared to move. If she did, whoever was on the stairs would know for sure that she was there . . . and yet she could ask whoever was calling to get the police.

In one swift dive she crossed the room, ready to pick up the still ringing phone.

'I don't think so.' A hand appeared and pressed the cradle rest disconnecting the call.

Chrissy swung round. And then she laughed with relief. 'Dawn! What are you doing here? You almost gave me a heart-attack.' The laughter died as Dawn lifted her right hand, which held a hypodermic syringe.

'But, Chrissy, that was the general idea!' Dawn laughed, but there was no mirth in it. 'First I'd like to talk and explain a few things to you – I like things nice and tidy, as you know. Let's go downstairs, shall we? Open a bottle, perhaps? You first.' And, with deceptive gentleness, she pushed Chrissy towards the narrow staircase.

The butler Floss had hired for the night – the one she always used and who knew her ways – moved discreetly through the throng, pausing every so often, whispering into an ear and pointing in the direction of Floss's library.

Floss waited, standing by the log fire, which was for show only since the boiler in the cellar heated the house quite adequately.

One by one they entered, and each in turn was invited to help themselves to a drink.

'Right. Is everyone settled?' Floss beamed around the seated group. 'I've a few words I want to say to you all. Glynis, are you comfortable there?'

'I'm fine, Floss, really,' said Glynis, from the side of the room where she felt more of an observer. She was worried, concerned that Floss's plan might misfire, but Floss was grinning as if she was enjoying the prospect of the game ahead. Floss had that indomitable bulldog look about her, which usually meant trouble for others. Glynis wondered if any of them knew Floss well enough to read the signs.

'Right. We'll use Christian names, it's easier. Dick, Craig, Giles, Matthew and Mark – the game's up. You've been rustled, rumbled, found out!'

'What the hell are you going on about?' Dick, Floss's brother-in-law, looked annoyed.

'What game?' asked Craig, smiling contentedly.

'Sorry?' Giles looked uncomfortable.

'Is this a form of charades?' Matthew sounded puzzled and Mark Fisher said nothing, but looked nervous.

'As you know, I'm a Friend of St Edith's and I see it as my duty to stop your little plan to privatise the hospital. You will – forthwith.'

A swell of male voices objected in unison. Like a school ma'am in charge of the class, Floss called for silence and sharply tapped a handy table. 'Your plans to run down the hospital services, sell the building for redevelopment, buy it back as a private hospital, make yourselves directors and cop a lot of money off the NHS. That little plan.' She smiled sweetly at them. 'I want an undertaking from you all tonight to stop what you're doing or I go to the relevant authorities – who, I should point out, are all here tonight as my friends and my guests, if you haven't already noticed.'

'Look, Floss, have you gone barmy? There *is* no scheme that I know of. Now, can I get back to the party?' Dick half stood, as if to leave.

'No, Dick. You may not.'

'He's not in on anything.'

'How interesting, Mark. Then if he's not in on anything there's something to be in on, is there?'

'You bloody fool, Mark,' Giles snarled.

'I didn't mean that,' Mark blustered. 'All I meant is, he's not one of our group.'

'I'm glad if he isn't – I don't want a smear on our family. But if he's not directly involved he's guilty of not being sufficiently concerned about his fund-holding practice to stop certain discrepancies – of pocketing, instead of ploughing back, any savings made.' Floss, making a stab in the dark, was gratified from his expression to know her assumption was right. 'I suggest you retire, Dick. You're too old, tired and lazy to have the responsibilities that go with your job.'

'Floss! You go too far.'

'My dear Dick, I haven't even started. Now, Mark, as we were saying. I think I should point out to you that Jake Shortley, the Junior Minister for Health, is in the drawing room. Would you like me to call him? You could have a little chat.'

'No, no, that won't be necessary,' Mark said.

'Oh, yes? You reckon dear old Jakey will go along with you, with this threatening? What about when his leader finds out about his bit of skirt who lives the other side of Thorpedale?'

'Craig, if you'd done your homework and checked your facts, which is essential if you wish to pursue a life of crime, you would have found out that the woman Jake visits on a regular basis is his sister, who, sadly, suffers from MS. Wrong information, Craig.'

'Don't say anything, Mark.'

'But then there's you, Craig.'

'You've got nothing on me.'

'Haven't I? Glynis, the faxes, please. How about this one and this?' She slapped them down in front of him. 'Pretty incriminating, don't you think? All those figures. And then, of course, we've the tapes. Do you want to hear the tapes of your phone calls? I especially liked "Burn the papers" . . . So dramatic, just like a spy film!'

'Wouldn't stand up in court.'

'It won't have to, my dear, now will it? You will tender your resignation, and recommend my nephew's promotion as you do.'

'That's nepotism.'

'Yes, that's the word. Of course, you can do it tonight if you wish. The Chairman of our NHS Trust is out there – no doubt having a drink with the Junior Minister. Now, Giles.' She turned to face him.

'I don't even work at the hospital. You've got nothing on me.'

'Haven't I? It might not be illegal to abuse the referral system of patients to the hospital. But stealing drugs and spiking Nurse Petch's drink – did you intend that she should die in that crash? I'm sure the Chief Constable and that nice Inspector Webster will . . .'

'Outside having a drink, yes, yes, we get the picture. But you can't prove it.'

'Oh, no? Glynis, the computer printout of the medical records of poor Mr Spike, aged ninety-four – if he were still alive, that is. Now that was naughty. And,' she held up her hand to prevent him speaking, 'I know from my own researches that it was you who phoned the police and reported poor Nurse Petch drunk and disorderly. What you didn't allow for is that Lynn Petch rarely drinks. She only took a few sips of your whisky which, of course, was far below the limit. The analyst's report showed traces of tamazepam. My, Giles, you do have a thing about that particular drug, don't you? A drug which, incidentally, Lynn had never before taken in her life. No, what foiled you, Giles, is that Lynn has such a low tolerance to both alcohol and drugs that that silly little amount made her distinctly incapable, but such a silly little amount was, of course, far within the legal limits. Bad luck there. And, of course, the GMC will lap up all this info on top of everything else. Oh, I nearly forgot – we'll have to tell them about the bribes you've taken from the pharmaceutical reps. Not very attractive, Giles,' Floss said darkly. 'You've been very quiet, Matthew. Cat got your tongue?' She turned to face him.

'I was amused, Floss. Who do you think you are, an Agatha Christie character?'

Floss laughed. 'Yes, it is rather like that, isn't it?'

'I must admit this is very entertaining. What am I supposed to have done?'

'You were part of the plot.'

'Prove it.'

'I can, if I want.' Floss crossed her fingers behind her back. She had no proof, but she was determined to get him for the way he'd treated Glynis who, she saw, had suddenly stood up.

'Of course, Matthew. I'm sure the authorities would be most interested in that little mishap of yours, all those years ago on a patient in Inverness.' Glynis smiled nervously. 'You do remember, when you accidentally cut into an artery – no one saw but me. Remember? Your assistant had rushed out to the lavatory – a gyppy tum. The anaesthetist was reading. And my assistant was inexperienced – her first day on theatres. Only I saw, and only I would have been stupid enough to cover for you.'

'You blow the gaff on that then your career would be ruined too, Glynis.'

'Yes. I was wrong. It would be just punishment.'

'Don't talk such twaddle, Glynis. We wouldn't even need that information,' Floss interrupted. 'I can, with your permission, Glynis, tell poor duped Wendy about you. How about that?'

'Ha! She knows. She's known all these years. I told her I had to keep in with Glynis or she might blow the whistle on my little mishap in Inverness. She thinks Glynis has been blackmailing me. For heaven's sake, why should I bother with the old bag for any other reason?'

Floss saw Glynis wince at his words, then bravely lift her chin. Nothing more could hurt her, she thought, and she mentally girded her loins.

'But Wendy knows nothing about your affair with her sister, Jenna, does she? Now that really is messy. And soiling your own nest – most reprehensible, Matthew, my dear. Glynis, come.' She held out her hand to her friend, who looked as if she was holding the desk for support. 'We shall leave you gentlemen to your deliberations. I want an undertaking, in writing, by midnight or we will have another little pow-wow in here with the relevant chiefs.' And she swept from the room with Glynis in dignified pursuit. Outside they hugged each other with glee, on Floss's part, and nervous relief, on Glynis's.

Chrissy sat straight-backed in the wing chair that had been her father's, Dawn sat opposite, the syringe at her fingertips, a glass of champagne in her hand.

'Sorry I can't toast you a long life,' she said pleasantly. 'This is good. Vintage. You can easily tell the difference, can't you? Ewan always said that.'

'I was right. I *had* seen you before, in Cornwall. Fleetingly. He pointed you out to me.'

'Yes. That gave me a little flutter when you asked if we'd met. I was brunette then. That's why you weren't sure. And, as I said, I've a common face.'

'You're not. You're very attractive.'

'Chrissy, don't waste what's left of your breath trying to get round me – it won't wash.'

'Russell will be here any minute.'

'No, he won't. I heard you on the telephone arranging to meet him at old Floss Yates's. There's no hurry – enjoy your champagne.'

Chrissy lifted her glass to her lips, but only sipped it. Her heart felt as if it were in her throat and that she would gag if she drank any. Her pulse was racing and she was sweating as terror seeped through her.

'I bet you thought it was Jazz who bumped off old Fortune? Silly Jazz, greedy Jazz.'

'But you were on duty that night.'

'Easy-peasy. I slipped into your ward when no one was looking and opened the fire escape. Then I ran down from my ward to your ward and, hey presto, you were regarded as a murderess.'

What was so chilling, Chrissy thought, was how normal Dawn sounded, not mad at all. Yet she had to be mad, didn't she?

'But why? Why kill that poor old lady? Do you like killing?'

'No, not particularly. But you don't understand, do you? I wanted to get to you. If they hadn't arrested Jazz, we wouldn't be here now. I wanted you to rot in prison, really. Trust Jazz to mess everything up. I'd have put money on her being the person nicking, wouldn't you?'

There it was again, that conversational tone which made everything even more terrifying.

'But why? What have I ever done to you? Because I got the oncology job and you didn't?'

'Don't be so stupid! Ewan, of course. He was my lover. Good God, haven't you twigged yet? He always said you were excruciatingly thick. We had a wonderful relationship – deep, spiritual. I understood him, you never did.'

'But, Dawn, I didn't kill him. I promise you that was all a dreadful mistake. He didn't mean to kill himself.'

'Oh, I know that. You see, I did.'

'I'm sorry?' Chrissy tensed in the chair, gripping the arms.

'I killed him.'

The walls of the room moved as if they were made of elastic. Chrissy felt hot then cold. The carpet became a blur.

'That shook you up, didn't it? It was so easy to do.'

'But the note?' Her voice sounded weak in her ears. She felt faint, was afraid she *would* faint and then what? As if she was reading Chrissy's mind Dawn picked up the syringe and played with it. Suddenly she lunged across the small space between them. Chrissy pressed herself further back in the chair away from the shiny needle, a small drip of fluid at its tip, which she watched, hypnotised, as it wavered an inch from her face. Dawn laughed and then sat in the opposite chair.

'Oh, Ewan wrote the note. I'm not a forger, for goodness' sake. At his mother's. I was there – that's who I got the insulin from, just took it from her bathroom cabinet. She liked me. She thought I was more suitable than you – a middle-class oik, she called you. She wanted someone upper class like me for Ewan.'

'You!' Chrissy snorted the word before she could stop herself.

'I am! And don't you ever forget it!' Again she waved the syringe dangerously close.

'He was devastated when you bolted to that hotel. He thought you'd gone for good. He wanted you back. He wanted you rather than me.' Dawn jerked her head as if such words were too difficult to say. 'I wanted all the things you had – the house, the lovely furniture, the glass, the money. We had money once, you see, until my father lost it all. Lloyds, you know,' she explained in that normal voice. 'And him. My Ewan. I couldn't have him, could I? If he didn't want me he certainly wasn't going to have you. It was all my plan, you see. I persuaded him that if he did what I said, he'd get you back. It amused him that his mistress was conniving to get the runaway wife back for him. I told him that I would inject him with just a little insulin, enough to make it look like a suicide attempt – only I gave the bastard the lot.' She laughed at that, suddenly harsh and shrill, her eyes glinting with excitement.

Chrissy looked at Dawn with horror and cowered further back in her chair. She felt so alone, so desperately afraid. And then came the memory of Ewan, the pain he'd caused her alive, the guilt when dead. In a flash she remembered the whispering looks, the innuendoes. Remembered the years of guilt, that wasn't her guilt. Anger replaced fear. The adrenaline of terror forged with the adrenaline of rage.

'You evil, mad bitch!' she screamed. She jumped from the chair and dived for the syringe but she was not quick enough – for Dawn had grabbed it and was waving it in front of her making Chrissy weave away from its lethal contents as, both standing, they danced a deadly dance.

Now, when Dawn laughed, Chrissy heard the shrill note of madness. With one leap she crossed the rug, got hold of a hank of Dawn's hair and tugged, and Dawn's laugh became a yelp of pain, which turned into a scream of agony as Chrissy's teeth sank into her arm and the syringe dropped to the floor. Chrissy swept it up and held it out in front of her like a weapon.

'Right. Now, how's it feel?' Angrily she waved the syringe. 'Scared?' Without taking her eyes from Dawn she backed towards the phone. Before she reached it the door burst open.

'Chrissy, are you here? What are you doing? Floss said –'

'Russell,' she called out, relief bubbling in her voice. For a second she glanced away. Dawn pushed her aside as she raced past her, past a startled Russell in the doorway, out of the cottage and down the path. 'Catch her! Catch her! She wanted to kill me!' Chrissy yelled, as she set off in hot pursuit.

Russell overtook her as they pounded across the springy turf of the cliff.

'Dawn!' she screamed, but the wind caught the name and tossed it away.

Dawn turned once on the edge of the cliff, silhouetted in the moonlight. She seemed to wave before she leapt into oblivion.

The night was long. They had witnessed the frantic efforts to rescue Dawn in case she was lying injured at the bottom of the cliff. Of her body there was no sign and the search for her had been cancelled until the morning. At the police station they had encountered a tearful and unusually subdued Jazz as she was being released from custody. Then they had to make their statements; their explanations of the events constantly repeated. Finally they were alone.

'Oh, Russ, will Christmas ever be joyful again?'

'I'll make sure it is – for you.' And his mouth pressed onto hers and he kissed her passionately, desperately, determined to kiss the pain and fear away.

6

St Edith's stood sentinel above the town. The patients stirred restlessly in their beds in their drug-induced sleep. The nursing staff scuttled about, finishing the preparations for tomorrow when every effort would be made to make Christmas as happy as they could for those too ill or damaged to be at home.

A and E was busy: a car crash, a drunken fight, a couple of domestic eruptions – normal for any Christmas – made the night speed past for the staff.

Two young men were stretchered in. The triage nurse assessed them: both would need intensive care, both were sent to the resuscitation room with their entourage of medical personnel.

Freddie Favour, who only a couple of hours before had played Father Christmas at Floss Yates's party, frowned over the figure on the treatment table. Tubes were inserted into the patient's arms and legs, a tube helped his breathing, but nothing could stem the blood pouring from the young man's chest cavity where the steering wheel had ripped into him. The smell of alcohol was all pervasive.

'No seat-belt, I suppose. Silly fool.'

The nurse at the patient's head finished cleaning the blood away. 'I know him,' said Freddie. 'How do I know him?'

'It's Buck – Buck Marston. He was in last month in a coma. I heard he'd discharged himself.'

'Why did we bother?' said Freddie. 'There'll be no coma this time.' He pulled the sheet over Buck's bruised but strangely peaceful face. From outside they heard the screams as Buck's wife denied he was dead. 'I'll talk to her,' Freddie said wearily.

In the Intensive Care Unit, the heat from the life-sustaining machines made the large room stifling. The nurses, lightly dressed against the warmth, tended the patients, from whom wires and tubes bristled, checked the dials, the screens, and reassured the frightened relatives that all would be well, that these two victims of the explosion would survive. They held their loved ones' hands, not really believing this could be the case.

On Care of the Elderly, Fred Clemence sighed his last, his wife of many years beside him. She wiped a tear from her eye. 'Poor Fred, he never really liked Christmas,' she said, as she bent to kiss him goodbye.

In maternity, Rose Noelle Basset, pushed her way into life and cried lustily at the sight of it. Her mother Rachel's euphoria was marred by the sadness that her husband, Andrew, was not here to greet his daughter. And she did what she had done many times in the past weeks: she cursed Buck Marston and wished him dead for taking Andrew from them.

The lights of St Edith's were fewer now as sleep and order settled back. St Edith's stood, a comfort to some, a place of pain and terror to others. There was a solidity about St Edith's in the bright Christmas moonlight, as if in some strange way the building knew it was safe – for the time being.